WHAT GOES AROUND COMES AROUND

PREVIOUS BRIAN MCNULTY BARTENDER MYSTERIES BY CON LEHANE

Beware the Solitary Drinker

WHAT GOES AROUND
COMES AROUND

CON LEHANE

THOMAS DUNNE BOOKS
ST. MARTIN'S MINOTAUR ⧗ NEW YORK

THOMAS DUNNE BOOKS.
An imprint of St. Martin's Press.

www.minotaurbooks.com

Book design by Jonathan Bennett

Library of Congress Cataloging-in-Publication Data

Lehane, Cornelius.
    What goes around comes around : a Brian McNulty bartender mystery / Con Lehane.—1st ed.
        p. cm.
    ISBN 0-312-32298-4
    EAN 978-0312-32298-4
    1. Manhattan (New York, N.Y.)—Fiction.   2. Bartenders—Fiction.
I. Title.
PS3612.E354W47   2005
813'.6—dc22
                                                            2004056477
                First Edition: February 2005

            10 9 8 7 6 5 4 3 2 1

To Paddy and Jimmy and their mother Cathleen

WHAT GOES AROUND COMES AROUND

I'd been back behind the bar of the Midtown Sheraton for about two weeks, after a six-month hiatus—the hiatus because my foot-dragging bartenders' union took that long to get my job back after the corporation fired me. The company and union both hoping, no doubt, I'd starve to death in the interval.

I was settling into, I thought, one of those quiet periods in life that folks with any sense clamor for after we've been exposed to too much excitement for too long. This particular afternoon, I was pondering the offerings in the *Daily Racing Form's* past performance charts for Belmont, hoping to get one more bet down for the afternoon race card, blissfully unaware that unresolved mysteries and ghosts of barrooms past were waiting just beyond the next race.

It was the lull between lunch and the cocktail hour on a Friday, and Alphonse, the manager, was huffily stomping through the lounge to let me know he didn't like that I was reading the paper. This was nothing new. He'd been hovering around me like a mosquito since I'd been back on the job, waiting for me to make a mistake so he could fire me again. At the moment, he was skulking around back by the service bar. But I didn't pay much attention, since I'd already done most of the prep and restocked the coolers for the night shift.

I worked mostly nights myself, despite the wear and tear on my psyche, because the money was better. And also because—even as I advanced into my forties—I was still afflicted with the delusion that I could make it as an actor. Working nights meant I could catch a morning audition now and again. Not content to be insulted by pompous hotel managers day in and day out, I went out of my way to be demeaned by supercilious stage managers every couple of weeks. I worked the Friday day shift so I could spend an evening with my son. On the rare occasions I actually landed a part, I switched with the day bartenders, who were happy to pick up the extra bucks on the night shift.

"McNulty," said Alphonse, rubbing the surface of the service bar with his manicured fingers. "This bar is sticky."

"Wipe it off," I suggested.

"Are you refusing a direct order?" He snapped to attention, pulling himself up straight to his full five feet six inches, presumably extending the military metaphor.

"You didn't give an order, Alphonse." I pointed out. The company wanted him to build an ironclad case against me so the union couldn't get my job back this time when he fired me. Alphonse was trying, but he wasn't much of a strategist. "Besides," I said, "you can't fire me for not wiping the bar. It has to be something serious."

Alphonse glared at me a few seconds, wiped his fingers on a bar towel, flipped it disdainfully onto the bar, then strode briskly out of the room, as if he had something important to do.

The two customers nursing scotches at the bar snickered as he left, enjoying what they mistook for good-natured bantering. I didn't get paid enough to be good-natured. And while Alphonse was a pretty good showman, good fellowship on his part was as phony as his European accent.

I didn't take much pleasure in provoking Alphonse. His nerves were shot anyway. He worked sixteen hours a day, made less money than I did, and worried himself sick over what his superiors thought of him. On this afternoon, he was rattled because a new regional manager was coming in. Maybe he planned to impress the higher-up by firing me on the spot. Alphonse didn't have real animosity toward me, just ambition.

In the corporate world of food and beverages, one rises quickly and falls even faster. Alphonse, still on the ascent, had passed a number of graying and boozy hotel managers on the way down. I'd seen more of them than he had, but I wasn't ambitious; I'd never wanted to rise any further than the front bar on the good nights.

A few minutes later, Alphonse returned to the lounge, trotting alongside a man who stood head and shoulders taller than him, Alphonse's fawning and obsequious manner suggesting the regional manager had arrived. The manager ignored him, striding swiftly and determinedly toward the bar, reading one of the balance sheets Alphonse had given him. Not looking at me, he ordered a Campari and soda.

I said, "Let's see your money first."

The man turned and lunged toward the bar in the same motion, his outraged expression on full throttle. But the corners of his eyes quickly wrinkled into a smile and those deep dimples formed in his cheeks. Big John had always admired audacity.

He looked directly at me for just a second. "Jesus Christ," he bellowed. "Brian McNulty. Hey, bro! How are you?" We shook hands and laughed heartily. I went back a long way with John Wolinski. A dozen or so years before, we'd been young and foolish together, working the stick at the Dockside Lounge in Atlantic City.

Alphonse's jaw dropped to the bar. When he recovered, he couldn't make up his mind whether to join in the laughter or stand aside looking stern. He did a little of both and took on the aspect of the village idiot. I poured John's Campari and soda and asked if he'd like a check.

"Put it on my check," Alphonse said nobly.

"I don't want it on your check, Alphonse," John said.

"It isn't going on my check," I said.

"Swing it, bro," said Big John. We both laughed again. Alphonse's Adam's apple bobbed like he was swallowing goldfish.

John and I made plans to have a drink when I finished my shift. In the meanwhile, he sat down at the corner of the bar to go over the inventory sheets with the trembling Alphonse, and I finished the prep for the night shift and mixed a few drinks for the few early cocktail hour tipplers. At about 5:30, the bar phone rang.

"John Wolinski," a man stammered. The voice sounded familiar, yet so far in the past, I couldn't catch up with it.

"Mr. Wolinski is the regional manager and is expected there," the voice said when I didn't answer right away.

Then it connected to its proper circuit in my memory. "Greg," I said. "Is that you?"

"Who is this?" His tone was formal and cautious.

"It's me, Brian. Brian McNulty." I hadn't seen or spoken to Greg Phillips since he and John and I quit working together a decade before. "What the hell is going on? Is this old home week? John's right here."

"Brian." Greg's tone softened into a semblance of the warm, friendly voice I'd known years before. "I wish I'd known you were in the city, man." He sounded wistful. "Man, I wish I'd known you were here before all this came down."

"What came down?"

"You don't wanna know."

He was right. I'd always been better off not knowing what John and Greg were up to. "I'll get John."

"Yeh, get Big John. He'll know what to do. He always does." Greg's mocking tone was not something I was used to when he talked about John in the past—not something Big John would be used to, either.

John listened gravely to Greg, then said a couple of things I couldn't make out. He spoke softly and seemed to be reassuring Greg. John was good at that: He was the guy you looked to when things went bad. Greg's cynicism aside, John always did come up with something. The only thing I heard him say clearly was, "It ain't like that, bro." When John hung up, he looked troubled.

I cashed out, with the bar clean and stocked and the first wave of cocktail hour patrons tended to—everything set up for Nick, the night guy coming on behind me. For, however little I cared what Alphonse thought of me, I cared what the other bartenders thought. I left the bar the way I used to leave it for Big John at the Dockside before he had me moved to the night shift to be his partner.

After John finished up his business with Alphonse, we went for a drink at the 55 down in the Village. The 55 is off Sheridan Square, a couple of doors from the Lion's Head. I don't know if it ever had a name, but in the years I'd been going there, it was known only by the numbers of its street address: 55 Christopher Street.

John and I were on our second drinks, laughing and telling tales of the old days, when I spied Greg in the doorway, waiting for his eyes to adjust to the dim light, giving the joint the once-over. He didn't take a step farther in than he had to until he was sure. It wasn't hard to get one's bearings in the 55: You came down a couple of steps into the joint; a long bar stretched from the front of the place to the back wall; there were bar stools and, a few feet behind the bar stools, a wall. Dull dark wood and dim lights—people came there to drink, not for the ambience.

Greg wore a lightweight black leather coat. With his granny glasses, his blow-dried blond hair, slightly long in the back to compensate for its receding in the front, he looked like an accountant on his night off. Because of his slight frame, his nervousness, his glasses, and his neatness, he was not someone who stood out in a crowd.

He also hadn't gained a pound in fifteen years. His movements were still quick and jittery, too, so that he probably burned up a day's worth of calories just standing in the doorway, casing the joint. Greg never seemed quite real. He looked like a caricature of the eighties now, just as he had seemed a caricature of the sixties when he used to dress in leisure suits, like a record company executive. He'd dressed stylishly and impeccably, but without any character. He wore clothes like a mannequin might. Nothing about how he looked gave you an entry into what he might be like as a person.

After he'd sized up the place and spied us at the bar, he came over to stand next to John, so that John would be between us. We shook hands all around, and Greg, throwing a fifty on the bar, ordered a round of drinks. It was a kind of a ritual—the way a top-notch bartender entered another man's bar. Still, Greg's arrival put a damper on things. He cuffed me on the shoulder a couple of times and looked me in the eye. But the heartiness was hollow. John didn't even try. He waited, somber and expectant, watching Greg, keeping his peace.

Greg seemed to be running in place while he stood at the bar with his drink. But he'd always been like that; his speed and finesse as a bartender grew out of his nervous energy. He asked how I was and where I'd been, but I could see him drift off into his own thoughts before I had a chance to answer. So I didn't say much, and no one minded. The expression in Greg's blue eyes, magnified by his glasses, gave away nothing. When he finished his drink, he said he had to get to work. John walked out with him. No one invited me, so I stayed put.

Just before he left, Greg wrote a phone number on a bar napkin and told me to call him sometime. He looked at me steadily as he handed me the napkin, so I got the feeling he meant for me to call sooner rather than later. I tried to read him, to get some sense of what was going on. But right then, you wouldn't have known from looking at Greg if he was glad to see me or hated my guts. Still, we'd been friends once. You didn't have to wonder whether Greg would watch your back. So if he wanted me to call, I'd call.

John waited impatiently, a sour expression on his face, until Greg followed him out the door. I sipped my drink and waited, minding my p's and q's. That's how it was in the old days, too. John and Greg always had more business going on than I did.

John was angry when he came back a few minutes later. His mouth was set tight, his eyes were hard, and he didn't speak. He had another drink, which seemed to do a pretty good job of putting the problem with Greg out of his mind. By the time he drove me uptown in his Eldorado, he was laughing and joking again. He got a real charge when I told him I'd never known anyone who owned a Cadillac before. We ate German sausage and drank St. Pauli Girls together at a small restaurant called Wine and Apples on Fifty-seventh Street, and he was himself again. Seemingly, I was, too.

"You haven't changed," said Big John after dinner. His tone implied that I should have. "I thought you'd be in Hollywood by now." He caught himself. "Not Hollywood. Broadway."

"Right," I said, "not Hollywood. Broadway. I'm an out-of-work actor with a higher calling."

He looked at me, the white foam of the St. Pauli Girl clinging to

his bushy mustache, letting me know he knew about dashed dreams
himself. I'd always liked his eyes, dark, lively, alert, kind, and tough,
all this through his glasses. His hair was thinner on top than it had
been, and he'd put on a few pounds around the middle, but not as
much as I had. "I knew you were working at the Sheraton," he confessed, then laughed. "I'm supposed to fire you."

John looked embarrassed. When he laughed, the dimples in his
cheeks flared, making him look boyish. I should have worried about
getting fired, but I knew Big John. Like Alphonse, he was ambitious.
But he was smarter and tougher than Alphonse.

"You remember what you said when I went out front from behind
the bar?"

"No."

"You wanna be the boss, you gotta fuck over your friends."

"My father told me that."

"Still a goddamn Commie."

"Me or him?"

"Both of you."

I wasn't guarded with John. In those long-ago days, following in
the footsteps of my father—who actually was a Communist—I'd
joined with the generation of student radicals bent on overthrowing
the system. Big John, on the other hand, took the system on—head-
to-head—for reasons that were not political but personal, that I never
did understand. The corporations screwed the customers, and they
screwed the workers; Big John understood this. But they were dumb,
too, said Big John, so he planned to con his way to the top—beat
them at their own game.

So far, it looked like his game plan was working, while as for mine:
The enthusiasms of the sixties had produced Ronald Reagan. Now, as a
hotel union steward, I had my work cut out trying to instill the toiling
chamber maids, dishwashers, and bellmen with revolutionary fervor.

John must have read my mind. "You and the fuckin' union," he
said belligerently, leaning across the table. "You stepped on a long-
term arrangement, you know."

"Oh."

"They were coming down to break your head."

"The union?"

"I told them I'd take care of you."

United Bartenders of America, Local 1101, didn't handle criticism well. The leadership was of the knee-break school of trade unionism, and for them I was a wise guy. Local 1101 hadn't let the membership ratify a contract since I'd belonged to it. So a group of us from the rank and file was pressuring them to do so, engaging in anti-American practices like holding shop meetings, publishing a newsletter, and running for office. I suppose my attempt to get elected to the local's executive committee and then filing a Landrum-Griffin charge when they stole the ballots violated the leadership's sense of propriety.

"How will you do that?" I asked John. "Are you going to fire me?"

Big John's eyes twinkled behind his glasses and the dimples returned to his cheeks. "I got a plan."

Watching Big John slip out from between his rock and his hard place, I remembered when he'd helped me organize the union at the Dockside, after it was taken over by a hotel corporation. We struck for two days. He was about to be promoted to his first management job, and the corporation managers threatened him, but he walked out anyway. I don't know how he explained things to the corporate bosses. But two weeks after we settled the contract, he got his promotion.

Charming, gregarious John could talk anyone into anything—even at times like this, when he was worried. "You're not even my biggest problem," he said significantly. His eyelids drooped over his eyes as they did when he got sentimental, especially when he might have to fuck over one of his friends. "Greg is."

Greg was neither ambitious nor charming, and John had been getting him out of scrapes since I'd first met them.

"What's the matter with Greg this time?"

"The company said he had to go." John looked to me for help. "He's on the sauce all the time."

Greg had always drunk too much. Forever, though, he was okay with me. When I'd shown up years ago, longhaired and shaggy, as a service bartender at the Dockside, it was Greg, not John, who took me under his wing and then hooked me up with John. I'd worked a couple of beer joints and thought I was a bartender; they learned me otherwise. The first thing they impressed on me was that they ran the bar—not the manager, who thought he did. The manager, Aaron Adams, was another story. Seeing John and Greg now reminded me I'd been young once and was less so now, with not much to show for the intervening years. John paid for our dinner on his gold American Express card. A couple of months before, I'd had to cut my green one in half and send it back.

After dinner, we moved a couple of blocks to the Carnegie Tavern, where, sipping scotch and waters, we listened to Ellis Larkin play the piano. Big John made friends immediately with the bartender, introducing himself and me, shaking hands, making clear he was a big spender and an even bigger tipper, both of which were true. He dropped a fin in the cup on the piano, so Ellis Larkin stopped over at the bar to say hello at the end of his set. I sat in Big John's shadow, as I'd done so often in the past while he charmed the gathering at whatever bar or hotel we happened into. Big John was still an event, even at the sedate Carnegie Tavern.

"Listen," he said when Ellis Larkin went back to his piano, "I got a plan to take care of you and Greg both. I got to get him out of that club for a while."

"Maybe we can collect unemployment together after you fire us."

"My big chance to fuck over my friends," John announced to the empty tables between us and Ellis Larkin's piano. John had this way of talking in asides, as if an invisible someone out there would understand him. A wry look, a thrown-off line, most of the time the joke on him, he wanted the world to know he was wise to himself.

"This is what we'll do," Big John said. "You're going to take over his job as bar manager at the Ocean Club. It takes you out of the union for the time being, and I'll take Greg out of the club for a while to work for me."

I came abruptly to my senses. "Not me. I don't want to be a boss."

"That's why it works," John said eagerly. "You can hold down the job for Greg. Other people, they'd want to keep the job. You don't

mind it's temporary." He paused, checking on how his pitch was doing, judging if he needed to ratchet up the presentation or might be
able to coast home.

"They wouldn't make me bar manager."

"It ain't up to them. I hire the bar managers."

"They wouldn't let you hire me."

That glimmer was back in his eye. "They already have. I told them
everyone's for sale—even you."

Despite the vision I conjured up of Brian McNulty, bar manager,
cavalierly whipping past the tuxedos clamoring at the bar to graciously
step behind to give the overwhelmed barman a hand, I saw the pitfalls
to this plan. I banged my fist on the bar. "No union, man. They can
fire me whenever they want."

John didn't bat an eye. "You'd be working for me."

"They could fire you, too."

This stopped Big John for a moment. But he bounced right back. "I
can get you a job if they fire you. You'll be an experienced bar manager."

"I couldn't handle the responsibility."

Big John looked at his drink. He then took a pad and a gold foun-
tain pen from his inside pocket and began writing. When he was finished, he ripped off the page and handed it to me:

> Mr. Brian McNulty will assume the duties of bar manager of
> the Ocean Club effective immediately. He has the guaran-
> teed option of returning to his position at the bar of the
> Midtown Sheraton at any time.

I handed it back. "Put in that I keep my seniority rights." We sat in
silence for a minute or two. Then I ordered another drink and told
John I'd sign on for the job at the Ocean Club.

In spite of my certain knowledge that it was all bullshit, I began putting on airs as soon as I realized I might now be a bar manager. Feeling
a bit paternal toward the man making our drinks, who'd taken a moment too long to notice our glasses were empty, I thought, Perhaps I
should remind him, in a kind but firm manner, to keep his head up.

Fortunately, I realized Big John hadn't said anything, and I decided to take my lead from him.

After a few more minutes of conversation, John made ready to leave.

"Drive me uptown," I suggested. "I'll buy you a drink at my neighborhood bar."

My neighborhood bar was Oscar's. I worked there after the Sheraton fired me and, despite some painful memories, usually stopped in for a nightcap on the way home. It was the kind of joint John would like, but he said he had to get back to the Sheraton. "Besides," he told me, "you gotta meet me at eleven at the Ocean Club." He looked me over with some misgiving. "You better wear a suit."

"I don't have one."

Big John rolled his eyes. He prided himself on his designer suits, silk shirts, and Italian shoes. For that moment, I wondered what it was that we had in common. He was cynical, more honest than most people. He was daring also, never an ass-kisser. Despite his faintly disguised contempt for them, the businessmen at the bars always loved him, and so did the dishwashers, even the hotel managers. When I thought for a moment, I realized the real reason I liked John so much—maybe the reason everyone liked him—was that, despite his cynicism, his bombastic personality, and his unbridled ambition, he was kind. This was why he risked his own job now, first to save me, then to send me out to try to save Greg.

When he mentioned the suit, I noticed that my clothes—a white shirt and black pants from the Sheraton, with my black bow tie hanging from my shirt collar by its clip—seemed a bit shabby, although I hadn't really noticed until I was promoted.

"You have to have three or four suits," John said.

"Forget it. I don't want the job."

"Just wear a shirt and tie tomorrow." He looked at my worn and shiny black chino slacks. "You have any other pants?"

"Another pair like these." John looked disappointed, so I said, "There's a Gap near my street. I can get a new pair tomorrow if you want."

Big John shook his head sadly and raised his eyes to the ceiling. Pulling a wad of bills from his pocket, he peeled off three one-hundred-dollar bills. "Get a fucking suit tomorrow."

I couldn't imagine paying that much money for a suit. You can buy one off the rack at Fowad on Broadway for $39.95. Fortunately, on the way uptown I remembered that my friend Carl, a doorman on West End Avenue for the midnight to eight shift, had an in to a suit. He had borrowed suits for us from a guy in his building for a funeral a while back.

I stopped off at his building on the way home. Carl, who wrote poetry during the long night's watch, was reading Baudelaire in his little shack off the lobby. He looked me over when I told him my news.

" 'The working class can kiss my ass; I've got the foreman's job at last,' eh?" he said.

"That's not exactly what I had in mind."

Carl said he'd borrow the suit before he left work in the morning and leave it with Harry, the day guy, so I could pick it up any time after 8:00.

At 11:00, sitting on the kitchen loading dock at the rear of the Ocean Club, drinking from a container of coffee I'd picked up on the way over, trying not to spill any on the borrowed suit, I watched a red tugboat push an oil barge down the East River. It had been a good hike from the Lexington Avenue subway stop, but I liked the walk because it was through a new neighborhood. Something interesting always turns up in a new neighborhood in New York—in this one, I found a store that sold Lionel trains and nothing else. In the window, the old orange engine pulled a coal car and some boxcars through hills and tunnels, past wooden railroad stations with ornate roofs overhanging the platform.

When I'd waited about twenty minutes, enjoying the sun and the peaceful lapping of the river and the gentle rolling of the barge or raft or whatever it was that the Ocean Club sat atop of, I realized once again I had a real talent for doing nothing. I was lulled into contentment by the gentle swaying and the warmth of the sun and the cool of the breeze.

Despite the suit, I felt comfortable on the loading dock, smoking cigarettes with the Guatemalan and Ecuadorian kitchen workers in their American Linen Service whites, with their gentle manners and shy smiles, all of them illegals.

Across the valet parking lot on the uptown side of the restaurant, a couple of white gleaming yachts bumped against the floating piers. Two of the kitchen guys who'd walked over to look at the boats began shouting, pointing into the water. The others, beside me on the dock, lost their sweet smiles. A couple ran over to take a look; the others took off. They went swiftly, right past the restaurant, and disappeared under the raised concrete roadway of the FDR Drive. By the time I sauntered over to take a look in the river, the others had gotten the message and hit the road themselves. I wondered if maybe the INS was coming in by submarine.

Instead, at the base of the hull of the whitest and gleamingest of the yachts, directly beneath the name—*Snug Harbor*—floated a body dressed in a tuxedo.

chapter two

By the time Big John drove up half an hour later in his dark blue Eldorado, the parking lot was crammed with police cruisers, fire trucks, and ambulances, while a police boat and a fire department boat bobbed around in the water next to the bulkhead. A dozen or more cops milled about the cars and trucks and boats. They took pictures, drew chalk lines, erected barricades, measured distances, and sectioned off portions of the area with long strips of yellow tape. Two divers, one from the police department and one from the fire department, both dressed like Martians, bobbed around in the water. Just as John arrived, the amphibious cops, using various riggings from the police motor launch, hoisted the body out of the water and onto the boat.

"What's going on?" Big John asked when he came back from next to the building where he'd parked his car.

"They found a body in the river."

Before I could say anything else, he strode over to the edge of the river, beckoning the police lieutenant over to him, as if he, Big John, had been sent by the commissioner to take charge.

"Can you quiet all this down? You're ruining our lunch business."

"You don't want any lunch business," I told John before the sputtering cop could speak.

John looked at me.

"All the kitchen slaves took it on the lam."

He walked away from the lieutenant as resolutely as he had walked over to him.

In the locker room, I took off my borrowed suit and hung it next to Big John's six-hundred-dollar job. We donned American Linen Service whites and went to work, John on the line, while I made sandwiches: chicken salad with pineapple, tuna and avocado, turkey clubs. Fortunately, the sous-chef, who actually knew how to cook and handled omelettes and such things, was French and had a green card, so he hadn't joined the exodus.

The next hurdle rose up before us at 5:30, when the dinner crowd rushed in, and Greg didn't show up for his shift. John sent me back behind the bar. The bar was new to me, but it didn't take long to find my way around. Greg had set it up, and it wasn't much different from the way I'd set up the bar at the Sheraton; after all, I'd learned it from him. Big John looked on approvingly as I worked my way through the first wave: martinis, Gibsons, perfect manhattans, wine spritzers, Rob Roys, a rare old-fashioned, stingers, whiskey sours, daiquiris. The crowd was older, senior partners and such, out with their wives on Saturday night. These guys had cut their teeth during the cocktail hour heyday in the fifties and could appreciate a well-made drink. The first sips were followed by satisfied looks that were like firm handshakes. As soon as I had things under control, Big John took off. To look for Greg, I guessed.

During the lull between cocktails and after-dinner drinks, I suffered a momentary lapse of concentration and stared out the window at the river while I fantasized about what the bar manager might be entitled to in the way of dinner and other amenities. When I looked up, Detective Sgt. Pat Sheehan stood leaning against the bar, watching me. At that moment, my heart sank with the dread one feels at the first undeniable harbinger of terrible news. The last time I'd seen Sheehan, he'd kept tripping over me while he was conducting a murder investigation in my neighborhood that I tried real hard, but unsuccessfully, not to get involved in.

"Hello McNulty," said Sheehan. "Fancy meeting you here."

"Nice to see you, too." I said, the note of suspicion in my voice as clear to him as it was to me. I approached him gingerly because I knew he was about to tell me something awful, though I had no idea what it might be. Sheehan wasn't the most gregarious of souls; he had no facility for small talk. Yet he stood now in the exclusive Ocean Club in his crumpled suit with the same aplomb as in every other place I'd ever seen him. He didn't need the authority of his badge because he'd developed an authority of a person that one finds rarely, but that I was experiencing for the second time that afternoon.

"It looks like you've happened into an investigation of mine for the second time," he said in a friendly voice. He stood in front of the bar, making no move to sit down or to go away.

"Not on purpose, you can believe me. What are you doing here? I thought you worked on the Upper West Side."

"I'm on loan to the Manhattan Detective Bureau for a couple of months. Now I might ask the same question of you. What brings you to these parts?"

"Well, you might say I'm on loan myself."

Sheehan's manner was such that when he made an effort to be friendly, it seemed so forced that I used to think he was insincere. Eventually, I learned that he was sincere—he just wasn't very good at being friendly.

We looked at each other long enough for me to become uncomfortable. "What is it this time?" I asked when the silence finally got to me.

"We found a body in the river, right outside your door."

"Maybe he fell."

"He fell with a knife wound in his chest and a concrete block tied to his leg."

"Oh."

"He got tangled in the lines of that yacht there, or we wouldn't have found him for years."

"I doubt it means anything one way or another to him," I said. "Maybe he came from the yacht."

"Maybe," said Sheehan. "We don't have an ID yet. Anyone missing from here?"

"This is my first day," I said, but I immediately thought of Greg.

I couldn't imagine someone stabbing him and dumping him in the river—and I didn't want to tell Sheehan, because I didn't want to jinx Greg.

"Who's the manager?"

"I don't know," I said, then added rather stupidly, "I'm the bar manager."

"You don't know who the manager is?" Sheehan repeated. I guessed he was giving me a chance to come up with a more plausible answer. But I actually didn't know who the manager was.

Sheehan tried a different tack. "Who was on the bar last night? I'd like to find out what went on here."

"I don't know." This time my voice wavered, and I dropped my gaze too quickly from his.

"McNulty," he said, "you'd lie to me if I asked you what time it was."

"I don't know what time it is."

Big John returned, making his usual bombastic entrance, bursting through the door, charging up to the bar. Sensing Sheehan's out-of-place presence at once, he turned on him like he'd found a slug in the church collection box. They faced each other like boxers just before the bell.

"John Wolinski, meet Detective Sergeant Sheehan." I felt like the referee.

Big John shook his hand. "You think you guys could keep people from dumping stiffs into our riverfront? This is a high-class joint."

It was a joke—one of John's asides to his invisible audience. If Sheehan got it, he didn't let on. John made a sweeping gesture toward the bar and me. "A Campari and soda, and give the sergeant a drink."

"No, thank you," said Sheehan. "Are you the manager?"

"He's the regional manager," I said.

Big John sipped his drink. "Is this one of those 'Nobody leaves the room' scenes, or can we go on about our work?" He looked Sheehan over. Sheehan was bigger than John by a couple of inches. They both towered over me, and I'm not tiny.

"You go on about your work, Mr. Wolinski," Sheehan said. "I'll do mine."

"Do you have a warrant or something?"

"No," Sheehan said. "You don't want to talk to me, don't."

"Nothing personal," said Big John in a conciliatory tone. "The company likes to believe that everyone who comes in here shits Baby Ruths. You understand?"

Sheehan seemed not to, so I helped him out. "You look like a flat-foot, Sheehan. We don't want you to scare off our customers. We deal with the executive class here. Brooks Brothers, not Robert Hall."

Sheehan was neither amused nor insulted.

"By the way," I said to Big John. "The stiff was wearing a tuxedo. Maybe that will make the corporation feel better."

"Thank goodness," said Big John.

When Sheehan left us to speak with Joseph, the manager, John sat at the bar alone, nursing his drink, and took counsel with himself. I began to restock the bar, but I didn't know where the juices and the fruits were kept. I didn't know how to requisition liquor or where to find the beer. So engrossed was John in his thoughts that I felt like I was interrupting an important conversation when I told him I didn't know where anything was.

"Go tell Joseph I said to find you a bar boy." Then he thought better of it and went himself, passing Sheehan, who was on his way back.

Sheehan stood in front of the bar again, facing me. When he spoke, he sounded more disappointed than accusing. "The manager said the guy who worked this bar last night didn't show up today."

"Did he tell you the entire kitchen crew left this morning?"

"No. He didn't. Illegals?"

I didn't say anything.

"Just when I began to think this place would be more cooperative than the last place you worked, I find they have secrets, too."

"Don't we all?"

Sheehan took a notebook from his inside coat pocket and shuffled through some pages. "We have an ID on the victim. Does the name Aaron Adams mean anything to you?"

"No." I held my poker face in place, picturing Aaron, in his grand manner, striding across the floor of the Dockside in Atlantic City,

menus under his arm, beckoning to a waitress, snapping his fingers at
the busboy, leading a bewildered couple, who had just stopped in for
a hamburger, to a secluded table. I tried not to picture what he'd look
like after he'd been dragged out of the river.

Sheehan watched me as if he could see my thoughts. "For all of
us—but especially for me—I hope this has nothing to do with you,
McNulty."

Sheehan left when the bar boy showed up. The bar boy wasn't a
boy at all, but a man of about my own age. He wore a white dinner
jacket just like mine, in the style of a cruise ship's officers' corp. He
introduced himself as Ernesto and apologized for his poor English.
He was dark-haired and dark-eyed, slightly built, and wiry. His color
was brown with a strong reddish tint, his features angular and sharp. I
liked him right away. He had a bright smile and a warm manner, but
there was also something hard behind the gentleness in his eyes.

I said, *"Mucho trabajo, pequito dinero,"* which was most of the
Spanish I knew. He patted me on the shoulder. I pointed to the fruit
containers. He galloped off toward the kitchen and had the juices and
the fruit refilled in five minutes. We looked into the beer cooler together. I mumbled about a case of this, a half case of that. He waved
his hand reassuringly, patted me on the back once more, took off,
and came back in minutes with four cases on a hand truck. He emp-
tied the beer coolers, cleaned them out, and put the new beer on the
bottom. He got ice without my asking him, wiped down the service
bar again, eyed me when a waitress came up for a couple of whiskey
sours, and, when I nodded, made them.

"You know Greg?" I asked when he had finished. We stood together
in the service bar, which was a little hut at the rear of the main bar.

He smiled. "Your friend?"

I said yes.

"Greg, he all right," said Ernesto.

"He trained me, too."

Ernesto nodded enthusiastically and patted me on the shoulder
again—a workable form of communication.

"You know where Greg is?"

Ernesto stopped nodding, but didn't say anything.

"He's supposed to be here," I prodded. "He didn't show up for work."

Ernesto shook his head, his eyes opening wide with worry. Probably he didn't understand what I was saying, but since I looked worried, figured he should, too. I didn't get a chance to ask him anything else because I caught a glimpse of Sheehan on his way back through the glass doors.

"Who knows what goes on here?" he asked as he slid onto a bar stool. I looked at the ceiling, then at the river. "I'll save you the trouble, McNulty. Get me a cup of coffee and ask the big shot if I could have a word with him."

There was no sense pretending I didn't know whom he was talking about, so I went in back and got John. He came out like a farmer who hears a fox in the henhouse, but sat down quietly enough beside Sheehan and ordered another Campari and soda.

Sheehan very deliberately put a teaspoon of sugar into his coffee. He watched it carefully, as if it might try to get out again, speaking to John without looking at him. "You got any idea where this guy Greg Phillips went?"

John's expression was as pious as an altar boy's. "I have no idea. But I'm sure he had nothing to do with this. The guy was stabbed, right? This is New York. Don't people get stabbed here all the time?"

"All the time," Sheehan said after a sip of coffee. "But people show up for work, too—even here in New York. Did this guy call in?"

John took his time answering. "He may have. I wasn't here."

"Can you find me someone who was here, and can I get this Phillips guy's address?"

"The hostess would know, and she has a list of addresses," John said wearily. He stood and waited for Sheehan, who finished his coffee at his leisure, then asked for the check. I said it was on the house. When Sheehan left, John came over and made a show of looking under Sheehan's cup and picking up his napkin and shaking it out in a vain search for a tip.

It was an old joke, and we laughed. But the laughter sounded hollow, mine and John's. He was a worried man. I'd seen men worried like him before, men who owed money they couldn't pay to people they shouldn't have borrowed from. John left as soon as the door closed behind Sheehan, without another word to me.

The night wasn't especially busy, but it would have been tough without Ernesto. The waiters and waitresses were tolerant enough while I kept them waiting for their drinks as I looked for bottles, or fumbled with the price list, or couldn't find the right glass. They usually waited for a few seconds while I stumbled around; then they asked Ernesto.

When John returned, not long before closing, he didn't seem any more inclined to explain himself than he had been before he left. At the end of the evening, when the last of the patrons had moved on and Big John looked as if he was heading out himself, I called him over.

"I'm ready to exercise my option," I said as he approached the bar cautiously. "Back to the Sheraton. . . . We'll make it a trade. Me and Ernesto to the Sheraton. You get Alphonse, a day bartender, and two waitresses, to be named later."

"Whoa," said Big John. "Wait a minute." His expression was bleak, his eyes sad. "Not you, too, bro?"

He sat down at the bar. I poured him some Glenfiddich and opened a beer for myself. Before he began speaking, I knew he'd convince me to stay. Even though I hadn't seen him in a good few years before last night, if I'd been in trouble—no matter how bad—Big John was one of the few people in the world I'd have gone to. We were bros. The kind who take the rap for each other if it comes to that. Years before, not long after I began working with him at the Dockside in Atlantic City, John didn't show up for his shift one night. The manager—it had actually been Aaron Adams—was going to report him to the hotel's general manager, who would have fired him. I was coming off the day shift and talked Aaron into letting me punch in on John's card. I worked his shift until he rushed in around 11:30, looking like he'd missed his own funeral. He sneaked up behind the service bar and called me aside. When I told him I was covering for him, he was genuinely shocked at what I'd done. There were tears in his eyes when he clasped my hand and said he'd never forget it. And like an elephant, he never did.

Even though I'd aged quite a bit, it seemed I was still a sucker for Solidarity Forever. "Okay," I said. "What's happening?"

"I don't know, bro." I could see in his eyes that his mind was racing over everything that had happened. "None of this makes sense."

"What was Aaron doing here? What about Greg?"

He took a large drink of his scotch and looked me in the eye, as bewildered as I had ever seen him. "Greg is gone," he said in a wavering tone that conjured up the supernatural.

"Gone where?"

"I don't know."

"How do you know he's gone?"

I felt a strong sense of the empty bar. The dull orange lantern lights on the walls reflected off the hardwood floor; two or three candles burned themselves out in their red globe bowls on the dark wooden tables. The lights were dim, but my eyes had adjusted to the peaceful half-light. I liked even this hoity-toity lounge late at night, now that everyone was gone and it belonged to me. Ernesto slipped around behind me, finishing up the restocking and the cleaning. Big John looked him over suspiciously.

"He's a good guy," I said. "Greg broke him in."

John followed Ernesto with his eyes.

"He doesn't speak much English," I said.

John paid no attention. "Hey, come here," John hollered. I didn't like his tone of voice; it was imperious and disrespectful. Ernesto's back stiffened; he held himself rigid for a moment before he turned.

I tried to smile reassuringly, but Ernesto ignored me.

"You work with Greg a long time?" John asked in that superior tone that bosses use.

Ernesto nodded.

"He used to drink all the time. Why didn't you tell anyone?" John sounded like a hanging judge.

Ernesto looked at him stonily.

John took people on like that. He came out punching at the bell. I
didn't like it, but it was his way. I got used to it, so I guessed everybody had to. "I could fire you," he announced to Ernesto. "This is the
new bar manager." He pointed at me. "He could fire you, too. Now, I
want to know what happened here. Where's Greg?"

Ernesto's expression darkened.

"Give him a drink," John said.

"Your friend?" Ernesto asked me, looking at John. His eyes were
dark and smoldering; the gentleness was gone. He clenched his fists,
stiffened his back, adjusted his stance, and waited.

"Greg's friend, too," I said, moving to get between him and John.
"He's our boss."

Ernesto looked at John, a smile crossing his face. He pointed. "The
boss? Him?"

I laughed out loud, while Big John sort of shook himself and rolled
his eyes, getting himself back together after he'd been knocked off his
perch. He'd sized Ernesto up—and maybe decided he was okay. John
wouldn't have taken my word for it, though, or Greg's, either. He
made his own decisions about people, and his standards were tougher
than mine.

Big John explained life behind the bar to Ernesto, the way he'd
once explained things to me. First, he told Ernesto, I was the boss; I
would take care of Ernesto. Ernesto was not to trust anyone besides
Big John and me. Next week, I'd put him on the schedule to work the
service bar one night. He'd also work as a bar boy on the two nights I
worked up front. Everything would work out well for Ernesto, because he was now one of us.

"Okay, bro?" said John clasping his hand thumb-to-thumb, the
way Black Power folks used to back in the sixties.

Ernesto listened and nodded without much enthusiasm. He drank
a beer, then went back to work.

"Talk to that guy tomorrow," John said after Ernesto headed toward the liquor room. "He knows more than he's saying. If he doesn't
talk, fire him."

John stared down my disbelief. "You're the boss; you can fire people—fuck over your friends whenever you want." I was still staring at him when he said, "Greg didn't go home last night."

"What's that mean? Do you think something's wrong?"

"*Wrong?* Of course something's wrong!" Big John's lip curled up at the corner, as it did when he was being cynical. "But maybe not what you think. He took off with his bank and last night's deposit."

chapter three

The lights from the Queens side of the river glittered and danced on the river's black water—that I'm told is made up almost entirely of effluent from half a dozen or so sewage treatment plants along the East River's banks. I finished up behind the bar, poured John another drink, grabbed a beer, and came around to sit down beside him. What I was thinking was that in the old days Greg never did much that John didn't know about. No one did. John was the boss. So it was hard for me to believe John didn't know what was going on with Greg now. I decided to be blunt. "Why did Greg call you yesterday?"

John seemed surprised by the question, as if he'd forgotten about the phone call, and paused for a stiff swallow of scotch before he answered. "I told you about that. He was going to get fired. I didn't want him to screw things up before I could fix it. I told him to sit tight. He said he would. That was it. I guess he didn't."

We sat in thoughtful silence, mulling things over, until I remembered the bar napkin Greg had given me at the 55. "Why did Greg want me to call him?"

"I don't know," John said. "Did you?"

"I was gonna call him today. I didn't know he'd disappear."

John digested this with a couple of nods of his head and a slug of scotch. "Greg's been actin' strange—strange even for him," he said, as if to himself. "I shoulda known somethin' was up." Once more, John shook himself like an old dog. "Maybe you didn't know. But Greg always had this secret side. You know, he'd disappear—sometimes for a couple of days, sometimes a week. He's been doing that for years. Maybe he was hitting on someone else's wife somewhere or went to hang out in whorehouses or lock himself in a motel room to do coke, I don't know—and I didn't care. He always covered himself—changed his schedule, called in sick—took care of him and me. Now, I don't know what happened."

"Aaron got murdered. That's what happened."

"What's that mean?" John snapped. All I could see was the light glinting off his glasses, but I could picture the challenge in his eyes.

I went straight at him. "Did Greg kill Aaron?"

John sat bolt upright. "Why would you ask that? What the hell are you thinking?" His tone was prosecutorial.

But he knew what I was thinking, whether he chose to admit it or not. This wasn't the first time I'd sat in a darkened bar late at night, trying to understand sinister happenings just outside the door. When I first went to work at the Dockside in Atlantic City, I walked into a tragedy. The job I took over had belonged to David Bradley, a friend of John and Greg, their partner at the bar, who'd died of a heroin overdose.

The really strange and horrible thing about his death was that he was found buried in a shallow grave. Then, a few weeks after I started work at the Dockside, before I'd really gotten to know John and Greg, there was another sudden death. The police found the body of Bill Green, a ne'er-do-well hanger-on, especially when it came to John and Greg. He'd been stabbed to death. The rumor going around at the time was that Bill Green had been with David when he overdosed and was the one who'd buried him.

Neither John nor Greg said anything to me about either death. But the other bartenders and the waitresses did. There were rumors. I overheard things. What I remembered now, as John and I sat once more in a dimly lit bar on the cusp of some crazy time warp, was the most startling rumor from those days: that Greg had killed Bill Green. This was what I heard. I never thought it was true. I never knew for sure it was untrue. Nothing like that ever came up again. Until now, almost fifteen years later.

"You remember what happened to Bill Green?" I said.

You would have thought I'd pulled a gun on Big John. He looked that shocked. John knew I'd heard the rumors years before. But none of us had ever said it out loud. I'm sure John no more expected me to speak of it now than he expected me to take off and fly around the lounge.

As I said, the main reason John and I became friends in the old days was that I had been loyal to him, so he would be loyal to me—and an important part of that loyalty was that I didn't ask questions about things that weren't my business. This reticence came from some kind of code—taken whole-hog from 1930s James Cagney movies—that I signed on for when I joined up with John and Greg: You take the fall yourself before you rat on a partner. He lies; you swear to it. You mind your own business. As the old bartenders said, "You work the bar deaf; you leave it dumb."

I didn't have to be told how silly all this should sound to a grown man. But back then, I had jumped in with both feet. I believed these guys would follow me into the grave rather than let me go it alone. And I wanted them to believe that of me, too. If there was anything about their business they wanted me to know, they'd tell me. If they didn't tell me, I didn't want to know. That was what John required of me and that was what he got.

John sighed and then drank before turning to size me up, his expression pained with disappointment, as if I'd broken the code and he would now have to drum me out of the brotherhood. "Greg didn't kill Aaron, if that's what you're thinking," he said simply, making clear by his expression and stiff manner that I'd lost some of my standing. "Someone found Aaron and killed him. Greg must've thought he was next, so he hit the till and took off. That's all. Something maybe was goin' on with him and Aaron, I don't know."

Properly chastened, I returned to sipping my beer and playing second fiddle. Just like in the old days, there was more going on than I knew. Once again, I should listen and do what I was told.

John sat in stony silence for a moment, but after a while, he seemed to come to terms with things. "You know, the fuckin' guy gets out of hand; this is what happens. I shoulda saw this comin'."

"You should have seen a murder coming?"

"Not a murder," John shook his head. He leaned toward me, making clear what he was saying was only between us. That quickly, I'd regained my standing. "Just that when things were finally startin' to go good for me. I shoulda known something would happen to fuck it up. I shoulda dumped Greg years ago. You know, you got family and friends from when you're young. You stick up for them. And this is what happens." John sounded mean—a lot meaner than I knew him to be; maybe as mean as he wanted to be.

"Like you should dump me now," I said. "You wanna be boss, you gotta fuck your friends."

"Dump you, too, you son of a bitch—you and your fucking union." John took off his glasses, and I saw in his eyes that the kindness and the sadness had returned. Funny how the two go together.

John wasn't going to dump me, nor would he, when push came to shove, throw Greg to the sharks, either. I didn't necessarily believe Greg hadn't killed Aaron. John would say he didn't, whether he did or not. Even if Greg were up to no good, this wouldn't ruin his chances with John. John had chalked up a fair amount of no good himself in his time. It was the way John and Greg stuck together—and that they cut me in—that had won me over when I first ran up against them years before.

I arrived in Atlantic City in 1973, when the city was on the skids, the hustlers doing the Boston Stand Around on the street corners, waiting for legalized gambling to restore the city's former grandeur and their bankrolls. I was on the skids myself. For years, I'd been driving a cab in the city, trying to get a break in the theater, trying to keep my marriage afloat. My wife never believed I could become an actor, never cared if I did. Finally, she got fed up with auditions, bit parts, and some other things and threw me out. I lost my real job—the one that paid the bills. I felt like I'd sold my baby son down the river. So I took to the suds—and I hadn't seen my kid in a couple of months. I was in Atlantic City, trying out for a part at a theater there. Some people from the Actors Studio were doing *Death of a Salesman,* and I got the first break I'd gotten in a long time: I got to play Biff in an Equity show, with some first-rate actors in the other parts.

The second break was running into Greg Phillips at the audition. He was a primitive actor—a couple of high school plays under his belt—and the competition was all trained actors, so he didn't have a chance, even though he was the only one who'd memorized a part. He was disappointed at not getting a callback but pleased I had, admiring me far out of proportion to my worth, because I was a professional actor, even if my credits were small, few, and far between. When I got the part, we had a couple of drinks together. I told him if I was going to do the play, I had to get a second job so I could pay my child support. He hooked me up with Big John. They got me the job at the Dockside. Later, they helped me get my son back.

"You remember when you and Greg took me back to Brooklyn to see Kevin?" I asked John.

He looked at me steadily and his eyes glistened. He shook his shoulders and waved me away.

Thinking about the Dockside and the time I spent at the shore brought back one other memory that flitted through my mind a couple of times. I'd been embarrassed to bring it up, but now I'd had enough to drink for sentimentality to overtake my better judgment. "Do you ever see Linda Moroni?" I asked, embarrassed down to my toes as I said it.

John started for a second, as if I'd snapped him out of a reverie; then he chuckled. "Funny you should ask. I forgot all about that . . . you and Linda. You were as cute as a couple of pups together." He looked me over warmly, as if he shared my regret. But I lost my courage and didn't ask the follow-up—shades of Gordon Lightfoot— "Did she mention my name just in passing?"

John dropped back into his reverie, and I began one of my own. Back during the Dockside days, John, Greg, and their cronies had any number of small-time hustles going on. John's father was a crook of some sort, and, I guess, the source of the penny-ante rackets. So because of this, John was top dog. But John had bigger ambitions than being a small-time hood. He was doing his best to make it in the corporate world. I knew about John's old man because John and I used to talk about our respective outlaw fathers—mine, the Communist; his, the grifter—when we drank together at the bar after closing. During our talks on those nights years before, I grew to understand John loved his father, despite the man's larcenous ways. Knowing about John and his feelings for his dad, even though I never met the man, helped me understand the contradictory and unfathomable relationship I had with my own father. It was funny, too, that John came to admire Pop. Despite his corporate ambitions, John saw himself as a workingman. He hated the corporate mucky-mucks, even though he was bound and determined to become one—so he liked that Pop spent his life taking them on. And when he and Pop met on his trips to the city after I moved back, they really hit it off.

For anyone working the stick, it wasn't hard to become corrupt. If you spent your life in gin mills, it was pretty easy to fall in with bad company: bookies, call girls, slot machines in the back room, coke, bennies, and amyl nitrite in the restrooms. If, like John, you knew all the numbers runners, bookies, and small-time hustlers as family friends from childhood, corruption was even more of an occupational hazard.

When I first knew John, he and Greg were tangled up in some kind of marijuana-transporting operation. Since I'd known any number of folks over the years who dealt pot, this wasn't any big deal for me. I smoked the stuff. Why should I care how it got to me? John told me about the marijuana transporting because he needed me to switch shifts with him now and again. He tightened me up with free weed, and I covered for him and kept my mouth shut. This was the extent of my criminal enterprises.

Added to this, in the circles we traveled, John's father's reputation provided an aura of romance—I was hanging out with Big John, the son of Charlie Wolinski, who had something to do with the mob from Philadelphia, who was seen in the company of Big-Nosed Sam or Little Mikie. When we'd come across one of the reputed gangsters showing off in a barroom, he'd nod to Big John, shoot his cuffs a couple of times, and buy us a drink. It was cool being the kind of bartender Louie Suspenders shook hands with before he ordered a drink. These small-time grifters were impressed when John became a hotel manager. He always treated them with the kind of phony respect they expected, so they didn't mind that he wanted legitimacy instead of the rackets.

Now John waved his arm around to take in the entire Ocean Club. "You know, Greg coulda been manager here." He stopped and, leaning on both elbows, kind of sagged over the bar, staring at the bottles on the back shelf. After a minute or two, he got up and went to make himself a drink. Behind the stick, he handled himself with his old sureness and confidence. He didn't pick through a bunch of bottles before he found the one he wanted. Remembering where the Glenfiddich was from watching me, he reached up to the back shelf, slammed his hand against the neck of the bottle for a solid grasp, picked it up, and poured in the same motion, pouring water from the small pitcher on the bar with his other hand at the same time, working on the rail, not spilling a drop.

He put the bottle back and took a long drink. Then, as he was drinking, the small video camera above the bar caught his eye. He looked at it for a long time before he picked up a bar towel and draped it over the whole camera, covering the lens. "I hate those fucking things," he said.

Watching him, I got an idea. "John. Maybe we can go over that film and find out who was at the bar last night. Maybe Aaron came to the bar. Maybe someone was with him. Maybe that's who killed him."

John looked at me with a patient, bored expression. "Those cameras don't watch the customers, bro. They watch the bartenders and the cash register."

He was right. They used them at just about every bar I ever worked at, even years before, back at the Dockside. Nearly every piece of equipment, from automatic pourers to computerized cash registers, was developed to protect the hotel corporations from their bartenders.

John stayed behind the bar, feeling his way around. "You know, bro, sometimes I wish I was still workin' the stick. I miss it, you know.

Being one of the guys. Like they say, it's lonely at the top." He said this without irony. Despite his charm and sophistication—and his meteoric rise in the corporate world—Big John was a simple man. Part of his fascination with me when we first met was that I'd been to college. He had that respect for a college education held only by people who'd never gotten one.

"Poor Greg," I said after a long period of silence. "How's he get himself into these messes?" Greg was the most fickle of souls. As far as work was concerned, he was fastidious, neat, punctual, meticulous. But in his own life, he was out of step with everything. If everyone dressed casually in jeans, Greg would wear a suit. If it was a wedding and everyone wore suits, Greg would show up in overalls. Despite his fastidiousness, he was always forgetting and always late. Most of the time, he got there—wherever it might be—when everyone was leaving. He wore an alarm wristwatch, which added to his image of robotlike efficiency; but it served mostly to remind him of events he forgot to show up for and places he should have been. He never got along with bosses, either, even though he tried. Aaron would tell him not to open the second bar station. Greg would give him thumbs-up and go on about his business. An hour later, Aaron would come back and both stations would be open. Aaron would holler. Greg would listen humbly. Sometimes he would say sadly to himself, " 'When, in disgrace with fortune and men's eyes . . .' " and Aaron would stomp out of the room.

Yet Greg was a stand-up guy. I'd never forget the afternoon he and John took me back to Brooklyn. John negotiated with my ex-wife while Greg and I walked around and around the block—it must have been a dozen times—until I saw John standing on the steps of my old house. He was holding Kevin and waving for us to come over. I got ahold of the kid and never let go. I've seen Kevin every week since then. It's not good enough, but Kevin is a forgiving kid; he takes what he can get.

I took a long drink of beer. "Poor Greg," I said again.

"Poor Greg, yeah," said John. "Poor everybody." When he wrinkled his brow, his glasses slid lower on his nose, so he pushed them back up, then looked searchingly at me. He pulled a wad of bills out of his pocket, thumbed through it, and spread the bills out on the bar. They were twenties and fifties and hundreds, a half dozen or more of each. "You know, bro, I look at these, and I know I could be stone-broke again tomorrow. I've spent fifteen years getting this far. You know what I had to do to make it—everyone thinking I'm a gangster because of my old man. Now I've been straight for a long time. But the company gets wind of this, nothing I did will make any difference. The fuckers'll rifle me in a minute."

John sat hunched over the bar and sort of rolled his shoulders to turn his head in my direction, his expression that of an honest man willing to take his medicine. It was far into the night, the sky bending toward morning. It seemed like we'd ended a million nights like this. "I gotta find Greg. . . ." John said to himself.

I suddenly felt tired, and when I get tired like that, I get cold, so I began to shiver slightly. "Do you think Greg is going to get killed?"

The question caught John by surprise, even though it shouldn't have. His expression at that moment was unguarded: He looked scared.

chapter four

I woke up the next morning with a sinking feeling, remembering I'd told John I'd help him find Greg. Why hadn't I kept my mouth shut and let him handle things? No sir, not me, not Helpful McNulty himself. Even when John tried to talk me out of it, I insisted. Now I was supposed to see Ernesto this morning—actually early afternoon—and worm out of him whatever it was John was sure he hadn't told us the night before.

When I checked with my service, I discovered John had already called with Ernesto's address. There was one break: He lived on 104th Street on the West Side, not far from me. Pop had called also, so I called him first. It was his fault I got myself involved in things like this, anyway. Battering me day and night all through my youth with his stories of man's inhumanity to man, the struggles of the wretched of the earth, the dignity of labor, and the insidiousness of inherited wealth, he'd stamped indelibly on my brain that the concerns of my fellowman were mine, as well.

Pop had called because he wanted to go to a ball game with Kevin and me when the Yankees got back into town later in the week. This, in turn, reminded me of John's boy, Robert, who was two years older than Kevin. Years ago, after I'd left Atlantic City and moved back to New York, John used to look me up when he came to the city with Robert, and we'd go to Yankee games together, he and I and the boys.

At Yankee Stadium, it isn't hard to pass for a real dad. Neither of us were real dads, but at the stadium during those night games when the Yanks battled the Red Sox for the pennant, we pretended we were. The last time I'd seen John before all this had been on Kevin's seventh birthday, at the stadium.

I told Pop I'd seen John, there'd been a murder at the Ocean Club, Greg was missing, and I was helping John look for him. He was disturbed by the murder but pleased John was in town and suggested I invite him to go to the game with us.

"Maybe," I said. "But we might be too busy looking for Greg."

"He has to eat and drink and sleep," said the old man heartily. "Look for him there."

"Where?"

"Where he'd eat or sleep."

"I don't know where he'd eat or sleep."

"You can ask. Nose around a bit." Pop was a big fan of the chase. He was also determined that I would accomplish things in life. I was a great bewilderment to him, right up there with the working class. He couldn't understand why neither of us would do what he thought we were capable of.

"Who was the man who got himself murdered . . . and why would he do that?"

"His name is Aaron Adams. But I don't think he got himself killed on purpose."

"This I can tell you," Pop said after a pause. "The better you know the victim—the more you know about how he lived his life, why he ended up at the place he died at the time he died there—the sooner you will know who killed him."

"I don't know if I want to find out who killed him. Suppose it was Greg?"

"Suppose it wasn't?"

"Actually, I'm worried about that, too. Someone might be after Greg."

"Who saw Greg last?"

"The bar boy, probably. John wants me to talk to him this morning. But he didn't tell us anything last night, so I don't know what good seeing him today will do."

Pop is a retired journalist, a charter member of the Newspaper Guild, and a lifelong Communist, prematurely retired from the working press by the blacklist back in the fifties. After that, he worked for unions until he retired, voluntarily this time. He'd been a top-notch investigative reporter before anyone heard the term, and, at one time, did internal investigations for one of the needle trades' unions, searching out arrangements between corrupt business agents and crooked bosses. The experience had jaded him: He didn't necessarily believe people were who they said they were, that things were as they seemed, or that you took anything on faith.

"Who is this bar boy?"

"His name is Ernesto. He's from Chile."

"That's all? I suppose it's beneath the dignity of a bartender to chat with his subordinates," said Pop, bitter sarcasm as much a part of him as his piercing look.

"I've only been there one day," I grumbled.

"And this job title, bar boy, I suppose he's eleven or twelve, not grown up yet?"

"He's grown-up," I said. "A man."

"So the degrading job title is so you don't feel bad paying him your cheap tips?"

"John moved him up to the service bar one night," I said defensively. I didn't have the heart to tell Pop that John had made me a boss.

On 104th Street, tiny brown-skinned boys and girls played in and among abandoned cars, worn-out mattresses, broken-down armchairs, and burned-out couches along the sidewalk and gutters. Men worked on cars propped up on metal milk crates along the curb; women in housedresses sat on the stoops. It was midday warm, almost summer hot. The upper-middle-class white people live west of Broadway in the massive gilded-ghetto apartment buildings on and off West End

Avenue. The low-wage working folks—once Irish and German, now Dominican, Ecuadorian, and Chilean—live in five-story walk-ups on the east side of Broadway, the neighborhood stretching north through the Manhattan Valley and east toward Central Park, where at some nebulous point it becomes Harlem. The people living in these walk-ups spend a good part of their lives outside because the apartments are cramped and stifling. Despite the detritus, these folks aren't any messier than the folks over on West End. They just don't have as many people picking up after them.

Given the activity, and the music from the parked cars and apartment windows, the street had a neighborhood feel to it. But the neighborly ambience broke down at each end of the block, where the dope dealers and their outriders, half a dozen nervous, watchful, slippery, streetwise kids, old beyond their years and destined for short and painful lives, patrolled Amsterdam and Columbus avenues. Their presence seemed to make everyone unhappier.

The woman I asked directions from had been laughing and chatting with her neighbor, watching her child from the stoop, when I stopped in front of her. She gave no indication of understanding English at all until I said I worked with Ernesto, and then, satisfied that I wasn't a Yuppie in search of dope or a collection man from Household Finance, she said, "Fifth floor rear." I should have known it would be the fifth floor.

Ernesto's wife, small and dark, with beautiful black eyes, opened the door while I stood in front of it, puffing from the climb. Three dark-eyed children of varying sizes, none of whom reached her waist, gathered around her skirts. She looked scared.

"I'm a friend of Ernesto," I said hopefully, though I didn't suppose I was really a friend or that he wanted me nosing around his home the day after I met him.

"Buenos días," Ernesto said from a doorway behind his wife. He smiled a cautious but friendly smile and didn't seem surprised. I liked the way his face creased and his eyes sparkled, and I liked the way a couple of the kids went to him to hang on to his leg while they watched me.

"You're up early for a bartender," I said.

"You, too." He pointed at the kids. "When they awake, no one sleeps in the neighborhood." He laughed.

Acutely aware of the impoliteness of my visit, I mumbled an apology.

"I expect you," Ernesto said.

I waited.

"Greg ask me not to say, so I no say."

"Don't say what?"

"Greg no say his friends. He just ask me no say." He held his hands out in front of him in a pleading gesture.

I held up my own hands in front of me like the proverbial Jewish tailor to suggest I shared his concern. I didn't know if he should trust me, either. "Maybe I can help him."

"I don't know," said Ernesto. He sized me up and thought it over. As he did this, I realized Pop had been right, as usual. Without actually thinking about it, I'd already judged Ernesto by his station in life, assuming that if I had the better job, I must be the superior person. But it became clear to me now as Ernesto weighed his options that he hadn't made the same judgment. After a few minutes, he reached for his jacket. "Let's see," said Ernesto. We took the train downtown then walked across to the club without speaking much.

In Greg's locker, which Ernesto opened quite deftly by listening to the rattle and fall of the tumblers on the combination lock, we found a freshly pressed bar jacket, a freshly dry-cleaned tie, two laundered and starched shirts on hangers, and a clean pair of black slacks with a sharp crease. Greg never recovered from navy boot camp; he was always ready for inspection. We also found a small leather toiletry bag with Old Spice aftershave, Right Guard deodorant, Tic Tacs, and a portable electric razor. When I switched the razor on, for no reason other than to see if it would buzz, I guess, Ernesto jumped a foot away from me. He laughed then, like it had been a joke, but the fear in his eyes bordered on terror.

I stared at him, holding the buzzing razor, until I realized what I was doing and shut it off.

Smiling sheepishly, he pointed to the union pin on my shirt collar. "I was union," he said.

I began to catch on, remembering Pinochet and the torture ship in Santiago harbor.

"You were in jail in Chile?"

With a grim smile, he touched the shaver, then his face, his fingers, and his testicles.

I put my hand on Ernesto's shoulder. I wanted to tell him he could trust Big John, but, though I knew I could, I didn't know if he could. This wasn't his business; why should he help? The expression in his eyes told me he'd had enough of being brave the last time around, in Chile; now he wanted to be home with his wife and kids.

I put the razor back in the leather bag, and Ernesto put the bag into Greg's locker and closed it. He opened his own locker then, pulling out a large interoffice mail envelope, tied closed but not sealed and addressed to no one. He handed it to me. In the envelope, I found an American Express card—even Greg had managed to hold on to his— a driver's license, a Social Security card, a Macy's card, and a check-cashing card from Sloan's, probably all of Greg's identification.

Greg's address was on his license, Seventh Avenue in Brooklyn. I wrote it down and gave the envelope back to Ernesto, telling him to put it in Greg's locker. Obviously, the police hadn't gotten to the locker yet. They would need to establish he'd flown the coop before they could get a search warrant and, lacking Ernesto's finesse, pry it open with a crowbar. It would be better for them to find Greg's papers in his own locker, rather than in Ernesto's.

I told Ernesto he could punch in and start his shift early, since we were already there, then asked again if he knew where Greg had gone, figuring if he knew this much, he probably knew more. John had suggested I threaten to fire him to get him to talk, but I figured I was above such things. Instead, I stood for a while in front of the lockers, scratching my head and looking perplexed. Ernesto stuck with me while I scratched my head, wrinkled my brow, and pursed my lips. He seemed to be rooting for me, but gave no indication that he would be of any help.

I began speaking as if to myself. "If I could figure out what Greg was doing that night . . ." Out of the corner of my eye, I sneaked a look at Ernesto. He smiled politely. "The tough thing is," I said to myself, "Greg may not know how to get in touch with me or John. If he knew we were looking for him . . ." I finally faced Ernesto, who began changing for work. "Look," I said. "You ask Greg. If you asked him, he'd tell you to tell me what was going on, so I could help him. Call Greg and ask him."

Ernesto continued dressing and just shook his head. The gentle expression evaporated. The hard look he'd taken on with Big John the night before came back. "I go to work now." He started to walk away.

When I called him back, he looked over his shoulder but kept going. My temper got the best of me. "Hey," I shouted. "Ernesto. You work for me. Don't fucking walk away like that."

This time, he didn't even look back. Two or three busboys, who'd come in to change for their shift, were watching. I could have sworn they were snickering. The more I thought about it, the more pissed off I got at Ernesto. When the Sunday-night bartender arrived around five o'clock, I went back and found Ernesto in the pantry area between the kitchen and the bar, where the waiters and busboys were getting supplies to set up for Sunday supper. I asked Ernesto again if he knew where Greg was. Half a dozen of Ernesto's fellow workers caught the drift of what was going on and had an ear cocked in our direction. Behind me, I heard the buzz of conversation—what's the word for asshole in Spanish? Ernesto, like a good basketball ref, walked away, trying to save me from myself. But I was too far gone; I needed to save face.

"Okay, Ernesto," I said. "Back in the locker room. I'm not finished."

He'd begun cutting up fruit and was slicing oranges, continuing to ignore me.

"All right, pal. That's it," I said. "You're fired!"

Ernesto glanced up from his cutting, his expression a mix of controlled rage, piercing hatred, pity, and disgust, as if he'd hoped for better from me. He finished the orange he was cutting, put down the knife, and headed for the locker room.

In the first flush of power, I felt the thrill of vindication. But after an hour or so, I began to feel like I'd murdered a baby. Corrupted by power on my second day. I couldn't believe what I'd done—taking away someone's job, sending the guy home to tell his wife and kids he didn't have grocery money, couldn't pay the rent. It was like stabbing him.

I worked the bar through the late afternoon, then watched the night bartender, Herb, for a while. He didn't need me, so I wandered between the bar and the small bar manager's office behind the liquor room until well into the evening. When I got tired of kicking myself, I called Ernesto's to tell him he could have his job back. He wasn't there, so I tried to explain to his wife, who didn't speak English, first that I had fired Ernesto, then that I was hiring him back. I don't know what the hell I ended up telling her.

After that, I sat and thought for a while, finally deciding to try to do something useful. I called John's office. No one answered but the machine said John would retrieve his messages frequently, so I told him I was going to Greg's apartment—one place he might eat or sleep—and asked John to meet me there.

I walked all the way across Thirty-fourth Street to Seventh Avenue and took the number 2 train to the Grand Army Plaza stop in Brooklyn. Years before, when a couple of lesbian real estate operatives first staked out the area, I'd gone out with a woman who lived on Eighth Avenue. For a while, it looked like they might be able to create a kind of Amazonia in that section of Brooklyn, but, like all good neighborhoods, it went to hell when the Yuppies found it and came rushing in to pay exorbitant prices to gentrify the place.

Along Prospect Park West, I joined up with a small troupe of young men and women in designer sweatsuits, hurrying home from their health clubs to their brownstones. The brownstones had been sandblasted and reworked into one- and two-bedroom apartments that were sold as co-ops by real estate agents named Fern. Seventh Avenue had been cleaned of drug dealers and junkies, just as if the town had hired a new sheriff.

On a corner in front of candy store and on the stairs of the stoop next to it, teenagers lounged, smoking cigarettes, reminding me of the Brooklyn of my youth. A pretty dark-haired girl wearing black chino pants looked at me as I passed. She hadn't filled out enough yet to fill her chinos completely, but she dragged on her cigarette and looked me in the eye with a kind of haughty flirtatiousness. I was surprised teenagers still smoked. Kids like me didn't know cigarettes would kill us back in the days we used to sit on the stoops smoking and trying to look tough; we thought the worst smoking could do was stunt our growth. I was disappointed these kids were like me, that there didn't seem to have been any progress. Something like panic came over me. I stopped in my tracks and hoped and hoped for my son, Kevin, that his life wouldn't be fucked up, that he'd be okay.

Greg's apartment was in a four-story building on Seventh Avenue— a street of storefronts in three- or four-story brownstone buildings with apartments above the stores. His was above a health-food store and had on one side what looked like a typical pretty good-food, refurbished restaurant, and on the other side was an old-fashioned neighborhood bar that seemed to have weathered the Yuppie invasion as it had various other neighborhood shifts over the years. I didn't have grand expectations in going to Greg's apartment; it seemed unlikely he or anyone else would be there. But I rang the bell and waited.

When no one answered, I went into an upscale place on the right to have a beer to help me think. The bar was too loud, with too much blond wood, too many hanging plants, and too many young men with overdeveloped pectorals, wearing sport shirts and cologne. I left and went to the bar on the other side. This one was quieter, clean, and un-adorned, with a dull wooden floor, a dark mahogany bar, wooden backed-bar stools, with a faded mirror and ornate dark wood behind the bottles on the back bar. A few elderly women, probably retired and lonely, sipped sherry or manhattans at the bar, their large handbags propped beside them. They looked like they were used to the place. A couple of older men stared vacantly at the Met game on the TV above the bar. At one end, a handful of younger men watched the game with more interest; none of them wore cologne. I ordered a draft beer from the bartender, who pulled himself away from the game to pour it. He didn't wear cologne, either. I asked him the score. But he didn't know and had to ask the guys watching. They had to discuss it themselves before someone made an educated guess that it was three to one, Mets in the fifth. Gooden was pitching, so three runs should be enough, I figured.

I drank my first beer before asking the bartender if he knew Greg. I spoke softly so no one else would hear, but he took a look around the bar, wrinkled up his mouth, and made it clear that he didn't like my having asked.

"He's an old friend of mine," I said. "We used to tend bar together." This cheerfully imparted bit of information didn't improve my standing. The bartender grunted, his expression even nastier than it had been, and went back to the ball game, not even bothering to refill my glass. I hung on; sooner or later, he'd have to come back my way.

Sure enough, on one of his passes to the service bar, he inadvertently looked at me, so I ordered a refill. Although he gave the impression he'd rather throw it, he set it down gently in front of me. I laid a five down, so he'd have to bring change. "He's in trouble," I said. "Maybe I can help him."

The bartender bent slightly toward me. "Look, I don't know who the fuck you are," he said. "Why should I tell you a fuckin' thing?"

Ah, the noble New York City bartender!

I sipped a couple of beers and watched Gooden bring it in, trying John's number a few times between innings, at first telling his machine where I was, then leaving nastier messages each time. After an hour or so, as fate would have it, I went to pee before I headed back to Manhattan. When I went to the men's room, I noticed that the joint had a rear entrance off a hallway next to the kitchen. There was a screen door leading out, which for some reason piqued my interest. Taking a quick look outside, I discovered the yard behind the bar connected to the yard behind Greg's apartment building. There was also a tree and a fire escape. I thought this over as I peed—although *thought* is too strong a word to describe the process. I could climb the tree onto the fire escape of the building the bar was in, go up that fire escape, cross the roof, and then go down the fire escape of Greg's building and take a look in the window of his apartment. Why did I want to do this? I have no idea. Nor did I have any idea then. It seemed the thing to do. Maybe in my cell-diminished brain I thought it was what Lew Archer would have done.

Up I went, feeling quite athletic for a man in his forties with a beer gut. I hoisted myself between the tree and the wall of the building until I could haul myself up onto the first limb of the tree. From there, I leaned over to the fire escape and got a foot and a hand on the rungs hanging from the first platform. Once aboard, again with some difficulty, I climbed the fire escape stairs. The adrenaline was pumping, my heart was thumping, and I was puffing like the little engine that could. Dodging the windows of the apartments above the bar, both of which were dark, I crossed the roof and came down the ladder on Greg's building.

A dim light shone from the window of the top-floor apartment, so I climbed back and hung over the ridge of the roof to take a peek. No one in Brooklyn, it has long been known, has window shades. A man and a woman were in the throes of ecstasy on a bed not more than five feet from my face. The man was on top, looking down at the woman. The woman had her face turned sideways on the bed, so she was facing the window; she was alternately chewing on her lower lip and opening her mouth, gasping, while the man went up and down like a pile driver and the bed rocked back and forth like the old Erie Lackawana. If her eyes had been open, she would have looked directly into mine. I slithered under the window and damn near lost my footing on the ladder between the top floor and the third floor. Fortunately, she didn't open her eyes.

The third floor was dark, as was the second—Greg's apartment. It was impossible to see anything. I looked around from my perch on the fire escape's landing, wondering for the first time if anyone could see me. There were plenty of windows facing me. But I didn't see anyone looking. I tried Greg's window. The latch was broken, so I opened it. Climbing gingerly through the window, I found myself in a bedroom. The bed made, no clutter on the surfaces of the bureau or night table, it was as neat as a hotel room, with not much more personality. Greg's neatness always made me uncomfortable; now here where his life should be, the neatness concealed too much. I didn't have a flashlight. But I didn't see any reason not to turn on the lights, so I did.

The next two rooms, in what was a good-sized apartment by New York standards, were as neat and nondescript as the bedroom. The rooms connected through internal doors, like a railroad flat, but there was also a hallway from the kitchen to the front door. When I got to the front—what should have been a living room overlooking Seventh Avenue—I found that it had been made into another bedroom. This room had a lived-in look: The bed—a mattress on the floor—was unmade; clothes dripped off the chairs. There were papers and other clutter on the surface of a wobbly bureau, magazines carelessly piled beside the bed. The magazines were *Penthouse* and *Playboy*. And a copy of *Jane's Pocket Book of Pistols and Sub-Machine Guns*.

This new wrinkle, which I might have guessed if I'd had half a brain, gave me something to think about. Should I wait there for the roommate to return, scare the shit out of him—and have him blow my brains out with his pistol or submachine gun? Or should I wait downstairs until I saw a light and then ring the bell and come back up? clearly the more prudent choice. Next, I had to decide whether to go back down the fire escape or use the front door and the stairs like a normal person. I chose the latter path and ran into two of the Seventy eighth Precinct's finest, standing with guns drawn on either side of Greg's door when I opened it. A couple more cops with drawn guns were at that moment climbing in the window from the fire escape, so it really didn't make any difference which route I'd chosen.

The officers in the hallway were as scared as I was, so they screamed and waved their guns in my face. I threw my hands up, shouting, "Don't shoot! Don't shoot!" and flattened myself against the doorjamb. This wasn't good enough for them, so one of them spun me around and kicked my feet out from under me, while the other slapped me on the side of the head with the hand holding the grip end of his pistol as I slid past. I partially blocked my fall with my hands, but my face, chin-first, still banged against the floor, which I noticed, stupidly, was pretty dusty. One of the cops held his gun on me while the other wrenched my arms behind my back and cuffed my wrists together.

"You're making a mistake," I advised them.

But as they pulled me to my feet and pushed me toward the stairs, I sensed we all knew who'd made the mistake.

chapter five

The boys from the bar next door found the cop cars and flashing lights more interesting than the recap of the ball game, so they came out to take a look, while the cologne scented sports from the other joint gathered around menacingly, as if they might take the law into their own hands. The cops pushed me into the backseat. One put his hand on top of my head so I didn't bounce it off the roof on the way in—a nice gesture, usually reserved for criminals they don't have a grudge against. They sped me around a couple of corners and off to the precinct.

With some difficulty, I persuaded the desk sergeant to call Sheehan, my old nemesis. I don't know what help I thought he'd be. I also called Peter Finch, a lawyer I knew from the West Side bars. His dad and Pop fought the labor wars of the 1930s together. Peter was of the breed of brash young leftist lawyers who had resurrected the National Lawyers Guild in the 1960s. Later, he transformed himself into a successful-enough criminal lawyer, whose unsavory clients bankrolled his humanistic legal support of the underdog—among whose numbers I counted myself. I left my SOS on his answering machine.

For quite a while, I sat on a blond wooden bench and waited until my turn for picture and prints. The cop who walked me through the booking process was a pleasant, chatty guy, who found common ground, as if we were fellow workers, just on opposing teams, like Gary Carter chatting with the second baseman of the other team after sliding in for a double—or, as in my case, after being thrown out stealing.

"You live in Manhattan?" the cop asked when he looked at my card. I sat in a straight-back chair, holding a number under my chin. "You'd come to Brooklyn for a B and E?"

"I grew up in Brooklyn," I said, realizing immediately this wasn't the answer I wanted to give.

"Me, too," he said. "Where?"

"Flatbush."

"Bensonhurst. So'd you know this guy?"

I said, "Yes . . . sort of."

"Have something of yours?"

"Not exactly. It's a long story."

"Usually is," the cop said as we moved to the next stage of the booking process. "Just relax your hand and let me roll it across the ink pad."

When the bars clanged shut behind me, I sat on a metal cot to contemplate my life to that point. Staring at a stained toilet against the back wall of my cell, I resolved to reform. The night passed slowly. I longed for sleep, listening to the groans and laments hollered out by my fellow felons—all of us, it seemed, innocent victims of ironic twists of cruel fate. I was tempted to tell my own sad story, but the voices gradually faded out, and I did eventually sleep, fitfully, waking now and again with a feeling of dread, then forcing myself back toward sleep.

The next morning, a burly, grunting oaf of a jailer woke me up, handed me a limp New York Corrections version of an Egg McMuffin and a container of soured milk. Sometime after that, he came back, opened the cell door, and pushed me down a series of iron steps to a side door and a waiting squad car. I bumped along Flatbush Extension on the springs of a lumpy vinyl seat and landed up, after sitting in traffic for a half hour, at the Brooklyn Criminal Court building on Schermerhorn Street. It was an edifice I'd often admired from the outside, and one of some historical significance because of the luminaries who'd been tried there over the years, but not a place I'd ever desired to visit.

After an interview with a well-meaning but overworked and jaded social worker type who seemed pleased that my arrest record was limited to a couple of roundups back in the sixties, I sat around for many more hours in a large locked room on benches with a small mob of smelly strangers, almost all of them younger, bigger, and meaner than me. When my name was called, I was walked through a door into a very busy courtroom, where, thank heavens, Peter Finch was waiting for me. Peter was his usual somber, dour self, but I wanted to hug him all the same. With his patrician features, which included thinning blond hair that belied his Irish-American roots, his conservative gray suit, and his well-modulated, precise diction, he seemed lawyerly and confident, which was a good thing, because I dreaded—with a loathing beyond my capacity to describe—the thought of that steel door slamming shut behind me again.

Peter had some discussions at the bench with a bored gray-haired judge, who in my estimation would never see seventy again, and a wet-behind-the-ears prosecutor. They threw around a lot of numbers and letters—the discussion of a one-ninety-fifty notice seeming to draw the most debate—and passed sheets of paper to one another, one of which Peter told me to sign. Finally, after another whispered gathering at the judge's bench, followed by a mini flare-up over an ROR—whatever that was—the prosecutor, looking as if Peter had beaten him out of his firstborn son, nodded okay, the judge mumbled something to me that sounded like a warning, and Peter nudged me toward the door.

"I tried to get trespassing. But the cops want to charge you with burglary because the window was jimmied," Peter said when we stopped to talk in the hallway. "The judge let you out on recognizance because he believed me when I said you weren't a risk. I'll talk to the ADA and see what he's willing to do about the charge. Right now, you're looking at a Class D felony."

I grabbed Peter's arm in panic. "A felony? I'm not a felon. I didn't jimmy the window. It was open."

"They say it was jimmied."

"They're lying."

Peter grimaced. "Why would they do that?"

I couldn't think of any reason why they would. Peter listened soberly while I told him all that had happened. "I've got a couple of cases in another court," he said. "Don't do anything that might get you arrested again, and don't talk to the cops about anything."

"I had no real desire to get arrested this time."

After thanking Peter, who ran off to his other case, I headed toward the door to get the subway out to Bay Ridge to pick up Kevin. My ex-wife would love this: his seedy father coming to pick him up after a night in jail.

"Not so fast," said a familiar voice from behind me, sharp and loud in the marble hallway. Detective Sergeant Sheehan caught up with me on the stairway.

"My lawyer told me not to talk to you."

Sheehan snarled. "Is that why you had the officer from the Seven-eight call me over here, so you could tell me you weren't going to talk to me?"

"I wanted you to help me. I wasn't trying to steal anything," I said.

"Greg Phillips's apartment." This was a statement. "What were you looking for?"

"Him."

"Why?"

"He's a friend of mine."

"I thought you didn't know him." Sheehan stood triumphantly two steps above me on the stairway, looking like the statue of righteousness. "Why should I help you out of a jam if you're just going to get in my way?"

"Don't you believe in justice?"

He looked at me long and hard. "I believe in good guys and bad guys, McNulty." In his broad, pleasant face, I saw an uncomplicated intelligence, the kind that was certain of its beliefs, knew right from wrong and good from bad. He was someone, unlike me, whose life revolved around certainties. He shook his head. "I suppose you don't know what your pals were up to?"

I didn't have to feign ignorance. But Sheehan rolled his eyes to

suggest he wasn't letting himself be conned. Even though he didn't believe me, he sounded protective, in spite of himself. "I'd watch my step,
McNulty. You may not be tough enough for these guys." He looked to
the ceiling, then glared at me. "A city full of innocents. You buy your
nose candy like you have nothing to do with the bodies strewn from
here to Colombia. . . ." His eyes like the steel cell bars I'd lately left behind, he made a short, quick, hard uppercut motion with his right hand.
"A professional hit, McNulty. The way you make a martini, this guy
uses a knife—up, under, between the ribs and into the heart—one
hole."

The force of what he said stunned me. "I didn't have anything to do
do with that," I said softly, suddenly afraid of this world where a person stabs someone else with an upward thrust of a knife, under the rib
cage, between the ribs, right into the heart. I did want Sheehan to protect me from it.

"A waitress said two guys stopped to see Phillips the night of the
murder. That wasn't you and the big shot by any chance?" Sheehan's
steely blue eyes bore into my soul.

"No. Not us. We didn't go there."

"Do you know where the big shot was?"

"He was with me."

"Till when?"

"I don't know. After midnight."

Sheehan turned to go. "Your lawyer told you not to talk to me? You
should listen to him. Better than that, you should stay out of my way."

Martha stood in the doorway of her modest East Ninety-first Street
brick row house, her favorite expression, disapproval, firmly in place.
She wasn't angry; the bitterness had dissipated over the years. Life had
dealt her a bum hand. She'd thrown it in. No hard feelings; they were
buried. Maybe they gave her indigestion or ulcers, but she knew how
to be a single parent and a divorced woman. I'd taught her to keep her
guard up.

"You're a wreck, Brian. Can't you stay sober the night before you
pick up your son?"

"I was sober," I told her. "I was in jail."

A smile began, but she quickly smothered it with indignation. Businesslike and respectable these days, she was no longer the slim girl in bare feet and flimsy summer dresses. Her cheeks were still hollow and her big gray eyes still pretty. Her hair was fluffy now, when before it had been long and straight. "Grow up," she said.

"Where are we going today?" Kevin asked, coming up behind his mother. He wore a black Grateful Dead T-shirt and ripped dungarees; his hair had grown over his ears and was flopping over his forehead into his eyes. Deep into the sullen, shuffling, and mumbling phase of a young man's life, he still had a bit of kid enthusiasm left.

"To the track."

"Good God, Brian, you'll never change," said Martha in the scathing tone of a scandalized Lutheran.

A perplexed and sad expression took the place of the sullenness on Kevin's face for a moment. As he looked from Martha to me, I could almost hear what he was thinking. Why, he must wonder, couldn't these two people who were supposed to raise him keep it together? Standing in the doorway, watching Martha hug her son, I tormented myself with the same thoughts. Here was Kevin about to turn fifteen, and I didn't remember him growing up.

"I saw Big John," I told them.

"Oh," said Martha. This time, she did smile, looking wistful, sadness in her eyes. "I hope he's doing well."

"He's a big corporate mucky-muck, now. He's doing fine."

Martha didn't share my disdain for the ruling class, and she liked John. For a while, years back, when I started seeing Kevin again—with Big John as matchmaker—it looked like Martha and I might get back together. But it didn't work out. We looked at each other now across those years, realizing in these few seconds of time travel that there was no longer any reason to work anything out. I didn't tell her about the murder because I was afraid she'd keep Kevin home if I did.

As usual, Kevin and I stopped off to visit Pop on our way to the Long Island Railroad station at Atlantic Avenue, where we would get the train to Belmont.

"I've stopped drinking coffee," Pop said when he opened the door. We usually drank coffee together, and I suppose he wanted to squelch my expectations.

"Oh?" I said.

"I've burned a coffeepot for the last time." He ushered us in and we sat down at his ancient oak dining room table. "Would you like a glass of water?"

"Is that it?"

"It's too early for beer."

"It's okay," I said. "No thanks." He was already suffering from caffeine withdrawal, so I didn't want to jangle his nerves any further.

"Good. What's new? Any trace of that friend of yours?"

"No."

"Have you been looking?" He was irritated.

I explained to Kevin as delicately as I could about Aaron's murder and Greg's disappearance. Since he didn't know Aaron or remember Greg and John was only tangentially involved, he wasn't all that interested. Then I told Pop about the rest of my adventures, leading up to my arrest.

"Don't worry. Finch'll get you off. All those lawyers and judges are in cahoots; they'll make a deal. What did you find in the apartment you broke into?"

"I didn't break in. The window was unlocked. Anyway, I didn't find anything, except that Greg has a roommate."

"That's something," said Pop. "But you might have discovered that by looking at the mailbox. What now?"

"I don't know. I'm going to the track. Maybe I'll win enough, so I can go away and forget all this."

"Yeh," said Pop. "You and the track."

Things at the track went predictably. We won the first half of the double, then lost the second and third races. We skipped a couple of races and won on an eight-to-one shot in the sixth. After collecting our winnings, we went to check out the paddock, which at Belmont has trees and lawns and benches and makes you feel like you're walking around the old plantation in Kentucky. Jose Garcia was standing in one of the saddling sheds, so Kevin went up close to the fence and hollered out thanks for bringing in our eight-to-one shot. Jose was gracious and pleasant. He glowed with a kind of bronze color and his dark eyes sparkled with the kind of joy about life I've always envied. You got the feeling he was one of the lucky ones who did work he loved. He walked over, asked Kevin his name, and shook his hand. Kevin came swaggering back from the fence like one of the horse owners who'd just given instructions to the jockey.

In the next race, Jose—who, despite his indomitable spirit, was near the bottom of the jockey standings for the fall meet—was riding another eight-to-one shot, this an also-ran, whose odds dropped to nine to one by the time the horses got out of the paddock and onto the track. Kevin and I were near the rail, so when Jose came by and hollered out, "Hello, my man Kevin," Kevin took this to be insider information. He was so excited, I couldn't bring myself to bet on the horse I'd doped out, so I put ten bucks on Step-and-a-Half—who by call to post had dropped to eleven to one—and he came in dead last.

"What the hell," I said. We bet on our pal Jose in two more races, but he didn't finish in the money either time. Still, he smiled and waved to Kevin each time he rode onto the track and seemed like he was having a hell of a time.

Maybe if he took his job a little more seriously . . . I told myself.

On the train ride back to Manhattan and then the subway to my apartment on the West Side, I forgot about the track and enjoyed being with Kevin, the brightest light in my life. I liked sitting next to him, wondering what he thought about. I didn't have to talk to be happy with him, just be near him.

"Do you want to go out to eat or get Chinese food and go to my apartment?"

"Chinese is okay, I guess," Kevin said. "Don't you ever eat decently?" His tone spoke volumes.

We were sharing hot-and-sour soup, moo shoo pork, kung po shrimp, and Chinese vegetables when the door buzzer rang. Kevin got to it first. It was Big John, whom he hadn't seen in years. Kevin's face lit up, and he danced out to the lobby to open the outside door, catching himself and restoring his sullenness before he actually reached the door. But Big John tousled his hair and lifted him off the ground with a big bear hug anyway, so Kevin couldn't help smiling.

There was enough food for all of us. But Big John wasn't interested. "I don't eat that Chinese stuff," he said. "They use cats."

"Cats?" Kevin was shocked. "For what?"

"For meat. They cook 'em."

Kevin dropped his chopsticks onto the table.

"They don't cook cats," I said. "That's an old wives' tale."

"Oh yeah," said Big John. "Did you ever see any cats around a Chinese restaurant?"

Big John had beliefs like this. He believed in old wives' tales and, despite his business acumen, had the prejudices of a Gypsy. John rarely ate anyway; I think he ate one big meal every couple of days, like one of those wolves who eats a moose and then doesn't eat again for a week. He'd always been like that. Drinking a beer, he watched us eat.

"We went to the track," Kevin said brightly.

"D'you win?"

"Nope," said Kevin.

"That's what used to happen when I went to the track with your old man." Big John took off his glasses and rubbed his eyes. "Those were good days, though, weren't they?" His voice had a sentimental lilt. "Who cared if we won? Everything was easy. Now nothin's easy."

Finally getting a word in, I followed up on the "nothin's easy" theme and told him about my night in the slammer.

Big John laughed heartily, nodding like an old uncle. "That sounds like something Greg would do, not you," he said when I finished my tale. "Jesus, I've spent my life and picking up after everybody—my father, Greg—and now you're gonna start?"

When I told John that Sheehan had asked if we'd been in the club the night of the murder, John banished the idea with a wave of his hand. "You didn't tell him we saw Greg before that, did you?"

"No. But Sheehan's developed a couple of theories of his own."

When I told him about the cocaine and the professional hit, John jerked to attention. "Maybe he was just fishing. . . ." But John didn't sound convinced and he looked really surprised, sitting for a long time deep in thought. After a few minutes, he came out of it. "You shoulda called my office, bro. The office can reach me no matter where I am." He stood and stretched. "But it's okay. I know Greg's roommate. Let's go see him. I can have him drop the charges."

John started for the door, but I held him back. "I've had enough of Greg's apartment. Besides, Kevin's staying overnight."

"Okay," said Big John. "I'll have him come over here."

He went to the phone and dialed. "No answer," he said, then dialed again. He handled the phone like someone who was used to it, the way he'd once handled the bottles behind the bar. This time, someone did answer, so he spoke into the phone like Conrad Hilton on the horn with one of his managers.

"That's right. Tell Walter John wants him." He waited a few seconds. "Hey, bro," said Big John. "I need to talk to you. . . . Now." He waited again. "No, that ain't good enough. I need to talk to you now, here on the West Side." He turned to me. "Where the hell am I?" I told him, and he told Walter. "Get someone to cover and come up here as soon as you can," John said in a tone of easy but unmistakable authority.

"You know," John said when he'd gotten himself another beer, "Greg was just about Kevin's size when I first met him. He was about twelve. We were playing baseball. . . ." John paused when he noticed Kevin's troubled expression. After some quick calculations, he figured out his mistake. A true storyteller, John didn't want to lose his audience. "Now wait a minute." He scrutinized Kevin. "You're a lot older than twelve. You must be sixteen or seventeen." Kevin rolled his eyes, as if to say anyone could tell he wasn't a twelve-year-old. But he was listening again as John went on with his story.

"Greg was a new kid. And he was small, too. This guy George said he was out at second, and he wasn't. George was big and mean—and stupid. He knew he couldn't push me around, so he tried Greg. But Greg wouldn't budge." John smiled and sat back, relishing both the memory and a healthy swig of beer.

Kevin, chopsticks poised in front of him—but eating with a lot less enthusiasm than before and sticking pretty much to the shrimp—looked like he was now afraid John wouldn't finish the story, so he asked, "What happened then?"

"Well," said Big John, who had been waiting for such attention, "I had to straighten George out." John's expression became solemn as he prepared for the moral of the story. "He wasn't out; he was safe," John said by way of explanation. Kevin nodded a bit uncertainly. Big John nodded, too, emphasizing whatever point it was he thought he had made.

As I stood up to get another beer for John, the phone rang. I answered it absently. A Spanish-accented voice said, "Mind your own business, bartender. Stick to tending bar, or you're gonna have big trouble." Then the phone clicked and the line went dead.

chapter six

When I told John about the phone message, he looked at me for a moment, then said, "Maybe that's good advice."

The phone call convinced me Kevin should stay at Pop's apartment for this visit or go home to his mother until life made sense again. He agreed to go to his grandpa's in the morning, no doubt remembering I'd almost gotten him killed once before.

We were watching a Yankee game on television, John and I drinking a couple of beers, when Walter showed up at the door an hour later. Standing in the foyer, he looked my apartment over like he was casing it. I didn't like anything about him. Not his cheerfulness, which was nervous and put-on; not his manner of dress, tight pants of a color between gray and white and of a material that seemed to be available only to gangsters and Greek greasy-spoon waiters on their nights off. He wore the same shiny open-collar, dress shirt and gold necklace, too, and had hairy chest that I believe is purchased with the shirt. He smelled of the same cologne I remembered from the unpleasant bar next to Greg's apartment in Brooklyn. Small-time punk was written all over him. If you hadn't turned and run already, his smile lit up like a warning sign: FORTY MILES OF BAD ROAD AHEAD.

"What's goin' on?" he asked John, ignoring me, even though I'd opened the door and now stood beside him. He shuffled around, his eyes settling on mine for a second, then on John's, then on my bookcase. He looked twice at the bookcase.

Big John spoke to me over Walter's head. "Walter thinks everyone's a punk like him." He grabbed Walter's arm in a gesture that seemed friendly, but he clenched the muscle with his fingers. "Brian and I go back a long way," he said quietly into Walter's ear, then let go. Walter backed off, his expression sullen.

"Do you want a beer, Walter?" I asked.

"I don't know, man. What else you got?"

"A beer," I said. "That's it." We looked each other over for a few seconds; then I started back toward the living room.

"Sure, man," said Walter urgently, hastily reaching an arm out toward me. "I'll take a beer." He was obviously someone who'd missed a lot of chances by holding out for more.

Seated across from us, next to the TV, he drank his beer and waited for John to tell him what to do. One of those people who think kids are like pet turtles, he ignored Kevin. But then, when I looked at Kevin, I remembered that even this jerk must have been a kid once—even he must have been lovable once—so I felt sorry for him.

"Walter," I said, standing beside Kevin's chair, "This is my son, Kevin. Kevin, Walter." When Kevin stood up and walked over to shake hands with him, Walter got flustered. He half-stood, then sat back down. He held out his hand awkwardly, then pumped Kevin's hand like he was running for mayor in Altoona.

Under John's questioning, we discovered Walter didn't know where Greg had gone, nor did he know what Greg had been doing lately. Big John, a look of mild disgust on his face, turned from Walter to watch the ball game. The Yankees were changing pitchers, with two runs in, two men on, no outs in the top of the seventh. I myself had turned *from* the game with a look of disgust.

Even though John wasn't paying any attention to him, Walter began to fidget. "Greg and I aren't that tight, man," he said nervously.

John looked up from the TV. "What have you been up to yourself, Walter?" he asked innocently.

"A little of this and a little of that," Walter said evasively.

It took a bit of hammering from John, but pretty soon Walter began to open up. A little of this was bartending in Bensonhurst one night a week, in addition to his regular gig for John at the service bar at the Downtown Club. A little of that turned out to be buying kilos of cocaine from a supplier in Bensonhurst, breaking it down, and wholesaling it with Greg to a string of bartenders in some of the better Manhattan clubs.

On the TV, a number of players from the Oakland A's were scooting around the bases, as the Yankees booted the baseball around the stadium; this summer wasn't going any better than the previous one. Good thing we had the Mets.

"How long's this been going on?" John sounded like someone had pulled a fast one on him. "What did Aaron Adams have to do with it?"

Walter said he'd never heard of Aaron.

Big John rolled his eyes and slumped back into his chair. He'd put on a few pounds over the years, so he had to struggle a bit to get back up after he had slumped back. Walter sat on the edge of his seat, alert, his ears pricked, ready to duck or run.

John tried for a tone of fatherly concern. "You guys weren't trying to get over on anybody were you?"

Walter's eyes darted around the room; he looked like a man about to break under questioning and squeal on his partner.

I could follow John's line of thinking. If Greg and Walter—and maybe Aaron—had tried a swindle on their supplier, this could explain Aaron bobbing to the surface of the East River. It was also reason for Greg to hide, and for Walter to be nervous—and me, too, after that phone call.

When I went to the kitchen for another beer, John followed me. Quietly, he told me he wanted me to take Kevin, get a cab, wait outside my apartment, and follow Walter when he came out.

"Just find out where he goes from here, just the address. Don't get out of the cab for nothin'."

"Will Kevin be all right?"

"Nothin' will happen if you do what I said."

"What about that phone call?"

"I don't know about the call, bro. But Walter's gonna have so much on his mind when he leaves here, he ain't gonna notice you followin' him."

"What if he takes the subway?"

He thought it over. "Let him go. This is just a dumb hunch anyway." He pulled a fifty-dollar bill and a couple of twenties off his roll and handed them to me.

I looked at the bills. "Do you think he's going to Chicago?"

John walked me back to the foyer and asked out loud if Kevin and I would go out for a cup of coffee so he could speak with Walter in private. When I got out on the street, I had a better idea. Kevin and I walked down to Oscar's. Sure enough, my pal Ntango was sipping a rum and Coke, his cab parked with its hood and trunk open in the bus stop outside. Ntango drove us back to my street. He waited on the corner with his lights out while Kevin and I hid in a doorway. When Walter came out of the apartment, Ntango switched on his lights, pulled up, and Walter climbed in.

When I told John about the change in plans, he chuckled. "I guess there's no chance he'll lose him in traffic." Then he got serious. "Who the hell is this cabdriver, anyway? Are you sure we can trust him?"

Ntanago is Eritrean and has the distinctive light brown skin color and semi-European features of his countrymen. He was part of a small colony of exiles living on the Upper West Side. I'd gotten to know a good many of them when I tended bar in the neighborhood, and I'd become friends with Ntango. We'd been in enough scrapes together for me to know the kind of man he was. Once, he'd risked his life when Kevin was in danger. He was one of those people who—because of their upbringing, I guess—put a premium on being part of humanity. They think their friends are more important than the glitter and gleam of the easy life and that an injury to one is an injury to all. In the "me first" culture of contemporary New York City, they stick out like sore thumbs.

Because Ntango was soft-spoken, African, and drove a cab, for most people he was one more invisible man. But Ntango was wise and tough. He'd lived through seven different kinds of hell and could eat punks like Walter for breakfast. "This cabdriver fought a couple of wars, climbed through mountain ranges, fought off plagues, and probably swam half the ocean to get here, so he could drive a fucking cab," I told John. "You can trust him. Relax and watch the ball game."

The score was nine to three as the Yankees went through the motions in the bottom of the ninth. The game ended with the Yankees heading dejectedly for the tunnel to the clubhouse and the A's matter-of-factly shaking hands with one another as if they were used to it. The Yankees hardly ever got to shake hands anymore. I remembered my dad and the ball game he wanted to go to, so I asked John if he wanted to go—assuming we got through with all this by then. He said he would, and I went to the refrigerator for a couple more beers. After Kevin went to bed, John rolled a joint. He lit it and we passed it back and forth a few times, sipping the beers.

An hour later, Ntango rang the bell. He drank a beer and we smoked another joint. He gave John the address of a Dr. Charles Wilson, an optometrist in Bay Ridge.

It was interesting watching John and Ntango size each other up. They were outdoing each other with graciousness. John wanted to know about Eritrea, but that wasn't something Ntango talked about, so John tried to interest him in the hotel business. Ntango had been a busboy, but he hadn't liked it. When John got out of Ntango that he had been a mechanical engineer in Eritrea, I could see the respect beginning to take hold. By the end of the joint, Ntango was a bro. John asked some questions about what Walter acted like in the cab. And he kept coming back to Dr. Wilson being an optometrist.

"That's strange," John said when Ntango told him for the third time. He was stoned and talking to himself.

"What?"

"What what?" John came around slowly to focus on me.

"What's strange?"

After an exchange of bewildered looks, John returned to his meditation.

When John stretched out on the couch, I got him a blanket and a pillow, then went to the bedroom where Kevin slept. I sat in an easy

chair, watching my son for a long time. Then fear began to creep in. It
came at me softly from all sides and hovered over me like a fog until I
fell asleep in the chair.

In the morning, John drove us out to Brooklyn to take Kevin to Pop's.
After that, he was going to pay a visit to the optometrist's office.

"Don't you think you ought to find out more about what's going on
before you go barging in on this guy?" I asked as we climbed back into
John's Eldorado in front of my father's apartment.

John had his hand on the ignition switch but didn't turn it. Instead,
he sat back with one hand on the steering wheel, the other on the ignition key. After a couple of minutes, he whacked the steering wheel
with the palm of his hand. "You're right. . . . What the hell am I doing?" John glanced at me out of the corner of his eye. "I gotta find out
something. Let's take a ride. You know where Union Street is? There's
a union hall there."

The hall was across the Gowanus Canal from Park Slope, in a section of Brooklyn once called Red Hook, lately deemed part of Carroll
Gardens by the real estate gougers. Italian longshoremen once lived
there, and their union hall remained, though their neighborhood was
filling up with Yuppies, their jobs had been taken by containers, and
their union hall had been sold to the Amalgamated Industrial Union,
an entity I'd never heard of.

A gray-haired woman sat at a desk in the carpeted outer office. Her
expression was on the sour side as she watched me come through the
door, but it blossomed into smiles and wrinkles when she spotted John
behind me. Beaming and giggling, she popped up from behind her
desk and galloped to the doorway to throw her arms around his expansive middle. John handled the adulation with good cheer, slightly
embarrassed, dimpled, and smiling.

"Why don't you ever come to see us anymore?" she asked him
"You forget your friends." Her eyes were dark and you could see the
pretty girl she'd once been. Her name was Joyce. She acted coquettish,
holding John's hand, smiling at him, possessively folding his hand under her arm as she led him to her desk.

"Frank," she said into the intercom on her desk. "A prodigal son has come home."

A few seconds later, Frank appeared in a doorway behind the desk. Probably in his sixties, he had a suntanned face, a healthy shock of gray hair, an expensively cut brown suit with a pale blue silk handkerchief in the breast pocket. In general, he looked well taken care of—prosperous. But his hands were thick and his fingers short and stubby; his head was large, like a bull's; his neck was thick; and his back so broad that it stretched the fibers of the suit jacket. Above his eye was a scar and in his eyes a light of intelligence. But even when his eyes smiled, which they did when they rested on John, they were like granite. He cuffed John around the shoulder and shook him. John both gave way and resisted, so they tussled, at great risk to the furniture. I wouldn't have wanted to be in between them.

"This is my friend, Brian," John said after the wrestling.

Frank stepped back from the tussle and looked me over skeptically. "He's the one you told me about?" His hard stare sought me out. "The guy who thinks he should be running the bartenders union?"

John stopped smiling; he looked hurt. After meeting Frank's eyes for a moment, he shook his head. When he spoke, his tone was aggrieved. "Brian's a good guy, Frank. That's what I told you. Those guys are wrong."

"It's okay," said Frank, waving a hand in my direction. "I'm glad to do a favor." He continued to look me over. "Kevin McNulty's son?"

I nodded.

"That figures. Is your old man behind this?"

My back went up. "Behind what?"

"Taking over the bartenders' union." Frank looked at me long and hard, then went on before I could say anything. "Your old man and I had some run-ins. But he wasn't anything like they said he was—those pissheads. The Commies were a pain in the ass, but they were tough, not like the whiners that came after them. I never had anything personal against your old man. When no one else would touch him, I offered him a job." Frank didn't move any closer to me, nor did he grow any bigger. But I had the impression that both things had happened.

"He said he wouldn't work for me," For a second, Frank's expression was pleading. "He didn't need to say that. But I let it go. He thinks he's too good for me. So where's he end up? Slopping through Pennsylvania for a hundred a week. And where's he now? You come to me to get the pressure off. You don't go to him."

My temper flared. But John gave me a hard nudge before I could say anything. "Frank put in the word for you when I asked him to." John's expression was as hard as I'd ever seen it. I bit my tongue.

Frank clapped me on the shoulder to show there were no hard feelings. He would treat me nicely, that pat on the back said, since— unlike Pop—I knew my place and accepted favors.

After we stood together for a few minutes in the center of the room while Frank cuffed John a couple of times, John said he needed to talk. Frank nodded. I expected to be ushered into his office. Instead, Frank led us out a side door onto Union Street. We walked to the corner, where, leaning on a mailbox, Frank listened.

"There's a guy in Bay Ridge I need to talk to," John said.

Frank listened.

"His name's Dr. Charles Wilson." John indicated by a slight gesture of his head that I should take a walk, so I did. The two men spoke a minute or so more; then we went back inside. We shook hands all around. Joyce hugged John. We left.

When we were in the car, headed back to Manhattan, I asked John how Frank Carlucci would find out about Wilson.

"Frank'll find out."

"Why did we talk outside and not in his office?"

John looked at me like I was an idiot, and then turned on the radio.

He dropped me at the Ocean Club, where I stumbled around the bar, the liquor room, and the bar manager's office again, checking the schedule, pretending I was doing something useful. I tried calling Ernesto, but no one answered the phone. Then after fifteen minutes of trying to get the electronic adding machine on my new desk to work, I gave up. The day shift was going fine, and I had a couple of hours to kill before the night crew came on. "An idle mind is the devil's workshop," my mother used to say. Rereading the story of Aaron's murder in a three-day old *Daily News,* I realized the address they listed for him was not far from the club. So I decided to take a walk.

Aaron's name was on a mailbox in a building on East Thirteenth Street, just below Stuyvesant Town. It was alongside the name Scott Cooper. Scott Cooper answered the bell through the squawk box, and it took five minutes to convince him to let me in. When I got upstairs to his apartment, I understood why. The apartment had been broken into and robbed a couple of nights before. That and his former roommate being murdered had understandably unnerved the guy. He was slight and soft-spoken to begin with, but at this moment, he looked like one of the winos lined up, waiting for the gin mill to open.

"Sorry about Aaron," I said. "I knew him a long time ago." I realized this sounded like a euphemism for some kind of fudge packing in the past, so I got a little nervous. But Scott didn't seem to notice.

"Yeah," he said when we sat down in his small living room. "Poor Aaron. I wasn't even surprised. It was as if he was trying to get himself killed." The man looked sad when he said this, not vindictive, and didn't seem to think I should be surprised by him saying it. So I tried not to be.

The apartment's built-in wooden cabinets were splintered in places and the front of a wooden drawer had been ripped off. Scott followed my gaze to the cabinets.

"The police who investigated the robbery told me that burglars read the paper and when someone dies or gets killed, they break into the apartment because they think no one will be there." He sounded as detached as the cops must have sounded. "The paper listed this as Aaron's address, even though he's been gone for months."

I was hard-pressed to feel too self-righteous about this breaking and entering, since at about the time this apartment was being broken into, I was breaking into an apartment myself over in Brooklyn. The subtlety of difference, I decided, would be entirely too difficult to explain, so I didn't try.

"Aaron was trying to live like he did when he was twenty-one," Scott Cooper said. "He couldn't come to terms with himself, and he couldn't hold a relationship together."

What I learned from this forty-five-minute conversation with Scott was enough to depress most people for a month: Aaron died addicted to cocaine and alcohol. At the time of his death, he was living in a not quite seedy hotel on Forty-fourth Street, using drugs and whatever money he could find to pick up runaway boys around Port Authority and the Christopher Street docks. When Scott told me all this, he looked into my eyes. His were timid and trusting—and filling with tears. I liked him. But the Aaron he described was nothing like the person I knew.

When I knew Aaron, he'd just joined the workaday world after a stint in Princeton, following a boyhood in private boarding schools. Aaron's family disowned him not long after that, according to Scott, because he came out of the closet at the wrong time in history. The Aaron I knew was Little Lord Fauntleroy, a dainty, pristine prima donna, the first person I'd ever met with manicured fingernails. Pudgy, his face round and cherubic, except for a sculptured goatee, he looked like a twelve-year-old in disguise. Without the goatee, he would have been the kid in grade school who carried a briefcase, wore rubbers over his shoes, and sat in the front row. Like most managers, he kowtowed to the powers above him and lorded over his underlings. We let him act the part, because the bar itself was firmly in our control. Spoiled all his life, he didn't know how to be hard—though he tried to be and thought he was. So he didn't fire any of us, even when he could have.

Scott, it turned out, was a social worker, and part of what he did was to help people walk through their sorrow and grief. Maybe we did that for the hour or so we talked together. I found out some surprising things about Aaron. For one thing, he'd talked about those days down at the shore with Big John, me, and Greg. For whatever it meant, he'd remembered that time as fondly as I did. For the more recent time, Aaron had been working as a maître d' at a black-tie East Side dining room. He might have been involved in a drug-dealing scheme with Greg and Walter. But Scott said he doubted it, because Aaron was so terrified of being sent back to prison.

Finding out about Aaron's life didn't tell me much. I didn't know what the hell Pop was talking about. All that hearing about Aaron's life did was make me want to go looking for a gas pipe. Instead, I went back to the Ocean Club and poked around behind the bar again, until the bartender made it clear I was getting on his nerves. Leaving the bar, I went back to the bar manager's office and tried to make sense out of the ordering book and the inventory forms. I sat at my desk and shuffled papers for a while, went up front and chatted with the bartender about places we'd worked and bartenders we knew, checked out the dark-haired, long-legged, aloof-looking cocktail waitress, and got in both of their ways. I was really disappointed that Ernesto hadn't shown up for work. I'd tried calling him again, but again no answer.

The next morning, John woke me up by ringing my doorbell. He was double-parked, so I couldn't do anything except throw on some clothes and follow him. He'd spoken to Frank, and the way was clear for us to visit the optometrist. I demanded breakfast before we did anything.

"If you can find us a place to park, I'll buy you breakfast," said John.

I took John first to La Rosita on Broadway. But there was no place to park. I saw a cab parked in a bus stop in front and guessed again that it was Ntango's, which it turned out to be. John pulled up along side. Ntango was reading the *News*.

"Don't you ever work?" I asked him.

"Hey, my friends, Mr. Brian and Mr. Big John." He looked up from the paper, smiling, speaking in his usual slow drawl that suggested there was no real hurry about anything.

"How do you get to Bay Ridge?" I asked.

"The Triborough to the Cross Island to the Belt."

"Where can we park and get something to eat?"

"There's a diner with a parking lot on a Hundred and twenty-fifth Street and the river. But you can park here in the bus stop; just put your hood and trunk lid up."

I happened to remember that Ntango had recently paid nine hundred dollars in parking tickets to get his cab out of the car pound, so I opted for the diner with the parking lot.

"I forgot to tell you. I have a new dispatcher," Ntango said, handing me a card through the window. "A high-class operation. Give me a call."

We got onto the Triborough after breakfast and a stop and go trip along 125th Street, during which John, who was gawking around, almost ran into the back of a bus. As we crossed the bridge, Big John looked over at me a number of times. His expression was guarded. "There's no danger from this guy," Big John said after a lapse, while I played with his car phone. "He's really a professional optometrist."

"Good," said I, although I didn't really have any higher regard for professionals than I did for gunmen.

"Good," repeated Big John. "That's why I want you to check him out."

"Me? I thought you didn't even want me to go with you?"

Big John's expression was stony. "It's safe, bro. I wouldn't send you in if it wasn't."

"Why?" First, I wasn't even supposed to come on this crusade. Now I was expected to lead it.

"I got my reasons." He watched the road in front of him. I watched the city skyline out my side window from the crest of the bridge—all that stone and steel and glass. No matter how many times I'd seen it, each time I was awestruck.

Not until we left the Belt Parkway and were driving down Fourth Avenue did John speak again. "The guy's name isn't really Wilson."

"You sure he's an optometrist?"

"Yeah, He's a goddamn optometrist." Perspiration beaded on his brow, despite the air-conditioned car. "He would know me. That's why I can't see him." Big John took me in with his soulful expression. Loyalty called.

"Okay! Okay! What am I supposed to find out from this drug-dealing optometrist with an assumed name?"

"Ask about Greg. See what he tells you."

When we pulled up in front of the office, John peeled off three twenties from his bankroll, handing them to me along with his business card. "Here, I got some things to do. Take a cab back. Call me at the office later and let me know what happens."

chapter seven

Dr. Wilson's office was in a square two-story wooden single-family house on a quiet tree-lined street of formidable single-family homes—shades of Bedford Falls—a block off Fourth Avenue in Brooklyn. DR. CHARLES WILSON was printed on a gold plaque on his door, and a receptionist stood guard in the outer office. The sentry was thin, with hair a color between gray and blond. She wore a white uniform, smiled efficiently but without warmth, the expression on her face a perfect mix of boredom and disapproval.

"I'd like to see Dr. Wilson," I said.

"Do you have an appointment?" She smiled sweetly, but her manner was supercilious: She knew damn well I didn't have an appointment. Instead of answering, I took a white pad with a drug company logo from her desk. On it, I wrote "Greg Phillips? Dead body?"

"Would you hand this to the doctor?" I folded the note quickly, almost catching her nose in it.

To all appearances, Dr. Wilson was a working optometrist, with eye charts, cabinets filled with instruments, and large machines with lenses and lights on arms with hinges, like a dentist's drill. He didn't have any patients, but it was still early.

"Interesting note," he said, standing amid his equipment and machines like a captain on a ship. "Who are you? Why do you think I know Greg Phillips?"

"Brian McNulty." John had said to leave his name out of this, so I did, and I didn't see any reason to bring up Walter. This left me with no believable answer to his second question.

The doctor was a good-size man—"husky," my mother would have said. His hair was gray, thick, and wavy, worn in a style left over from the Sinatra era. He had a full mustache, also gray, and large eyes that gave him a startled expression, like a vaudeville comedian rushing out onto the stage with a gag. And because he had dimples when he smiled, he seemed harmless and friendly. He sized me up, seeming unperturbed by my nonanswer, but persistent all the same.

"Someone told you I knew Greg. Who was it?"

"I can't say."

"Well, I can't say, either." He held out his hand. "Nice meeting you. Have a good day." He seemed pretty cocksure as he stood there waiting for my next move.

Since I didn't have a next move, I told him about Aaron being killed and Greg disappearing. "I understand you and Greg had business together. I just want to make sure he's okay. Do you know where he is?"

"I want to know why you came to my office," the doctor said, his eyes lively and penetrating, his manner gruff and down-to-earth, like you might expect from a bookie or a nightclub operator, not modulated and precise, as you might expect from a doctor. "And why you think I have any information for you."

I wasn't getting anywhere, and I had to do something. John said to leave his name out of this. But he hadn't said anything about not dropping Walter's name, so I did.

"A person named Walter told you I had business with a person named Greg? Is that it?"

"Not exactly, but close enough. Walter's Greg's roommate, and you know goddamn well what I'm talking about, because Walter came here last night. A friend of mine followed him."

The doctor looked worried for a moment, but when he spoke, he had a twinkle in his eye. "Let's say, for the sake of argument, that I did know this Greg Phillips. Why would I tell you?"

"Because I want to help him. He's in trouble."

"Suppose he is," said the doctor. "What can you do to get him out of trouble?"

He had me there. "I don't know. . . . A friend of mine and I—" I stopped, realizing I was treading on dangerous ground.

But the good doctor was right on it. "This friend," he said, raising an eyebrow, "what's his name?"

Taking a deep breath and feeling like a fool, I said, "I'm sorry. I can't tell you."

"Oh? I'm supposed to provide you with all kinds of information based on a bunch of wild allegations you throw at me. But you don't have to answer my questions. Is that how it is?" He watched me squirm for a minute or two without losing his twinkle or amused smirk. "This friend wouldn't be John Wolinski, by any chance?"

Well, if I was befuddled before, I was surely twisted now. Big John had hung me out to dry. Of course, I didn't have to tell Dr. Wilson about John. Walter would have told him.

The doctor was downright jovial, and I must have looked as bewildered as I felt, because he laughed again and cuffed me on the shoulder. Suddenly, he bent down and looked at my face quizzically. "Have you had your eyes checked lately?"

"No," I said carefully. "Why?"

"You're squinting."

Actually, my eyesight had been growing dimmer; I had to squint and move the book closer and then farther away from me when I read at night. I'd been ignoring the symptoms. Now I was scared I was going blind.

"Are you really an optometrist?"

This time, the doctor's eyebrows went up and down a couple of times. "What did you think I was?"

I got flustered. The guy was toying with me. He knew whatever Big John knew and I didn't, so I was making an ass out of myself.

With a warm smile, the doc threw a paternal arm over my shoulder and led me toward a chair. "Look, I'll tell you a secret. I do know Greg. I've known him a long time. But I don't have any business with him." He sized me up once more, continuing in his paternal tone. "If you know Greg, you know he wouldn't kill anybody—whatever else he might have been doing."

I knew nothing of the sort. To my mind, no one was the kind of person who would kill someone—yet they did, all the time. But I let it go. "Greg's in trouble," I said again.

The doctor had a twinkle in his eye. "If Greg's in trouble, Greg will get himself out of trouble. It's nice of you to worry about him, but it's not your business."

"I don't want to get into anyone's business," I persisted. "Why don't you just tell me where I can find Greg?"

"No," the doctor said carefully. "For one thing, don't be so sure I know where he is. For another, even if I know where he is, there's no reason for me to believe telling you would help him."

This doctor had a pretty good hold on his composure and was unlikely to tell me anything if he didn't want to. But I took one more shot. "Where were you Friday night?"

The good doctor's expression slipped for a fraction of a second—an instantaneous flash of alarm that I wouldn't have seen if I hadn't been looking directly into his eyes. When he spoke again, he'd lost his good humor; his expression was severe. "Trying to tie me into this isn't going to help Greg. I'd drop it if I were you." He stared at me for a moment to let me know he meant business, then picked up some papers from his desk, stuck his nose into a file, and turned his back on me. This is one way doctors get a leg up on the rest of us, who don't have files to look into.

"Make an appointment, and I'll check your vision—on the house," Dr. Wilson said as I turned to leave; his tone was friendly, his manner professional and paternalistic once more. "Don't worry about Greg."

As I left, I noticed three or four people in the waiting room. It looked like an optometrist's office after all. Everyone glanced up when I came out of the inner office, probably to make sure I had both my eyes and wasn't tapping along with a cane. One guy, a dark-skinned Latin-looking guy, glowered at me like I'd stolen his appointment.

Considering I might want to talk to the doc again, I signed up to have my eyes checked the following week. Sourpuss called a car service for me, and I went outside to sit on the stoop and wait for the cab. I was reading my *Daily News* and waiting patiently when the doctor's door opened and the Latin guy walked down the steps and right past me, still scowling. I watched him walk toward Fourth Avenue and get into a car that someone else was driving—a fire engine red Jeep Cherokee.

When I noticed the Cherokee pull slowly from its spot next to the curb, a poorly maintained early-warning system in the back of my mind began sputtering. Just as the car stopped directly in front of the doctor's office and Mr. Scowl opened the door and stepped out, the old warning system kicked in—about a minute too late to be of any use.

I don't like stereotypes, it told me. Brooklyn has many Latino lawyers, doctors, and hardworking family men. But a Cherokee in Brooklyn? Driven by a mean-looking Latino?

My adrenaline started pumping, and I suppose I attempted to move, but I don't remember. I do remember Mr. Scowl raising a long-barreled handgun. Bang went the gun, and I thought I was dead.

The next thing I knew, I was on the sidewalk at the bottom of the stoop, a searing, burning pain ripping through my left leg. Mr. Scowl stood calmly next to the door of the car, watching me, his angry glare saying it was my fault he'd had to shoot me; then he climbed back in. The Jeep drove off slowly down the street as I stared after it, too dazed or too dumb to read the license number.

I rolled over on the sidewalk, trying to sit up, watching my blood soak my pant leg; then, I began to shake—from shock, from fear, from pain, I don't know. I got dizzy and couldn't have stood up if I'd wanted to. I kept seeing that gun barrel and feeling the bullet go through my heart. But it hadn't. The guy shot me in the leg, and, strangely, I felt grateful for that.

Dr. Wilson was beside me before I saw him. No one else seemed to care that a man had been shot on this quiet tree-lined street. Since I was a stranger and had been shot by strangers, why should they care? All we were doing was giving the neighborhood a bad name and putting a dent in property values. This, I thought about later. For the moment, I thought of the nearness of death. I wanted to see my son.

But the doctor had strong arms and someone helped him. The

strong arms felt good—safe and secure, something to hang on to in this cruel and dangerous world—until, halfway up the porch stairs, I realized he might be taking me inside to finish me off. I started struggling, twisting away from the arms that supported me, but the arms held. When I'd twisted far enough, I could look into his eyes. They smiled reassuringly.

"You'll be okay," the doctor said.

Once more, I believed him. I believed him, I realized, because I needed to. He would have to be my hero; all my other choices were used up.

Dr. Wilson sat me on a chair in the inner office, wrapped a great deal of gauze around my wound, and, with the help of this other guy, who had come from somewhere, carried me to his car.

"Where are we going?"

"To the hospital. I'll take you to Kings County. They have a lot of experience with gunshot wounds."

"It's too far away. What about Coney Island?"

The doctor seemed to be figuring out how to say what he wanted to say, and the process must have been distasteful to him, because his face was contorted with the effort.

"It would be better for me if this shooting didn't take place in front of my office." His expression wasn't exactly pleading when he looked at me; it was more like embarrassed. I was pissed that he was concerned about his own well-being while I bled in the seat beside him, though I did take some comfort from the fact that I was bleeding on the leather seat of his Mercedes.

"Yeah," I said huffily. "Just tell them you found me while you were jogging in Prospect Park."

"I won't have to tell them anything. But they'll report a gunshot wound. You might just say someone tried to hold you up and you resisted. A young black guy wearing tennis shoes and a gold chain around his neck is as good a description as any. That's what they'd expect you to say." He smiled.

"How about if I tell them it was a white guy in a three-piece suit, carrying an attaché case?"

The doctor's brow wrinkled.

"Doesn't everyone know they're crooks, too? They are, you know. Look at you; you're a crook. Everyone I know who wears a suit is a crook." My head was spinning; I couldn't stop babbling.

"Put your head down between your knees and close your eyes. You'll be okay," said Wilson in a reassuring voice. "I'll make it worth your while to keep me out of it."

"Everyone can be bought," I said. My eyes closed. I felt dizzy and nauseous, but my head cleared a little. "I got shot near Prospect Park. A guy picked me up and drove me to the hospital. I don't know who shot me." I looked over at Wilson; he looked straight ahead. "It was a white guy in a business suit."

Wilson pulled into a semicircular driveway that might have been in front of a suburban hospital, except that here weeds and a few scraggly shrubs fought for life in a patch of dirt on an island where there might have been lawn. He stopped at the Emergency Room entrance, which had a glass and chrome entranceway tacked onto the ancient brick building. A hospital cop helped him get me out of the car; someone dressed in white brought out a black vinyl–covered stretcher.

I was wheeled through the self-opening door into a room stuffed to the gills with life's unfortunates of every size, shape, and color: folks with bandaged heads and bruised faces; drooling, yellow-eyed old men; fat girls with tiny babies; old women in housecoats; teenage boys in dungaree overalls laid out on stretchers like mine. One young black guy, who had a white bandage soaked with blood on his forehead, was handcuffed to his stretcher. Next to him, in the line of stretchers against the wall, an ageless black man, his face sunken in around the area where his teeth would be, stared blankly into the hallway. Those not lying on stretchers and staring at the ceiling sat vacant-eyed on pink-and-yellow plastic bowl-shaped chairs, their expressions blaring out misery and interminable waiting.

The orderlies wheeled me briskly through the waiting room into a large space that had been subdivided by doors and curtains into cubicles. Here, too, the hallway was teeming, like a city street. The walls were an unhealthy shade of green; the people moving about were dressed in anemic green scrub suits, white nurse's uniforms, or blue police uniforms. A few of the young black guys, here, too, were hand-cuffed.

I was wheeled past a door marked WOMEN and another door marked MEN into a small examining room marked TRAUMA. One of the scrub-suited people—an orderly, I guess—looked me over, pulled off the top level of gauze, and said, "The surgeon will be right in." The orderly was young and big, and strong. I expected him to be gruff and unsympathetic, but his hands were gentle and his voice kind. He looked into my eyes. "Do you feel weak, like you'll pass out?"

I said yes.

"You've lost some blood, but it looks like a flesh wound. The surgeon will have you fixed up in no time." His gentleness stunned me into peace. Instead of being terrified, as I had been on the trip through the waiting room, I felt like a child, drifting into the perfect human kindness around me—it wasn't only my eyes; I needed my head examined. But I closed my eyes. When I opened them again, I looked into the bemused brown eyes of a very pretty woman. Her skin was a stunning color between olive and reddish brown, and there was a faint blush of pink on her cheeks. Her hair was close-cropped and curly. I couldn't stop looking into her eyes, and she kept smiling. Then she moved to the end of the table, where she cut and peeled the remaining gauze from my leg. It hurt a lot and I yelped.

She said, "Sorry," as if she really meant it.

"I'm going to stick a needle in your leg," she said with a bemused, almost secret half smile, while her eyes kind of danced. So I smiled, too. Then she jabbed me with the needle, and I yelped again. "That was to numb your leg," she said. "I'm going to have to dig out that bullet, which will cause you more harm than the bullet did going in."

She seemed competent and sure of herself. But I kept wondering if she was doing all this, what exactly would the doctor do? It wasn't un-til a middle-aged black woman in a white uniform joined her and be-gan putting pads around my leg and washing it with various things, and this beautiful woman came back, wearing a green surgical gown, holding her hands in front of her, and the nurse put gloves on her hands that I realized she was running the show. While she was fishing around on a tray through an array of silver-bladed instruments, I said, "Hi, Doctor."

She looked at me with that amused smile again. "Hi yourself," she said. Then she began working on my leg, and it hurt. She struggled also, leaning hard against my leg, her face down close to the wound. After a few moments, she held up a long tweezers and plunked something onto a metal tray. Various instruments were exchanged and she began stitching me up. In another few minutes, she had finished and walked out of the room.

"Where'd she go? I asked the nurse. I couldn't believe she was gone. I wanted her to be with me always.

"Another patient," the woman said in a tone of absolute disinterest.

"Am I finished?"

"Yes."

"Can I go?" I began to sit up, but she pushed me back.

"You might have a little trouble walking when that anesthetic wears off," she said. "Stay put."

"Will the doctor come back?" I could hear the whining in my voice.

"What for?" the nurse scolded.

Embarrassed because the rebuke suggested I was being a baby, I said in as dignified a tone as I could muster, "I thought there might be something else to do," and tried to look pathetic.

"Not unless you get yourself shot again," the nurse said in the same tone she probably used with her grandchildren.

Dr. Parker did come back to give me a prescription and tell me to see her at her clinic in three days. Nothing could have made me happier.

"Are you okay?" she asked, helping me off the examining table. "You're going to be in some pain. I'm giving you painkillers and a prescription for an antibiotic. Also, you've lost some blood, so if you try to do anything, you'll probably pass out and fall down."

"Great!"

She looked at me, still bemused, her eyes dancing.

"You must really like your work," I said.

"Sometimes."

"You did a really good job. I'm glad you were my doctor." She didn't respond, so I said, "I'm really glad I get to see you again."

Still with her secret smile, she turned away. I stared after her until the nurse interrupted my reverie. "The police want to see you," she said.

The police interrogation, if that's what it was, consisted of ten minutes with a round-faced cop, who took as much interest in my answers as a census taker. I told him I was shot on Prospect Park West around noon. No witnesses; no description of the assailant, except that he was young and white. The guy asked for my money; I said I had none, so he shot me. Would I come to the precinct and look at some pictures? the cop asked. I told him I was too weak at the moment. Would I attend a lineup if called? I said I would. That was it. Before I sat down with the cop, I'd found the card Ntango had given me that morning in my pocket and called to have him pick me up at the Kings County ER. I had no idea how long he would be, but he turned up right as I finished talking to the cop.

"How were my directions this morning?" he asked after watching me thump out the door on my crutches. "Did you have an accident?"

"Brooklyn has not been good to me lately," I said.

chapter eight

I asked Ntango to drop me at Pop's apartment, which was only a few blocks from Kings County, and tried to give him fifty bucks from the money Big John had given me.

He refused to take it. "This is not a fare, Mr. Brian. This is helping my friend." He called me Mr. Brian in a joking way, that was friendly and mocking without being either diffident or disrespectful. He finally settled for twenty bucks because it was Big John's money and I said I would claim it as a business expense.

When Pop answered his bell, I said, "I've been shot." Realizing too late I'd phrased that badly, I heard the clatter of his footsteps on the stairs and saw his pale, worried face in the front door's window before I had a chance to explain. New Yorkers have grown accustomed to a son's body on the doorstep.

"I'm all right," I said.

"Thank God."

"You don't believe in God," I reminded him.

He frowned. I noticed more wrinkles in his brow and that his hair was changing from gray to white. "Your mother's influence."

When we got back upstairs to his apartment, I smelled the coffee boiling on the stove and told him so.

Spewing curses and blasphemies, he dashed for the kitchen. When he came back carrying the glass pot in front of him like a cat he was about to heave out the door, he said, "It's your fault this time."

"You would have burned it anyway. You always do. Besides, I thought you were off the stuff."

He grumbled while he got me a cup, then grumbled some more while we drank the scorched coffee. As I told him about the shooting, he listened, his lips compressed, his eyes searching the ceiling in this thoughtful Solomon-like pose he'd developed over the years.

"This city," he said bitterly. Years of fruitless struggle echoed in his voice. My father loved New York, and he loved people. For a lifetime, he'd fought the good fight: the workers against the bosses, the poor against the rich, the peacemakers against the warmongers. Now his own street was home to teenage thugs who carried guns as an emblem of manhood and peddled drugs to buy gold chains, sheepskin coats, and ridiculously priced sneakers manufactured by poverty-stricken children. Neighbors were mugged in his doorway. Although he wouldn't admit it, he was afraid of his own block. However much longer he lived now— ten, fifteen years—it would be a sorry exit. A life of battles in vain.

I wouldn't say this to him. Despite these momentary lapses, Pop's optimism barreled on toward the New Day. Every time six people got together to complain to the landlord, he saw the coming of the revolution.

I used his phone to try to reach John at his office. He wasn't there, and the saccharine-voiced receptionist wouldn't tell me where he was.

"You got shot by a gangster?" Pop asked when I hung up.

"And I got stitched up by a beautiful surgeon. There is a bright side."

Pop lowered his bushy eyebrows like a bull lowering his head. "What now?"

"I'll go home and wait for someone to call me."

"Who will call?" asked Pop, still looking ferocious.

"The surgeon, I hope." I went over to lie on the couch because my leg started to throb.

His expression a mixture of sympathy and exasperation, Pop looked me over. "You're pale. Sleep. You need iron; I'll go get a steak."

I woke to the smell of steak broiling and heard my father in the kitchen. Now I really did feel like a kid again. I thought about my mother and wished with all my heart she were alive. I felt a craving for all of us to be together and longed for something I'd felt when I was young that I couldn't now name. It wasn't any great memory of youth, just nostalgia for calmness and predictability and a sense that everything would always be as it was.

Pop and I drank Pilsner Urquells and ate steak, french fries, and salad. Over dinner, I mentioned Big John and our meeting with Frank Carlucci. Pop's pace of eating slowed, but he didn't say anything.

"He remembered you," I said. "He offered you a job and you wouldn't take it."

Pop put down his fork and rubbed his temples as if they pained him. "After World War Two, the Left fought the gangsters for control of the unions on the docks. Some good men got killed. I don't say Carlucci killed them. He wasn't one of the gangsters; he was a strong union man in the beginning. Later, he went with the winning team. Thanks to the bosses, the government, and the witch hunts, the gangsters won. Carlucci offered me a job later on because he knew which side he should have been on."

"Does he still know the gangsters?"

"I would imagine."

"John said he kept the bartenders union from leaning on me."

"Frank Carlucci likes to do favors that don't cost him anything." Pop picked up his fork, but he ate lethargically. Before I could say anything, he went on. "Union leaders wearing suits and shooting their cuffs. Tough hoods. Bah!" I thought he would spit on the plate in front of him. "They rolled over in front of the bosses."

After a long swallow of beer, he said angrily. "You're not thinking clearly." The anger came on suddenly and curled his lips at the corners, so it looked like he was baring his teeth at me. "John drove you to that doctor's office—and left you there. Why?"

I felt weak in the knees, the way I did as a kid when my father yelled at me. He didn't mean to this time, either, but he made me feel dumb and humiliated because I didn't know the answer.

I tried to call John again, but he still wasn't in. The receptionist was no more helpful this time than the last. "Look, lady," I said. "This is important. I've just been shot."

"I'm very sorry, sir. Maybe you should see a doctor, sir," she said sweetly, and then added in a cheerful, reassuring tone, "I'll give Mr. Wolinski the message just as soon as he comes in, sir."

I called my service, too, which I might have thought of before if I hadn't been popping the Percocet pills twice as often as I was supposed to. There was a message from Big John telling me to sit tight and he'd call me. The last part of the message was, "Tell him I got a line on the guy we're looking for."

Back on the couch, I stared at the ceiling, which was a dusky brown now, not having been painted in many years. I doubted my father would ever think to paint it without my mother nagging him. I tried to make sense of why I'd been shot. Someone wanted to scare me. And it worked. They probably wanted me to stop doing something. And that might work, too. But I didn't know what to stop doing.

A thought came to me from far away in my unconscious: Bosses get shot by disgruntled former employees. Now, it's true I didn't work for the Post Office, but I was a boss now, and I did have a former employee who had every reason to be disgruntled.

"I wonder if Ernesto had something to do with this," I said out loud, even though I didn't really believe it.

"Who?" asked Pop.

"The bar back . . ." I said tentatively. "He wouldn't tell me what happened with Greg. Then he didn't come back to work after—" Here, I lost my nerve.

Pop wasn't having any of it. "After what?"

"After I fired him," I mumbled.

"You what?" Pop bellowed. "How could you fire the man?" Suspicion clouded his eyes, then the dawning of understanding. The other shoe had fallen.

"I'd been meaning to tell you. It's a long story. John made me a bar manager—to cover for Greg—before all this crazy stuff started happening."

"You've been meaning to tell me?" roared Pop. "You mean you've been meaning not to tell me—but it slipped out."

"It's temporary, I'm telling you . . . a favor to John. . . . And I didn't mean to fire Ernesto. I tried to hire him back. It was an accident. . . . I was trying to get him to talk."

"You were a boss for how long?"

"It was an accident, I tell you . . . a mistake."

That night, I stayed at Pop's, despite the chill brought about by my class treason. Then early the next morning, at his prodding, I called John's office again and was told by the tight-assed secretary that he was out of town.

"I thought you were going to tell him to call me."

"I gave him your message, sir." Her tone implied that if I had any standing in the world, he would have called.

"So now what?" I asked Pop over coffee and bagels at his ancient wooden dining room table. "Should I look for the guys who shot me?"

My father stopped, his coffee cup to his lips. "Why would you look for them? If you found them, they'd shoot you again."

"Good point."

"Where does John live?"

"I don't know."

"Wait," my father grumbled; his mouth half-full of bagel, he went for the Manhattan phone book. In a minute, he was flapping it in front of me, pointing to John's address and phone number. "Try that, Sherlock."

I called and got the same recording as the other night: John would return all calls within an hour. I left my number. Then I wrote down his address: Ninth Street in the Village.

I went home on the subway, seated all the way, thanks to the compassion of my fellow New Yorkers. The only difficulty came when I switched to the local at Ninety-sixth Street and had to stand for a few minutes of debate between an elderly man and his wife as to whether I was faking or not. While they debated, a woman wearing a nurse's uniform and speaking in a West Indian accent called me from across the car to give me her seat. I sat down heavily and tried to concentrate on the pain in my leg to make the couple feel guilty. I had years of expensive training as an actor that I didn't want to go to waste.

When I got home, I decided to rest and then go down to the Ocean Club and pretend I was working. Maybe Big John would turn up. I called and left a message with Ntango's dispatcher, asking him to pick me up around four. After reading for a half hour or so, I fell asleep. When the doorbell woke me, I expected Ntango; instead, I found Detective Sergeant Sheehan. As usual, I opened the door in a daze, while he looked alert, his face clean-shaven, his blue eyes bright and inquisitive. I quickly thought over a few explanations for my leg before realizing he already knew.

"How you feelin'?" He sounded sympathetic.

"I have a sore leg."

"So I hear." He walked into my living room, not really sniffing as he went but giving that impression.

"Who shot you?"

"I don't know."

"In Prospect Park . . . What were you doing there?" Sheehan looked over the books in my bookcase, then walked over to look out the window.

"I don't remember."

"McNulty, people get shot in the leg as a warning. They stray into someone else's territory; they owe money to a supplier; they're suspected of freelancing. It's a trick of the trade." He pulled himself away from the window, stood up straight, and looked down at me, even though I was still standing. "And the trade ain't bartending, McNulty."

Once again, I was sure Sheehan knew the answers before he asked the questions, so it was foolish to lie to him. I told myself he couldn't know all the answers and that, whatever he knew or thought he knew, I didn't have to tell him anything. Since his eyes bored into mine like a drill, I really had to brace myself. I was sure people confessed to him all the time because of this penetrating look and his complete self-assurance that made you think he already knew anyway.

"If you want to stick to your story, there's nothing I can do," said Sheehan. A flash of anger, a wisp of sympathy, and then his eyes closed slightly. When he opened them, the sympathy was gone; he was a battle-scarred, jaded cop looking down at another dead body in an alley. "Suit yourself, but let me tell you something, just between you and me. A bar jacket hanging in this guy Greg Phillips's locker had fibers on it that came from a tuxedo, the same kind of cloth the deceased wore. They were on your bar boy's jacket also.

"Ernesto?" I lost what little composure I had left.

Sheehan's expression changed ever so slightly to something between a smile and a smirk. "That's him. He's gone to join your pal in cloud-coo-coo land."

"He's missing?"

Sheehan nodded. "Duty requires me to explain that harboring either one of them is a criminal offense. One more bit of information: The deceased was a pansy. Does that mean anything to you?"

"A what?"

Sheehan looked irritated. "A queer."

I stared at him incredulously.

"A homo."

"Jesus, Sergeant. I thought the New York Police Department had grown up."

Sheehan frowned like a schoolmaster from a Dickens novel. "Don't tell me you're a fucking bleeding heart, on top of everything else?"

I maintained my stern expression.

Sheehan grunted a couple of times. "Whatever you call him, I imagine you still don't remember him?"

I told him I didn't.

Sheehan's face broke into, what was for him, a broad smile. "Funny . . . You used to work for him."

"Is that right?" I feigned shock. "I've always said I worked for more managers than I can remember." Still, Sheehan's detective work impressed me. He'd traced Aaron back a dozen or so years to the Dockside and gone over the employment records.

"I understand you had some trouble with him there." Sheehan had taken out his car keys and was rattling them in his hand as he stood in the foyer. "Something about a union."

"Bosses don't like unions. Probably not even yours. Am I a suspect now?"

"There's this coincidence. You. Greg Phillips. The big shot . . . Wolinski. The deceased. All of you together years ago in Atlantic City. All of you together when this guy gets fished out of the river." He turned those blue searchlights on me for a final time as he stood holding the doorknob. "By the way, you know where I can find the big shot?"

"I honestly couldn't tell you," I said brightly.

He nodded, pursing his lips, as if he expected as much; then he left.

When Ntango showed up, I debated a couple of minutes and then asked him to stop on 104th between Amsterdam and Columbus. He perked up because he thought I was after a packet of blow. Instead, I hobbled up five flights of stairs on my crutches to Ernesto's apartment.

His wife's deep, dark, tear-filled eyes told a story words couldn't keep up with. The kids watched from behind her skirts, or from their playground on the cracked linoleum of the warped kitchen floor. All those dark eyes beseeched me to do something. A walk-up, the smell of chicken and rice; worn, dark, and littered hallways, garbage-strewn streets; the neighborhood whacked out on cheap wine, heroin, and cocaine. All this she could take. But not the cops after her husband—not again.

I gave her my address and phone number. She looked at it blankly. "For Ernesto." Her eyes met mine once more, questioning.

"What can I do?" I shouted at her, waving my hands. "I don't know where he is. I don't know where the fuck anybody is!"

She shook her head. "Ernesto."

"Shit," I said.

She looked bewildered and scared of me. I patted her on the shoulder. I tried a reassuring smile and felt my face redden. I patted her shoulder again. Three kids. I didn't know if she had any money or any food even. I didn't know what she should do next. I didn't tell her to have three goddamn kids. I didn't tell her to come to America. Why the fuck was it my fault? She watched, her head tilted slightly, her eyes still questioning.

I gave up and handed her a bunch of crumpled twenties from the

stake John had given me. It didn't look like I'd be buying a suit anyway. She looked at them and at me. "Food," I said, "the kids. I'll get it
back from Ernesto."

She stood in the doorway, holding the twenties in her hand, watching me bump and stumble down the stairs. When I opened the door of
the building, I didn't see Ntango's cab, so I panicked, practically pitching myself off my crutches down the stone steps of the stoop. Ntango
and his cab had disappeared, too! But then I saw the cab pulled in at a
fire hydrant down the block, where he was buying a dime bag of pot
through the window. We drove downtown through the gathering evening traffic. Ntango toked up a joint; we passed it back and forth while
I told him what had been going on. He nodded sagely but didn't give
me any encouragement.

John wasn't at the Ocean Club; neither was Ernesto. No one knew
whether John would be in later. No one knew whether I was supposed
to work that night. No one cared that I'd come in. No one would care
when I left. I said a couple of encouraging words to the bartender,
called Ntango's dispatcher, then left.

Twenty minutes later, sitting in the backseat of Ntango's cab, feeling
drained and depressed, staring at the Sherwin Williams paint sign on
the Queens side of the river, I got this feeling I sometimes get that I
don't want to go home, even though I know I should. The feeling, com-
pelling as it is, doesn't always tell me where I might go instead of home.
So, this time, on a hunch, I asked Ntango if he'd take a ride to Brooklyn. I directed him to Bay Ridge and Dr. Wilson's office. I thought I
might look around the place I was shot. Who knew what I might find?

Instead, when we got there, I had another hunch. We parked across
the street and waited; I had no idea what for. I gave Ntango a couple
of Big John's twenties, about what he'd make for the fare to Bay
Ridge and some waiting time. We didn't talk, just waited and watched
the house. I expected I might get an idea of the comings and goings
around Dr. Wilson's office, or perhaps see someone—maybe Greg,
maybe Big John, or the guys from the red Cherokee—who might help
me make some sense of what had been happening.

My instinct served me well. After an hour—or maybe longer—of watching the sun leaving Brooklyn and the darkness creeping in, I saw one of Ntango's sister ships glide to a stop in front of Wilson's office, and Walter the Sleaze climbed out. Hunched up into a light windbreaker and carrying a little ditty bag, like a sailor home from the sea, he took a look around, saw our cab—stuck in among the rest of the cars on the block like the purloined letter—paid it no mind, and headed toward Wilson's house. My heart beat faster; I felt a kind of rush, like I do on the rare occasion when my horse starts to pull away in the stretch. We waited another half hour, until the lights went out in the office and two shrouded figures carrying overnight bags slunk out the side door and got into Wilson's Mercedes. I'd expected Walter would be alone and was prepared to pounce on him. But Wilson tagging along changed my plans.

Ntango followed Wilson's Mercedes out Fourth Avenue to Fort Hamilton Parkway, up and over the Verrazano Narrows Bridge, onto the Staten Island Expressway, out through the foul-smelling garbage mountains of Staten Island, over the Outerbridge Crossing, and then south on the Garden State Parkway. By then, I had a pretty good idea I was headed toward my old stompin' grounds. I gave Ntango a C-note from John's dwindling stash, took a joint from him, toked it up, and sat back to follow where life led.

chapter nine

A couple of hours later, we turned off the Garden State Parkway onto the Atlantic City Expressway. Stoned, I'd daydreamed on the way down about my life in Atlantic City years before. Ntango stayed a couple of lengths off the pace, keeping the Mercedes in sight, even though it moved at a pretty good clip. After a few miles, the expressway turned into a city street that ran straight to the casino hotels backed against the ocean. Ntango followed the Mercedes past acres of blacktop, employee parking lots with herds of blue-and-purple and black-and-green tour buses with names like Bally's, Harrah's, and Trump in gaudy lettering on the side. We headed for the gleaming glass and bright lights, the slums sliding past us on one side, the bus depot on our left.

Riding into Atlantic City after so many years, I felt like I was coming in for a landing at a spaceport. Glass and steel skyscrapers, thirty stories high, shimmered in front of me, oblongs and squares, pillars and obelisks, glittering monuments to greed. The stately brick and white-trimmed Claridge was the only building among dozens pressed against the sea that had been there in my time. The Dockside had been razed to make room for the Sands. Yet, barely a block off the main thoroughfare, the dilapidated, lopsided wooden-frame houses of the porters, maids, and kitchen workers hadn't changed by so much as a bucket of paint.

The Mercedes made a left onto Atlantic Avenue and then a right into the valet parking zone in front of the Claridge. Ntango followed. Before he'd even come to a complete stop, the doorman opened the cab door and was attempting to lug me out. I didn't want Wilson or Walter to see me, so I came out backward, my head bent. By the time I looked up, the Mercedes's taillights were rounding the far turn toward the valet lot, and the culprits had ducked into the hotel. So there I was: out of the cab, hoisted onto my crutches, tottering on the sidewalk like Dufus Dumbfuck. Fortunately, Ntango had his wits about him and climbed out of the cab, turning it over to the parking valets. I didn't want to go into the casino to look for Wilson and Walter, because with the crutches, they'd clock me in a minute, so I asked Ntango to find them and keep an eye on them while I figured out our next move. He'd recognize Walter from the other night, when he drove him to Brooklyn.

Ntango set off, while I secluded myself—shades of Sidney Greenstreet—behind a potted palm, discreetly reading a copy of the *Atlantic City Journal* I picked up off the bellman's desk. I sat there long enough for Ntango to lose track of Walter and Dr. Wilson and the C-note I'd given him. After he gave his report, I hobbled over to the pay phone and tried to call Big John. The tape on his home phone continued to promise to return all calls within an hour. No one had seen or heard from him at the Ocean Club. Next, I called Pop to tell him where I was, in case Kevin was looking for me. I told him that while I was in town, I might check out a couple of Greg's old haunts.

While we were speaking, Pop remembered someone he knew in Atlantic City. "Sue Gleason," he said, "an editor at the *Atlantic City Journal.* Look her up, and you'll save yourself a month of trying to find your way around." Pop's newspaper cronies were scattered around the country—blacklisted founding members of the Newspaper Guild or writers on the old reader-supported *PM,* they wrote for years under assumed names, and were these days, many of them, writing for senior citizen newsletters. Other of his comrades were from the younger generation that had tried to revive radical journalism in the sixties and had sought out Pop and his ilk for workshops and seminars. Sue Gleason was of the latter group.

Pop was on a roll once we got on the topic of digging up information. He told me about city directories, phone books, property lists, driver's license bureaus and marriage licenses, and on and on. "Sue Gleason can help you with all that," he said. "And be sure to check the police and court records."

This sounded too much like work, so I didn't pay much attention. I thought I might look for bartenders and waitresses I'd known in the old days, folks Greg would most likely search out if he were back in town. At the top of the list was Linda Moroni—the blond, blue-eyed Italian-American waitress I'd once loved and lost.

For the time being—recognizing a strategy once I found one—I told Ntango I was going to sit behind the potted palm until something better turned up, so he went back to the craps table to try to recoup his losses. The two hours of sitting that followed provided me an opportunity to watch a few hundred people walk through a doorway. It also gave me time to wonder what the hell I was doing in Atlantic City. I suspected myself of altruism on the one hand, and on the other hand, I wondered if I might be suffering from a form of senility that made the past more palatable than the present. I owed Greg. I didn't want to forget that. But already I'd gotten myself thrown in jail and shot trying to catch up with my old pal. The trouble here, I thought, might be deeper than a prudent man should delve into, if he has a choice. And I did have a choice.

At least I thought I did. But at just this moment, Greg appeared in the doorway that led from the casino into the lobby. Like the last time I saw him, in the 55, he didn't take a step farther in than he had to until he'd cased the place. But he couldn't see me behind the potted plant and my copy of the *Atlantic City Journal.* Greg wore the same light jacket he'd had on the last time I saw him, topping it off this time with a beret. Three steps behind him was Dr. Wilson, and alongside Wilson was good old Walter.

As soon as Greg was fully into the lobby, I hauled myself out of my chair and hobbled toward him. I came from behind, so he didn't notice me until I spoke. By then, I was right next to him. "Greg," I said. "It's me, Brian."

He jerked to a stop and turned. His face froze. But in less than a second, he unfroze, put his hands out in front of him, and shoved me in the chest so hard, I pivoted on my crutches and tumbled over like a bowling pin onto the stylish red rug of the Claridge lobby. By the time I righted myself, the trio had hightailed it out of there.

The security guards were solicitous as they picked me up and dusted me off, but there wasn't much they could do. They did say I could come up and watch the videotapes the next morning if I wanted to try to identify who had pushed me. But I already knew who'd pushed me. After a bevy of solicitous assistant managers had fawned over me long enough to make sure I wasn't planning to sue, someone went for Ntango, he retrieved the cab, and we headed out. "Which way?" he asked at the end of the driveway.

"Go to the next block and turn left," I told him, sounding more decisive than I felt. Turning left was what I remembered; it was the road to Greg's and John's house of a dozen years before. Perhaps they'd be waiting on the porch, drinking beer. Maybe, too, Linda would be there in her summer short shorts, with her shirt tied up under her breasts, her eyes brightening the way they used to when she smiled at me.

The city quieted just beyond the last space-age hotel. Here, the rambling, ornate seaside mansions along the beach roads toward Margate held their ground against the onslaught of the noveau greed. Despite being the summer vacation homes of the rich, they were familiar and welcome, promising elegance and charm, something civilization might need after all, like a Henry James novel. On a side street about three miles from the last casino, I found the house Greg and John once lived in. It was smaller than I remembered, with stone steps and an old-fashioned porch wrapping around three-quarters of the house. Neither Greg nor John sat on the porch, nor was Linda anywhere to be seen. I'd hoped that seeing the house would help me get my bearings. But, aside from a brief rush of nostalgia, my thinking was as muddled as ever.

On the way out, we'd passed a few rooming houses with vacancy signs. I suggested we go back to try to find a room for the night. These guesthouses were large and wood-framed. With their broad facades, airy wraparound porches, gables, and second-floor porches, they harkened back to an era of family vacations and oceanfront relaxation that was more optimistic than ours. Our era's frenzied and frenetic pastimes were played out in the garish, bright, and glittering casinos towering over the beach and the boardwalk.

We got a room from a thin woman who wore glasses and puffed nervously on True Blues while I filled out the registration card. I paid cash in advance. When she first watched me thump up the porch steps, I think she expected I would pay off the cab after Ntango dropped my bags in the room. When she looked at the card and realized he was staying, a pained look came into her eyes that suggested I'd betrayed her; she chomped down hard on her cigarette filter but didn't say anything. I hoped she'd ask about my leg, so I could tell her it was a gunshot wound. But she didn't.

The room on the second floor was clean and white, with large windows facing the ocean a couple of blocks east. The windows were open, and billowy curtains gathered in the sea breezes. I took a bath in an ancient tub, despite having to hang my wounded leg uncomfortably over the side, and felt a new rush of nostalgia, this one for my childhood.

"So," said Ntango when he'd finished his own bath and we'd sat down on the easy chairs that came with the room. "What do we do now that you have found your friend?"

"He didn't seem all that glad to see me, did he?" I went over and lay on the bed, my sore leg stretched out in front of me. "What I should do is forget this whole thing."

"You say this in a way that suggests you won't," said Ntango. "Why would you keep looking?"

Why indeed? I thought about this for a few minutes before I answered, maybe telling myself as much as answering Ntango. "A couple of reasons, I guess. One, I don't know what's going on with Greg. Maybe he's in trouble. Maybe those guys grabbed him or something and he was protecting me by pushing me down. I want to hear his side of the story and find out why Wilson and Walter came charging down to Atlantic City.

"I shouldn't have started this. But now someone shot me. And my old friend John is screwing me around. And someone got killed. And my other friend, Greg, just knocked me on my ass. So now I'm in the middle of this mess. I suppose I think someone should explain something to me. If nothing else, they should tell me why someone killed poor Aaron, and then they should tell me why someone shot me, and what I need to do to keep someone from shooting me again. I can't believe John or Greg had anything to do with me getting shot, but I suspect the explanations start with Greg. As long as I know he's here—or was here at least—I'd like to track him down and ask him something before he knocks me down again or does something worse."

Ntango nodded slowly; his long face and drooping eyes made him look sleepy and slow, but I knew otherwise. He relaxed back into a small chair with round wooden arms and a padded seat and backrest covered in a floral pattern that was a replica of a chair my mother used to sit in to sew. His eyes darkened with sadness. "Once I looked for my father," Ntango said quietly. "I was eleven. My father was a teacher, an important man in our village. Almost every evening, he went to meetings, of the cooperative, of the village council, sometimes to Asmara to a convention of the union. One day, the government troops came into town, so my father went to a meeting. When he didn't come home that night after the meeting, my mother went before breakfast the next morning to ask, and she found he had not been to the meeting. She was afraid, but she came back home to us. When she fed my sisters and my brother, I left to look for my father. I walked through the village and asked everyone who knew him. The soldiers stopped me once and told me to go home. But I kept at it all day and went to every single person I saw in the village. Late in the afternoon, I walked out into the countryside. I would have followed the road as far as it went, hundreds of miles to Asmara, to find my father. I knew he was somewhere. I knew he would not leave me. I kept to the road, jumping off whenever I heard or saw anyone, and watching from the brush. When it got dark, I remembered I had not eaten all day. I was afraid of the dark. But I kept thinking my father was somewhere, needing me. Finally, I was so tired, I just sat by the road until I fell asleep. I forgot to hide myself, and I was found by the soldiers, who took me back to my village and delivered me to my mother's house." Ntango stopped speaking; he watched the billowing white curtains. I could no longer see his eyes.

I imagined my own father gone, and my search for him; I imagined Kevin searching the city streets and back alleys, looking for me. During most of my waking time, I hid from myself the knowledge that in places all over the world children searched for their parents along dirt roads.

How do you put yourself into someone else's life? I couldn't imagine Ntango's life. I wondered if I could imagine Greg's. He might be in a room like this one—the walls closing in—wondering what he should do next. He might be a few blocks from me right there in Atlantic City. It's a good place to hide, this resort city, where the average vacation lasts four hours. When I woke up in the morning, Ntango was dressed and sitting in the same chair, looking out the window toward the ocean. "The meter is running," he said softly. His mask was back, not an unkind face, not a game face like Robert Parrish's, but impassive, as if nothing concerned him.

In the Atlantic City public library, my first discovery was that someone had stolen the city directory. There was no listing for Linda in the phone book. She could have left town years ago. This was enough investigating for me, so we headed toward the *Atlantic City Journal* and my father's protégée, its managing editor, Sue Gleason.

Ms. Gleason was around my age, not particularly tall, on the stout side, wearing a loose-fitting skirt and blouse, so she looked comfortable and seemed exactly the size and shape she should be. Her movements were quick, whether answering the phone, which rang the moment we approached her desk, or typing into her computer, which she did with the phone receiver tucked up under her chin, saying "Um-hmm" a lot. She gestured with her eyes toward chairs in the cluster of desks around her, so we sat down and waited. Before we'd left the guesthouse that morning, I'd called to tell her who I was, so she smiled at me often during the phone call, as if I were more important than the other things she was doing, even though I had to wait for her to finish them.

When she hung up the phone, we all shook hands. She asked about my father but seemed too involved in the present to be especially wistful for whatever past they'd shared. I told her I'd come back to Atlantic City after a long time away and was looking for people I'd known a long time ago. She wrote the names down as I gave them to her. "Greg Phillips? Linda Moroni? Any of them gamblers? Might any of them work for a casino?" She referred again to her list. "Dr. Charles Wilson? Walter who?" I was afraid she was a little put out as the list got longer, so I didn't even mention Ernesto or Big John. Unperturbed, she acted as if every day someone came in looking for half a dozen people for no particular reason.

I didn't want to tell her about Aaron being murdered. But I soon realized she didn't have much enthusiasm for the chase, so I leveled with her. "A guy was murdered in New York a couple of days ago," I said. "He used to be my boss down here in Atlantic City—at the old Dockside. And then someone shot me in the leg when I went to talk to this optometrist who knew Greg. . . . Greg worked at the Dockside, too. I forgot about Walter. . . ." Here, I got hung up because I didn't know how she'd handle the drug part, so I skipped over it. "Walter's Greg's roommate. We followed him and Wilson to Atlantic City last night. . . . Wilson's the optometrist."

She listened patiently; there was even a spark of interest in her eyes. "What about this Linda Moroni?"

I felt myself blush. "She's someone I used to know." I stammered like a fourteen-year-old. "I thought she might have seen Greg or—"

"Why?"

"I don't know. . . . I just thought she might have." Realizing this might sound evasive to someone not right up on my line of thinking, I said, "Let's just forget her for now."

"You may have hit a lucky break. The security director at the Claridge used to work at the Dockside—and I know him pretty well. Fortunately for you, he's obsessive; I don't think he's ever thrown anything away." Sue Gleason reached for the phone again, spoke to the man, and found out he'd kept some files from when the Dockside went out of business. The Dockside had changed owners and then went bankrupt, she explained. The owners skipped town, so Paul kept all the files in case any legal trouble cropped up. He still has them somewhere and he thinks they include a lot of old employee ID pictures. "I gave him the names and he's going to check. He said to drop by later and he'll give you what he has. The photos might help if you make the rounds of the casinos looking for any of these people, especially for the girl. You can't tell about the name; she might have married."

This gave me pause. The idea of Linda being married knocked me back on my haunches, though I don't know why it should have. Did I really think she was waiting back there on the porch?

"You could to go to the Cape May county courthouse; look up marriage records for her and property records for her parents. That would take quite a bit of time but might get you going in the right direction."

"That's okay," I said. "It's not so important."

Ntango and I watched Sue Gleason go to work again, dialing the phone, typing now and again on her computer, riffling through a Rolodex on her desk. It was as if she had compartmentalized herself so different parts of her could work simultaneously and independently. Still smiling in my direction, she searched through her notes in preparation for something else.

"Uh," I mumbled.

She replied, "Um" quite distinctly to show she was listening attentively, but she didn't look up from her notebook.

"My father said we should check the police records."

"Good idea." She went for the phone once more. Again, she spoke to a person she seemed to know well. Again, she began writing—writing quite a lot, actually.

She hung up and looked over her list, which, because of the pictures, now included John. "A Wolinski here seems to have made quite a name for himself," she said. "But not John. Charles, who would be almost seventy now. Maybe a father or uncle?"

She looked at me. I shrugged. It might very well be John's father Charlie.

"Greg Phillips appears once for assault and battery. Coincidently, I know the man he assaulted—Ralph Ettinger."

"Ralph?" I said. "He assaulted Ralph?"

She looked up from her notes; for the moment, I had her full attention. "You know Ralph?"

"Do you?"

"I did a story on him a few years ago. There's a building at the far end of Park Place, in the inner city. It has a soup kitchen, a used-clothing store, a radical bookstore, and some offices. He runs an organization called Jobs and Justice for Atlantic City. From there, he launches quixotic sorties against the impregnable casinos and jousts with the city government."

I knew Ralph from the sixties. He was a red-diaper baby, like me, and a community organizer, who disapproved of my high-roller life around the hotels of Atlantic City. I used to go to some of the demonstrations he organized and was a halfhearted participant in some community-organizing drives. I introduced him to John and Greg and the other hotel people, trying to get them involved in the movement, such as it was, but they didn't hit it off. Like too many radicals I knew, Ralph was puritanical and disapproving. It sure was curious that he'd get into a fight with Greg.

Cape May Courthouse is twenty or thirty miles south of Atlantic City, back on the mainland. Ntango drove there at a leisurely pace along Route 9, the main north-south road in that neck of the woods before the Garden State Parkway opened in the 1950s. The area hadn't been much disturbed since, except for an occasional self-storage compound, gas station, or convenience store. The trees were tall and broad, the houses, set back from the road, looked well cared for and comfortable in their setting.

We found the courthouse without much trouble. Leaving Ntango to nap in the cab, I hobbled off. Armed with clear directions from Sue Gleason that I was within my rights and not to take no for an answer, I withstood the bullying of a couple of clerks and began pouring through their records. Linda Moroni was the first name I looked for.

I tried voter-registration records and found Moroni's on the first shot. Her parents lived on Sixty-seventh Street in Sea Isle City. I didn't find Greg or any other Phillips. I tried birth certificates and found Linda again, born February 19, 1952, but no birth certificate for Greg. In the marriage-license records, I found Linda once more— on an application for a marriage license, along with Ralph Ettinger.

Alone at a small wooden table next to a large wooden counter, in a large room of dull gray file cabinets and mustiness, I stared at the names for a long time, trying to weather the jolt of disbelief and disappointment that shot through me. Linda loved me. Even though I'd left her, and even though I'd had no plans to see her again until last night, somewhere in the great ocean of foolishness—my unconscious—I'd harbored the expectation that she would be there, still in love with me, when I came back. Ralph? Why would she marry Ralph?

chapter ten

Ntango dropped me off at the Atlantic County Opportunity Center, a three-story rectangular brick building—a dead ringer for the parochial school I'd gone to in Brooklyn until fourth grade. Then he went to check with the security director at the Claridge to see if he'd come up with any photos. The front wall of the building listed a number of organizations, each on its own small wooden plank. Jobs and Justice for Atlantic City was on the second floor—a precarious trip for the hobbled, up the worn wooden stairs, but I made it.

In a shabby office with metal desks and filing cabinets, worn wooden floors, curtainless, unwashed industrial-size windows, and faded green walls, I found Ralph Ettinger sitting at a computer. I'd expected a mimeograph machine. His expression, pleasant enough and interested when he looked up from the screen at the thumping of my arrival, clouded with suspicion when he recognized me after a few seconds. Ralph never had much warmth or passion. Steady and unvarying, he kept to his work, without the righteous anger against injustice or the joy of belief that most of us felt in the halcyon days of our vigils for peace and freedom. He'd been an up-and-coming party leader in those days; I didn't know if he still was. I didn't know if anyone was anymore.

"Brian McNulty, Ralph," I said.

He smiled anemically, holding out his hand. I shook it. Having expected a friendly reunion, I felt uncomfortable—the feeling you get when you overstay your welcome and are sober enough to realize it. So

I got to the point: I wanted to find Greg and Linda. I didn't say why.

"I haven't seen Greg in years," Ralph said. "He was your friend, not mine. The last I knew of him, he worked at the Sands with Linda when it first opened. Now Linda's at the Claridge." I wondered if the flutter of happiness I felt when he mentioned her name was apparent to him. I had a feeling it was.

Trying to make conversation with Ralph was like making small talk with my ex-father-in-law, but I kept trying. He gave me a cup of stale coffee from a stained and discolored Mr. Coffee machine near the wall, sat down on the corner of the desk, and pushed his own chair out for me to sit on.

I asked again when he'd seen Greg last. He didn't remember. Then I asked him about the assault charge.

This pissed him off. "That was a long time ago," he said curtly. "I'd rather not go into it." So he didn't. I didn't press him, realizing that, although we'd pretty much kept it under wraps in the old days, Ralph and I disliked each other. The more I thought about it, the angrier I got that Linda had married him. He never asked why I was looking for Greg. And he didn't tell me that he and Linda were married. But he did give me an address and told me she'd be home. I was glad to leave him behind, and still curious about what had happened between him and Greg.

Ntango was waiting for me in front of the Opportunity Center. The security guy did have pictures, it turned out, of Greg, Linda, John, me, and even Aaron. Ntango gave me the pictures, then dropped me off at the corner of Linda's street, a few blocks from the ocean, not far from the house that Greg and John once lived in, about a mile over the Margate border. He said he was going to hit the casino again and would meet me back at the rooming house—if I could get there myself, which I assured him I could. Propelling myself down the quiet street on my crutches, I pretended I was the wounded war hero limping home. The houses on the street looked the same: small single-story bungalows, white, blue, or yellow, all of them cozy—the real estate term for cramped.

Linda's house sat on a plot of small round polished white stones, which is what passes for a lawn in that part of the country. There were few trees along the street, and those were scrawny and weirdly shaped by the elements; in Linda's front yard, one twisted scrub pine on one side and one bayberry bush on the other served as shrubbery. The sparse terrain was nature's way of reminding the inhabitants that barrier islands belong to the sea, not to them.

She was waiting at the door. Her eyes as bright and her smile as beguiling as I remembered. Whatever it was that had captivated me years before hadn't faded. To stop myself from gawking, I put out my hand to shake hers. She took it and held it. Then she came into my arms and kissed me on the lips. The kiss was quick and light, but lingered for just a second.

Her eyes sparkled, her lips were faintly red with lipstick, her cheeks flushed. She wore a blue summer dress and was as slim as she was as a girl. Being near her felt the same as when I first knew her, during the nights we talked for hours on the boardwalk and the days we walked on the dunes. She loved me then without illusion and with no pretense. Because I had come from the radical movement, she saw me as someone who, like her, rejected falsity, though I'm sure I wasn't as honest with her—or myself—as either of us thought then.

"Oh, Brian, I always knew you'd come back."

"I wish I'd known," I said.

She held my hand; her eyes were as blue as the sky. "I want to know all about you." She tugged at me, almost pulling me off my crutches. "Come in. What happened to your leg?"

"Nothing serious." I followed her inside to a boring brown-and-beige living room, the kind you might expect to find in this one-story bungalow. What gave the place life was that it was cluttered with the paraphernalia of infancy: a stroller, a plastic walker, a playpen—nowadays called a play yard, in an attempt to belie its true nature—various oddly shaped, brightly colored objects of no particular purpose—and, in my limited experience, of no particular interest to infants—a contoured seat of a size to fit the baby, and a number of rubber ducks and rabbits that squeaked when I either stepped or sat on them.

"The baby's asleep," Linda advised me as she led me to the couch and took my crutches. She spoke the word *baby* adoringly, despite her attempt to be offhanded.

"You married Ralph." I said, more accusingly than I'd expected to. Already, I felt as if time stood still and I'd never gone away.

Her eyes twinkled as she looked at me through her long eyelashes. "What'd you expect me to do? Wait for you?"

I stared at her.

Sitting down next to me on the couch, she stroked my hair. "Oh, Brian, we could have had four or five babies by now if you'd only stayed."

I couldn't think of anything to say. My heart was pounding. I didn't know why I hadn't stayed with her. I was crazy during that time. Just divorced, with a kid in Brooklyn whom I hadn't seen in months, I didn't know why I did anything. Things I wouldn't do now had seemed right then.

"Ralph waited for me for a long time. He was as patient as you should have been."

We fell back into talking as easily as we used to. We were attuned in a special way. If we hadn't seen each other for twenty years, we still would have been perfectly at ease together.

"You seem happy."

"I am," said Linda, her eyes glowing. "And you?" She sounded mildly sympathetic. "Are you still unhappy?"

She touched my arm. The openness of her affection confused me. It was as if we were beginning a romance. But I should have known better. Linda wouldn't stop caring for me once she'd begun. She wouldn't hide her caring, either. I'd spent three months with her, and she'd engulfed me with such passion that I'd run away.

She leaned closer to me, her lips inches away. I reached for her. "Can I kiss you?" I whispered.

"You already did," she said matter-of-factly. I slunk back against the couch. But her expression didn't change; she still acted like I belonged to her. "Ralph said you were looking for Greg. Why?"

"It's a long story. Actually, I found him last night, and he knocked me on my ass."

She tilted her head, scrutinizing my face to see if I was kidding. Satisfied I wasn't, she said, "That's weird. But why would you come here to ask me about Greg?"

I wasn't quite ready to tell her why, and she was polite enough not to push. I told her I hadn't found Greg or his family listed in any of the directories and asked if she was sure he'd grown up in Sea Isle City. She was sure. She remembered him in high school, she said, and went to get her high school yearbook. He was there all right, under *P*, but he was Greg Peters, not Greg Phillips.

"What do you think of that?" said Linda. "I never even knew he changed his name."

"Not much is as it seems."

I thumbed through the yearbook, looking for a picture of Walter. There was a Walter Springer, his blond hair slicked back in a pompadour, à la Bobby Rydell. It could be the same Walter, but I couldn't tell for sure, and Linda didn't remember him. John wasn't in the book because he'd graduated a couple of years before them.

Linda looked at Greg's picture for a long time. "He sure was a strange guy. I've known him since we were kids and never really known him at all. John was the only person he cared about—and you." She turned to look at me. "I don't think you even knew how much he watched out for you." Linda laughed. "When you started at the Dockside, you were the worst bartender we ever saw. The waitresses would have hung you if it wasn't for Greg."

She was right. If I hadn't known then, I realized later Greg had my back the whole time. And Linda was right about what a closed book he was, too. Although he lived even more in Big John's shadow than I had, Greg lived his own life, too, and that part he kept pretty much to himself. He'd become my friend before John had. And he made me a bartender more or less in his likeness. A real journeyman, he was meticulous, as close to perfection as anyone got at a trade. I learned from him to pour with both hands, to keep my head up, to plan so that nothing—not the juices, nor the fruit, nor the beer, nor the ice—ever ran out, no matter how busy it got. After a while, the waitresses even liked it when I worked the stick. But when push came to shove, of all the bartenders, no matter how handsome or charming, as in John's case, or solicitous, as in my case, it was Greg the waitresses most wanted to work with. They came to the Dockside to make a living; most of them hated the work. Greg didn't keep them waiting—no backups on the service bar—Greg flew, so they made money the nights he worked.

I could still picture him in his blue bar jacket, clean and pressed as if for parade-ground inspection. Every other day, he walked in carrying a fresh bar jacket in a dry cleaners' bag. His shoes were always shined, his shirt ironed, every hair in place. He moved into the bar with the bearing and aplomb of the acrobat walking out onto the stage. He believed working the stick at the Dockside was the best job in the world, and he had paid his dues to get there.

The front bar was a bit different. Greg had little charm and not much interest in the patrons. His fastidiousness paid his way. The customers liked to watch him. He won them over by his mastery behind the bar. When he made a drink, his hands moved like a magician's. His movements were like close-order drill. And even if he never said more than three words to a customer, the guy's glass was never sitting there empty. The bar surface shined like brass; the glasses sparkled. So any hail-fellow-well-met assumed Greg was a jolly good fellow, even though he wasn't.

During my first few weeks at the Dockside, he taught me the bar. And after work, on rare occasions, he took me into his life—his own life, not the one he shared with Big John. We went to small neighborhood bars and softball games, a mom-and-pop restaurant in Ocean City, an old-man shot and beer bar in Sea Isle, and a gin joint that a couple of black guys he'd been in the navy with had opened in Wildwood.

Linda broke in on my thoughts. "Does this have anything to do with John?" she asked in the tone that suggested she already knew the answer.

"Why?"

Her eyes, which were always so clear and expressive, narrowed with concern. "Greg never did anything without John being close by."

"Maybe he did this time," I said more to myself than to her. "You remember Aaron Adams?"

She nodded.

"He's been murdered."

Fear flashed in her eyes. First shock, then fear. She still held on to life strongly enough for willful and sudden death to be terrifying. "And?" she asked, her eyes frozen open.

"It happened where Greg worked."

"When?"

"The other day."

"Which other day?"

"Friday night."

She drew back from me. "Why did you come here? Did John send you?" She grabbed at the front of my shirt. "Why did you come here?" she screeched again. The tone of her voice sent shivers through me. The change that came over her was awful. I was stung by what she said—until I remembered the baby.

"I'm sorry," I said, standing up. Linda, already standing, moved closer to the hallway that undoubtedly led to the baby's room, to stand between me and the baby. I tried to calm her. "This doesn't have anything to do with you. It doesn't have anything to do with me. I shouldn't have come here. I wish I hadn't."

Her eyes, still clear, were open wide. She cringed, as if she thought I might hurt her. But after a few minutes, when she'd calmed down, she insisted on hearing every detail of what had happened. So I went through the whole litany. Aaron was fished out of the river. John and I talked to Walter. I went to see this guy Dr. Wilson and got shot. I followed him and Walter to Atlantic City. I found Greg, and he knocked me on my ass. I didn't know what the hell was going on.

"Where's John?" she asked.

"I wish I knew."

I started to tell Linda I couldn't have endangered her or the baby by

coming there, but then I stopped before I began. I didn't know why
Aaron had been murdered or why I'd been shot. I didn't know why
Greg had run off or why Walter and Dr. Wilson had driven to Atlantic
City to meet up with Greg. I didn't know where John was. I didn't
know if someone was stalking me. I should have been more careful. I
didn't want to see the fear in Linda's face or the fierceness she summoned to challenge the fear. I wanted to remember how pretty and how
happy she looked when I first arrived. Now her eyes reddened and filled
with tears.

"Oh, Brian," she cried, then ran across the room into my arms,
burying her face against my chest, knocking me against the back of
the beige chair. "I'm afraid, horribly, horribly afraid."

"Why?" I hung on to her shoulders because she was the only thing
holding me up. "What are you afraid of?"

She lifted her head from my chest. "Don't you remember?" Her
face was blotched and red, her eyes wild.

My own horrors started climbing up out of the murkiness. "What?"
I hollered back at her.

"You really didn't know what John and Greg and Charlie were doing when you were here, did you?"

"What do you mean? Doing what? You mean, Charlie John's father?"

"Yes, you didn't know Charlie?"

I shook my head. "I knew about him, but I never met him. You tell
me. What was going on?"

Linda's eyes were red and wild-looking. Her hands were clasped
tightly in front of her to stop them from shaking. "Much, much more
than I would care to remember. Do you know why you got your job
at the Dockside?"

Linda and I faced each other, both of us grim-faced and rigid with
tension. "Because that guy David Bradley died." My voice shook.

"David Bradley was murdered. The overdose was on purpose."

My blood turned cold. "How do you know? That was a rumor. All
we knew was that he overdosed."

"And Bill Green."

I felt the cold wind at my back. Bill Green was the guy who'd given

David the dope he overdosed on. They found his body a couple of weeks later in a shallow grave, a knife wound in his chest. "I know what you're thinking. But you don't know what happened, any more than I do. And what does any of that have to do with what's going on now?"

There wasn't any reason to believe Aaron being killed had any connection to deaths so many years before in Atlantic City. Yet what was scariest about what Linda had said was how the tumblers clicked together. Something out of the past was coming after all of us.

I sat Linda back down. "Let's go over this again."

"No!" Her expression had hardened. No longer was she my sweet little Linda. "Just leave me alone."

"Did you know Walter?"

She shook her head. "I told you no."

"Look, I know John's father was some sort of second-rate racketeer. What else do you know about him?"

I put my hand on hers. She took a deep breath and almost smiled. We both began to calm down. She held my hand and squeezed. "All those guys—Bill Green, David, John, Greg, who knows who else—they ran errands for Charlie. Numbers, sports betting, bootleg cigarettes, stolen liquor, pot. You know, all that stuff." Linda began to sound more like a battered B-girl, and less like the angelic mother.

"I think I was born yesterday."

Her eyes locked on mine for a long time until the defiance softened into a smile. "Brian, Brian . . . you worshiped those guys. I used to wish you'd be like that with me."

"So my friends were gangsters, and I was too stupid to know it?"

"They were kids, Brian. They weren't gangsters. We grew up in the shore towns, where you couldn't even find a place to buy groceries in the winter, not to mention have fun anywhere. That was the romantic life. You knew it, too. You liked it. I saw it in you. You weren't like John and Greg and the other bartenders, but you wanted to be. You wanted to be a high roller. We all did, even before any of us ever saw one. Now I see a thousand of them every day and the glamour has sure worn off.

"If you'd known Charlie, you'd have loved him. He was generous and funny and even more charming than John. Those guys went to him. He didn't have to come after them."

I felt foolish. Everyone, even Linda, had known what was going on and I hadn't. Now I was mad at all of them. "Who killed David, if he didn't die accidentally? And who killed Bill Green?"

Linda weighed her answer before she spoke. "This is what I know. Bill Green killed David by giving him a hot shot because David had twenty-five thousand dollars on him. The money belonged to someone else, and that someone else killed Green to get the money back."

"Did the money belong to Charlie?"

"I don't know. It was all rumors. I don't know if any of this is true."

We sat quietly for a few minutes.

"What did Aaron have to do with any of that?"

"Nothing, as far as I know."

Linda sighed and laid her head back against the top of the couch. "Why did you ever decide to come and see me now?" she asked quietly. "What on earth made you think I knew anything about Aaron being killed?"

"Nothing, Linda, believe me. In my wildest dreams I didn't think you had anything to do with this. I just thought of you. I wanted to see you again. I thought maybe you'd know where Greg was. It gave me an excuse to see you. That was the only reason."

She scrunched up her pretty face to peer intently at me, as if by doing this she could tell if I was telling the truth. When she smiled, I figured she was satisfied. "It's not your fault," she said, "that things don't stay buried in the past."

chapter eleven

Linda said she'd drive me back to the rooming house on Atlantic Avenue on her way to work. I was hoping she'd come out of her bedroom dressed in a short-skirted cocktail waitress uniform, but, having given up waitressing in favor of dealing black-jack, she was dressed now like a riverboat gambler—black slacks, a white shirt with ruffles, and a string tie. Still, she was as cute as a button. I stared after her longingly, withstanding the compressed lips, wrinkled nose look of disapproval from the matronly babysitter, who had just arrived.

"Second shift is the best for me," Linda said as she backed her Toyota out of the driveway. "This way, I can be with the baby all day. Ralph can be with her at night, so we only need the babysitter a couple of hours a day."

On the drive in, I found myself not wanting to let go of Linda again, so I pushed my luck. "Maybe I'll sit in on your game later," I said hopefully.

"No. . . . I don't want to take your money." She looked over at me in this imploring way I remembered so well, that had always irritated me because it seemed to be asking me to do something I wasn't able to do.

"It's not inevitable, is it?"

"The house is the sure thing," said Linda.

When I tried to get her to tell me more about the time when David Bradley and Bill Green died, she said it was awful and looked like she would start crying again. "You came at the end. Everything was crazy, everyone running around making up stories. Charlie hadn't been out of jail long. Everybody was trying to cover for him, so he wouldn't get sent back."

"Get sent back for what?"

"I don't know. . . . It wasn't like we thought he'd done anything. Those guys were connected to Charlie, and he was just out of prison and still on parole and couldn't afford to have the cops suspect him." She sounded irritated and banged the little car in and out of gear. "I don't know why you're dredging all of this up anyway."

"I didn't bring it up. You did. How did Aaron fit in?"

"Aaron? . . . I told you. He didn't have anything to do with anything. He was the boss. Besides, he was gay. You guys barely talked to him."

"What about Walter?"

"I told you I didn't know any Walter."

It was stuffy in the little car. She pulled over and we sat there in front of the rooming house. I tried once more. "What is it that scared you when I told you Aaron had been killed?"

She looked scared again.

I put my hand on her shoulder. "Look, Linda. Do you know some reason Greg would have killed Aaron Adams?"

She looked like a little girl. I couldn't imagine her not telling the truth. "No," she said. "I don't."

"Well, then, what?" I was exasperated.

She pulled her knees up in front of her so she could turn her whole body to face me. "If I tell you something, will you just forget about everything? Go back to New York and leave me alone?" The look in her eyes was pleading and winsome. If at that moment she'd put her arms around my neck the way she used to, I would've promised her anything. But she didn't put her arms around me, and I didn't promise.

"Just after David died, Greg told me Bill Green had killed him." She sat rigidly in her seat, her eyes locked on mine. "When Bill Green died . . ." Her face was puffy, her eyes red again and glistening with tears. "I can't say this. I just can't say it. You know what I'm going to say. . . . Don't make me say it." She began wailing, and when I tried to put my hand on her shoulder to calm her, she whacked it away. "It doesn't have anything to do with Aaron. It doesn't have to do with anything. I don't know where Greg is."

She shook her head and buried her face in her hands, managing to make clear between sobs and hiccups that she wanted me to go. So I left Linda crying in her car and hobbled up to my room, lay down for a nap, and drifted off to sleep with the thought gnawing at me that Greg might do better for himself not being found.

Sue Gleason had invited Ntango and me for dinner to find out how we'd done on our search. So when Ntango returned from the casinos, with a few extra bucks in his pocket this time, we went. She lived in an open, airy, nautical-looking two-story modern house facing the ocean. It was on the same side of Atlantic City as Linda's, but in a more upscale neighborhood. Ntango and I sat on a soft and billowy dark brown couch across from a large bay window, drinking Jamaican rum and grapefruit juice, watching the moon rise over the dark and shifting water.

I told Sue about not finding Greg in the directories, then later finding him under a different name in the high school yearbook. She thought about that for a few minutes. "I'm not sure what it means," she said finally, sitting back comfortably in the stuffed easy chair that matched the couch. "He might have changed his name simply because he didn't like the name, or he might have because he wanted to conceal his identity. But it wouldn't do any good if he had a record and wanted to hide it from the casinos. They use fingerprints."

"Maybe he has two lives," Ntango said. We both turned to stare at him. He sipped his drink, smiling with his eyes. "That's what I'd like to have. When you said two names, I thought that I'd like to be two people. Some days, Ntango driving a cab. Some days, another man, living in the country maybe."

We let this register, then Sue said, "It's been done. Housewife in the morning, hooker at night."

"I doubt that Greg's a hooker," I said. They both looked at me. "Or a housewife, either," I added weakly.

"You've created quite a puzzle for yourselves," Sue said. Somewhere in the course of our conversation, she'd begun writing on a pad. She noticed me watching her. "These are just obligatory letters."

"Do you ever do one thing at a time?"

While we talked, she continued to write her letters, interrupted by an occasional trip to the kitchen, where she was cooking dinner. I tried putting together the whole story, with an eye toward connecting the past murders to Aaron's recent murder. But as I unraveled the story, it became clear I hadn't come up with anything to connect the past and Aaron's murder, except Greg.

"This person Charlie sounds interesting," Sue said. "Do you know where he is now?"

"I remember vaguely that a few years ago John had said his father was semiretired and lived out in Arizona."

"What did he retire from?" Ntango asked.

"From being a gangster, I guess." Then I remembered that in addition to his nefarious activities, John's father had a respectable job. But if I'd ever known what it was, I didn't remember.

We talked for a while longer but didn't come up with any new ideas to explain where John was, what Dr. Wilson and Walter were doing in Atlantic City, why Greg had two names, why he'd pushed me down in the casino, or how I might go about finding answers to any of those questions. So after sea bass and white wine, Ntango and I left to relax at the casinos before heading back to New York.

While Ntango sought his fortune from the craps table, I lurched off in search of my own treasure. It took twenty minutes of thumping between the casino tables, but I found her. Her face tight with concentration, she was raking in the house's winnings. When I approached the table, she looked up and her sparkling smile broke through the weariness in her face. She was glad to see me after all.

"I have a break in fifteen minutes," she said. During those seconds that she looked into my eyes, I felt perfectly happy. For that moment, being with her was the only thing in the world I wanted.

With a few minutes to kill, hoping the gods of probability would take pity on a cripple, I laid my crutches down and took a seat at the blackjack table next to hers. Fifteen minutes later, Linda, shaking her head sympathetically, stood beside me for the last hand and watched the dealer drop a four of hearts on top of his king-six to beat my nineteen and scoop up the last of my fifty bucks in chips.

"What are you going to do now?" Linda asked.

"I'm going to give up rambling, gambling, and staying out late at night. Let's go for a walk." I took her by the craps table to meet Ntango, but since he held the dice and had just made his point, we didn't want to get in the way, so we left.

"I'll go with you if you promise not to talk about this afternoon," Linda said.

This time, I promised.

As we walked away from the table, Linda slipped her arm through mine and pulled herself tightly against me. "I'm glad we get another chance to say good-bye. Seeing you just appear in that crowd around the table made me so happy, I almost cried." Her face, pressed against my arm, was as softly colored as a child's.

For some stupid reason, I felt tears well up behind my own eyes as I looked at her. "The ones who should be crying are those poor suckers you keep fleecing at the table," I said.

She hugged my arm, causing my crutch to wobble.

"Can we go outside?"

Her forehead wrinkled with worry for a second; then her face brightened. "I'm not supposed to, but I don't care. I used to go out all the time to smoke a joint before I got pregnant."

"I actually happen to have a joint." I patted my chest pocket as we walked through the doorway and out onto Pacific Avenue.

"We can smoke it on the boardwalk." Linda let go of my arm and walked slowly beside me. "Just like old times," she said wistfully.

We sat on an old wooden-slatted bench set on stone haunches that had withstood a century of Atlantic storms, while somewhere in front of us the surf rolled, the hushed roar drifting in on the darkness. I lit the joint and passed it to Linda. When I first knew her, she was the world's sweetest flower child. We got to know each other by sneaking out the kitchen door and smoking joints in the alley behind the Dockside kitchen. The first time we ever kissed was in that alley, next to a Dumpster.

Now, on the bench on the boardwalk, under the stars and a moon that was three-quarters full, my face brushed by the damp wind from the ocean, I put my arm around Linda, and she rested her head on my shoulder. There really wasn't anything to say. When I bent over and kissed her, her mouth moved gently against mine for a few seconds, but except for that, she remained perfectly still.

"Whew," she said when she pulled away from me, a dazed look in her eyes.

"Maybe if we close our eyes, we'll drift back in time."

"That would be wonderful." She turned toward me. Her breathing was rapid and shallow, and it excited me. In the darkness, her features were less distinct, so her expression didn't give any extra meaning to her words, yet I felt her eagerness. But in a second, she changed. "We can't do the things we used to do, Brian." She stared at me, and I felt the chill of her anger.

I didn't say anything.

She wrestled with herself for a moment, then came closer to me again, nestling her head against my chest. For what seemed a long time, we watched the sea beyond the darkness. When we walked back to the casino, taking the long way, I felt an odd mixture of contentment and longing—and there still wasn't anything to say.

About twenty feet from the front door of the Claridge, Linda stiffened beside me. Instinctively, I looked up. There, bursting through the doorway at his usual stampedelike pace and barreling down Atlantic Avenue toward Resorts International, was Big John. I hollered his name but caught the sound in my throat, so it came out a hoarse whisper that only Linda heard.

Stunned for the moment, I watched John. "I'm going to follow him," I told Linda as we pressed against each other and the wall of the building.

"Why?"

I couldn't explain. It seemed like what I should do. "Don't worry. I'm just curious. I'll call you later. Would you get Ntango at the craps table and ask him to catch up with me?" With that, I hoisted myself up, despite the increasing pain in my armpits, and went hippity-hoppity down the avenue.

Ntango caught up with me near the Resorts' entrance on the street side. I kept John in sight while Ntango negotiated with one of the local cabbies at the hack stand in front of the hotel. Sure enough, John handed the valet a ticket. Ntango waved me over. I ducked into the cab, but Ntango went to stand at the corner of the hotel—too near Big John for my money; I couldn't guess what he was doing. When the attendant pulled John's big Eldorado out of the lot and stopped about fifty feet in front of us, Ntango sidled up behind it, almost brushing against the back of the car. He crossed the street and then crossed back again behind the cab and climbed in beside the driver.

"Hey," said the cabdriver. "Good idea." The cabbie was big and round and very dark. He looked like he'd been poured into his seat at the beginning of his shift and wouldn't get out again until someone pulled the stopper at quitting time. He had a green-black-and-red flag on the dashboard and a decal on the back of the front seat that said JESUS LOVES YOU.

Ntango and the driver exchanged smiles, and when John's car pulled away, I saw that a portion of the taillight had been blacked out. Ntango had covered it with tape he'd borrowed from the driver.

"Taillights look a lot alike," Ntango said.

I took note of the irony of using Big John's money to pay for following him. Despite what I'd said—or not said—to Linda, I did have a pretty good idea why I was doing it. I didn't trust Big John now. That was one reason. But there were other things, too: outrage that he'd left me to get shot; curiosity, after all these years, about what he did do when I wasn't supposed to know about it. I felt like I was claiming my right to something. I'd paid my dues with a bullet in my leg.

He tooled the Eldorado around a couple of corners, then out Ventnor toward 694, heading toward the Atlantic City Expressway and then either Philadelphia or the Garden State Parkway. I had a sinking feeling that things were going wrong. Here I was in an Atlantic City cab with the meter running, possibly heading for New York, while the

New York cab I'd hired was sitting in an Atlantic City parking garage. Lew Archer never ran into this kind of trouble. Fortunately, Big John's car passed the ramp for the Garden State Parkway north and began winking with its bandaged eye, indicating he would go south on the Garden State.

The cabdriver was good at his job. He exchanged pleasantries, talked about the light traffic, and in general tried to act like this cab ride was no different from any other. A couple of times, he mentioned the speed— John was doing over seventy—and he hinted he might be wondering why we were following this guy, but he didn't come right out and ask. About twenty minutes down the parkway, just after the second toll-booth, John's signal blinked again—this time the good eye—and he turned off the parkway at Exit 17. The sign said SEA ISLE CITY, the town he, Greg, and Linda hailed from. We were going back to the roots all right.

Turning right at the end of the exit, we followed him across the coastal wetlands, the reeds and the water flat and dark outside the window, the black asphalt road stretching across this anomaly, neither land nor sea, for a mile or two, then over a bridge onto the island. A multistory white stucco condominium loomed in front of us, aspiring toward Palm Beach or Fort Lauderdale; a nightclub beside it glowed in garish panels of red and green lights. The street into town was wide and quiet until it crossed the main drag and then dead-ended at the ocean.

There was a grass island in the middle of the street we drove in on and on the far side of the street were some new one-story brick buildings, the spiffiest of them housing the police station. On the other side of the street, a large faded red lobster clung to the side of a shedlike building that sat on pilings out over a canal; beyond that lay rows of frame houses, mostly painted white or wearing those dark brown shingles peculiar to the seaside.

John turned a block before the main drag. From this street, looking beyond the first row of buildings, I could see brown sheds, weathered piers and pilings, and open boats, broad across the beam, seaworthy vessels that looked like they worked for a living. Real life existed beyond the condominiums, hanging on by its fingertips against gaudy prosperity and beach life. We drove along a street of mostly single-story houses with patches of white stone for front lawns. The street was lined with parked cars, many wearing Pennsylvania license plates. John drove slowly, and we dropped back a good distance behind him. The bridge we'd come over, I guessed, entered onto the island in the middle, because after a block or two the street signs were in the Fifties.

It was right about Fifty-eighth Street that headlights flashed behind us, and I heard the roar of gas and air being sucked into a powerful carburetor. For a second, I thought it was the cops. But it turned out to be one of those four-wheel drive all-terrain vehicles that they advertise during Jet games. It looked enough like the red Cherokee from Brooklyn for me to throw myself onto the floor of the cab, but the contraption roared past us and then past John without a fusillade of bullets directed at either of us.

The cabdriver dropped back farther behind John, but since no other cars moved on the street, I felt conspicuous. Beyond the houses outside the car window, the darkness seemed endless. I guessed from the depth of the darkness that the ocean was to our left and the bay to our right, and that the island was no more than a few blocks wide at the point we were passing. I wasn't exactly lulled to sleep by the ocean breeze. I was tired, I'd left New York what seemed like days ago, I'd traveled many miles in distance and time, I'd had a couple of drinks and smoked a joint, and I wasn't as alert as a hunter should be.

Somewhere in the Seventies, Big John's car sped up—shot forward might be more accurate. The cabdriver looked over his shoulder at me. A command decision was required. "After him," I shouted in a cavalry-charge voice. Who the hell did I think I was?

John's car disappeared around a corner to the right, far in front of us. But the blacked-out taillight served its purpose, so I felt pretty slick, sitting forward now on the edge of my seat, leaning against the back of the front seat, the better to provide direction. When we spun around the corner into the street John had turned into, we found ourselves bearing down on the bay a block in front of us. A street lay parallel to the bay, and when the cabdriver skidded to a stop at the intersection, we were there at the corner of left and right with the bay in front of us.

"Which way?" asked the cabdriver.

The question became moot, however, because John's car was parked with its lights out alongside the curb right at the intersection. The cabbie once more looked to me for leadership. But I was stymied. Like the family dog chasing the passing car, I had absolutely no idea what to do now that I'd caught it.

"Uh," I said, feeling I must say something. This sound, intimating that I might have a plan after all, attracted the attention of Ntango as well as the cabdriver, so they were both looking at me when the cab door on my right side opened and a snub-nosed gun got in, followed by Big John.

He seemed surprised to see me.

"Brian!" he shouted. His face, following the gun into the cab, was cement-hard. As soon as he recognized me and spoke, the cement cracked, making way for his smile and his dimples. "Jesus Christ, bro."

Taking Ntango and the cabbie into his confidence with a wave of his hand, he said, "Look at this guy," gesturing toward me with his gun. In almost any situation, Big John was prone to lecture. This one of danger, desperation, and intrigue was no exception. "This guy is a rock," said Big John, cuffing me around the shoulder with the gunless hand.

Ntango and the driver stared fixedly at him, as if they were already dead, for despite his cheerful expression and manner, Big John continued to hold the gun.

"You're on the job, right, bro?" Big John shook his head some more, continuing to marvel over those qualities of perseverance and determination he seemed to have rediscovered in me. "I shoulda known. If I told you to track Greg down, you'd do it—even if you had to go over me." Sitting beside me, he leaned against the backseat. "Jesus, bro, you almost did us both in." He gestured toward the front seat. "Either of you guys got a smoke?" Dragging on the cigarette Ntango gave him, he said, "What a fucking life!" Then he pushed himself forward to put the gun in his belt.

"Can I assume you no longer plan to shoot us?"

John chuckled and gave me an affectionate shove with his forearm as he settled back into the seat. I introduced him to Ntango and the cabdriver who said his name was Bub Williams. John leaned forward again and shook hands with them in that twisted, backhanded, brotherhood way left over from the sixties.

"What the fuck is going on?" I asked him.

Big John got his feet tangled up in the crutches and lifted them up. "Whose are these?"

"Mine," I said. "I got shot."

Big John raised an eyebrow.

"What the fuck is going on, John?" I tried to sound angry and menacing, but actually I was glad to see him.

chapter twelve

I told John how I got shot. Then I yelled at him. "Why did you leave me there, goddamn it? You told me it was safe."

John's eyes softened with sorrow. I didn't know if he was sorrier for me getting shot or for himself being misunderstood. "I wouldn't cut out on you, bro. . . . I didn't think anything would happen." His drooping eyes would have made a basset hound seem cheerful. "I got a call Greg was playing blackjack at the Claridge. I left you a message. I called you a couple of times. I didn't know anything had happened to you. I never expected there'd be trouble."

"Well, who shot me? You told me that guy Wilson was safe. Who is he?"

John shook his head. "It wouldn't have been him. I don't know what happened." His basset hound expression returned.

But I wasn't buying it, so I persisted. "Where've you been? Where are you going now?"

John answered in the same placating tone. "I kept missing Greg at about a dozen different places all over Atlantic City. That's why I'm still here. I should be back in New York."

"Well, I found him."

As I told John about our encounter, he looked troubled. "You sure he knew it was you?"

I nodded.

"You sure of the other two guys?"

"I'm sure."

John nodded, calculating, like he might do when figuring out where to place his next bet. Sitting back against the seat, he thought things over. I did some thinking, too, looking out the cab window at the calm black water of the bay and the marsh grass stretching like Oklahoma wheat beyond the water toward the backlit sky and the floating dots of headlights back on the mainland. A thousand gulls shrieked like banshees from their nesting places in the marshes. Life as I knew it was back there across the bay, distanced from me now, hushed by the expanse of water and marsh of the Inland Waterway.

"You followed me from AC," John said into the silence of the night. "I wouldn't have known it, except your headlight is out. This one-eyed car with a dome light was on my tail from the time I left the hotel."

"Shit," I said.

John kept his own counsel for a few moments. Seeming to decide something, he reached in his pocket for a wad of bills. "How much you want for this trip?" he asked Bub.

Bub looked at me, then at Ntango. "We're with Brian," Ntango said quietly.

"He's coming with me," John said.

Ntango's smile was as soft as his voice; nonetheless, it was clear we would all die that night at the edge of the bay before Ntango would leave. It came home to me, as it often did, that real danger lurked never far from single men who live the nightlife we'd chosen: A couple of drinks with the wrong woman, a brushing of shoulders in the doorway of an unfamiliar gin joint, and you're in the alley fighting for your life.

"It's okay, Ntango," I said, leaning toward the front seat, clasping him on the shoulder to calm him. "Despite appearances, John is my friend."

John squirmed and began a couple of times to say something. He admired Ntango's loyalty, so he tried to put things right. "You guys did a good job," he said with the pomposity of a general bestowing a medal. "Things got a little bit confused. But you guys ain't gonna go wrong sticking by Brian."

While I hoisted myself out of the cab and onto the crutches, John leaned in the front window and handed Bub a C-note, then elaborately shook hands with both Ntango and Bub again.

"I'll see you back at the rooming house," I told Ntango.

Sitting alongside John in the plush Eldorado, I picked up his car phone, pretending, as my mother would have said, that I was somebody. "Does this really work?"

"Of course."

"If I had one of these, I could call my service more often," I said.

"What for?"

"In case my agent has called with an acting job."

"How often does that happen?"

"Never."

A familiar look of bewilderment passed across John's face as he tried once more to understand why I did things for which there seemed to be no reward.

For a moment, I fiddled with the phone, then said, "This whole charade might make a pretty good movie itself. Maybe I should call my agent and offer him a part."

"He can have mine," said John, who hunched wearily over the steering wheel as he pulled away from the curb.

I did call my service and found that my agent hadn't called. But there were messages from my ex-wife, who needed me to call immediately, as usual. Another from John Wolinski, saying he'd gotten tied up. He'd left a 609 number for me to call. The last call was Ernesto, who said his call was very important but didn't leave a number.

"Why the gun?" I asked when I hung up. For some perverse reason, I didn't tell John about his call or about Ernesto.

John's expression hardened. "It's a fucking jungle. You can't ever stop watching your back." He looked with disgust at my leg and crutches. "Even you, someone takes a pop at, for Christ's sake."

I wasn't sure how to take this idea that the gunman had lowered his standards by shooting me, but I wanted out of the deal anyway. "You know, this guy Walter scares me. So does Wilson. Why don't we drop a dime on both of them?"

John arched an eyebrow. "Yeah, and let them have Greg, too," he grumbled. "And maybe I'll turn you over to the union thugs. I'm the boss; I don't need no friends. That's only for working stiffs, right?"

Preaching, I've discovered, always comes back to haunt you.

Feeling gabby, for some reason, I told John about going to see Linda.

"Linda? Why'd you go see her?"

My face started burning; I could feel myself turning red. "She's married to Ralph Ettinger now."

John nodded, his face screwed up with distaste.

"Greg was arrested a few years ago for assaulting Ralph. Do you know anything about that?"

John shook his head. "The guy's an asshole."

"But why?

John shrugged his shoulders again. Then he looked at me quizzically for a moment, his expression one that had always made me feel like his little brother. "I'm sorry you got dragged into this, bro. But we'll get it straightened out."

He drove a few blocks more on the dimly lit, car-lined, deserted streets and pulled up across from a small one-story house, this one also set on a bed of whitish rocks. On a street of massive structures with flying bridges and picture windows, it had neither. It was just a small cinder-block house with small windows, set on a small lot, with a plain cement walk leading through the polished round stones.

"Let's go." John was out of the car and up the walk, so once more I hobbled after him. There was a ramp leading to the porch, which made it a lot easier for me than climbing the steps.

I don't know what I expected, so I don't know if I was shocked when Greg opened the door. But open it he did. I don't know if he was surprised to see us, either. His face registered the fact that we were there with the same expression he used to greet various calamities behind the bar—a stiffening of his mouth, a clamping down of his eyebrows, a quick push with his finger to get his glasses back up on the bridge of his nose. Nothing more.

"John! Brian!" he said heartily. "This is a surprise. Come in! Come in!" This was more enthusiasm than I'd seen from Greg since I'd known him. Nothing in his voice suggested shame or fear or even consternation at being found. He acted like he didn't know we were looking for him, like he wasn't in hiding—like he'd never knocked a gimp off his crutches in his life.

"Do me a favor," he said softly as he stood back to let me walk past him and into the house. "My name is Greg Peters."

The hallway and the tiny living room off of it were as neat and polished as any bar Greg worked. The furniture was too large for the living room, a kind of fake colonial style with thick wooden frames for the couch and easy chair. But the room was as neat as pin and as clean as a cat's whiskers, as my mother would have said. I stopped beside John at the alcove entrance to the living room while we both looked at a dark-haired woman sitting at the end of the couch. A wheelchair stood beside the couch, and I knew right away that the chair belonged to her.

"John and Brian are friends of mine, former clients," Greg announced.

"I'm Sandra," the woman said, holding out her hand so graciously that I felt chivalrous when I walked over and held it briefly. I liked how her hand felt, her touch. I liked her; there was a lively light in her dark eyes. She seemed sensitive. Some feeling came from her that I connected to right away. She held out her hand to John also, who, dimples flaring, swooped down on her like Sir Galahad, while I, awkward and flustered, moved aside. The wheelchair loomed up before me like an iceberg; I didn't know if I should acknowledge it or not, say I was sorry she was crippled or pretend it was no big deal. I know I kept looking at it and then at her.

Big John had no such difficulty. He sat down in the chair and began wheeling himself across the living room. "This yours?" he asked her.

Laughing, she said yes.

"It's hard work," said John. "Don't your arms get tired?"

"Not when you've used it as long as I have." She smiled, but sadness like wisps of her black hair drifted across her eyes.

"Do you two auger doom from Greg's secret life?" she asked, and I almost dropped right there. John didn't miss a beat with the wheelchair. In fact, he was doing a wheelie as she spoke. She made a grand effort at happiness, but I saw the rage and bitterness, and also despair. Beneath the placid smile and the self-control lurked anger much larger than any I had ever felt.

"How about a drink?" said Big John.

"Jeez, I'm sorry," said Greg Peters. "I don't drink."

That did it even for Big John. He crash-landed his wheelchair into the solid-oak coffee table.

"It's been a long time," I told Greg, although it had been only about twenty-four hours since he'd pushed me over in the hotel lobby.

"Too long," said Greg with more of his fake enthusiasm. He looked at me steadily, a rather superior pose for someone in his position, I thought.

"It's good to see you, too. How've things been going?"

He smiled ruefully. " 'My grief lies onward and my joy behind.' "

John danced in place during all this, like he was waiting for the bell, then gestured with his head toward the door. "Maybe we could go out on the porch for a minute," he said. "Brian can entertain Sandra."

Greg's eyes narrowed, his brow wrinkled, and he pushed his glasses back up on the bridge of his nose again. His eyes searched out mine, lighted there for a few seconds, reminding me we were stand-up guys who watched each other's back, that if it came to taking the rap, each of us would take it silently and alone.

"You take my husband's Shakespeare in stride," Sandra said when Greg closed the door behind him and John.

"I met Greg at an audition, years ago. I guess it's something we have in common." I was immediately captured by Sandra's eyes. The sympathy and kindness in her manner drew me to her, so, knowing her less than five minutes, I was ready to pour out my heart. I don't talk to people about acting—the one thing besides Kevin I really care about. Talking about it seems self-indulgent, like feeling sorry for myself. But I told Sandra more in those few minutes than I'd told anyone ever before. I just opened up and babbled about what it was like to struggle for nearly twenty years and yet have nothing to show for it.

Her own suffering, I realized, gave her sympathetic understanding, rather than the bitter jealousy it would have given me. Already, I wanted to stay with her. Her deeply tanned skin perfectly matched her dark eyes and hair. Her face had lines at the corners of her eyes and the corners of her mouth—she wasn't a child. Her neck was long and graceful and her face thin, with the bone structure slightly angular, so that you wanted to touch her face, like you might want to touch a statue when looking wasn't enough and you needed to feel it.

I guess I looked at her for a long time, because she said, "Do I make you nervous?" Her eyes were gentle, but they persistently followed mine. "It's okay, I make most people uncomfortable. They don't know whether to notice that I'm crippled."

"I noticed," I said stupidly. This was only part of what made me nervous, though; the rest was the strength of the attraction I felt for her. I think she noticed; maybe she felt it. But she changed the subject.

"Greg doesn't want me to talk about his work, so I won't ask you. But that's strange, don't you think, keeping his work secret?"

"Naw," I said, hoping to get off this subject, too, before I got myself in trouble. "Work sucks. Why talk about it at home? I don't blame Greg. It's not like he's Monsieur Verdoux or anything."

She raised an eyebrow. "I certainly hope not."

Realizing this, too, might be dangerous ground, I tried again. "You're from here? I mean you grew up here?"

With some difficulty, Sandra changed her position on the couch and then nodded. "I couldn't bring myself to leave. I love the ocean and the beach."

I nodded. "What I like about it here is that it's not part of the mainland."

She laughed lightly. "I never thought of that. Why would you care?"

"I figure maybe you're less responsible for all the crap that takes place back on the mainland if you don't actually live on it. . . . Technically, I don't live on the mainland, either." She looked at me blankly. "Manhattan," I said.

She smiled again and said, " 'No man is an island.' "

Her face took on that angelic, searching one's memory look of a fourth grader in a spelling bee. She recited:

> "No man is an island, entire of itself; every man is a piece of the continent, a part of the main; if a clod be washed away by the sea, Europe is the less, as well as if a promontory were, as well as if a manor of thy friends or of thine own were; any man's death diminishes me, because I am involved in mankind; and therefore never send to know for whom the bell tolls; It tolls for thee."

Her voice was melodic and perfectly tuned to the words.

"You're a poet," I said.

Her face flushed, and she looked quickly away from me, casting her eyes down into her lap to fiddle with a small quilt that was tucked around the top of her legs. "That wasn't me. That's John Donne."

Obviously, my village idiot pose was convincing. "I know. But you are a poet. I can tell from your voice, the way you say the poem."

She looked up, her eyes glistening; then just as quickly she was fiddling with her quilt again. "I have," she said. "I do." She looked up again. Though she was still embarrassed, her face was brightly happy. "I mean, I write poems. But that doesn't make me a poet."

"Oh? If not that, what? Out-of-work actor, out-of-work poet, who's to throw stones?"

She laughed again, a happy tinkling sound.

When John and Greg came back in from the porch, I didn't like the strain I saw in their faces. Hard faces on hard men. Sandra saw it, too—it was the flicker of fear in her eyes that made me turn to look. She was no fool. After a few seconds of uncomfortable silence, with John and Greg standing next to each other in the hallway like strangers on a subway platform, John asked for the bathroom, so I was alone with them.

Sandra kept her eyes on Greg's face, worrying at him until he spoke.

But he spoke to me. " 'One woe doth tread upon another's heel,/So fast they follow.' " Once more, remembering he'd asked me to call him the night Aaron was killed and I hadn't, I felt like he wanted to tell me something.

"If I can help, call me in New York," I said. "I'm in the phone book."

When John emerged from the bathroom, he looked us over like a disapproving parent. "We need to get going," he said, already galloping toward the door. My eyes met Sandra's for a second. Hers seemed to ask for help, too. When my eyes met Greg's, his were so sorrowful, I felt guilty.

In the car, John sat like the Sphinx, so I didn't interrupt the silence. Soon enough, I would know what was going on—too soon probably. I watched the endless sky as it stretched out toward the sea on the far side of the island. We were a couple of blocks from the ocean.

"I want to see the ocean," I told John.

He was preoccupied. "The what?"

"The ocean. I want to see the fucking ocean. It's right over there."

John turned toward me. "Why do you want to see it?" he asked suspiciously.

"Because it's there. It's one of the wonders of the world. If you got a chance to go see the ocean, you should go see it."

"You want to look at the goddamn ocean? Now? With all this shit coming down!"

"Now! Especially now!" Our eyes met. "You used to sit and look at the ocean, too. You used to know something about your goddamn soul."

Big John stared at me; then he seemed to let go. At the next corner, he turned and drove to where the street dead-ended against the sand dunes.

Without speaking, we climbed out of the car. The horizon glowed pale blue; the white-capped slate gray waves rushed against the beach and slid away again. John walked ahead. I hobbled on behind him, until my right crutch sank too far into the sand and I went headfirst down the slight decline of the sand dune, landing on my forehead and my shoulder while the errant crutch whacked me on the side of the head for good measure. John halted his trek to look back at me sprawled on the sand.

"You need some help, bro?" he asked.

I didn't answer. When I got myself somewhat righted, I made my way a little bit closer to the water, then sat on the sand, watching the horizon for the paleness that came well before the rising sun. John stood at the edge of the sea, looking like he would command the waves to cease. I expected he would tell me what he'd talked to Greg about sooner or later. For now, he was digesting it. I admired his ability to meet a situation squarely without bemoaning his fate. I would sit around whining, "Oh no, why me? Why now? How could this happen?" Big John expected nothing from the gods; life's unfairness never surprised him. Instead of whining, he worked out a plan. This is what he was doing now, standing in front of the ocean while the battle raged: life against him, him against life.

For the first time since I'd known him, John looked small to me. Against the massiveness of the ocean, he seemed downright tiny. After a while, he came and stood over me, then sat down. His awkward, lumbering movements, as, grunting like an old walrus, he bent himself this way and that to park himself beside me finally on the sand, regained for him his real-life stature.

"Well, bro, there's the ocean. Did communing with your soul tell you anything?" He spoke softly, so even though he was putting me on, I could tell he wished it had.

"Not a fucking thing," I told him. "A couple of days ago, I was tending bar, minding my own business. Then you came along. Since then, I get thrown in jail and shot in the leg. Greg knocks me down. You climb into my car and stick a gun in my ribs. I don't know if I have a job, and even if I have a job, I can't work because I can't walk. I should have listened to Pop and not gotten mixed up with people who are slicker than I am."

Big John watched the sky over the ocean; it was still dark but now had a hint of gray. "We got a lot of trouble," John said.

"I thought I just said that."

John ignored the comment. "I know now what was going on. These guys tried to do something on their own. They didn't cover their bases; they didn't make the right connections. Anything could have happened. Still could." John shook his head. "Now I gotta undo this mess. But it ain't goin' to be easy. I made that gig for that stupid bastard at the Ocean Club, and I had something better lined up. But he had to go off doing this."

"What did he go off doing, and what do you have to do with it?"

"Me? What I got to do with it? . . . Nothin'. . . . Nothin' and everything. Greg decides he should be top banana. And he got this Sandra thing going on. Can you believe this? Something like this was going on for years, and I never knew."

"You didn't know? Didn't you know Greg was using a fake name?"

John nodded. "That part I knew. He said it was because of income tax he owed, so I didn't think nothin' of it. But this Sandra thing? It's goin' on for years, and we don't know anything about her, and she don't know anything about who he is and that he bartends in New York? . . . He's a goddamn drug-dealing drunk and she thinks he's some kind of pillar of the community—Mr. Fucking Prim and Proper? How do you figure that?" John's eyes were question marks. And I was baffled, too. Ntango was right: Greg had a double life. But why? As far as I knew, he didn't have anything to hide from—at least not until recently.

"You didn't know anything about this?" I asked John again.

John shook his head, as if he still didn't believe it. "Not until a few hours ago. I ran into one of Greg's old navy buddies. He said, 'Greg's probably at Sandra's,' like I should know all about it—and I had no idea what he was talking about. 'Greg's been with her for years,' he said. So I'm trying to cover myself, actin' like I forgot and tryin' to find out the address. The guy musta thought I was a complete fool."

"Why would he do that? Why would Greg not tell anyone about Sandra? Why go to all this trouble?"

John lifted his arm and gestured to the sea and sky around us, as if to let me in on the universe's unanswered questions, too. "Only Greg can answer that, bro. But the life we know about's the one we got worries about." John watched the ocean for a long time again, then spoke without turning toward me. "Look, bro, you know where I come from."

I nodded because he seemed to want me to, even though I didn't know if he could see me.

"A long time ago, I buried the past. I got everybody else out, too, including Greg. Now he has to be a wise guy. He has to have a hustle. And it ain't just him." John sounded unsure of himself, like this big powerful machine that was skipping and missing and barely running on one cylinder.

"Is that why Aaron was killed?"

John picked up handfuls of sand, sifting them through his fingers and staring out over the ocean. When he spoke again, it was quietly and sincerely. "Look, bro, I'm gonna ask that you forget about all this. Forget about Aaron being killed. I know it ain't right. It shouldn't have happened. But no one can do anything about it now." I started to say something, but he held up his hand to stop me. "I know you don't want to stop. But there are things going on I can't tell you about. I have to fix them myself. If I don't, you'll find out everything soon enough anyway."

"Does this have anything to do with David Bradley and Bill Green?"

John's reaction was extraordinary. He froze in midbreath and stared at me. Then he shook his head. "Who told you that?"

"It just came up."

"How could it come up?" Then he caught the scent. "Linda," he said.

"Not Linda. . . . I was here then, too, remember?"

"Jesus Christ," said John. "Every fucking chicken I've ever known is coming home to roost." He lifted his gaze to the sky, like he was going to bellow. Instead, he said, "Sometimes not knowing is better than knowing, bro. Let me take care of it."

"What about whoever shot me?"

"I'll find that out, too. I promise."

"What about Greg?"

"I'm finished with him. He's not going back to the corporation no matter how this shakes out. He can start another fucking new life."

This reminded me of Ernesto, so I asked John what would happen to him.

"Who?"

"Ernesto. The bar back. I fired him, and I want to bring him back."

"Stay away from him. He ain't goin' back, either."

I started to ask why. But I remembered what Sheehan had said about the fibers on his bar jacket. "Ernesto called me."

"What for?"

"I don't know. He left a message, but he didn't say."

John shook his head.

"Does he have anything to do with this?"

John raised an eyebrow. "I wouldn't go meeting him in any dark alleys."

After wrestling his way out of the sand and onto his feet, John held out his hand and pulled me up. He looked disdainfully at my gimpy leg. "You can't work the stick like that. Hang around the Ocean Club another week or so and keep an eye on things for me. You're management now, so I can keep you on the clock until you're able to work again."

Together, we trudged away from the dark water, the paler sky, and the rhythmic beating of the surf against the shore.

chapter thirteen

After a long drive in silence back to Atlantic City, John dropped me off at the rooming house—tourist lodge, if you listened to the landlady—telling me he'd see me back in the city in a day or two.

Though I was tired enough not to care about anything, I did notice that Ntango wasn't in the room. It surprised me. Something wasn't right about his not being there, but it didn't scare me. I figured he'd stopped off at the casinos when he went to get his cab and maybe he was on a roll. I dropped on the bed in my clothes and slept for an hour or so. When I woke up, Ntango was the first thing I thought about. I looked toward his bed. He wasn't there. I jumped up, found one crutch, got to the pay phone in the hallway, and called John. I woke him up.

"What the fuck could have happened?" he shouted, but his voice was thick with sleep and duller than it might have been.

"I don't know." My panic rose. I hadn't eaten in a long time, so I was jittery.

"I'll be over in a half hour." His voice wasn't as muddy.

"Hurry up."

"Okay, bro," he said quietly. "I'm on my way." I felt like his thick arm had just gone around my shoulder to steady me. Forty minutes of pacing later, John showed up with coffee and bagels, which we ate in the car on the way back to Sea Isle City. He had a hunch. For my part, I tried not to have a hunch. My mind raced from one unsavory possibility to another, each of them centering on the SUV I'd seen and dismissed the night before. As we came down off the bridge leading into town, I saw Bub's cab parked among the cruisers in the parking lot next to the police station. I froze.

"I knew it," John said.

"What?"

"They arrested them."

"Oh?" This was a startling turn of events, and I didn't know what we were going to do about it. But it seemed like John did. He parked in the police parking lot and marched right through the front door of the cop shop, with me bouncing along in his wake.

"Who's in charge here?" Big John demanded, bellying up to the desk like it was the bar at the Bucket of Blood. I knew we were in trouble: Big John had caught the scent of injustice.

"Who the hell are you?" the middle-aged, sour-faced desk sergeant asked right back.

John looked him up and down a couple of times. "I'm John Wolinski. This is Brian McNulty. You have two friends of ours in your lockup, and you'd better have a goddamn good reason for them being there."

"Sit down," the sergeant said. "I'll get to you."

John took off his glasses, then put them back on and leaned toward the sergeant as if he might grab him by the lapels and lift him out of his chair. "I'll ask you one more time who's in charge; then I'll call the chief."

The sergeant, in a grand gesture of defiance, placed the phone on the desk and slid it toward John. Staring at the sergeant with that imperious expression of his that wrote *buffoon* on the forehead of the victim, John pulled a small address book out of his pocket, looked in it, then dialed a number.

"Bob? John Wolinski here. . . . Good. I'm fine. Fine. How are you?" He laughed. "Great. . . . Actually, you can do something for me. I'm talking to a dunce here at your front desk."

The dunce stared openmouthed at Big John as he told the chief about Bub and Ntango. When he finished the tale, John handed the sergeant the phone. The cop listened, looked at John, at me, at John again, his brow wrinkled, his expression pained, as if he couldn't quite grasp what he was being told.

"We picked up these two guys," he said into the phone. ". . . Suspicion." He screwed up his face. "Just suspicion." He snarled at the receiver. "The cab had a headlight out." The snarl edged his voice when he spoke again. "They were suspicious." Then, softly, as if imparting a secret he added, "One of them's a foreigner." He listened, brow wrinkled. "I don't know from where; he wouldn't tell us. And he didn't have any papers." He glared at John, and his mouth got square.

When he hung up, he didn't look at John anymore. "Okay," he said, shuffling through some papers. "Just hang on. We're gonna release 'em." He picked up the phone again and mumbled into it, then looked behind him toward the squad room. As luck would have it, some of the crew who'd worked the graveyard shift the night before had stayed for some overtime on the day shift. Two young cops, who turned out to be Schmidt and Lunsford, the arresting officers, stuck their noses around the corner as Ntango and Bub came from the lockup to the desk.

"What gives?" asked Schmidt. He had close-cropped blond hair and a fresh-looking round face; he looked innocent, a big, chunky farm boy, like a guard or tackle on a high school football team. He seemed genuinely interested but not particularly concerned. And he didn't have the nasty arrogant edge I'd come to expect in cops.

The sound of bristling and stiffening and the clatter of rattling belts, cuffs, keys, and flashlights coming from the squad room melded into a creaking silence. Four or five of Sea Isle City's finest gathered around. From behind them came a red-faced, white-haired man in a gray Anderson-Little sports jacket that didn't match his brown dress slacks. New York City Irish Cop Retired was printed on his forehead. He had quick blue eyes and, without much change of expression, made clear it would take a lot to impress him.

Bub and Ntango came to the side of the desk, picking up the envelopes with their belongings. I thought about tugging on the hem of John's jacket.

"These guys get locked up for driving down the street?" asked John. "And you wonder why blacks holler about police abuse?"

"That's not true," said Schmidt. He sounded like he believed it.

John hunched himself down into his shoulders. He took in Schmidt and all the cops around him. Then his eyes rested on the older man. "Why'd you lock them up?" he asked him.

The older cop took a step closer, spreading his hands toward John. He looked like someone quick on his feet. "You're wrong about this black thing. I worked with lots of black cops who would've locked 'em up, too. What're they doing in Sea Isle? That's not a tough question. Instead, they're wise guys." The man spoke in a placating, calming manner, but without backing down.

Big John wasn't going to back down, either. "They don't have to tell you why they're here. They have a right to take care of their business, just like Brian and me." I winced, wishing John hadn't said that. I didn't want this hard-eyed guy to start wondering what our business was.

"Look," the older man said. He didn't exactly smile, but his voice took on a buddy-buddy edge. "Maybe we made a mistake. We're trying to protect the good people from the bad guys. Sometimes good people suffer a little inconvenience so we can get to the bad guys. We're letting them go. We're sorry for the inconvenience."

John gently rocked back and forth as he stood like the colonel before the assembled troops. "It's more than inconvenience. Some solid citizen says, 'Hey, there's a nigger walking down my street; he's probably robbing something.' So you go check it out. This poor bastard's walking home from a twelve-hour day cleaning someone's cellar for four or five bucks an hour. He's walking because he can't afford a car, and there's no bus out in that wealthy neighborhood. He don't want to be hassled. He's had a long day. He's tired. You come up and say, 'Hey, you, what're you doing here?' Maybe you even say it politely. 'Excuse me, sir, where you going? Do you have any identification?' He's tired of the bullshit. So he says, 'Go fuck yourself. This ain't South Africa.' The guy's fed up with the landlord, the bill collectors, cleaning people's cellars, walking home when sixteen-year-old white kids are whizzing by in their sports cars. You stand in front of him. He brushes by you to keep walking. Boom. You grab him. He resists. Now, you say, he's assaulting an officer. He's into the slammer. You say he's a bad guy. But he ain't. He's a working stiff."

Big John walked to the far side of the room and wrapped his thick arm around Bub's shoulder, while the pleading look in Bub's eyes suggested he'd just as soon return to the lockup.

Ntango bowed slightly toward the assembled police force and said, "Gentlemen, if I am free to go?" They more or less tumbled over one another assuring him he was, and we moved toward the door.

"I'd still like to know what all of you were doing in Sea Isle" was the white-haired cop's parting shot.

John and I followed Bub's cab back to Atlantic City.

"How'd you know they'd be in jail?" I asked John.

"I grew up in these towns. . . . I know how these people think."

"How did you get the chief to let them go?"

John turned and winked at me. "We go back a long way. He owed me a favor."

Now it was time to get out of Atlantic City. I wanted to get back to my own slightly depraved normalcy. I couldn't keep up with Big John. We gathered at the Claridge and said good-bye to Bub. Ntango said he needed a couple of hours' sleep before driving back, so I decide to try to see Linda one more time, in the light of day, to say good-bye. When I called her, right after John, Bub, and Ntango went their separate ways, she said she'd meet me in the lobby of the Claridge because she was coming in to pick up her paycheck anyway.

I ate a hamburger in the hotel coffee shop for just under seven dollars and waited. She arrived fresh and pretty in black shorts and a red T-shirt. Bright-eyed, well rested, beaming with good health, she made me feel like a stumblebum. I wouldn't have been surprised if she'd sat a couple of stools away, but she sat down right beside me and pecked me on the cheek. "You look like someone fished you out of the gutter," she announced.

I told her I caught up with John and tracked Greg down, and that everything was okay, so I was going back to New York. She didn't buy it, pestering me instead about where Greg was, what John was doing, and what the hell was going on. I didn't tell her. "Yesterday, you didn't want anything to do with all this," I said. "You got your wish. It's all over."

"No," said Linda. "It's come back." She twirled toward me on her stool. "This time, it's not going to end so easily." Her eyes bore into mine, and then they softened with tears. "It isn't your fault."

Every time I saw Linda, I brought her to tears. I had no idea what she was crying about and no idea how to comfort her, so I waited while she pulled herself together. I wanted her to tell me what wasn't going to end so easily this time and what might have seemed to end easily last time. But she didn't, though she did agree to look at the videotape of Greg and his pals with me. I wanted to try one more time to see if she recognized Walter.

We got ourselves escorted to a security room on the floor below the lobby. Two security guards sat watching dozens of TV monitors that were picking up the action from all over the casino. When the security guard rolled the video from my encounter two nights before, I caught a glimpse of myself from the back hobbling into camera range; then the video picked up Greg and, behind him, Walter and Dr. Wilson. Just as Dr. Wilson hove into view, Linda sprang from her chair toward the screen. "My God," she blurted out. "That's Charlie."

"Who?"

"Charlie," she said. "John's father."

chapter fourteen

On the trip back to New York, I could no longer ignore the burning pain in my leg. It had begun in earnest that morning, and the longer it went on, the surer I was that the leg was gangrenous and would have to be amputated. My future rose before me: Brian McNulty, the one-legged bartender. When I looked under the bandage, that whole part of my leg was bright red and puss was seeping from the wound. I stared at it as if I'd found maggots there.

By the time I got to my apartment building, I knew I needed to do something about my leg, so I asked Ntango. He said I should go to the ER at St. Luke's, right there on Amsterdam Avenue. But I asked him if he'd take me to Brooklyn. Maybe I could find Dr. Parker, the beautiful surgeon who'd taken the bullet out of my leg in the first place. When I went inside to call to try to have her paged at Kings County, I picked up an official-looking envelope someone had slipped under my door. By some miracle, I reached her and she gave me directions to the clinic she was working in. Ntango drove me to Kings County.

As soon as I caught a glimpse of the surgeon in her clinic, I realized there might be life after Linda after all. If anyone was to chop off my leg at the knee, I wanted it to be Dr. Parker. I wanted to see that reluctant smile one more time before I drifted off to sleep and woke up with a stump. But this meeting with Dr. Parker in the surgical clinic—a tomblike cavern with ancient marble floors, worn wooden benches, and a smattering of Brooklyn's walking wounded of all shapes, sizes, and ethnicities—began under a dark cloud. No smile from the doctor this time: I'd messed up her handiwork. As soon as she got me into the examining room, she began complaining about bandages needing to be changed, pills taken, wounds washed, and patients listening to their doctors. I nodded in abashed agreement until she washed out the sore—using lye for spite, from the feel of it—and I screamed.

She stopped swabbing to look me in the eye and tell me I was acting like a baby.

"It hurts," I whined.

When she finished rubbing my leg wound with salt, she wrapped it up in a fresh bandage and handed me a bottle of pills. "You're infected," she said in a biblical tone. "These are antibiotics. If you don't take them on time and for the full course, you're going to end up in the hospital on an IV."

"Will I lose my leg?" I was trying to keep a stiff upper lip—I was raised in Brooklyn; I should bite the bullet—but the question slipped out. I was putty in her hands. I liked how strong and efficient she was. I even liked the way she ripped my leg to shreds.

The secret smile slipped out in spite of herself. "Not if you take your medicine like a good boy."

I watched her in her long white lab jacket and her gabardine slacks, her blue blouse opened a button at the top along her graceful neck. She seemed to be through with me and had turned to her clipboard. But I hung on.

"Uh," I said. She turned. I barreled forward. "You wouldn't, by any chance, want to have dinner with me?"

"Tonight?"

I was sure that meant no. "Why not tonight?"

She smiled. "Where?"

I thought this was also part of the argument, so I stared at her blankly.

She asked again. "Where?" With that half smile, she looked bemused and a little puzzled. Her smile was like my father's.

"Where?" I asked her back.

"Where?"

"I don't know." It dawned on me she was saying yes.

"How about Chinatown?"

I was thrilled. Mainland China would have been fine. I racked my brain trying to remember the name of one of the twelve hundred restaurants in Chinatown, most of which I'd eaten in at one time or another, but I couldn't remember a single name.

Dr. Parker didn't seem worried. We decided she'd pick me up at Pop's apartment on Cortelyou Road, which was only a few minutes from her clinic, and we'd search out a restaurant from there.

I found a gypsy cab in front of the clinic, and Pop buzzed me in a few minutes later. He was sitting at his round dining room table, reading a book of Maksim Gorky stories, when I hobbled in.

"You're still limping," he said, putting the book down carefully after finishing the passage he was reading and marking the page with a bookmark.

"I didn't change the bandage, so it got infected." I felt guilty in the same way I once did for not doing my homework.

Pop appraised me in his fashion. "I see. You have one good leg; that should do you."

"No. I'm getting it fixed." I found myself smiling. "I'm having dinner with the doctor tonight."

"That should do it."

Poor Pop. Despite his quick wit, he felt the pain of my failure as his own. I had my own kid; I knew how it felt to believe you'd messed up a child's life.

"I need your advice."

He nodded.

Standing behind his chair, I looked down at his gray head and wanted to hug him the way I did Kevin, but I couldn't. I didn't even remember hugging him when I was a kid. I went over what had happened since I saw him last. He didn't know what to make of the fact that both Greg and John's father had more than one identity. When I told him John wanted me to forget the whole thing, he seized on it immediately.

"So why don't you give up?" He has this peculiar way of pretending to sound convincing when he means the opposite.

"I guess I should."

He glowered at me for a moment, the intensity in his eyes at the level where he could see through steel. This was his temper at half throttle. "Make up your mind."

"I don't know what to do. . . . Someone was killed a long time ago. Maybe it had something to do with John and Greg. Maybe it didn't. Maybe it has something to do with Aaron getting killed."

Pop didn't seem surprised. If anything, the expression in his eyes hardened a bit. "Your friends are corrupt. In John's case, that's a shame, because he has so much to offer." He rubbed his hand across his eyes—a familiar reflection of his own angst.

In another of my ongoing efforts to show Pop I was something other than—or at least in addition to—a ne'er-do-well, I showed him the official-looking letter I'd found under my door when I got back from Atlantic City. It was from the Labor Department, upholding our rank and file challenge to the bartenders' union's election. I had neglected to tell John I'd taken my battle with the bartenders' union to the Labor Department when they stole the shop stewards' election.

Pop was as pleased as punch. "You need to pay attention to this now." He looked at me steadily, like he must have looked when he spoke to the workers at rallies. "The men you're challenging in that local are ruthless. They control by terror. You need a plan to fight them; you don't have time for John and his shell games." The old man paused. Fear flickered in his eyes. "You need to begin working on the new election. You may need to ask the Labor Department for protection."

Before he got carried away, I told him he was wrong on a couple of counts. Number one, John had made me a boss. So, technically, I wasn't in the union anymore. And I couldn't really go back to the bargaining unit until I could walk again. Number two, John had gotten me out of the unit precisely to get me away from the union thugs. And finally, John had been a big help when we organized the union down at the shore and might be able to help with this one.

The old man looked skeptical. "John has a good heart. But he wants to be a boss too much to help you with the union. You can't trust someone who wants to be a boss."

He stopped to look at me because I'd begun to laugh quietly. Once more, I felt this overflowing affection for him. At times like this, it practically gushed. However he'd done it—and I still didn't know how—when push came to shove, it was my old man I'd follow. His values, his way of being, that's how I was—his image and likeness. "You wanna be the boss, you gotta fuck over your friends, right, Pop?" I laughed at his perplexity. "Look," I said more quietly. "John has been a good friend to me, whatever you think of his workplace politics. You used to like him, too."

Pop sat back down to his book. He opened it but looked up at me. "I'm glad you beat the bastards. I hope you keep after it." The expression in his eyes reminded me of a lake I'd been on once long ago in New Hampshire. The water was so clear that when I looked down over the side of the rowboat, I could see twenty feet or more through the water to the bottom. "I'm an old man. I can't tell you how to live your life." He picked up his book, but before he started to read, he again turned to look at me. "Forget what I said about John. I do like him. I'd like to see him again. Is he coming with us to the ball game tonight?"

"*The ball game?*" Then I remembered I was supposed to take Kevin to the ball game. "Shit. What about the doctor?"

Pop was unsympathetic. "You said dinner. Have an early dinner."

Dinner? What about a walk from Chinatown up through Little Italy? An espresso and a latte? A few drinks at the Village Vanguard? A nightcap uptown at the Terrace, a joint in my apartment, dim lights, Lester Young on the stereo, a tentative first kiss, soft caresses?

I called the doctor's office, but she'd already left. A few minutes later, the doorbell rang, and I buzzed her in. While Pop poured her some coffee from his perennially scorched pot, I told her my dilemma. She laughed and said she'd love to go to the ball game. I called Big John, who actually was at his office for a change. He hemmed and hawed until I reminded him Pop was going. "Great," said John, "just like the old days." He was remembering the 1978 season, when he used to bring his son up from New Jersey to go to the stadium with me, Kevin, and, Pop. He and Pop, die-hard Yankee fans, were the best of buddies. I was a Mets fan myself, but I never actually admitted this to either of them.

When Kevin arrived, he seemed impressed that I'd gotten myself shot. "Are you going to go after them?" he asked.

"After them?"

"Yeah . . . get a gun and track them down. You can't just let someone shoot you and get away with it."

The law west of the Pecos. Kevin was serious. This is how young men thought in Brooklyn, the best efforts of parents, teachers, police, and pillars of the community notwithstanding. You settle scores the manly way. How could I explain to him that there were better routes to becoming a man, when everything around him argued something else? Be a man. Track them down. And the truth was, part of me felt that way, too. Why wasn't I such a man?

What I did do was tell Kevin that my getting shot was tied up with the killing at the Ocean Club and that all of it would get cleared up sooner rather than later. "I need to work some things out with Big John," I said.

This reassured him, "You and Big John can handle it," he said confidently, then thought about it some more. "But why would someone shoot you?" He seemed to agree with John's assessment that I was hardly worth shooting. Kevin was less impressed that I was bringing along a doctor for a date. "A lady doctor," he whispered to me in the kitchen. "Jeez, Dad!"

We ordered a pizza. After we ate, Dr. Parker drove us all to Yankee Stadium. Thus began Dr. Parker's first date—with three generations of the McNulty clan and Big John Wolinski. As we were crossing the bridge over the Harlem River at 155th Street in thick traffic and the stadium was in sight, she was gleeful, "I love the Yankees," said Dr. Parker.

Pop, in the backseat, perked right up. "Me, too." He'd seen Gehrig and Ruth and King Kong Keller, DiMaggio, Mantle, and Whitey Ford. Not only had he been a known Communist in Brooklyn during the height of the McCarthy era in the fifties; he'd been a Yankee fan, too. Bad enough to wear SAVE THE ROSENBERGS buttons; he wore a Yankees cap on the subway.

Big John said to meet him at the general admission booth in front of Gate E. When we found him, he'd already bought a string of tickets. A few minutes later, he was down next to the mezzanine-level railing in whispered but intense negotiations with a short, stubby usher. When I saw him pushing something into the man's hand, I realized he was bribing the guy to get us into some box seats that wouldn't be used that night. Soon enough, we were about eight rows back in the boxes behind third base.

Being at the stadium like this naturally reminded us of times past. John was quick enough to sense what was missing and brought it up himself. "Boy, I wish Robert was here," he said.

"How is the boy?" I asked, knowing I was treading on difficult ground. John had a strong sense that he should do right by his son but knew he'd fallen down on the job over the years.

"Robert's in military school. He got in some trouble, so his mother thinks she can't handle him anymore. I'm paying for him to go to one upstate, and he's doing good. He comes home once a month. Maybe we can all get together again the next time he comes down."

Guidry was pitching, and Big John had two hundred bucks on the game. As Guidry strode out to the mound for the first inning, it was clear that he, like Pop, John, and the rest of the smattering of fans, was pretending it was still 1978. The Red Sox disabused him, and us, of this notion with four runs in the first inning. John and Pop complained about George Steinbrenner and talked about the economy. Kevin raved about the wonderful seats and watched for foul balls. And I held hands with Dr. Parker, stoically braving the pain in my leg. The Yankees lost seven to two.

We left John at the ballpark, without my bringing up the question of his father versus Dr. Wilson. I didn't want to get everyone else involved, for one thing; for another, I didn't want to mess up my date with Dr. Parker. I did tell him there was something I wanted to talk to him about, and he said to call him at his office. Dr. Parker dropped me at my apartment after the game and took the rest of my family back to Brooklyn. She promised we'd go out again on a night when she could stay out later—then she bit my lip when she kissed me good night.

I was back in my own apartment for all of fifteen minutes, still starry-eyed from Dr. Parker's kiss, when the phone rang. Maybe the phone rings differently when it senses anxiety; maybe I have a sixth sense. Or maybe I'm just used to getting bad news. Whatever the reason, I knew before I answered the phone that this call meant trouble.

"Mr. Magnolia?" the voice inquired in a thick Spanish accent.

"No," I said.

"Yes," the voice insisted, with the slight quickening of panic people unfamiliar with a language get when what they're saying isn't understood. "Brian Magnolia."

"Right. . . . Brian Magnolia. What do you want?"

"I call for Ernesto Hermanos."

Remembering the phone call to my service, I felt my pulse quickening.

"Come to Ninety-two East One Hundred and eighty-ninth Street tonight."

"Now? You're nuts. Why would I do that?"

"Because you are a friend, señor," the voice said with a solid note of conviction, as if friendship and loyalty were commonplace. The guy must not have been in the country long. But before I could straighten him out, he hung up.

At midnight, on East 183rd Street, in the bowels of the South Bronx, an adult man has about the same potential for survival as he does in a squad-size firefight in pretty open terrain. But I'd been tricked by someone—my fucking father, probably—into believing I had a duty to respond to people like Ernesto, who, I'd been told since birth, were the salt of the earth. Political correctness notwithstanding, I was scared shitless. For sure, I wasn't about to go to the South Bronx on the Lexington Avenue subway at night with a bum leg.

Of course, the first person I thought of was Ntango. When he dropped me off at the hospital earlier in the day, he'd told me he was going home to sleep. I trekked over to his apartment on 109th Street on my crutches on the off chance he'd kept the cab. I was in luck. He answered the door in boxer shorts, sleep and irritation wrinkling his normally impassive face. Standing in the doorway with that regal bearing of his, he made me feel like a messenger disturbing the king with bad news. Not only was I the messenger; I was also the bad news.

"You wouldn't by any chance want to take me to the South Bronx tonight, would you?" I asked. I still had some of John's stash left after paying Ntango for the Atlantic City trip, so I said—as if it meant something—"I could pay you."

Ntango's face clouded; a rush of anger smoldered behind his eyes.

I looked at him helplessly, shrugged my shoulders, and held my hands toward him, palms up. I explained about the phone call and Ernesto.

Ntango's calm returned, and with it his long-suffering sympathy. "One adventure after another, my friend."

There are neighborhoods New York has given up for lost. Buildings are burned-out hulks; others are abandoned and stripped of all their wiring, plumbing, and most of their wood, all of them with sheet metal or plywood covering what once were windows and doors. Here, the streets are littered with debris that includes everything from the rusting bones of old cars to beams and joists of a building's former life. Yet the streets are not deserted, nor are the buildings. Winos and junkies live in the four- and six-story brick shells—and some families, too, with small boys and baby girls. Some of the children still played that night in the darkness after midnight on the block Ntango detected would house 92—if by any chance in the world the building had a number. A couple of buildings still had windows and light—probably through bootleg hookups providing electricity for the entire block. There was even a neighborhood grocery store in a narrow building surrounded by abandoned and boarded-up storefronts; it shone through the Lindsey riot gates like a campfire from deep in the woods. When Ntango slowed to try to catch a number, I looked into the store and saw a young Hispanic guy looking back from behind a bullet-proof window.

Clusters of young men, who leaned against the fronts of other buildings, watched us with some interest, since we were the only car moving on the street. I got the clear sense that nothing of society as it's generally known penetrated this street. I felt like the guy with the white hat in the old Western, riding into the mountain camp of the outlaws, where lookouts watched from high places, the law had no authority, strangers were not taken kindly to, and where those strangers, once having crossed the threshold of the badlands outlaw town, were at the mercy of the outlaws.

The number 92 was faintly visible on the weathered doorjamb of a building with corrugated-tin windows. To say that the entrance—a sheet of tin peeled back like a jaggedly opened can of sardines— looked foreboding is to mince words. Nobody in his right mind would walk through that entrance. Ntango stopped the cab and watched me out of the corner of his eye in the rearview mirror. "There's light," he said. "But if you get out of the cab, I'm leaving. I'll gather the fare from your estate."

A sinister darkness settled around the cab. "I came all the way up here," I told Ntango. "I ought to just go in." I pictured myself getting out of the cab and marching up to the door. But in reality, I didn't move a muscle. Just sat in the backseat. *Huddled* might be a better word. Cringed.

Taking matters into his own hands, Ntango gave the horn two short toots, the sound ringing out through the neighborhood like shots. But it worked. The tin door waggled and shook and two men pushed through the doorway. Both were short and stocky and had wavy black hair, bushy eyebrows, and thick black mustaches. With their furtive manners and hard-chiseled faces, they looked like extras from a Pancho Villa movie, except that one of the men smiled at us, his expression almost shy.

"Mr. Magnolia?" the smiling man inquired.

I said, "Yes," and looked at him, I'm sure, with eyes as wide as manhole covers.

"It's better inside," he said. Then to Ntango: "You, too." Nodding toward the door, "Alberto will watch the cab." Alberto didn't move or change expression, but by the breadth of his shoulders and the darkness in his eyes, he gave clear indication the cab would be safe.

We crawled through the corrugated tin to a dank and dark hallway. The musty smell of desertion seeped from the walls. The warped wooden floorboards creaked and trembled, so that I expected to fall through to a pit below. The apartment had a steel fire door, which seemed appropriate for this cubicle in Desolation Row. The room we entered was lit by a single lightbulb in the middle of the ceiling. Three men sat at a table as if this might be the regular Friday-night poker game. One of the men was Ernesto. Everyone looked up. A sea of gently smiling faces made me feel like I was the thug.

Ernesto rose from his seat. He seemed unsure whether to hold his hand out toward me, so I held mine out toward him, and we shook hands. I liked that his grip was gentle rather than firm. "I'm very glad you came," Ernesto said. "And very sorry for causing you so much trouble."

"No trouble," I said cheerily.

"Much trouble." Ernesto's dark eyes softened with sympathy. Everyone nodded sadly, even Ntango. I myself suspected a bit of difficulty might lie ahead.

"So what's up?" I asked Ernesto. He noticed my crutches but didn't say anything. Instead, he looked over his shoulder at an older man who sat at the table. The man, maybe in his late fifties, wore glasses and had gray hair. He was dressed in workingman's clothes—the thick green cotton shirt and pants you'd expect to see the building super wearing. He was squat and short, his skin dark and somewhat reddish, his eyes dark and clear, and his expression straightforward. The whole group was like this. No posturing. No role playing. No one trying to impress me. No one trying to scare me. Just a group of regular working guys. I expected someone to switch on the ball game and offer me a beer—uh, *una cerveza.*

The man at the table, despite his diffidence, looked me in the eye, taking my measure, and in doing so seemed quite formidable. "Mr. . . ."

"Brian. Brian McNulty."

"Brian." He nodded and seemed pleased. When he smiled, the

dimples in his cheeks reminded me of Big John. He raised an eyebrow ever so slightly in Ntango's direction.

"He's with me," I said. "Ntango Tivugla."

The man bowed respectfully toward Ntango.

The gray-haired man, his face etched with the resignation and wisdom you find in men who've seen a lot and gained very little in life, spoke slowly. "Ernesto said you would help him. The police think he killed a man." The gray-haired man stopped smiling. Each word seemed carefully chosen, filtered through his own language, carefully crafted in mine. "I want to make no mistake. Ernesto say you understand some things . . . political things."

"Actually, there's a lot I don't understand . . . and maybe we should keep it that way." I had an idea that Ernesto and his friends were up to the sort of political shenanigans frowned upon in better Republican circles, so I tried to look blank while everyone in the room waited for my move. They waited a long time. These were patient men. The tension was palpable. Something was expected of me.

"So?" I said.

Everyone reacted as if I had made a major pronouncement. The men nodded to one another, then nodded at me approvingly. A wave of relief rolled across the room.

Ernesto gestured toward the chair next to him, so I sat down. "Everyone is very nervous. . . . They let me send for you, but they weren't sure."

Somehow, I'd gained their trust, but I didn't want it. Someone had switched the dice.

"The problem . . ." said Ernesto, his dark eyes even darker with seriousness. "For us, deportation means death." His body rigid with the tension of the fugitive, his haggard face showing the strain of his life, he went on: "Greg is a friend. I don't want to turn on him, but—" He left the sentence unfinished. What they really needed me for up here was to finish their sentences.

"After we close," Ernesto said quietly, "Greg take me outside. He show me the body under the cloths near the boats. I help him carry to the river. We tie the bricks and throw him in."

"Did you recognize the guy?"

"I never see him."

"You never saw him when you threw him in the river, or you never saw him before that night?"

"I see his face," Ernesto said. "I never see him."

"Are you sure he wasn't there earlier, that he didn't come there regularly?"

"I never see him."

"Did Greg kill him?"

Ernesto shrugged his shoulders and looked quickly and instinctively at the older man. But the older man's eyes never moved off of me, nor did his expression change. "He's dead when I see him," Ernesto said.

"The police have evidence—fibers on your bar jacket. That's why they're looking for you."

Ernesto didn't flinch. "I didn't kill him. . . . This, what I told you, happened."

"Did you know anything about drug dealing?"

He looked into my eyes for a long time, thinking it over. Then he brushed his nose a few times with his hand. "Lots of cocoa. Greg. Everybody—" He gestured again like he was shoveling blow into his nose. "All the time."

"How about you?"

He smiled with a kind of boyish shyness, shaking his head, as if burning out your nasal passages and scrambling your brain was the province of sophisticated Americans alone.

"What do you want me to do?"

"We want that you know what happened," the older man said. "Ernesto helped your friend. Nothing else. He wants to see his family."

"And he can't until this is over, right?"

The expressions on the faces of all the men in the room suggested they were proud of my bravery and devotion to the cause. When I looked in Ntango's direction, he made clear he was the cabdriver and had no other connection to the project.

"I understand the problem," I said to Ernesto. "I just have no idea what I could do to help."

Ernesto bent forward, rounded at the shoulders, which accentuated his slight frame. He looked like a boy who was tired and afraid. "I don't know, comrade. Perhaps you knowing, that will help."

When Ntango and I went outside again, we found Alberto leaning casually against the cab. Though his body was relaxed, his eyes were alert. The cab was untouched. Ntango was quiet as usual as we drove away, so I went over the whole story with him again on the way downtown.

"Many intrigues," Ntango said. "But I don't know why those men wanted to see you tonight."

This bothered me, too, I had to admit. They wanted to assure me Ernesto hadn't killed Aaron. But there was something of the "She doth protest too much," about the summons. I didn't think Ernesto did kill Aaron. So why go to all this trouble to throw me off the scent? Why did these guys care what I thought?

These *compañeros* wanted me to keep the cops away from Ernesto. Big John wanted me to forget the whole thing. Pop wanted me to regroup the workers of the world under the banner of the bartenders union. And all I wanted to do was turn the clock back a dozen years so I could marry Linda, or, failing that, spend the night with Dr. Parker.

"So where are we now?" I asked Ntango.

" 'Ay, there's the rub,' " said Ntango. I looked him over carefully. This Shakespeare thing of Greg's was catching on. "Your problem is one of goodness," said Ntango.

Ntango the oracle. I never got a chance to ask what he meant. He pulled up to the curb on the service road at the Riverside end of 110th Street. We got careless. Too late, I heard something—doors opening or doors closing. An unnatural sound of movement. Peering out the cab's back window, I saw the front end of what looked like a small truck that had pulled up close on our bumper. I knew instinctively, in the way a doe hears the click of the hunter's gun, that they were after us. Maybe it was the stocky, shadowy shapes of the men who had gotten out of the truck. Even before they reached us, I knew they would come for us. Even before I recognized the red Cherokee, I knew. In the glow of the streetlight, I saw cruelty frozen on a man's face and the glint of a gun barrel as someone opened the door on the sidewalk side of me. At the same moment, someone else leaned in the front window and poked at Ntango with a gun, jumping around outside the cab, speaking rapidly and angrily in Spanish, as if Ntango was arguing or fighting with him, when, in fact, Ntango in his calm, soft voice was telling him, "I don't have money. I'm a cabdriver. . . . Look, my friend. . . . How much money do I have? Take it."

I knew Ntango was wrong. They weren't after money.

The guy at the rear waved his gun through the open door and reached to pull me out of the cab. As he pulled me toward the door, Ntango caught on. He'd never shifted the cab out of gear while we were stopped, so he floored it. The open back door took out the guy who held the gun on me. I heard a shot. The cab sped out into 110th Street and hooked into the curve that led to Riverside Drive, where it careened into an uptown bus broadside. Just before the cab hit the bus, Ntango slumped against the window.

chapter fifteen

The cab's intercom radio was turned off. So, hanging over the front seat, I tried to get it to work. Finally, I did, and by pushing buttons, hollering, and answering stupid questions, I got across to the dispatcher what had happened and where we were.

Ntango hadn't moved. The guy with the gun had been at point-blank range. I sat there in the dim, wobbly light of an ancient Riverside Drive streetlamp, in a cab crumpled against the side a New York City bus, barely aware of the few worried faces looking down at us from the bus. I expected that Ntango was dead and that if I moved him, I would find the white mush of his brains spattered against the window.

In those terrible moments, I wanted to get away from him; I huddled into the far corner of the backseat. Then all of a sudden, I didn't feel so afraid anymore. I leaned forward, reached over the back of the seat, and held his hand. When I squeezed it, I felt a slight response. I sat like this for the few minutes—I have no idea how many—it took the EMS ambulance to arrive. They came with red lights flashing and siren wailing, then jumped out of the truck with instrument bags and stethoscopes and began working over Ntango. Then they dragged him out of the car, placed him on a stretcher, and stuck an IV line into his arm.

When the paramedics had prodded and poked Ntango enough and had finally slowed down, I asked one of them, a stocky woman in an olive green medic's suit, her dark hair tied back from her face, if

Ntango was alive. She said it looked like he'd gotten a small-caliber bullet in the back of his head, but he wasn't dead. I wanted to ride to the hospital in the ambulance with Ntango, but a police cruiser arrived and a truculent young cop, who looked like a fourteen-year-old with a mustache, told me I had to stay and answer some questions.

"I'll do it later," I said, edging toward the back door of the ambulance. "I want to go with my friend."

The mustachioed 14-year-old unbuckled the flap on his holster. His partner, a Hispanic guy, who also had a mustache but looked his age, came alongside me and touched my arm. He spoke softly. "We'll take you to the hospital after we ask a couple of questions," he said, and then patted my shoulder. I realized I was shaking, and since I really didn't know what to do, I grasped for the cop's kindness.

"Thanks. Do you think Ntango will be okay?"

He nodded toward the EMS truck. "These guys are the best." His hand gripping my arm, he walked me to the police car, helped me into the backseat, and, with the door open, stood looking down at me. I didn't know whether he thought I might keel over or I might run off. But he kept a pretty good watch over me. After he asked my name and address and Ntango's name and address, the other cop called the information in on their radio. I described what had happened, trying to gloss over exactly where we'd been and exactly what we'd been doing.

"What were you doing tonight, Mr. McNulty?" the formerly truculent but now politely stern younger cop asked me again. He sat in the front seat and awkwardly twisted his body, encumbered by leather belts, handcuffs, a flashlight, a holster, and the other accoutrements of policehood, to face me.

"I told you. We went for a ride."

"No one goes for a ride to the South Bronx."

He had me there. In my initial state of shock, I'd told him where we'd been; now, if I'd had a third leg and was able to stand adequately on the other two, I would have kicked myself in the ass for doing it. I couldn't think of any plausible reason for us to be in the South Bronx, either, except to buy drugs—or else the real one, which I didn't want to tell him about. I was mulling over a possible explanation when I heard my name come back over the cop radio, mixed up with a bunch of numbers and letters. The sound of my own name crackling through the radio startled me and seemed to have a similar effect on my companions, who stiffened noticeably and became warier than they'd been.

"Are you sure you didn't recognize the assailants?" the good cop asked.

"I told you no," I said wearily.

From a misguided sense of loyalty, I didn't want to tell the cops about Ernesto and his pals in the Bronx until I knew if they had done this. From an equally misguided sense of loyalty to John and his father, I didn't want to tell the cops about the Cherokee and the first shooting until I knew for sure who was telling the truth. This combination left me tongue-tied when it came to explanations. It turned out not to make any difference, because just then the mild-mannered cop with the Spanish accent told me that I had a right to remain silent, that anything I said could be used against me, and that I was entitled to a lawyer.

"What the hell is this?" I screamed at him. "I'm the fucking victim. You said you'd take me to the hospital to see Ntango."

He still looked sympathetic. "Sorry, pal, this comes first."

"There's a charge pending for Brian McNulty, Six twelve West One Hundred and tenth Street. That's you, right?" This was from the cop in the passenger seat, who had regained his former truculence now that I'd been identified as a criminal.

"A charge?" Then I remembered my escapade at Greg's apartment. "That's a mistake. I was released. You can ask them."

"Yeah, well, we're gonna unrelease you." He turned to open his door. "Get out of the car. I'm gonna frisk you."

As I opened the door, I doubled myself over to drop the joint I had in my pocket into the gutter. But the cop was quick; he bent and picked it up. "Now what's this?" He came up in my face and held the joint in front of my eyes.

"It looks like a joint."

"Is it yours?" The expression on his face was triumphant.

"Nope. You can have it."

He bumped his chest against mine, knocking me backward a step and forcing me to catch my footing with my sore leg. Particles of spit spewed from his mouth when he yelled at me. "I saw you drop it."

"Not me."

He spun me around and pushed me against the car. Without my crutches, I had to use my bad leg again to steady myself, and it hurt, so I yelped and cursed. As soon as my back was turned, he slapped me hard enough on the back of the head that my forehead bounced against the doorframe of the car. "Nothing there," he said, laughing, then spread me against the car and patted me down the rest of the way. His partner looked embarrassed.

They took me to the lockup at the Twenty-fourth Precinct, where I sat on a wooden bench in a holding cell populated with drunks and junkies, muggers, rapists, slashers, and shooters. I had tried to explain that an injustice was being done here, but I could tell by the blank expression on the booking cop's face that injustice meant no more to him than justice did. He didn't care what I'd done or not done, if I went to jail or if I got away. He was a factory worker with twenty years in at the same machine, attaching the same part, turning the same valve. He wanted his shift to end and to go home to some sanity in his life before he had to come back and go through this again.

"Look, pal," I said. "Could I call a lawyer?"

"Later," he said without looking up.

I stood my ground, but I could feel panic grabbing at my voice. "Could you call Sgt. Pat Sheehan at the Detective Bureau? He used to work up here."

At this, he looked up, exhibiting the first spark of interest he'd shown all evening. "Sheehan? Do you want to confess to somethin'?"

I started to say no, then realized this might be my only chance. "Yes, but only to Sheehan."

I waited on my wooden bench, contemplating the human misery around me. It was hard to believe, taking in the anguished faces and the twisted bodies of the men and women draped over benches and staring at ceilings and walls, that these were the perpetrators; for all the world, they looked like victims.

Sometime later, maybe an hour, maybe longer, a slim, gentle-looking cop in a perfectly pressed uniform called my name. When I stood up, he steered me by one crutch to a scarred and battered room off a scarred and battered hallway, where Sheehan sat on the corner of the query room table. His face was red, but he didn't look angry; it was just his usual impatience, suggesting I was wasting his time. His eyes bore into mine. "I was in the neighborhood, McNulty. You're lucky."

"I'm sorry, Sergeant. My friend Ntango, the cabdriver, got shot tonight. I want to get to the hospital."

Something flickered in his eyes. "The tall, light-skinned black guy?"

I nodded.

"He's African or something."

"Eritrean."

"How bad?" There was a small resonant chord of sympathy in his tone.

"I don't know." My voice shook. "He got shot in the head."

"Who shot him?" Despite the sympathy, Sheehan's eyes were still piercing.

"I don't know."

"Were you with him?"

I nodded.

"The same guy?"

I didn't answer.

Sheehan, perched on the table, surveyed me from head to toe, as if he were looking for something. He seemed perfectly patient doing this, and patient meeting my eyes. This scrutiny made me nervous, so I looked away. When I looked back, he was still watching me. For these moments, I liked him. I wished we could be friends. But I felt a distance, too. I didn't know if it came from me or from him, but I suspected from him. We weren't ever going to be friends. I was his work.

"Well, now you got a misdemeanor possession to go with breaking and entering rap in Brooklyn." He watched while I squirmed. Sheehan was the kind of guy where begging wouldn't do you any good. He knew what I'd asked him. He knew what was right. I'd have to wait for him to decide. So I waited, and I squirmed.

"Call your lawyer," he said finally, having made up his mind. "If he'll do the paperwork, I can take you to check on your friend."

I called Peter's number. He was usually near the phone this time of night, since many of his clients worked nights and often needed legal assistance during the wee hours.

"That was pretty stupid," Peter said. "I might have gotten the charges dropped. Now you'll end up going to trial."

"Forget about that for a minute. Ntango's been shot."

"Shot!" said Peter."

I told him Sheehan would help get me out if he did whatever lawyers do to get people out of jail.

"I can ask for bail. If you weren't already out on recognizance, I could just get you released."

"Bail's okay. Can you put it up, and I'll pay you back?"

I told Sheehan Peter was coming down with the bail.

"Let's go," he said.

I felt grateful; I'm sure it showed in my face. But before I could thank him, Sheehan sidled up next to me. "We can talk on the way."

I signed the release forms and regained my possessions. Sheehan told the booking guy that my lawyer would be in to do the rest. As I'd surmised earlier, this guy didn't care if it was a jail break.

St. Luke's was only a dozen or so blocks up Amsterdam from the precinct building. I tried to be cooperative as Sheehan asked his few questions, but I couldn't tell him about Ernesto because that would get him and his friends in trouble. I couldn't tell him where Greg was. And I didn't want to tell him about Dr. Wilson now that I knew he was John's father. My discretion made our little chat somewhat strained. But I did break down and tell him the whole story about the second coming of the red Cherokee. I left out Dr. Wilson and the address, but the rest of it was what had happened.

"The second time." Sheehan said. "The same guys?" We were headed up Amsterdam. He drove easily, keeping up with the cabs, timing the lights, switching lanes, using the mirrors as much as the windshield. Concentrating on driving, he spoke without turning toward me.

"You were shot in the leg as a warning the last time, right?" Sheehan glanced quickly at me. "I don't think they were warning you this time. What do they want you to stop doing?"

"I have no idea. I don't deal drugs. I don't owe bookies any money. I can't stop doing something if I don't know what it is. I don't think they meant to shoot me. I think they wanted to take me somewhere."

"Yeah," said Sheehan. "To a vacant lot in Canarsie."

Ntango was in an OR recovery room when we got to the hospital. The chief surgical resident told us he'd been shot in the lower part of the head; the bullet missed the brain and came out behind his ear. There was swelling near his brain, so they surgically released some of the pressure. He was unconscious and the resident didn't know when he'd wake up or how he would be when he did.

There wasn't much more to say, and they didn't like us hanging around, so Sheehan and I went outside.

As soon as the door closed behind us, Sheehan lit a cigarette. "I should take you downtown and put the screws to you," he said, not unkindly.

We stood on Amsterdam Avenue in front of St. Luke's Hospital. Across the street was an apartment building that some of the hospital workers lived in. A couple of blocks up the street, Columbia University began. A couple of blocks east, the end of the campus backed up against Morningside Park, and beyond the park stretched the howling Harlem slums.

"Your old buddy Aaron Adams lived a pretty sordid life. Did you know that?"

"Oh?" I said, deciding not to mention my talk with Scott Cooper, Aaron's former partner. "The Aaron I knew was rich. He went to boarding schools and graduated from Princeton."

"Sounds like a different guy. This guy Aaron worked at a fancy restaurant as a maître d', where he made maybe five hundred a week.

When he was murdered, he was living in an SRO on Forty-fourth Street, the kind of hotel I don't like to walk into by myself. He was a pervert, a drunk, and a cokehead, and he'd done time. On the first conviction, he got released to rehab. The second, he did a three-year bid at Greenhaven." Sheehan looked thoughtful; I'd say wistful, if I'd thought him capable of it. "We used to call them pansies. Fairies. But a life like his would scare me to death."

We contemplated the morning light coming to Amsterdam Avenue. Then Sheehan put his cop hat back on. "That bar boy is from Colombia, right?" He dragged on a cigarette, leaning his back against the front wall of the hospital.

"Not Colombia." I didn't hide the irritation in my voice. "He's from Chile."

This gave Sheehan only a second's pause. "The way it looks, he sold drugs on the side. Aaron was his customer. Something went wrong."

I stared at Sheehan. I could feel my eyes narrow with suspicion. I hoped Sheehan couldn't see it. "That's speculation, though, isn't it? How does Greg fit in?"

"He doesn't; he's an accessory, probably got scared and ran. That's why I'm not going to hammer you for helping hide him out." He watched a cab pull away from the curb, then turned to face me. "There's one piece that doesn't fit yet. I'm told two guys came to see the bartender that night, an older guy with gray hair and a younger guy. It may be nothing, but we got to check it out. When we find them, we'll tie things up." Standing up straight, he took a step away from the building and flicked his cigarette butt, spinning, out into the middle of Amsterdam Avenue. "You don't have any guesses who the two guys might be, do you?"

Once more, Sheehan looked like he knew whatever it was I was keeping from him. Once more, with difficulty, I fought back the urge to tell him. I shuffled a little under his scrutiny. "Sorry, I have no idea."

Sheehan lit another cigarette in the manner of a man little concerned about the outcome of the conversation. "Just be careful. Life ain't worth nothing to these Latin drug people."

"Unlike us nativist Americans, eh?"

Sheehan looked hurt. "These guys are vicious."

"Vicious how?"

"Bringing in dope. Smuggling illegals. Murder. Terrorism."

"Terrorism?" I raised an eyebrow.

Now Sheehan looked irritated. "If you want to get those guys in the red Cherokee off your back, you take it up with that Ernesto guy." He smiled. When he did, I realized that unlike most people, who look better when they smile, he looked much better when he didn't. "That is, of course, if you can find him."

I turned down a ride, so Sheehan walked down the block to his car, and I propelled myself toward home along 112th Street. All the way there, in the gray dawn light, I kept picturing Ntango's sleepy-looking half-closed eyes that masked his really alert intelligence, his soft voice and gentle manner, qualities that only the foolish took for weakness. I hadn't really known how much of a friend he'd become until I felt the empty space now without him.

When I woke up later that morning, I stayed in bed, pretending to myself I was still asleep. Sheehan had things figured out wrong, I decided. But he could probably grab Ernesto and make the charge stick anyway, for all I knew of the processes of justice. And, for all I knew for sure, he might have figured things out right.

I went back to the hospital, my heart filled with dread, to check on Ntango. There was a lot more activity now—the day shift, I guessed— though the chief resident was still there, deep dark circles under his eyes, doing paperwork and conferring with someone new every ten seconds, it seemed. But he did take a moment to look me in the eye with a large degree of sympathy.

"You can sit and wait," he said. "Or we can call you when something changes." He looked away and then back again. "He's getting stronger. I'm feeling more confident than I did last night."

I thought I should wait with Ntango until he woke up, and I did sit by his bed for quite a while. But the sight of the tubes in his nose and mouth and the IV line in his arm and the sound of the monitors beeping, plus the medicinal antiseptic smell were making me sick. I also

wanted to find the pricks who'd shot him, and I wanted to begin looking for them by talking to John and getting the lowdown on the
phony optometrist—his dad. I wanted to get the loose ends tied up
and then come clean to Sheehan with the whole story, with the possible exception of the freedom fighters in the Bronx, and let the cops
figure out what the hell was going on.

I thought about calling my friend Carl, the doorman, to sit with
Ntango, but he worked nights and slept during the day. He also got
pissed if anyone called while he was sleeping and usually hung up on
them. Then I thought of Kevin. He'd been a real trouper when his
grandfather—my ex-wife's father—was dying, visiting him in the hospital almost every day, and he was really fond of Ntango. I called his
mother at work and asked her. She didn't like it much but said she'd
leave it up to Kevin. So I called Pop, told him Ntango had been shot,
and asked him to get Kevin and see if he'd be willing to keep watch
over Ntango at the hospital.

Since Kevin had known Ntango for years and had tooled around
the city with him in his cab any number of times, and since he knew
Ntango loved him like a son, he readily agreed to spend a couple of
days with me and take his turn sitting with Ntango.

"The same guys who shot you shot Ntango?" he asked when he arrived an hour or so later, his teenage sullenness bowled over by wide-
eyed astonishment. "What are you gonna do now? Are the cops after
them?"

"Sort of," I said evasively. "First, I have to talk to John and
straighten a couple of things out. Then we'll go after them. This isn't
TV, Kevin. Problems don't get settled so easily. In real life, the good
guys don't always win—the good guys aren't even always the good
guys. The punks who shot us are puppets—working for someone,
probably someone who makes a lot of money off them. We need to
find out who and what's behind this before we can stop them."

"Yeah," said Kevin, his awe receding, his eyes closing, the sullenness
returning. "When you track them down, maybe you can lecture them
to death."

chapter sixteen

I finally reached John at his office the next morning to tell him Ntango had gotten shot. He didn't say anything for a long time. Then he said, "I don't understand this, bro. I don't know why anyone's after you."

When he asked where we'd been the night it happened, I told him the truth—that we'd gone to the Bronx to talk to Ernesto.

"What'd you do that for?" It was both a question and an accusation.

"He called me. He's got problems, too."

"Problems! You're goddamn right he's got problems!" John's tone was controlled but near the edge of an explosion. "You should've stayed away from him, like I told you. Who the hell knows what he's into?" John's voice went softer. "I'm sorry about your friend. You better lay low until we figure out who's after you."

I wasn't in the mood for John's brush-off right then. "Look, John, Ntango got shot because someone was after me. If you won't tell me everything you know about what's going on, I'm going to the cops."

I could sense John stiffen through the phone line. But he pulled himself together. "Listen, bro," he said soothingly. "I ain't gonna let anything happen to you." He paused for a moment. "I got an idea. . . . Let me put you up at one of the hotels until this blows over."

I barely heard what he said. I just went on. "What's your father got to do with this, John?"

There was no sound from the other end of the phone for a long time. "Maybe you better come over to my office," he said finally.

John's office was on the forty-first floor of a glittering glass building on Sixth Avenue, a couple of blocks south of the New York Hilton, near Rockefeller Center. The building and its companions, clones of Lever House over on Park Avenue, were built during the late fifties and early sixties, when America's future looked bright and the bankers and real estate sharks wanted nothing to do with the past. I preferred granite and marble myself.

The lobby of John's building turned out to be where the marble was after all, variegated off-white polished stone with deep blue lines. The lobby ceiling must have been four stories high. The marble surrounded me like the cliffs of heaven. A gigantic black metal abstract sculpture in the middle of the lobby looked like a pile of arms and legs. Still, if only because of sheer size, it was imposing. If the lobby was intended to humble those who entered the building, it worked on me. I looked over my shoulder a few times to see if the security guards were on their way to give me the heave-ho.

I told the elevator starter I wanted the forty-first floor. He directed me to a bank of elevators whose first stop was the fortieth floor. On the forty-first floor, the elevator doors opened into a carpeted reception area. At the front desk was a young blond woman with a very pretty smile, white teeth left over from an Ipana commercial, a corn-fed complexion, and blue eyes that saw what they wanted to see and nothing else. She looked like she'd come to the job straight from cheerleading school in Iowa. I wondered if she was the one I'd argued with on the phone when I was trying to track John down.

"Mr. Wolinski, please," I said.

"Whom shall I say is calling?" she responded daintily. She looked with some curiosity but without any obvious sympathy at my crutches.

"His proctologist."

"Name, please," she squeaked.

"He'll know."

John came out of his office, wiping a grin off his face. As always, he moved decisively, taking large strides, his eyes bright and alert. As usual, he looked healthy and robust, with the energy of three or four people. As usual, I was dragging myself through the morning.

"How's your friend doing?" John asked.

"He's the same as he was—in a coma."

John let that register. "That's rough, bro. You know if there's anything I can do—"

I held out my hands in a helpless gesture.

"Does he got a good doctor? A good room? Insurance?"

"Actually, I don't know if he has any of those things. I don't think he has insurance."

"That, I can take care of. Jane will help you fill out an employment application for him and backdate it a couple of months."

John said he was tied up for a few minutes and would leave me to fill out the forms for Ntango. He saw me watching Jane, the Ipana secretary, as she sat back down and crossed her legs. "Jane"—he raised an eyebrow in my direction—"you give Mr. McNulty here whatever he wants while he's waiting." He made a kind of comically obscene gesture to suggest what Jane might do for me. But she didn't see it, and he didn't really mean it. When she saw us both looking at her, she blushed, pulled her skirt down, and tucked her knees in under her desk.

"Don't let John pick on you," I said as he ducked back into his office to finish a phone call.

"Oh, not Mr. Wolinski," she gushed. "He's wonderful."

Trying to look like someone who'd been in an office before, I self-importantly looked through my pockets as though I might find something of value there. What I did find were the Dockside photographs Ntango had gotten from the security chief at the Claridge. On a whim, I showed them to Jane.

"Did you ever see any of these people before?" I dropped the stack of pictures in front of her. She looked at them in wonder. "That's Mr. Wolinski," she said. "He looks so young and handsome. And that's Mr. Phillips," she said, looking at Greg. "This man was here just a few days ago, but I don't remember his name." This time it was Aaron

Adams she pointed to. "And this one . . ." She held it up, looked at me, then at the picture again. "Is this you?"

I smiled a little sheepishly.

"You must be a lot older now," she said without a trace of irony.

I couldn't finish the forms because I didn't know Ntango's Social Security number. I said I'd get the information and bring it back. Then John summoned me to his pale blue-carpeted office, which had floor-to-ceiling windows and a shiny wooden desk about the size of a tennis court. There were abstract pastel paintings on the pale gold walls, a good-size, comfortable-looking couch beneath them, and what looked like a liquor cabinet against the far wall. The carpet was so thick, I bounced across it. I was afraid to sit on the couch, so I stood by the windows, leaning on my crutches, looking out over the spires and towers of the city through a haze that made everything gray.

Sitting at his desk, reclining in his high-backed leather swivel chair, John waited for me to speak.

"Quite a spread you got here," I said.

John waved an arm at the expansive office. "I've been promoted again. The president called me in. 'Wolinski,' he said. Not Mr. Wolinski, not John—just Wolinski." John leaned forward, warming to his story even though he had an audience of only one. "He puts his arm around my shoulder and leads me into this office. He shows me my nameplate with 'Vice President' on it. I tell the guy I have enough titles. This time, I want more money." John glanced at me over the top of his glasses, making it seem that the joke was just between us.

"My apartment isn't this big," John said. Like much of what he said, this sounded both funny and regretful. He showed me around the office: bar, refrigerator, stove, private bathroom with a shower, closet with three or four suits and four or five pairs of shoes. The phone rang. He spoke briefly to someone I assumed was the manager of a hotel in Philadelphia. I didn't really listen, but I heard enough to know it was about food and beverage costs being too high. "If you don't have a bar manager who can get the right bar cost, I'll come down and find one," John said. He flashed me a look of pure disdain for the man he was speaking to, then hung up.

"What was that all about?"

John smiled conspiratorially, then opened his desk drawer and started pushing buttons like a mad scientist. A speaker on his desk played back the conversation, the placating and unctuous voice of the manager, the decisive, ironic voice of Big John. He laughed at my expression as I listened. "Maybe I'm paranoid," he said. "But I keep a record of my phone conversations."

"Just like Nixon," I said.

"That's funny," said Big John after a pause. "You're right. Nixon screwed by a tape recorder."

I watched John curiously. His expression was strange—ominous—like he was about to tell me something. Instead, he shut off the machine and stared out the floor-to-ceiling window. "You know," he said after some time had passed, "I come here in the morning and sit at this desk and wonder what the hell it was all for. You give up everything in your life for something and then when you get there, what you were after ain't there anymore. You know what I mean?" His voice was almost tearful. "You ain't gonna believe this. But I miss working the stick."

"You're right," I said. "I don't believe you."

My irony was wasted; John was back in Atlantic City in 1973. "I loved being a bartender: the front bar on Saturday night, a good crew behind you. We were kings of the mountain. I miss that—you know, it really is lonely at the top."

"The money probably helps you suffer through," I said, though not unkindly.

John chuckled. He knew the choices he'd made.

I knew what it had cost him, too. Over the years, except for Greg—and, I guess, me—he'd fired most of the people who'd been his friends. I remembered when he fired Ben Finch. John had been food and beverage manager of the Dockside for a few months. We all thought it would be heaven. But the corporation called in the note. John and I sat at the bar for hours one night after closing; he'd long since switched from Campari and soda to scotch. The company had sent him a spotter's report on Ben. John had saved Ben a couple of times before—for missing work, for being drunk, the first time he was caught stealing. According to pretty much any standard, Ben deserved to be fired. But he hadn't done anything any of the rest of us, including John, hadn't done. If John had covered for him, he'd covered for John, and for me, too, as I had for both of them.

"I tried, bro," John had told me that night. "I even went up to New York to the corporation." What he wanted was for me to tell him that it was okay to fire Ben. It wasn't that he thought it was. He just wanted me to make it easier. But I couldn't. That was the night I told him that he wanted to be boss, he'd have to fuck over his friends.

John's expression this morning was regretful, too, but nothing like that night. I suppose after a time you get used to fucking over your friends.

"So, how did you find out about my father?" John asked pleasantly.

"I looked at the videotape of Greg in Atlantic City. Linda recognized him."

John lurched forward to lean his elbows on his desk. "Videotape? What videotape?"

"Security had a videotape of when I ran into Greg in the lobby."

John screwed up his face. "It used to be you could just live your life. Now there's a fucking replay for everything you do. And Linda? Is that going on again?"

"No," I said quickly. "She's married and has a baby."

John looked at me with this bewildered expression. He started to say something, but after a few seconds he shook his head and compressed his lips, like he'd reluctantly decided against it. He leaned far back in his chair so that it reclined. "I shoulda told you about Charlie myself. But I didn't want to get you mixed up in it. That's my old man, Dr. Wilson. He came back from Arizona and set up practice here without my knowing it. It's a long, twisted story. But Charlie doesn't have anything to do with you or your friend getting shot."

"How do you know?"

"He doesn't have any reason to come after you, number one. And number two, that ain't what he does."

"Maybe he doesn't want anyone to find out who killed Aaron Adams."

John looked at me over the top of his glasses, his expression suggesting I was a half-wit.

I stood in front of his desk, leaning on it with both hands, ready to go to the mat. "I'm gonna ask again, John. How do you know he doesn't have something to do with killing Aaron?"

Leaning forward, elbows on the desk, John rested his chin in his hand like a wise old judge. "He didn't kill anybody, bro. But it's almost as bad as if he did. Just him being in the neighborhood when this came down makes for a big fucking problem." John took his glasses off and slumped back against the back of the chair again, staring at the space in front of him long enough to remind me of a junkie nodding in a doorway.

Then, when I began to think his depression was permanent, he jumped up. "Let's go."

Already in full stride, he'd reached the door before I was able to ask where we were going.

"To see my old man."

On the drive to Brooklyn, he said, "You got a lot on your mind, Brian. I know that. You wanna think I'm gonna let someone do you in, I can't stop you. But you could do what I say and lay low—go back to the shore and stay in my apartment at the hotel, or I'll put you up at one of the properties here in the city. Let me straighten this out."

I'd begun following John's lead the first day I met him and never felt it was the wrong thing to do. But years pass; things change. I wasn't a kid anymore. I no longer took goodness on faith. So I told him I didn't want to hide. I was about to ask him about his secretary recognizing Aaron's photo but then decided to hold off.

Dr. Wilson's cool and efficient receptionist remembered me. "You're appointment was at eleven," she said with a condescending smile. "You're late."

I stopped in my tracks. "My what?" Then I remembered I'd made an appointment to have my eyes checked. "I forgot," I said.

The receptionist, her eyebrows arched, her mouth a thin line, embodied disapproval. "There is a charge for a missed appointment," she said with fake understanding in her voice and ice in her eyes.

I stared at her with my fading eyes.

John listened to this exchange with some interest and then, as the receptionist stared at him with her mouth open, strode past her desk and opened the door to the examining room.

Dr. Wilson, Charlie, or whoever he was, must have just finished with a patient, who was poised to open the door from the other side as John barreled through from our side. Once the guy caught a glimpse of John's expression, he passed through the doorway quickly and headed for the street.

"What the hell do you think you're doing?" Wilson demanded. His words were angry. But he looked like he was seeing a ghost.

Ignoring his father's protestations, John calmly sat down in the examining chair. "Who's trying to whack Brian?"

Noticing me, Dr. Wilson switched tracks and became charm itself, "Ah, Brian," he said, ignoring John. "Feeling better?"

"Better than I'd be feeling if those fucking thugs of yours had caught up with me the night before last." I sat down at the small desk in his examination room.

His expression didn't change. Once more he stood in front of his gigantic eye-examination machine like Captain Ahab. "I assure you, Brian, I sent no one after you." He pointed to the examining chair. "Why don't you sit down here. I don't have a patient, so I can at least examine your eyes while we talk."

I looked suspiciously at him, his chair, and his eye-examination machine. John stood up to let me sit down; he had a smirk on his face.

"How's the leg?" Wilson asked. "Healing okay?"

"It's infected," I said testily.

He blinked but remained unruffled. "Sit down, Brian. I'm actually a pretty good optometrist."

I sat in the chair and Dr. Wilson looked through the big machine, snapping various lenses on and off. He projected letters on the far wall and asked me to read them. He said "um" and "ah" just like a real doctor and looked appropriately noncommittal with just the slightest tinge of worry. John watched with amused interest. They reminded me of each other. Not so much in looks as in manner and charm. They were both warm, good-natured, likable men.

When he finished, Dr. Wilson looked me over. "You need glasses for reading or any kind of close work. Your distance vision will hold up for a while longer."

"What's wrong?" I gripped the arms of the chair with the panic of a drowning man. "Why are my eyes failing?"

"Age," he said offhandedly. "It happens to everyone. Your eyes show signs of wear, just like the rest of you. But don't worry. The glasses will help you to read and see things up close. In a year or so, you'll need to have your eyes checked again."

"That's it? I'm not going blind?"

"Certainly not," said Dr. Wilson.

Things were looking up. Not only was I not going to lose my leg, as long as I took my medicine, but I wasn't going to go blind, either, if I wore my glasses. All I needed were a few props, and I could still run with the field.

Wilson offered to make me a pair of glasses on the house. "It'll take a couple of hours. You can pick them up tonight—I'll be here late— or tomorrow." He gave the glasses and his notes to someone dressed in white who came through a door from a laboratory-type room behind the examining room, picked up the tray Dr. Wilson handed him, and went right back out.

The more I saw of Big John and Dr. Wilson—or Charlie— together, the more they resembled each other, as Charlie was a slimmer Big John, dated by a wavy 1950s hairstyle and a natty but out-of-style jacket and a tie as wide as the back of a bus. As they stood together now, there were two sets of eyes twinkling behind glasses, and two sets of dimples flaring. Sparring like boxers after the opening bell, they worked through each other's irritation and each other's toughness. At the same time, they both seemed to wriggle with antici-pation, too—like big cuddly dogs when the master comes home. This standoff went on for quite a while before the younger one went over and swallowed the older, slighter man in his big bear hug.

"Brian," John hollered. "Here you have my old man. What're we gonna do with him?"

The eye doctor dropped his imperious professional air. Smiling with his eyes, he shook my hand heartily, as if he were meeting me for the first time, while laying his other arm almost tenderly on my shoulder. Holding me with his glittering eye, he said, "Believe me, I had nothing to do with your getting shot."

I told him the story of my return match with the Cherokee.

He shook his head. "I'm sorry. If I could help, I would."

John picked this moment to sigh audibly, like a whale spouting water. "Jesus Christ, you just can't stay away, can you?"

The senior Wolinski smiled shamefacedly.

"Let's try again," I suggested. "Why was the guy who shot me in your waiting room?"

"I told you the truth. He wasn't connected to me."

"Why was the guy in your office?"

Wilson shook his head. "The receptionist said he came in right behind you and sat in the outer office until you left."

"She'd recognize him, right? Like from a mug shot or something?"

Wilson looked troubled. "I told you I'd prefer being left out of this." He came closer and, with a new series of facial gymnastics, tried to look earnest. "The cops wouldn't find those guys even if she did identify them. They're probably out of the country by now." His face took on an expression of benevolent camaraderie, which on him looked like a false mustache. "I thought we had a deal."

"That was before they shot my friend."

John stepped in again. "Look, Charlie, you gotta play straight with us. You know what happens if we don't get this cleaned up? You know what happens to you if you get one more rap?"

The older man looked startled. "I don't know why that guy was murdered. Just like I don't know who shot Brian."

"I suppose you didn't make a hasty trip to Atlantic City to see Greg, either," I said.

Wilson looked away. I could practically hear his brain scrambling for an answer. "We had business there. But it wasn't murder. You're barking up the wrong tree."

When I got out of the examining chair to pace around the office, John took my place in the chair. He was calm and under control. "Those answers aren't good enough, Charlie," he said quietly.

The doctor tried to regain his professional status by grabbing a chart off the desk and looking at it. "I'm busy, John. I have patients."

Leaning back into the examining chair, John crossed his ankles like he was settling in for the long haul. "Whatever was goin' on is over." he said evenly. "That's number one."

"You don't know what you're talking about. You'll find out I had nothing to do with any killing."

"I will find out," John said. "Just like I'll find out whatever it was you and Walter and Greg were trying to get over."

John began turning some of the knobs on the big eye-examining machine. He got a light to go on, and he twisted a big round knob. Then he got up to go look in the machine from the doctor's side, swinging it around as if it were an antiaircraft battery. "Why didn't you stay in Arizona?" he asked from behind the big gun. "You're too old for the rackets."

Charlie shifted his eyes uncomfortably, trying not to look at me or John.

"I set the good doctor up in a practice in Arizona," John said to me. "The whole family was going straight at the same time." John backed away from the examining machine.

Charlie's expression softened. There was less worry and some warmth in his expression. "Ah, John. This practice in Bay Ridge opened up. It was a gold mine."

"You mean a perfect front. You think you're pretty slick, putting me on with that phony receptionist in Arizona who said she'd give you a message."

Charlie went over to his machine, looked through the scope, shot an irritated glance in John's direction, turned a few knobs, turned off the light, and pushed the arm of the machine back into position. "C'-mon, John. I was dead in Arizona. I didn't know anyone. No friends."

"Those sharks you deal with aren't friends." John angrily banged the back of the examining chair with the heel of his hand, swinging full force, as if he would knock it out of its moorings and across the room. "You're back what? Six months? Already, look at all this." John looked at his father with pity and disbelief. I was having a hard time staying with the conversation: The son telling the father it was time to retire. The father not wanting to. This should be normal enough, right?

"It was harmless, John," the older man pleaded.

"Harmless?" John exploded. "There're bodies all over town."

"I don't know about that," Charlie said desperately. "I don't know about that. It was just a little dealing." He tried to enlist that doctorly manner of ending the conversation again, busying himself in the files and papers he'd picked up from the desk. But this time, the folders rattled in his hands and some papers spilled out onto the floor.

When the papers fell, John and his father knelt down facing each other to pick them up. Their eyes met and something happened between them. They reached an understanding, so that when they stood up, Charlie was calm again.

I felt outnumbered, but I asked anyway. "Did you go to see Greg the night Aaron was murdered?"

Charlie didn't flinch. "No."

"What about Walter?"

"No."

"Could he have killed Aaron?"

"No."

"Did Greg kill him?"

Charlie's eyes hardened up. His voice went harsh. "Why do you care so much who killed this guy? What's he to you? None of us killed him."

I guess I expected John to say something—to stick up for me. When he didn't, I got flustered. "I just want to know what's going on." I said weakly.

"There's a lot more reason for you not to want to know," Charlie said. Then immediately, his charm reemerged, the dimpled smile and twinkling eyes taking away the threat that had seemed so ominous just seconds before. "I'm telling you for your own good."

chapter seventeen

On the drive back to Manhattan in John's plush Eldorado, I asked John, "Is he really an optometrist?"

John chuckled. "That's Charlie."

"What's that mean? Is he or isn't he? Does he have a license? Did he study optometry?"

John was still laughing. "You saw the license. It was hanging right there on the wall."

I sputtered. I was tired of being flimflammed. "He's not a goddamn optometrist. He's a fraud. He probably makes the glasses out of windowpanes."

"What can I tell you?" John chuckled some more.

The story, according to John, was that Charlie had learned to grind glasses in a prison optical shop during one of his sojourns. When he got out of jail, he worked as an optician for a while for a small-time optometrist in Philly. When the guy retired, Charlie bought the practice, did some reading, practiced on his friends, and learned how to examine eyes and use the equipment to make lenses. He sold the place in Philly and opened one in Atlantic City. "No one ever bothered him. People don't complain about the glasses he makes. Self-taught. Self-made. The American way, right?"

"How'd he get a license?"

John rolled his eyes and raised his eyebrows.

"It's fake?"

John sighed deeply. "People get addicted to coffee, to drugs, to cigarettes. My old man's addicted to larceny. When I was growing up, from when I was five until I was twelve or thirteen, my father was in jail. He got out and became an optometrist. I was a kid. What did I know? I knew about policy slips, loan sharking, the football pool, Thoroughbreds and Standardbreds. We had a garage full of boosted cigarettes one week and hijacked booze the next week. Optometry, racketeering, it was all the same to me. Booking numbers for me was the same as a plumber's son fixing sinks. By the time I was sixteen, I was running a crew. Charlie taught me, and he took Greg under his wing, too. You got to understand; as far as I knew, we were the good guys. The only people who ever got hurt were guys who did you wrong."

"Greg, too? What about Walter?"

John nodded. "Greg, yeah, as much a part of it as I was. Not Walter, though. I didn't know him then."

"And David Bradley and Bill Green?" I asked, revisiting the unanswered questions and unclaimed bodies of the past.

John turned on me sharply. "David was a bro; you know that. Bill Green was a punk. What do they have to do with anything?"

"I don't suppose you want to tell me what happened to David and Bill Green." I pretended to look out the windshield of the car, but I could feel John's hawk eye boring into the side of my head.

"There's nothin' to tell."

"Bullshit, John," I turned to glare at him, while, this time, he stared straight ahead.

"This is ridiculous," John shouted to the plush ceiling of the Eldorado. "Why the fuck is someone shooting at you? Why is my fucking old man in the middle of this? Why can't you all just leave me alone?" We drove slowly in thick traffic. After a while, John said softly, "Sorry, bro, I've got too many things coming at me." His jaw tightened and his knuckles went white on the steering wheel. "If the old fucker gets caught, he goes back to the slammer for good. A habitual. And, as soon as the company hears about it, I'm gone." John glowered at me as if it were my fault. "He was all set. He didn't have to do this."

"Did he have anything to do with Aaron getting killed?"

"He didn't kill Aaron," John said softly.

I waited a few minutes; then I went on. "If it's all the same to you, I think now is the time to clear up a couple of other things."

John curled his lip and tightened his eyebrows but didn't say anything. The irritation level was already pretty high in the car. "Go ahead," he said without enthusiasm.

"Let's talk about cocaine dealing, strong-arm tactics, lying, cheating, stealing, and murdering. Does that cover everyone's hobbies?"

"Some of us play golf, too," John said. He leaned back against the seat, driving with his wrist draped over the top of the steering wheel. We were doing about ten miles an hour in bumper-to-bumper traffic on the Gowanus Expressway heading into the Battery Tunnel, so it didn't make much difference what he did with the steering wheel.

"You know who brings cocaine into the country?" Big John asked. "The government," he answered with a satisfied smirk. "The CIA brings it in from Colombia. You think those drug cartels are outlaws? Those days are over. Now they're all businessmen."

"Talking about businessmen," I said. "You're secretary told me Aaron Adams came in to see you last week right before he was killed."

John looked toward me; then his eyes darted away. He relaxed, sinking lower into his leather seat. He looked like he was ready to give up, staring at the taillights of the Love Taxi in front of us.

Finally, he came to a decision. "You remember Arizona?"

I remembered.

"After a while, I needed Aaron to cover for me at the Dockside, so I cut him in."

I'd known John and Greg were flying to Arizona and driving back rented cars stuffed with bales of marijuana. But we thought, So what? We were all outlaws anyway—the counterculture; everyone smoked the stuff. But I couldn't picture Aaron covering for a dope dealer. A Nixon Republican, he was the soul of the establishment. When push came to shove during the union campaign, he relished the oncoming strike, strode through the picket line like a peacock when it came, and cried for the National Guard when I took down his new sports car. He came speeding up to the picket line with his black paint–spattered red

Triumph, craning his head out the side window on the driver's side because he couldn't see through the smashed windshield. He came for
me, and my knees shook, but John grabbed him around the neck.

"He did it," Aaron shouted, the finger of accusation pointed so
truly at its mark. "You'll pay for this." Tears glistened on his cheeks.

"You don't know who did it, Aaron," John said calmly. "Tell the
company to pay for the damage."

I would have been surprised back then to know Aaron covered for
John. But then John had always assured me that everyone was cor-
ruptible.

"These days I'm making good money," John said now. "But for
years after I came out from the bar, I didn't make two-thirds of what
you guys were making behind the stick. Those corporate whores, they
thought I was just another shithead hotel-management graduate." Big
John looked over his shoulder as if "they" might be still be coming after him. The bitterness in his voice was as resonant as my father's was
when he used to rail against the bosses. "I used their mails, their couri-
ers, their banks and their credit, and their corporate cars. Half their
management people worked for me on the side. When they were paying me twenty-two thousand and laughing, I picked up another thirty
on my own. By the time they moved me up to thirty-eight, I moved
myself up to eighty." John's expression was aggrieved, like someone to
whom an injustice had been done. "I haven't done any of that for a
long time. I've gotten to a place where I don't need to anymore. But
back then I had everyone in on the deal, Greg, my old man—and, for
a time, Aaron. Later, I worked out gigs for Greg and my old man. For
my old man, retirement in Arizona. For Greg, the Ocean Club, where
he could pull down nearly a grand a week. By then, Aaron was long
gone, strung out on coke and booze. He didn't want my help."

Once more, like so many times in the past, John was trying to jus-
tify himself to me. He wanted me to say what he'd done was okay,
though I couldn't understand why he cared what I thought. On a
good week, I made maybe six hundred bucks. On a bad week, I made
three hundred, and half of it on any week went for child support.

"I told Charlie I'd front him the nut to set up something easy—like a liquor store—far away from Philly and the shore, somewhere he wouldn't get into trouble anymore. That was five years ago. I told myself, That's the one good thing you done. Whatever else, you took care of your old man. And I took care of Greg, too. I was gonna work him up into management.

"Now you see, right? Greg and my old man, they start out on their own. Who needs Big John?, they think We'll do it ourselves, right? Now look at this fucking mess I got to straighten out."

The story was good, but not good enough to throw me completely off track. "So why did Aaron come to your office?"

"He wanted a job, a management job. He was on the skids." John gestured with his open hands, letting go of the steering wheel. "He was hinting about dealing for me. But I didn't catch on. He must've known what Greg was up to. This time, I was the simpleton. I told him I'd get him something in a hotel if he was willing to leave town. He told me to fuck off. He's hinting at somethin'. But I don't know what it is. Maybe he was threatening me. But I didn't pay any attention. What'd I care? He's almost a stumblebum. That was the last I heard from him. When this thing came down, I kept it quiet that he'd been to the office. It was just a lousy coincidence. And I couldn't afford for it to get out."

"So then he went to see Greg?"

"I don't know."

Another thought occurred to me, and I blurted it out. "Where'd you go after you left me the night Aaron was killed?"

John rolled his eyes to the roof of the car again. "You see what I mean? Even you! You're ready to send me over when you hear Aaron came to my office. Imagine what the cops or the company would do. I shoulda thrown him out the fuckin' window then and none of this would have happened." John got a faraway look in his eye and cocked his head in my direction. He looked almost sheepish. "That night Aaron was killed, bro, after I left you, I was with someone I shouldn't have been with. And I really would hate like hell to have to say who it was." His eyes met mine.

"'She walks these hills in a long black veil' sort of thing?"

John nodded. "More than you know, more than you know." He banged both hands against the steering wheel. "You see what happens? Greg never told me. I didn't even know my own father was in New York. What does that tell you?" John glared at me. "These high rollers—my old man and Greg—they shouldn't be going to the bathroom without supervision."

"Where does Walter come in?"

"A year or so ago, he's just there one night with Greg. Greg said I knew him from the shore. I didn't remember. I still don't. But I said okay."

"Just shows up one night? You don't know where he came from?"

"No." John's eyes turned smoky, like they did when he was troubled. "You know, there's another thing. I was busy. Not paying attention. I didn't think about it." His voice trailed off. "I wasn't conning anyone anymore. So like a dope, I think no one's gonna be conning me."

When we got back to midtown, John asked me to go up to his office with him.

"Ah, success!" I said, pole-vaulting across the plush carpet on my crutches. Starting to think I felt at home in John's sumptuous office, I sat down on the couch. John picked up the phone and ordered some coffee, which was delivered in a silver pot by Jane, the blond receptionist. I felt embarrassed as she poured the coffee at the ornate round table in front of the couch. I thought she should get some coffee, too, as long as it was being poured. But she smiled just as brightly as she had when I met her, so maybe she didn't mind pouring coffee. Big John seemed not to notice her. You probably get used to this, too— pretty young women pouring you coffee—just like you get used to ragged and hungry homeless people sleeping in your doorway.

The coffee was actually good. "Maybe she could leave the pot," I suggested.

"She'll bring it back." John chuckled for a minute when he realized I was embarrassed. He bent forward to lean on his desk and shook himself gleefully. "If I push that buzzer, she'll come right back in. If I dial a couple of numbers and holler into the phone, four or five regional managers'll come running, knocking each other down in the doorway to get in first."

He looked up at the ceiling and held out his arms like Moses presenting the Ten Commandments. "None of them could hold a candle to you or me or Greg behind the stick. They were assholes when I worked for them, assholes when I worked with them, and they're assholes now that they work for me.

"And you know, Brian"—John got up from his desk and walked over to sit beside me on the couch—"what you said was true. I never forgot it for a minute. The people out on the floors who make the hotels work, the maids who run up to the nineteenth floor to make up a room for someone getting in early, the waitresses and bartenders the customers come to see—like you and me at the Dockside. Well, I can tell you for sure this fucking corporation don't give a rat's ass about any of them."

We sat for a few minutes once John finished speaking. I remembered how we used to spend time like this just talking—about everything—hour after hour, drunk or sober, hanging out on the slow afternoons while the bar back ran the bar, sitting in the dark drinking beer after closing time, driving around to half a dozen joints on our nights off. We had in those years a closeness I didn't have with anyone anymore, and I missed it.

"So," I said, leaning back into the soft couch, trying to balance my coffee cup on its saucer, then leaning forward to put it on the coffee table. When I sat back again, I sank down and couldn't reach the cup.

"So what?" asked John, who seemed quite comfortable on the couch, sitting back, resting his arm on the side of the couch.

"What's next?" I was getting irritated. I leaned forward for the cup again and felt like I was bobbing for apples.

"Take a week off, until you can use the leg again. By then, things'll be back to normal."

"I don't want a fucking week off," I shouted angrily, jumping up and causing a shooting pain in my sore leg. I had enough of the couch and the coffee table and the cup and saucer. "How the fuck do you drink coffee all bent up, with your nose touching your knees, for Christ's sake?"

John's smile was slight, just a whisper, but enough to make me smile, too. "I'm gonna have a lunch counter put in for when my friends drop by," he said.

"I need to call my service." I hobbled over to the phone on his desk. I'd left my number at the hospital in case anything happened with Ntango. But the hospital hadn't called. There was a message from Greg, though. No number. The message was that he needed to talk to me, so he'd call back. And he said to be sure not to tell anyone he'd called.

"Well?" John asked when I hung up.

I was a little flustered not telling him about Greg. But Greg said not to tell anyone, so I didn't. "Nothing. No news about Ntango. I'm gonna go to the hospital now."

John stopped me at the door, his expression somber. "You gotta watch your back, Brian."

"Thanks. I'll call you." I stopped in the doorway. "One more thing. What's going to happen with Greg?"

"You know, I've been bailing Greg out of things since he was twelve years old. Thirty years we've been partners—Butch and Sundance." John sounded like a mother who was at her wits' end because of a mischievous child. This was John's real nobility: Despite the compromises he'd made along the way, he remembered where he came from and he cared about his friends. The sentiment was genuine, too, and it went both ways. Any of us who were John's bros believed we would take a rap for him—if not any of the rest of us, certainly Greg—because he would do it for us. Big John's eyelashes drifted over his eyes; he nodded his head slowly. "Maybe Greg's taking off like that was the right thing to do." He took off his glasses; his expression changed, and he switched tracks. "You know Greg well enough. Maybe he's covering for that bar back."

This slowed me down a bit. John was right that Greg would disappear rather than rat on someone. But John had turned the tables on me. Ernesto and his *campañeros* in that burned-out hulk of a building, because they were part of my father's worldwide movement for the final triumph of the little guy, demanded loyalty, too. John's principles of loyalty, as rock-solid as they were, were personal; mine, as flabby as a damp handshake, were global—my legacy as a red-diaper baby. I didn't believe John. Ernesto was too easy a mark.

Still more or less able to read my mind, John came over and stood beside me. "Look, bro, I ain't saying Ernesto did it. I ain't saying let the guy take the fall, even if he did do it. We can take care of him, get him out of the country, back to his own country. Let him stay a few months or a year and the whole thing will blow over."

"He can't go home; they'd execute him."

"Oh?" said Big John, raising an eyebrow. He seemed impressed. "What for?"

"He's a revolutionary."

"Jesus," said Big John.

"I've got worse news. Sheehan told me that the night Aaron was killed two men came to see him—an older guy and a younger guy."

John exploded. "My old man?"

"I don't know. That's what he told me."

John took off his glasses and drew his formidable bulk into an oratorical stance that Demosthenes must have first developed. "Goddamn them!" He punctuated this with sharp forward thrusts of his head like he might be hammering in a stake with it. "Look at the stupid son of a bitch: mixed up with revolutionary bar backs, a third-rate punk for a roommate—and on top of it all, bringing my old man into the deal!"

John's expression mellowed into a look of weary resignation and his voice took on the timbre of hard-won wisdom that it often did. "Look, Brian, I don't know what Ernesto or Greg or my old man or even Walter did or didn't do. I don't give a shit, either. I told Greg someday I wouldn't be able to fix it. If I didn't have my old man to worry about, I'd let 'em all go to hell."

When I left John, I was going to take a nap. Instead, on a whim, I called Dr. Parker at the hospital. She'd given me her beeper number.

"Hi," she said brightly. "I hoped you'd call. Have you taken your medicine?"

"Shit," I said. "I forgot."

"That's okay; you'll look cute with one leg. I'm off now. What are you doing?"

As usual, I wasn't doing much, so she said she'd drive up to my neighborhood and we could have dinner. An hour later, she showed up.

"My friends told me that bartenders are corrupt," she said as we waited for twice-cooked pork and Hunan shrimp at the neighborhood sit-down Chinese restaurant. "They sleep with all their women patrons." Her sleepy expression—she'd been on call the night before—was content; her dark lashes drifted over her green-gray eyes as she spoke. I wondered if she might be innocent after all. Like that guy with a candle, I was still looking for one honest person.

"Are you innocent?" I asked.

"Hardly," she said. Her eyes opened wide for one moment. "What do you mean?"

The sordidness of the past few days passed through my mind; everything about it depressed me. I didn't like what John had become, or Greg. I didn't know what I had to do with them anymore. I didn't like my own life, either. I didn't know if I liked anyone's life very much. But, most of all, I was worried about Ntango's life. "Bartenders are corrupt," I told her. "Your friends were right." What I really wanted to do was to talk about Ntango. But I didn't know how. Because she sensed something, she kept quiet and waited, so I finally told her that a friend of mine had been shot.

She stared at the ceiling for a long moment. "I thought you were getting ready to tell me you were married." After I told her all about Ntango, she said she'd go with me when I went to look in on him and would talk to his doctors if I wanted. I said I did.

When we got to the hospital, Kevin saw me as I was entering Ntango's room and came running to meet me. "He's awake," Kevin said. "He just woke up." Very proud of himself for bringing this news, he sized up me and Dr. Parker before letting us go past him into the room. "You have to be quiet. And you can't stay long. Just say hello."

Ntango was alert and able to speak, although he slurred his words. "Brian," he said, that immense kindness sloshing around his soft brown eyes. "I'm glad to see you."

"I don't know why," I said. Along with the kindness in Ntango's eyes, there was fear that hadn't been there before. A bullet in the head wouldn't overcome his graciousness, but it could shatter his spirit.

He and Dr. Parker got along fine; I could tell he enjoyed her examining him as much I'd enjoyed her taking a bullet out of my leg. She spoke to the surgical resident on duty, and when we left Ntango's room, she told me his recovery was going great and he'd be fine.

"What now?" she asked in the hallway.

"I could go to Bay Ridge to pick up my new glasses," I told her, as if that explained my life in a nutshell. "Maybe I'll ride out to Flatbush with you and we can take Kevin home, too."

Kevin wasn't so anxious to leave, but I told him he'd done a great job, and Dr. Parker asked him questions and discussed Ntango's condition with him as if he were a consulting physician, so he felt pretty good about things when we dropped him in front of his mother's house an hour later. Dr. Parker said she'd take me out to Bay Ridge to get my glasses, so, not long afterward, we turned off Fourth Avenue onto Eighty-fourth Street in Bay Ridge just as a blue van pulled up in front of Charlie's office. Using the same purloined letter strategy Ntango and I had used the last time around, I told Dr. Parker to nestle her Volvo in among the parked cars.

The man who got out from the van's passenger side and walked toward the office looked a lot like Ernesto. There was no reason on earth to believe the man I saw was Ernesto, but I needed to make sure, so I got out of the car and hobbled up the street a little ways to where I could stand behind a tree and see him in the light of a streetlight when he came out of the office. I stood there a long while, and when I got a good look at the guy on his way back, I was sure beyond a doubt it actually was Ernesto. I debated asking him what he was doing, then thought better of it. I waited until he was back in the van and then hobbled back to the car.

Dr. Parker started the engine when I got in, but I told her to wait until the van was out of sight before she pulled out. The van, however, didn't leave immediately. The driver slid out of his parking space, stopped, then quickly reversed, until, before I knew it, I was eyeball-to-eyeball with Ernesto's pal Alberto, the guy who'd guarded Ntango's cab outside of the South Bronx tenement. The exchange lasted for no more than a second before he dropped the van into gear and sped off.

chapter eighteen

A few minutes later, I picked up my new glasses from Charlie, who spent a few minutes fitting the frames to my head. I didn't mention having seen Ernesto during this time, and neither did he. Dr. Parker dropped me at the R train stop on Eighty-sixth Street, and I rode a series of rattling, creaking, stalling-between-stations trains back to the Number 1 train stop at 110th Street. When I finally got home, I poured myself into bed. In the morning, my eyes popped open around 6:00. I tried to go back to sleep, but my eyes stayed open and my brain started running. So, around 7:30, I got up, plugged in my phone, which I had shut off the night before, and called Pop, but he wasn't home. Then, my service called with an urgent message from the night before: a message from Greg that I should come to Sea Isle City right away—it was a matter of life and death.

The message scared me enough that I decided to go, but I went to check on Ntango first. He was sitting up in a chair, groggy but content, despite his slow and slurred speech. He said he wanted to get out of the hospital and was worried about how he'd pay the bill. I told him John was going to fudge some forms and get him on the Ocean Club's health insurance plan, so he didn't have to worry about the bill. But he still wanted to get out of the hospital, so I told him I'd call Dr. Parker and ask if she could get him out.

I went back home and called John's secretary, the pretty and bubbly Jane, and gave her the information she needed to finish filling out

Ntango's forms. When I asked to speak to John, she said he wasn't available. "This is important," I said. "Tell him it's Brian."

"I'm sorry, sir, but he's at a meeting at one of the properties and left instructions not to be interrupted. I'd be happy to take a message."

I hung up.

I tried Pop and missed again. Finally, I called Dr. Parker on her beeper, and when she called back, asked her if she would go see if she could get Ntango out of the hospital. I also told her I wouldn't be around for a couple of days. My leg was feeling better, but Dr. Parker said I should use the crutches for a few more days. When I finished this call, I packed a couple of shirts, some underwear, socks, and such things, took the subway to Port Authority, and got the bus to Atlantic City, where I'd change to one for Sea Isle.

Even with an hour layover in Atlantic City, I got to Sea Isle City in the middle of the afternoon, disembarking with the assistance of a kindly old lady at a stop in front of a small grocery store deli that the driver assured me was only a couple of blocks from the address I'd gotten from Greg. I hoisted myself along a quiet block of small older houses and then a block of larger and more garish newer houses. You could date the change from a quiet working-class beach town by the size of the houses. Something happened in the early eighties that required everything built after that date to be expensive and ostentatious; there wasn't room for simple bungalows anymore.

Those few minutes of walking along the quiet, clean, and sun-drenched streets, pushed gently from behind by the prevailing ocean breeze, in the freshness and warmth of a late-summer afternoon, generated a bit of optimism even for me. Everything might work out after all, I told myself. Problems have solutions. People sometimes live happily ever after. Maybe this time Greg would explain everything. I'd go back to New York then. Ntango would recover. Maybe Dr. Parker could learn brain surgery and lobotomize me, so Ntango and I could sit quietly in the park, feeding the pigeons most days.

As I walked up the steps leading to Greg's house, a voice from the porch startled me. I jumped but recognized immediately that it was Sandra.

"Who is it?" Her voice trembled.

"Me . . . Brian McNulty. A friend of Greg's. We met last week."

"Oh yes," she said. "Thank goodness."

The fear in her voice scared me. The red alarm clanged. "Where's Greg?"

"I don't know." It was the tone of premonition one hears in the voice of a miner's wife when her husband's fellow workers show up on the doorstep.

"Why are you scared? What happened?"

"I don't know." Her voice shook. "Last night, he was in the living room; then he was gone."

She sounded shrill, and because I didn't want her to get hysterical, I tried to act calm. "Maybe he went out for a drink."

"He doesn't drink."

"Fuck," I said.

"What?"

"Nothing. Did he leave by himself?"

"No. Somebody came for him."

"How do you know?" I stood in front of Sandra's wheelchair and bent close enough to her that I was hypnotized by the terror in her eyes. She seemed to stretch up out of the chair toward me.

"Something terrible is happening," she said. Then her voice went cold. "And you know what it is. Tell me!" she screeched.

I stepped back, as if I she had shoved me. "Why do you think something's wrong?"

"He was hiding. He was afraid. He went out last night for a long time. But he came back. He didn't say he was going out again. I was sure he wasn't. But all of a sudden, he wasn't here anymore." Her voice rose as she spoke, and accusation sharpened the tone, until it was a screech again. "How can you not tell me?"

I felt like I was on one of those ancient torture devices that spread you out on the ground and then began pulling you in both directions until you either gave up or split apart. I wasn't about to tell her that Greg Whoever She Thought He Was led a distinct and separate life from the one he lived with her, that he might have committed a murder, and that he might now be murdered, murdering, or picked up by the police. This is a mouthful for a strong person on a good day—not something to tell a crippled, borderline-hysterical woman.

"I don't suppose you have a drink?"

She shook her head.

"Look," I said, shoring myself up under her withering eye. "I don't know what's going on myself, but I'll try to find out."

"Why did you come here?" Those eyes relentlessly pursued what she seemed quite sure I was hiding. "Why won't you tell me what's happening?"

To get closer, I knelt down on the wooden floor in front of her and put my hand on top of hers, where it rested on the arm of the wheelchair. "Greg called me. He wanted me to come here. But I don't know why."

Her eyes shifted from mine; the stiffness of her body slackened. "What should I do?"

"I'll look for him. Is there anyone who can stay with you?"

She shook her head. "No one I want to call. I'm okay."

I wanted to get started looking for Greg, but I didn't want to make calls from her house, where she could overhear me. I needed to talk to John. I'd noticed a small Days Inn when I got off the bus, so I hobbled back and registered for a room, since I didn't want to conduct my business from a phone booth on the corner. The first thing I did was put in a call to Big John. This time, I threatened to wring sweet Jane's pretty neck if she didn't get me through to him, so she said she'd try to reach him to see if he wanted to call me. I grumbled and fumed, but that was the best I could get. I gave her the Days Inn number. Then I made a few more calls, one to my father, who still wasn't home; one to Linda, hoping she'd help me look for Greg, but she didn't answer, either. Finally, I called Sue Gleason to see if she heard about Greg being arrested or anything worse. She offered to check the police stations along the shore to see who had been arrested, then said very quietly she could also check the hospitals and the morgues.

"By the way," she said. "I found some old news stories that you might be interested in. Should I mail them to you?"

"I don't know how long I'll be here. Hang on to them until I call you." I left her my number at the Days Inn, too. Not knowing what else to do, I went out and asked around the neighborhood: a shoe-repair store, a dry cleaner, a liquor store that was attached to banquet room–type restaurant with a large empty oak floor, and then back to the deli. No luck. I picked up a cold-cut grinder at the deli and a couple of bottles of Beck's at the liquor store and went back to my room.

When I got back, a little red light on my telephone was blinking. The message was that John Wolinski had called. I called him right back at a New Jersey 609 number. A switchboard operator answered and put me through to a secretary, who put me through to a man with a deep-voiced European accent, who begged my forgiveness for one moment.

John spoke then in his crisp businessman's voice, "Wolinski here."

"Wolinski where?"

"Brian?" He sounded impatient. "What is it? I'm in a meeting."

"Greg's missing."

"What?" John sounded even more irritated. "Where are you?"

"In Sea Isle City. Where are you?"

"Goddamn it," said John.

I explained what had happened.

John was quiet for a moment. When he spoke again, it was with the voice of a serious businessman. "You know what's going on. Maybe he had to take care of something that couldn't wait. I'll see what I can find out, but I have to finish up here. If you don't hear from me or he isn't back by dinnertime, call me again at this number."

The beers with lunch made me sleepy. I turned on the TV and found an old Peter Lorre movie, but dozed off anyway. When I woke up, the sunlight had faded and the shadows from the telephone poles along the avenue had lengthened. I walked back to Sandra's. She was sitting on the porch in her wheelchair, looking bright and hopeful when our eyes met, then darkening quickly.

"What happened?" It sounded like an accusation.

"Nothing."

"Where did you look? What did you find out?"

"Not much," I said guiltily. I didn't have the guts to tell her I'd been asleep most of the afternoon. "I checked around the neighborhood and made some calls. I sort of hoped he'd come back."

She looked sad.

"I'll look some more tonight. I think John will come over, and we'll be able to get around better with a car."

"A car?" She sounded surprised. "I saw a car pulling away from the house last night."

"What kind of car? What did it look like? Did you see the license plate number?"

She shook her head. "I don't know one car from another." She wrinkled her brow and thought for a moment. "There was something odd about the car, but I don't remember what. I can't picture it."

"Was it a cab . . . a taxi? It wasn't a red Cherokee, by any chance?"

"A what?"

"Never mind."

"I told you I don't remember."

Sandra seemed to be holding up well enough, so I went back to the motel and called John.

"I'll be there in an hour," he said, and hung up.

We agreed to meet at the Driftwood Lounge, the antiseptic-looking bar with the attached liquor store and the ship's lounge floor. When I got there this time, I found a bit of a crowd, mostly chinos and polo shirts. I ordered a shot of Jameson and a glass of water. When I'd finished the shot and ordered a second, this one mixed, I noticed out of the corner of my eye someone who was out of place. Bartenders develop this sensibility if they want to last—a kind of sonar that goes off when someone who isn't right for your bar comes in.

This guy attracted my attention as he was leaving, hurriedly. He didn't fit in because his face was darkly reddish and sharply featured, not white, like everyone else's in there. He was out the door by the time all this registered, so I followed him out into the quasi darkness and stood in a deserted intersection, watching a traffic light blinking yellow toward me and red in the other direction. A car pulled out of a space across the street, so I ran toward it. The man was by me before I got a good look. But the quick glimpse I did get confirmed my impression of a dark-skinned Hispanic with Indian features, dressed in workingman's garb.

I went back, finished my drink, and asked the bartender, a smiling, tanned, muscular young blond, if he knew the guy who'd just left. He looked blank, as if it were a surprise to him anyone had left, then shook his head—another sign the profession was going downhill.

Could Alberto or one of his pals have followed me? I tried to remember if I'd seen someone on the bus, or if anyone had been behind me on the walk to Greg's house. I should have noticed someone following me along the quiet street, but I didn't come up with anything. It was disappointing to think Ernesto—whose standing had already slipped a couple of notches—and the rest of the salt of the earth were stalking me.

A little over an hour later, Big John slid onto the bar stool next to mine. I'd been nursing Irish whiskey and water for about forty-five minutes. He ordered a double Johnnie Black on the rocks. I told him what Sandra had told me, but I didn't tell him about the guy who'd left the bar earlier. "I don't have the slightest idea where to begin looking," I confessed.

John took several sips of scotch before he said anything. He didn't look as worried as I felt, giving the impression, by his bulk and carriage and the way he had of surveying wherever he happened to be, as if he was in charge, that he would now, in fact, take charge.

"What a fucking day," John said. "The asshole manager of that Atlantic City property got himself punched by one of his bartenders last night."

I waited for John's analysis.

"He's a good bartender," John said, a barely perceptible smile around his mouth. "I told Bernard he couldn't fire him, so I spent the afternoon pretending I gave a shit whether Bernard walked out or not." John took another drink, looked around, and let himself shrink a little bit. "Actually, I would have been in big trouble if Bernard had walked out."

I didn't enjoy the story as much as I might because I was impatient and nervous. "What are we going to do?" I asked John.

He swallowed the rest of his drink, then shook his head. "What the hell are you doing here anyway?"

"Greg called me last night and told me to come here."

"Last night?" John asked. "What did he say? Why did he want to see you?"

"I don't know what he wanted. It was a message. What do you think he wanted?"

Big John shook his head, "I don't know. Maybe Sandra knows."

"She doesn't. She didn't know he called me. She doesn't know what's going on. She just saw him leave in a car."

Big John looked into his empty glass, then set it down on the bar and turned to face me. "A car? What kind of car?"

"She didn't know."

"Great," said Big John sardonically. "Never mind. Let's go."

And go we went, in Big John's Cadillac, hurtling through the night along a straight stretch of road through a thin strip of sand dunes, the bay glittering in the moonlight on one side and the ocean a stone's throw beyond the dunes on the other, until we slowed for a bend in the road and a large barnlike gin mill loomed before us, set back from the road against the bay.

The place was spacious—high ceilings, well lighted, with a wraparound bar like a corral and a few wooden tables—the kind of place you'd bring the family for fried fish or come to watch a Monday-night football game. John shook hands with the bartender, ordered a drink, as did I, and conducted a whispered conversation. Before he went for our drinks, the barman bent over and whispered something to John. They both rolled their eyes in the direction of a group of barflies at the far corner of the bar. I turned and saw an apparition: Charlie. John's face worked through variations of irritation and toughness, but his eyes smiled, too, before he walked over and swallowed the other man up in his big bear hug.

I shook hands with Charlie like we were old friends. The older man's grip was firm. His eyes danced when he looked me in the eye. Pumping my hand heartily, he put his other arm around my shoulder. He had John's sincerity and that same fullness of life that made the

room around him seem not large enough. When they were together at
the bar, everyone else receded into the background.

Charlie Wolinski, having traded in his white doctor garb for a gray
suit from another era, looked like an old-time Broadway hustler. With
his gray hair, thin gray line of a mustache, and a pale blue handkerchief
in his breast pocket, he carried himself with a kind of disreputable
suaveness. Yet, even with this reprobate style, his air of solicitousness
and charm suggested concern for someone else's comfort.

Charlie's cronies acted like they'd known John for years. John, being John, paid attention to each and every one of them with a kind of
dutiful and ritualistic politeness, which resulted in a good deal of
backslapping, hand shaking, and waving at the bartender to order a
round of drinks. Taking command, John ordered the first round for
the entire bar. Not long after this was delivered, Charlie bellied up
and ordered another round.

When things quieted and the spotlight was turned off, John said, "I
thought you'd be at the craps table at the Claridge."

"Soon," Charlie said cheerfully.

John asked his father quietly if he'd seen Greg.

The older Wolinski's smile flickered and a tiny cloud passed over
his eyes as he told John he hadn't seen him.

"What about Walter?"

No change in expression this time. The senior Wolinski was steady
on his feet.

But John wasn't easily sidetracked. "Look Charlie, what the fuck
are you doing?"

Charlie let out an audible breath. He didn't know which way to
turn; and when he turned toward me, he had the worried look of a
boy in trouble.

"Is Walter in town?" John bore down on the older man.

His father didn't answer.

John waited.

No answer.

"Were you with Greg today?" This time, John didn't wait for an answer or no answer. "Where's Walter?"

The older man's poise continued its disintegration. Sweat beaded on his forehead; he licked his lips as if they were dry, even though he'd been sipping a scotch and water. "Nothing's wrong with Greg. There's a deal going down; that's all."

John, too, sighed audibly. He raised his arms in exasperation and spoke to the ceiling. "Jesus Christ, you just can't stay away."

The senior Wolinski smiled anemically.

"Where's Greg?"

"A small house on Eightieth Street. He stays there with a woman named Sandra."

"He's not there," I said. "He left there last night with someone."

Charlie looked at me blankly. Then he looked at John. His brow wrinkled. He seemed to say something to John with his eyes but didn't speak. Nonetheless, John's brow wrinkled, and he seemed to be digesting some news.

"As far as I know, that's where he is," the older man said to me. "He left us last night to go home."

"Walter?" I asked.

"Back in New York by now. We finished last night." By now, Charlie looked almost haggard. Without his smile and the color in his face, the ravages of age showed through, making him look gray and old. When I shook hands with him before I left, he put his arm on my shoulder. "Take care of that big galoot, will you?"

Back on the road again, I asked John, "Did you know we'd find your father there?"

"I thought we might."

"Do you believe him?"

John shrugged.

We chased back through the sand dunes to a couple of joints in the neighborhood of the Driftwood where we started. In most of the places, John knew the bartender; in some places, he knew no one. But he always introduced himself, shook hands, and had a drink in each joint. I quit trying to keep up with him after the third place.

We drove on through the beach towns, stopping at neighborhood bars, soft-lighted cocktail lounges, cavernous white table-clothed, sea-side restaurants, through Stone Harbor, onto Wildwood, and into Cape May. Back to the mainland and north on Route 9, past played-out cornfields, truck gardens, and boarded-up vegetable stands, stopping at each roadside gin mill, each one with a neon-lit Budweiser or Miller sign piercing the darkness half a mile before we reached it.

Even though I knew John would rather stare steely-eyed into the darkness in front of the headlights as we hurtled from bar to bar, I felt better when he talked, so I kept asking him questions. "Why do you think Greg is still here? What do you think happened? How do you know he didn't go back to New York?"

"Just a hunch" was all John said. "I hoped I'd find him at some of the joints where we used to hang out."

As the night waned, it became clear that Big John had no more idea where Greg was than I did. But he kept on as if the sheer force of his will would find Greg. The bars were closed by the time we pulled back into Sea Isle. John was a burned-out hulk, groggy, asleep standing up, barely able to drive home from the last joint. I practically had to lug him along the second-floor cement walkway of the Days Inn to my rented room. He poured himself onto one of the beds, where he fell asleep on top of the bedspread in his Pierre Cardin suit. I lay down on top of the other bed in my Gap jeans and was asleep before I had time to think. But my sleep was restless, filled with dreams, whose ominous symbols woke me every few moments, then slipped away before I remembered what had scared me awake.

The ringing of the phone woke me. It was like a dentist drilling into a nerve. Fully alert, I sprang for it, bracing myself for the message.

It was the front desk, telling me it was checkout time.

The phone woke John also. I could tell by the suspicion in his eyes as he looked around the room that he didn't know where he was or how he'd gotten there. "What's happening, bro?" he asked tentatively.

"We got married last night," I told him.

After checking out of the motel, I left what little there was of my stuff in John's car, and we walked the couple of blocks to Sandra's.

I was trying out using only one crutch, and it worked pretty well.

Sandra opened her front door before we knocked. John shook her hand. But when I took her hand, she held on and pulled slightly, not forcefully, but gently, as if she wanted me to hug her, so I did, awkwardly, banging my elbow on the wheelchair and craning my neck to get my head next to hers. Her hair was as fine and wispy as a baby's. Her arm strong against my neck, her cheek soft against mine. I felt a stirring as I held her and my lips brushed the softness of her cheek. A feeling more powerful than I expected crackled between us and I held her longer than was proper.

When I finally let go, Big John asked her what Greg had been doing that night, right before he left, what he'd said to her, who he talked about. I guessed he was trying to find out if she knew Greg was hooked up with his old man. She didn't know much. Greg had spoken on the phone, but she didn't know to whom, nor anything he talked about. He was nervous and pacing, she said, but he didn't tell her what was bothering him. John paced the room himself as she spoke. I sat across from Sandra, wishing this hadn't happened to her. She had a gentleness and caring about her, like Saint Francis among the beasts. It didn't seem right she should suffer like this.

Back in John's Eldorado again, we headed for Atlantic City to check a couple of Greg's old haunts there. John made some calls on the way, to set up a meeting when he got to Atlantic City and another meeting that night back in New York. Finally, he called Walter at the hotel service bar where he worked. I could hear Walter's voice over the car phone, high-pitched, almost squeaking, as sleazy as ever, insisting he hadn't seen or heard from Greg. His tone was sly and wary, so you couldn't believe him if you'd wanted to. Once again, I felt the urge to wring his neck.

"Tell Walter we need to see him tonight," I told John.

John shook his head and grimaced in my direction. He was asking Walter about people Greg might see in Atlantic City.

"Tell him we'll be there tonight," I said.

John calmly questioned Walter while snarling and violently shaking his head at me, using that peculiar body English one uses only when being interrupted while on the phone.

"Tell him, goddamn it. I'll go myself. I'm going to talk to that son of a bitch."

"Where you gonna be tonight, Walter?" John asked finally, turning a baleful glance in my direction. "Well, stay there. Stay home till I come by there or call you." He hung up and turned on me. "What the fuck is the matter with you?"

"Walter's going to tell me something tonight. There's a key to all this, and Walter knows what it is."

John rolled his eyes. "Now you're a fucking psychic. Jesus, bro."

chapter nineteen

I had John call Linda for me from the car. My psychic powers suggested we go see her also. John said no, but I insisted, so he said he'd drop me off there if it was okay with Linda. He dialed the area code and numbers, then handed me the phone. Linda's voice, bubbly and enchanting when she answered, cooled considerably when I told her I was with John. She became cautious, said she had no time, but finally agreed when I told her I was the only one stopping by.

The sky was clear and blue over the coastal wetlands as I hobbled up Linda's walk. When she opened the door, she was nervous; the strain showed on her face. "Where's John?" She looked past me, as if he might be hiding behind the scrub pine in the yard. "He didn't come with you?" Satisfied that he hadn't, she calmed down, hugging me then and giving me a peck on the lips. "You, I like to see," she said cutely. "Come in." She wore cutoff dungarees and a T-shirt that draped over her breasts and didn't quite cover her midriff. Barefoot, her legs tanned golden brown, she walked like a princess, with that girlish air of unconscious and natural sexiness she'd had when I first met her. I followed like a pup dog.

When I sat down on the couch and asked how the baby was, she sat down beside me and told me that she'd finally fallen asleep after having been awake since 6:30 that morning. She talked about the baby as if she were the most pressing and important subject in the world—and perhaps she was.

I told her Greg was missing again.

"You came back to Sea Isle because Greg called you and wanted to tell you something? Now he isn't here? Maybe he went back to New York to tell you, if it was so important."

"Maybe. I'm not used to dealing with people who lead two lives. I don't know which person to look for." I recounted to Linda most of what I'd been doing since I'd seen her last, about Ntango getting shot, finding Charlie again in Sea Isle City, about Dr. Parker and I discovering a link between Charlie and Ernesto.

I thought she'd ask about Greg's double life or Ntango getting shot. But something else caught her interest. "Who is Dr. Parker?" she asked, her brows furrowed and sparks shooting from her blue eyes "You don't take long to forget me."

"I never forget you."

She smiled and blushed. Then she asked about Ntango. "The poor man. He got shot just because he was with you? Oh, Brian." Her eyes were wide with sympathy.

Taking advantage of her pity, I leaned toward her and put my hand on her shoulder. "Is there anything you haven't told me?"

She shook her head and looked away from me.

"What do you think Greg wanted to tell me?"

Linda shook her head once more. "I don't know."

"Take a guess."

She looked down at her lap. "Brian . . ." she said in the tone she probably used when the baby spilled her pabulum. "Stop trying to be like Charlie and John and Greg. You aren't like them. You could be so sweet, if you only tried."

"I thought I did try." Realizing I was whining, I went on to other things. "Why didn't you want to see John?"

"He brings back bad memories."

"What are the bad memories?"

"I'd rather not say."

Surprised by her answer, I looked at her carefully, but her expression was frank and open and fresh, as it usually was.

"Tell me more about John and his father."

"Tell you what? I could write a book. Charlie was the Duke of Sea Isle City—a celebrity, all rumors and reputation. The fastest gun in the west sort of thing. But no one knew what he did. No one ever saw him do any of the things he was rumored to do. For all any of us knew for sure, he was the village eye doctor. Everyone liked him. Even the priests. Charlie's reputation rubbed off on John, even though he never said anything about it, or tried to bully anyone because of his father. In school, he was the guy everyone thought was so tough that he never had to fight. He would break up the fights. All the guys wanted to hang out with him. All the girls wanted to date him."

"Did you know Charlie was in the rackets?"

"No one really knew. But everyone knew all the same." Linda smiled wistfully. "Sea Isle was a small town. The whole shore was a small town. I don't know how to say this—they were just there."

"Did they ever kill anyone?"

"Charlie?" Linda looked startled. "He . . ." She stumbled over the words and looked at me for help.

I tried to help. "How about Bill Green?"

The color left her face. "Don't ask me about that."

"What did Greg have to do with Charlie?"

"Greg worshiped Charlie. He would have done anything for him."

"Did he?"

Linda caught the double entendre right between the eyes. She let out a small gasp and her hand went to her mouth. I waited while she battled her snakes.

"Brian," she pleaded. "You're asking me about people I've known all my life. They are what they are. They've never hurt me. They always helped me whenever I needed them."

"Didn't John get out of the rackets? Didn't he go into the hotel business so he wouldn't be like his father?"

"John was an altar boy, an Eagle Scout, an honor student. I'm serious. He really was all those things. He won an award from the American Legion for a patriotic speech he wrote and gave at the high school. He volunteered for the navy and won medals. John did everything he could to be respectable. Except his life was different from that of all the other kids. He knew the gangsters from Philadelphia and Atlantic City. But he'd never tell you about that or even let you ask about it. And he was always one hundred percent loyal to Charlie. No matter what his father did, if Charlie needed him, he went. And Charlie needed him pretty often."

"How did Walter fit into all of this?"

"I don't remember that man . . . Walter. He could have been here. I told you before: I just don't remember him. I knew that girl Sandra, though—the girl Greg's been living with—I think. She went to high school with us." Linda sat on the couch with her legs pulled up underneath her. The upper part of her body was straight and erect, so she seemed taller, and she leaned toward me slightly when she spoke. "I liked her; she was cool. She dressed in black and wore a big silver peace symbol on a chain around her neck. She got hurt in a boating accident. A bunch of drunk high school kids in one of those big powerboats ran over her raft out in the bay."

Linda said that Sandra told the Coast Guard she was stoned, and the raft didn't have any lights or markings or whatever it was supposed to have, so she never got much money from the accident, except for her medical expenses.

"Did Sandra and Greg know each other?"

"I don't think they were friends or went out together. But if I remember right, Greg was one of the kids in the boat."

"Why in hell would she be living with a person who helped cripple her?" But when I thought about it, I began to see a possibility. Greg, as strange as he was, had a strong sense of duty: he did the right thing, though it would be the right thing by his own lights, not anyone else's. Like John, he made his own right and wrong. If Greg had been in the boat that hit Sandra, he might have tried to make up for it.

"Was John on that boat?"

Linda shook her head. "John was already out of school by then, running with the wise guys. He didn't pay any attention to high school kids."

"Except Greg?"

"Yeh, except for Greg, and whatever prom queen or cheerleader he took for a fling." Linda looked pretty when she was angry, her eyes glowing with fierceness, her mouth set hard but her lips still soft, so pretty and innocent, like a prom queen herself, but always with this fiery passion just below the surface. There was health and energy and vigor to her, and always the wild passion ever so lightly veiled. I wanted to grab her right then and wrestle all that angry energy into love, like we'd done once upon a time. Her eyes glowing, her lips wet and slightly parted and pouting, I believed she was calling me to her.

"Oh God, Linda—" I said. In spite of myself, I must have moaned, and I might have lunged for her. But she sprang up from the couch and away from me, then stood looking at me strangely and expectantly, a wild look in her eyes.

Her voice high-pitched, her face flushed, her eyes startled, she cried, "You can't come back and start this up with me again. You just can't do it. . . . I have a baby. I won't give that up. I can't. . . . This is my life now: Ralph and the baby." Her voice grew stronger, the expression in her eyes harder. "Jenny needs Ralph, too. She loves him more than anything. It would be too horrible." She got tangled up in her words and went on more slowly. "I won't let anything—nothing in the world—change it. Go away. Forget John and Greg. Leave me and my baby alone. Go away!"

She put her hands to her face and began crying in earnest, her passion in this as strong as the other passion, so that her face scrunched up, tears rolled down her cheeks, her shoulders shook, and wailing rose from her soul. When I moved toward her, she held her hands out in front of her as if to ward off a vampire. I stopped.

"I'm not asking you to give up anything," I said weakly.

"You aren't asking me to give up anything?" Her voice rose with disbelief. "You don't mean to wreck my life? But you came here. Now you come here again. You're going to ruin my life."

"No."

"Yes you are," she screamed. She sobbed into her hands, while I stood back and watched her. When she finally stopped crying, her face was a mass of red blotches where it wasn't pale, and puffy and streaked around her eyes. Her shoulders were stooped, her eyes bloodshot.

My head was whirling because I didn't know myself what I was doing there. I hadn't stopped to put together what anything meant. I just wanted to find Greg before it was too late, even though I couldn't shake the feeling that it already was too late.

"I've made so many mistakes," Linda said sadly. "I've done everything wrong. Poor Ralph doesn't deserve someone like me, a wife who doesn't even love him the way she should. If it wasn't for Jennifer, I would wish I was dead."

"There're enough dead people already," I said. "Don't say that. Everyone makes mistakes."

"Not like me."

"Sure they do. Look at the mistake I made coming here to see you."

She smiled, a thin smile, a tiny light in her eyes. "Oh, Brian, so much has happened, so much I wish was different. But it would have had to happen years ago, and it didn't." The smile went away; her eyes glistened with sadness. The chasm between us opened wider with each passing second. We smiled at each other, embarrassed; we'd run out of things to say.

Linda came over and took my hand in hers. "What are you going to do now?"

"I need to make a couple of calls, then hook up with John. Can I use your phone?"

The first call I made produced all the news I needed. It was to Sue Gleason. She told me the police were at that moment digging up what they expected to be a body in an abandoned landfill in Strathmere.

"Where's Strathmere?"

"Near Sea Isle. It's the upper part of the same island. An old man walking his dog this morning found what they think is a grave. It wasn't there two days ago." Her voice dropped into a meaningful yet jaded reporter's tone. "That's not the only reason I suspect it might be your friend. These news clips here that I've been saving for you . . . Maybe you ought to come take a look at them. Can you get over here now?"

"Yeah, I'll be right there." My heart had gone cold in my chest. I'm sure what little color there'd been in my face had drained completely out of it.

"What is it?" Linda asked, clutching at me.

"They may have found Greg's body. I've got to call John. I need a ride to the *Journal* office."

"Don't call John." Linda began scurrying around and ran to get her daughter. "I'll take you. Ralph will be home any minute. Here, hold Jenny." She lifted and pushed the baby toward me, then dashed off down the hallway.

So I held Jennifer, who was as light as a pillow. She squirmed this way and that to get a better view, looking me in the eye, reaching out to grab a tiny fistful of my hair, hanging on to it like a bulldog. When her father came through the door a few minutes later, he didn't take any more notice of me than if I were the plant stand; totally enchanted, he reached for the baby. But once he had her in his arms, he turned on me, hate burning in his eyes.

"What are you doing here?" he asked in a tone usually used to say, "Get the fuck out of here or I'll kill you."

"It's a long story," I said, hoping Linda would get back, so I wouldn't have to tell it.

She did. But Ralph wasn't pleased to see her, either.

"I'm going to Strathmere with Brian," she said, either not noticing or ignoring his fury on purpose.

"No, you're not," said Ralph, surprising us both. "All that's over. I told you to stay away from them."

Something in his voice—probably murderous rage—scared the baby, so she began screaming. Linda reached for her, and after a bit of a tussle, during which the baby's screams reached an earsplitting crescendo, Ralph reluctantly let her go to her mother.

As soon as he let go, he turned on me. "Are you leaving?" he asked. But once more it wasn't a question.

I held up my hands in a placating gesture. More was going on here than met the eye. For reasons of his own, Ralph had decided to make a stand; this was the defining moment for him and his family: wife and baby were at stake. I tried to tell him without actually saying so that this wasn't a romantic tryst—though, if the truth were known, through no fault of my own. "Take it easy, Ralph," I said in the tone I used to calm belligerent drunks, though Ralph was sober as a judge—just momentarily insane. "There's a good chance that Greg's dead, that he's been killed; that's why Linda's taking me to where the cops are digging up a body."

"Good," said Ralph with an uncharacteristic snort. "I hope they find Wolinski buried beside him."

"Don't be an asshole, Ralph," Linda said, her voice not at all soothing.

"You're not going." Ralph's hands were balled into fists, probably more from frustration than menace. But when he made a move toward her, I put my hand on his shoulder to stop him and calm him. Instead, my gesture popped his cork. He swung one of the balled-up fists in a roundhouse that glanced off the side of my head, just above my left ear.

More to keep from putting too much weight on my damaged leg than anything else, I grabbed for him. In this case, the easiest handle was his almost shoulder-length hair, so I grabbed it, but I lost my balance anyway. Rather than put my full weight on the game leg to catch myself, I hung on to his mane and took him to the ground with me.

Linda screamed, and this time the baby really kicked out the jambs, raising a wail that pierced the heavens. Ralph too was screaming bloody murder because I'd yanked out a fistful of his hair, and I screamed right back at him. "Get off my leg, you asshole!"

Since I managed to get back on top and had a good hold on another clump of his hair, and since Ralph seemed genuinely concerned about the baby, whose screams were now alternating with hiccups, he quieted, so I let him up. He and Linda stared at each other for a long minute as the baby quieted to sniffles and hiccups, and after a few moments of heavy breathing by all concerned Linda handed Jenny to him.

"I'm taking Brian to Strathmere," she said.

Ralph tried to glare at her, but since he wasn't much of a fighter to begin with, his one punch and its aftermath had pretty much knocked the fight out of him.

As Linda and I drove away from her house, there was a strained silence. She seemed shaken to the verge of tears by what had happened, while I still had a good deal of adrenaline pumping through me, and neither of us knew quite what to say. I felt like Ralph had caught us in the sack, and he, it seemed, had the same impression.

"Ralph didn't seem in a very good mood," I said finally. "Is he always that grouchy when he gets home from work?"

Linda looked over at me and with some effort managed a tiny smile. "Poor Ralph" was all she said.

I decided to leave it at that. I'd blundered around in their life too much as it was. They deserved to be left alone to work out whatever it was between them—among them, I guess, would be more accurate, since the tyke seemed to have something to say about things, too.

Linda seemed to want to move on to other things also, because after a few blocks she said, "You know, even though I said all those things about Charlie, he wasn't so nice, really, and most of all, he wasn't so nice to John. Charlie always talked big about how John was going to be a success. But he never did anything to help him. He was sort of a phony.

"He never said he wanted John to be like him—and John didn't want to be like him—but I think Charlie really did. John wanted more than anything to be respected for doing good, like a judge or something, and he could have gone to college. He could have gotten a scholarship to go to NYU. But he needed his father to come up with part of the money, and Charlie didn't do it.

"All of us wanted John to go. We told him, 'Screw Charlie.' But you never could tell John anything about his father. John decided college was a stupid idea and he didn't need it." Linda turned to me, bewildered and angry. "Why would he worship Charlie? The only things Charlie did for anyone, John included, were things that didn't cost him anything. Even for his own son, he'd only do the things that didn't cost him anything. Why would he worship Charlie?"

The late-afternoon breeze off the ocean blew in through the car window. We drove past hotels that rose garishly into the blue-gray wash of sky above the ocean. The shore was a pleasant place as afternoon became evening. I knew about fathers and sons. I had one of each. "Charlie's the only father he had," I told her.

Linda waited in the car when we got to the newspaper office. Sue Gleason had gone to cover a story, but she'd left the news clips in a manila envelope with my name on it. When I got back to Linda's car, I opened the envelope and took out the photocopies of the articles. The first one was dated June 18, 1975. It told of a man's body being discovered buried in a garbage dump in a town called Strathmere. The next article, from the following day's paper, said the body found in the Strathmere dump had been identified as that of David Bradley of Atlantic City, who appeared to have died of a heroin overdose, and that the police were investigating.

Another article, dated July 30 of the same year, reported that the body of a man, identified as William Green, had been discovered in the Strathmere dump. He'd died from a stab wound to the chest. A note from Sue Gleason said that there was only one dump in Strathmere—the one where the police were digging up a body right now. Sue's note also said that the police listed the Green case as open and unsolved, and while the newspaper articles didn't make any connection between the two deaths, she'd been told the police had found the first body on a tip and the second body when one of the investigators went back to the dump looking for evidence.

"Why did you get these?" Linda demanded when she had read the articles.

"Do you remember?"

Linda stared in front of her while I pulled from my memory's foggy ruins a dim vision of my younger—and considerably slimmer—self, wearing a bartender's white jacket, standing at the bar in the semi-darkness of after hours with pert, lovely young Linda. She wore her waitress's short-shorts, sailor suit that accentuated the contours of her adorable ass, and was talking to me in that absolutely sincere way she had that made the rest of the world disappear while I listened to her. Her hand was on top of mine and her bare leg pressed against me. We were waiting for Greg and John, who were holding a private conversation in the liquor room.

They were taking care of whatever serious and important business they were often about and that I paid little attention to, especially when the alternative was rubbing my hand along the soft nether down of Linda's thigh. I was particularly impatient this time because it was the night after Linda and I had slept together for the first time, and I really really wanted to do it again. That night, we'd heard about Bill Green's body being found. Greg had come in earlier and waited while John finished cashing out. He stood at the end of the service bar with us for what seemed like an hour, looking stricken, until John whisked him off into the liquor room.

Now, years later, Linda and I sat trancelike in her little car. "The night they found Bill Green's body . . . do you remember?" I asked again. "Did you think Greg killed him?"

Linda clutched the steering wheel and nodded very slowly. Then she let go of the wheel, adjusted herself in the seat to face me, and kind of cocked her head to the side. "I thought you knew, but I guess you were still too new. We made up a story to cover everyone—for the time when Bill Green was killed."

"Who made up the story?"

"John."

"Who else was in on it?"

"I don't remember. . . . Everyone, I guess, or everyone who needed to be—waitresses, bar boys, busboys."

"Charlie?"

"She nodded.

"And Aaron wasn't?"

She hesitated, her expression beseeching. "Maybe he was. . . . I don't know. Maybe they needed him because he was the boss and all. Everyone was just helping John and Greg." She reached toward me, her eyes filled with that sincerity again. "We didn't know what they did. We were just helping them, like they would have helped us." She laid her hand gently on my arm; her eyes locked onto mine. "John and Greg weren't murderers, Brian. They wouldn't hurt anyone if they could help it. You would have helped them, too." She took my hand; her eyes glistened. "Besides, I wasn't interested in what they were doing. I was paying attention to you. I thought I'd met the man I was going to love for the rest of my life." She smiled, and her smile was sadder than her tears had been.

"Will you take me to Strathmere?"

"Why? Can't you forget about all this? It's going to get worse and worse."

I didn't answer.

Linda shrank up into herself, as if she were shivering. "No," she said. "You won't forget about it. That was part of what I knew about you."

chapter twenty

Linda drove quickly out of Atlantic City, then south on the Garden State Parkway. The sun sank toward the horizon on the inland side of us, its rays of purple, orange, and pink splayed out against the horizon. The air was brisk and fresh from the prevailing winds. It was that kind of gorgeous late-summer, early-fall afternoon when every breath you took brought with it vague and unexpected joy. It wasn't the sort of day to look for a body in the Strathmere garbage dump.

"I don't want to do this," I said. "I must be nuts."

Linda had been stone-faced since we left Atlantic City. Whatever had come over her took away her girlish charm. Sitting rigidly straight, gripping the steering wheel with both hands, she looked possessed. Soon we were driving along the same narrow, sloping blacktop road through the dunes that John had taken the night before when we were looking for Greg. It felt and looked like an old country lane. The houses, which were only on one side of the road because the ocean was so close on the other side, were small lopsided wooden bungalows, this finger of land, a few feet higher than the bay on one side, the ocean held back by dunes on the other side, yet to be discovered by the prosperous and garish.

We turned onto a dirt road that led into the tall marsh grass between two matching weathered shacks. At the end of the road, backed in against the bay, mounds of unidentifiable debris rose like hills, but not as markedly as the stench. It smelled like the Staten Island landfill and looked like it, too, with a hundred seagulls parading on and hovering over the place.

Linda looked like she was waking from a nightmare. "God, this is awful. It's horrible." She glared at me accusingly, opened her door, and stepped out. I followed suit, stepping onto the spongy, speckled brown dirt. It looked like all of the eggshells ever eaten in New Jersey had been ground up and spread over the dump. My crutch sank into the ground and got stuck, so I put it back in the car and took my chances limping after Linda.

An ambulance and three or four cop cars, their lights flashing meaninglessly, were parked ahead of us. EMS medics, uniformed cops, and some plainclothes cops were gathered around a pile of twisted and rusted hunks of metal, ancient appliances, large wooden crates, and splintered skids. There were scrape marks on the ground where a stove or an old washing machine had been dragged across it. A section of dirt nearby looked freshly turned over. Two cops were digging and the rest were watching. They all looked up when we drove in. But they were intent on the digging or watching the digging, so no one came immediately to intercept us.

I could see a body that was partially buried, and I tried to pretend it wasn't Greg. But I recognized the top of his head, even though his face was still covered with dirt. My chest tightened up; I couldn't catch my breath. Linda screamed and grabbed at my arms as I stumbled toward the body. The nearest cop tried to grab me, but I got by him, despite my stumbling gait. Slicing my hand on the edge of the stove, I used my arms to vault past him, dragging Linda with me. I looked down and saw my own blood on my hand and on Linda's T-shirt. Her face stained with tears and dirt. She was saying, "Stop," as she must have been all along without my hearing her. "Stop," she said again. "What are you doing?"

"Greg's in there," I screamed at her. He was dead. I knew that, but I wanted the cops to dig him out because I felt like he was smothering. "He's my friend," I tried to explain to the cop who came to grab me.

After some effort, Linda calmed me and the cops down, so they let us stand together near her car, watching the rest of the excavation. The guy in charge was the jaded, retired New York cop John had argued with when we sprung Ntango and Bub. I'm sure he liked bodies buried in his dump even less than he liked people of color driving his streets at night. I expected he might have a question or two for me.

Linda continued to cry, her head pressed against my chest for a few minutes as we leaned together against the front fender of her car. I kept my arm around her shoulder. My other hand, wrapped in a clean cloth diaper from her car, began throbbing, but the bleeding stopped. I thought about Greg and his two lives. In the end, they didn't make any more or less sense than what one life added up to. He'd fought the chaos by his order and neatness in physical things—the way he dressed, the way he set up the bar, the methodical way he worked— and by some strong personal belief in right and wrong that made him loyal to his friends and led him, I guessed, to the life he had led with Sandra. But the chaos caught up with him anyway; he'd ended up murdered and buried in a garbage heap.

The police captain, whose name was Carney, was brusquely polite and clearly suspicious. I told him a long story about Sandra calling to ask me to look for Greg, a reporter friend of mine telling me about the police finding a body, and how, fearing the worst, we'd come to find out. I told him who the body was, using the name Peters.

"Do you know who would want to kill him?"

I shook my head.

"What can you tell me about him?"

"Not much," I said. "I hadn't seen him in years until a week or so ago." I gave a true, if somewhat abbreviated, account of what I knew of Greg's life. As soon as the police began checking on Greg, they would be back anyway, so I didn't want to waste time now.

The captain surveyed the dump and the bay beyond. The sun was in full decline, moments away from dropping beyond the horizon. "I'm going to need to ask you a few more questions," the captain said.

I nodded.

"Do you have a local address and phone number?"

I gave him the hotel number John had given me, answered a few more questions, and then Linda drove me to the bar I'd seen Charlie in the night before. I called John to tell him we'd found Greg. His response was a long silence. After a while, he said, "Say good-bye for me when they take him away, bro."

"I'm sorry."

"It's a bleak fucking life, ain't it?" Then after another silence, he said, "You better go tell Sandra."

"Me?"

"It should be one of us . . . one of his friends."

"What about you?"

"I gotta finish something here; then I'll try to make some arrangements. You need to handle this, bro."

"I can't believe how awful everything is," Linda said as we drove away from the bar after a stiff drink. She dropped me off at a liquor store a few blocks from the street Sandra lived on, refusing to come with me because she wanted to get back to her baby and Ralph. I picked up a fifth of Rémy Martin and managed to hobble to Sandra's house, leaning on the crutch, carrying the fifth. The steady breeze off the ocean died down as the sun sunk beneath the bay. It was a pleasant evening, with a hint of chill in the air. I had no idea at all what would comfort Sandra.

She opened the door as soon as I knocked, wheeled herself back from it, and looked at me with accusation in her eyes.

"I'm sorry," I said. "Greg's dead."

"I knew it." Her expression didn't change.

I had nothing else to say. I might still be standing in that doorway if she hadn't recovered her senses and told me to come in.

Moving forward seemed to unlock my brain. "I have some brandy. It would be good for you to drink some." She nodded, so I went to the kitchen and poured some into teacups. When I returned, she was at the entry to the living room. I put the drinks on the coffee table and, more decisively than I do most things, went over and lifted her out of her wheelchair and carried her, with her arms around my neck, to the couch. I sat down beside her. For a little while, we didn't talk. After she took a few sips of her brandy, she slipped her hand into mine. We sat there like that. At one point, I asked if I should call someone to stay with her. She said no. So I stayed.

"I do want to know what happened," Sandra said after another long lapse. "Just not yet." When she looked at me, her eyes were moist and sad and apologetic. "You don't have to stay."

"I want to."

"I want you to, too." She squeezed my hand and began to cry.

After maybe an hour, I began to feel light-headed and remembered the last time I'd eaten was a sandwich at the motel the afternoon before. I walked to the market near the liquor store, where I bought a couple of steaks, potato chips, lettuce, and fresh Jersey tomatoes. Back at Sandra's house, I grilled the steaks in a frying pan, washed the lettuce, sliced the tomatoes, and made up plates for both of us.

"I don't think I can eat," Sandra said when I presented her plate.

"You gotta eat," I said. I had no trouble myself. She took a few bites of the steak, ate the salad, then gave the rest of her steak to me.

"I'm ready now," she said. Some color was back in her face. Her eyes were clear, her chin up. "You can tell me what happened."

"He was murdered. They found his body."

"Where?"

I couldn't tell her the dump, so I said, "In some marsh grass on the road to Strathmere."

"How was he killed?"

"I'm not sure. The cops think he was stabbed."

It took a few minutes for her to take this in. Then she faced me unblinkingly. "Now you can tell me what you wouldn't before," she said firmly but not unkindly.

"It wouldn't have helped if I told you before."

She nodded.

Maybe I was supposed to protect her from the truth. But I didn't think it was up to me. I told her everything that had happened, from the phone call Greg made to the Sheraton almost two weeks ago to the present, about Greg's jobs in New York, Aaron's murder, the connection to Charlie and Walter, and the deaths of Dave Bradley and Bill Green many years before.

Her expression didn't change throughout all this, so that by looking at her, I wouldn't even have known if she'd heard me. I didn't try
to explain anything, just straight out told her. When I finished, we sat
together again in another long silence.

"God, to be this close to someone who did all that and not know
anything about it." She shuddered. "To have so many buried secrets.
Poor Greg. I guess I never knew him at all."

I guessed I didn't, either. Greg was a good pal, if he liked you, loyal
and generous. But he was cold, too, not someone you'd grab in a bear
hug. He never lit up a place when he arrived like John did. But then, I
don't suppose I brightened up very many places myself.

"I don't even know what he felt about me." Sandra's tone was
quizzical, rather than sad. "For the first time, I'm wondering now what
my life with Greg was all about. . . . Isn't that strange? Greg was with
me for ten years, and I never wondered why he stayed with me."

I watched her carefully because her calmness seemed unreal to me,
like the flat, dead air in front of a storm. Her voice tightened as she
spoke, and rose in pitch. I expected the look in her eyes to go wild any
second and for her to begin shaking and writhing in hysteria. I took
a strong slug of cognac to brace myself. But she stayed calm.

"I'm actually glad he had another life, though I'm sorry it led him to
this. His life with me was so impersonal. In a strange way, I feel closer
to you than I ever felt to Greg." Her expression was fixed and staring.
"I can't stand the idea of his being lifeless and stuffed in the ground."

Something, I guess, did snap, or perhaps just loosened—maybe the
cognac took hold—because her words began pouring out. She talked
about her whole life from the time of the accident till now. Greg had
begun coming to see her right after the accident. So he must have been
involved with her even back when we worked together at the Dockside.

"Didn't you know he was a bartender then?" I asked her.

"I was so self-absorbed for so long after that accident, I didn't notice or care what anybody did. Greg came to the hospital. I knew him
a little bit from school, but he wasn't one of my friends, just a quiet
kid, a little bit odd, not much interested in school. At first, after the
accident, a lot of kids came to see me. They had car washes and dances

to raise money for me. Gradually that all stopped. But Greg kept coming. He became indispensable. I was hateful, vicious, mean to everyone, especially my family, who I hated even before the accident. Greg put up with me. He took the place of my brother, who joined the navy, and my mother, who couldn't cope with a teenage daughter, much less a crippled teenager. Greg was there, always there, whenever I needed him. He helped me find this place, helped me move in, and then he moved in, too—at least for some of the time."

"But why the secrecy? Why did he never tell any of us about you—not even John?"

Sandra didn't know the answer to this. But as I asked her, I suspected I did. Big John took up too much room in Greg's life. John needed people around him and he was great to be around—generous, loyal, funny, considerate. Wherever he was going, he'd take you with him. John didn't like to go anywhere or do anything alone; he needed his bros. You were amply rewarded for being with him. He attracted women; he had friends or made friends everywhere, so you were always welcome and always the center of a good time. But there was a price to pay. Whatever you did, you did on John's terms. John didn't share top billing. So, the way I figured it, Greg needed to get out from under. But he couldn't completely break like I had. He needed John as much as John needed him. When I looked back now to our time together in Atlantic City, I remembered Greg's attempts at finding his own life—the gin joints he took me to, some folks he introduced me to who didn't know John. He often said, "There's someone you gotta meet—someone you'd really like." And I wondered now if one of those persons might have been Sandra but the right time never came for me to meet her.

"So that's what it's been?" I asked. "You didn't wonder where he went or what he did when he was away from here? You didn't mind him being away?"

I was drawn to look into her eyes that were brown and soft, but also turbulent and exciting. "It wasn't the sort of relationship you might think," she said. "I don't know how to say this. I'm sure it's as awful as it sounds. I didn't love Greg. He took care of me, and I needed him very much, and I was very grateful to him. But I never got close to

him at all. It was like I was a wealthy woman and he was my servant."
Her eyelashes veiled her eyes, and her cheeks flushed. "We never made
love," she said quietly. "Sex never came up—I guess he didn't think of
me that way, or he just thought I couldn't do it or wouldn't care, and
for a long time I didn't care or wouldn't do it, and that's how our relationship evolved. I loved him, but like a brother, I guess—and I think
I was like a child to him, someone to take care of."

When she told me all this, a peculiar and inappropriate question
presented itself to me, which I realized had been lurking in my addled
brain all along. I wondered if she could make love—and if she could,
how. Maybe the brandy. Maybe my warped need to desecrate propriety.
More likely, though, it was those beautiful brown eyes, the warmth and
the kindness in them. I wanted to make love with Sandra. I wanted to
go to bed and hold her. I had since the first time I looked in her eyes.
But now? How could I possibly think about this now?

Before she'd told me all this, I'd recognized I was attracted to her.
The feeling since the first time I'd seen her had been so strong as to be
illicit—enough to make an alley cat feel guilty. My friend dead, and
me coveting his wife, or the person I thought was his wife. She had
this openness to life, like Linda, where she accepted her feelings, let
them live even if they were sensual, sexual—maybe illicit—not afraid
of her emotions. I liked Sandra. I liked how I felt sitting next to her. I
wanted to touch her. What I felt about her and maybe from her was
emotional and physical.

When I looked at her again, tears trickled down her cheeks and her
eyes were liquid. "I would have," she said. "But he didn't want to. He
was so cold that way, like a stone statue."

I took her in my arms and held her, my face against her tear-stained
face, until I felt her rising in me. Then I kissed her on the lips, and her
lips pulled against mine and her hands caressed the back of my neck
as gently as feathers.

"You're a strange man, Mr. McNulty," she whispered. "Please don't
let go of me until I tell you it's okay."

We clung to each other for hours on her couch while the flat color
of the evening light changed to darkness.

"I want to lie down in my bed with you," Sandra whispered.

I had felt a plastic bag like an IV bag against her body while we sat together on the couch. She told me it was for urine. When she got off the couch, she wheeled herself to the bathroom. When she joined me in the bedroom, she'd taken off her pants, and when she raised herself out of the wheelchair and onto the bed, she put the bag, which was empty, on the floor under the bed. She did it discreetly, like a woman might put in a diaphragm, not exactly hiding her action, but doing it in such a way that even if it didn't escape notice, it might at least escape comment. There was still a tube coming from under her underpants. I watched the whole process more intently than might be proper, so she laughed at me.

"Does it come out?" I asked.

"No, the tubes stay in."

She loosened her hair from the clips that had held it back, so that the hair, long and thick and sparkling and brown, flowed luxuriously over the pillow as she lay back. Smiling like a Madonna, gentle and sad, she said, "I want you to lie with me and hug me. I don't know if I want to make love with you."

"Do the tubes bother people?" I asked.

"Do they bother you?"

"No," I said warily.

We held each other again in her bed, naked now. She patted one of her legs, which was thin and withered, and said, "This one never came back."

I touched her and felt where the tube entered her and just below it the opening to her vagina, which was moist as I touched it. Master of the bon mot, I asked if she felt anything.

"Mmm," she said, putting her hand on top of mine where it rested against her. "You must think I'm awful to do this now."

"No." I started to say I understood, then realized that I really didn't.

Sandra squeezed my hand. "I'm really afraid. . . . I need to be close to you tonight. It's been so very long since I've been close to anyone." She cried again, so I held her. She cried for a long time, and emotions being the confused things that they are, the sorrow became something else. We kissed for a long time, each kiss as gentle as the first one. And then she took my cock in her hand and held it. "Please come inside me," she said. "Come very gently inside me, please." So I did, sliding gently into her wetness, and though she lay still, her hips unmoving, inside her was alive and wet and burning hot. I moved gently inside her for a long time until she came, and when she did, I came, too. She moaned and writhed, the upper part of her body moving, and when she came again, she screamed in anguish or ecstasy—I wasn't sure which. But gasping and moaning she came in waves, and when she had finished, she cried and cried, as if she would never stop.

I held her head against my chest until she fell asleep, and then I did also, sleeping restlessly until I heard banging in the distance and realized it was finally morning and someone was at the door. I sprang from the bed, ready to go out the window, pants in hand. But Sandra calmed me. "Who could it be?" she asked. "Who could it be who would care?"

Who indeed? At the door, his eyes alert behind his glasses, his quick glance from me to the bedroom door letting me know he knew I'd just gotten out of the sack with Sandra but not whether he cared or not, laden down with bagels and cream cheese, doughnuts, and a restaurant-sized thermos of coffee, properly somber and appropriately attired, stood Big John there in the doorway. "I thought Sandra might need something," he said.

"What I need is company," said Sandra, wheeling up behind me. She'd gotten herself into a robe and into the wheelchair and looked less disheveled than I did.

"I can't stay," John said, then looked at me and at her again and came in.

chapter twenty-one

As we talked over coffee and bagels, John did most of
the remembering, beginning with when he and Greg
were kids playing baseball and Greg stood his ground against the first
baseman twice his size.

"What about Greg's family?" Sandra asked.

"There's only his father, and he's in a nursing home," John said.

"What about a funeral?"

"I'm going to arrange for him to be cremated and his ashes thrown
in the ocean. That's what he'd want."

"How do you know?" I asked.

"I know." John's tone was sharp, as if I doubted him. He didn't
like being challenged, but he caught himself, shrugged his shoulders,
and kind of shook himself back into his rightful place as chief
mourner.

There was an uncomfortable moment and then Sandra spoke.
"Who could have done this?" She shifted her gaze from John to me.
"Why would someone kill Greg?" Now we both looked at John.

John shook his head. "It must be Greg was doing somethin' none
of us knew about. . . . But we'll find out who. We'll take care of it."

Part of this wasn't exactly true, as John and I knew some things
Greg was doing—and whom he was doing them with. John didn't
know I'd told Sandra about Charlie. Rather than bring it up now, I
took my lead from Sandra. If she didn't bring it up, I wouldn't.

"We were bros," John said. "back-to-back. You never believe your bro will die like that." He watched Sandra, as if he expected her to do or say something, as did I. But she didn't; she closed her eyes. "What was Greg like these last few days?" John asked when she didn't say anything. "Was he scared? Did he say what was botherin' him?"

Sandra opened her eyes. "No. He wasn't afraid. Looking back, I get the feeling he'd accepted his fate, as if he'd been told by a doctor he hadn't long to live."

"What'd he talk about?" John asked her. There was toughness to his tone that I didn't like—as if he was accusing Sandra of something.

Sandra caught it, too, and her answer sounded as tough as John's question. "He said, 'What goes around comes around.' "

I didn't like how the conversation was going. Maybe John was mad at Sandra for sleeping with me—saw her as betraying Greg. I could see why he'd think that, but I wanted him to stop pressing her. So I tried to get him started in a different direction. I turned to Sandra. "Do you still not remember the car you saw Greg leaving in? Did you ever see a red Cherokee parked on the street or passing the house?"

She looked confused. "A what?"

"Whatever went around, in Greg's case, came back in a car," I told John.

Big John, his brow wrinkled, took the bait.

"A red Cherokee," I said patiently. "It's like a cross between a car and a van and maybe a jeep." Sandra tilted her head, as if she hadn't quite heard me right. "And it's red," I said testily. "Sort of boxy . . ." I glowered at her as she continued to look at me quizzically. "Like a station wagon. . . . It fucking says Cherokee on it," I said, raising my voice.

Sandra listened with some concern, then shook her head. "I don't remember. I told you that I can't tell one kind of car from another."

Before I got myself in any deeper, John raised an eyebrow and gave me a meaningful look to warn me that I was scaring her, so I backed off.

But Sandra wasn't having any of it. "Who has a red Cherokee?"

"I don't know," I said. "Forget it."

"You wouldn't have brought it up for no reason."

I looked to John for help. He gave me that "You fucked up again" look, then tried to rescue me. "Brian got jumped last weekend by some goons. He's wondering if they might have been the ones who killed Greg."

"Might they have?"

"I don't know. Neither does Brian."

Something in Sandra's bearing changed, a new level of sharpness, as if she suspected she was being had. "I understand that both of you are somehow involved in Greg's death." She looked from John to me and back to John.

"I already told you—" I said.

John looked at her as hard as she looked at him. He didn't owe her or anyone an explanation. After the standoff, he stood and looked down at her. "I'll let you know as soon as they finish with the autopsy. . . . You coming?" he asked me.

I looked at Sandra. She nodded her head slowly, her expression tired and sad. I kissed her on the cheek. She put her small, cool hand at the back of my neck while she held her face against mine.

As soon as we were out the door and had reached the end of the walk, John lit into me. "What the hell is with you?"

The rebuke stung, coming at me sharply out of nowhere, like a slap. Thinking he was talking about me taking Sandra to bed, I began to stammer an explanation, beginning with the age-old "It's not what you think."

But John shook his head and waved me off. "Jeez, bro," he said sadly. "You didn't have to start tellin' her everything about Greg. What good's it for her to know all the crap that's been goin' on?"

Before I could tell John what I'd really told Sandra, he started the Eldorado and prepared to pull out of his parking spot, and I saw that Sandra had wheeled herself out onto the porch of her house.

I opened the window and hollered to her, asking when I would see her again.

"Call me," she said.

"I will . . . When should . . . ," I yelled as we were pulling away.

She had a strange expression on her face, watching us pull away. I guess she didn't hear me.

"Forget all that," John said. "Right now, we're about to get pulled over." The police cruiser was beside us before I could turn to look.

"Mr. McNulty?" the policeman on John's side asked politely. The other cop stood behind and off to my side of the car, his holster unbuckled and his hand on his gun. I got out of the car.

"We'd like you to follow us to police headquarters, please," the first cop said.

Trying to keep John from getting hauled in, too, I said, "I'm McNulty. I'll ride with you." The cops looked at each other. "Some identification, please," the cop said to John, who showed him a license. "You don't want to drive to headquarters?"

"No," John said. "But I'll be back in a half hour with a lawyer for Mr. McNulty."

The cop waved a hand good-naturedly. "Nothing like that. Just a couple of questions. He won't need a lawyer."

John didn't share the cop's good humor. In fact, when John's narrowed eyes and piercing stare settled on the cop's face, the man snapped to attention like an enlisted man being called to task for taking liberties with the captain. John turned to me. "Wait till I get there before you talk to them."

I nodded and walked to the police car. The cop stopped me. "It's just a formality. But I have to frisk you before you get in the car."

At least this time I was clean. Nonetheless, this was my third involuntary ride to the cop shop in the last ten days; I was obviously doing something wrong. As I ducked into the backseat of the cruiser, I caught a glimpse of John staring at me.

At the police station, I was led into a room with fluorescent lights, a linoleum tile floor, blank green walls, and a blond wooden table. We didn't stop at the desk, nor did anything suggest they wanted to book me. The young cops, their thick chests and lumpy arm muscles bulging through their blue short-sleeved shirts, were relaxed and polite. Carney, the white-haired, red-faced captain I'd already met too many times, came into the room a few seconds after I sat down on one of the straight-backed wooden chairs. He was stuffed into a puke green summer suit, whose pants fit too tightly against his thighs and stopped just below his ankles. He sat down across from me.

With his eyes locked on mine, he said in a more pronounced New York City accent than I'd heard him use before, "You're beginning to be a suspicious character."

"I haven't done anything," I said pleasantly. But I was nervous. I'd been grilled before by cops and had always done poorly under interrogation. For some reason, cops immediately suspect I'm guilty, even when I'm not. What's worse, I usually begin to doubt my innocence also. This guy was no slouch, even if this was a hick town; already, I was beginning to suspect myself.

"So why don't you just tell me." The captain settled back in his chair, trying to cross his legs but getting hung up because of the tight fit of his pants. This irritated him, and I could see in his face that he would take this irritation out on me.

I slouched down in my chair as I thought befit a suspected felon. "Ask whatever you want," I said. "I don't have anything to hide." But as soon as the words were out of my mouth, I remembered John had told me to wait for the lawyer before I said anything.

Taking me at my word, the cop asked, "Why were you at the dump?"

"I'm not going to answer any questions without a lawyer," I said.

He winced, then glared at me. "Asshole," he said under his breath as he got up and left the room.

I stared at the blank walls for almost an hour before John and the chief of police showed up. The chief pumped my hand like I was a long-lost relative and called the captain aside.

"Let's go," John said while the chief and the captain talked.

"That's it?"

When I started for the door, Captain Carney began to protest, but the chief waved him off. "It can wait," the chief said. "You've got enough to keep you busy."

The captain looked disgusted. "Don't leave town," he said to me.

"I beg your pardon," John said to the captain.

"I want to be able to reach him," the captain replied.

"You can reach him through me."

We all looked at the chief, who nodded, and the captain stomped away.

As we walked through the glass doors toward the street, I held myself back from making a break for it. John's pace was sprightly enough, but every nerve in my body urged me to run.

We didn't talk again until we hit the Garden State Parkway. When we hit the first tollbooth, John turned to me, as if he'd been pondering something. "How'd you know they'd find his body in that dump?"

"A friend of my father's called me when she heard it on the police scanner." I steeled myself. "She also gave me some old newspaper articles. David Bradley was buried in that dump; so was Bill Green."

John nodded. "I thought of that, too, as soon as you called. Bill Green buried David's body there fifteen years ago; then someone dug a hole for him, too. Now Greg. Strange stuff."

Taking a deep breath, I dove in. "Maybe it was Greg who dug the hole for David Bradley."

John's mouth went square and he hunched his shoulders a couple of times, like he did when he was getting mad and didn't want to say so. "You used to be much better at minding your business and keeping your mouth shut. Lots of things are possible, bro. But only one thing happens."

We glided through the empty marshland in John's sleek and quiet Eldorado, while seagulls, terns, egrets, and all their waterfowl cousins screeched and howled from the depths of the swamps. Why did they holler and screech like that? I wondered. For food? Attention? Was it some kind of primordial angst? I thought about bellowing out the window myself.

"Lemme put it this way," John said, leaning his large form back against the leather bucket seat, draping his wrist over the steering wheel. "Something happened a long time ago. Maybe I don't know any better than you do what it was. Maybe I, for one, do mind my own business." He glanced over at me, his eyes bright behind his glasses. "But for the sake of argument, let's say whatever you think happened then did happen, right?"

I nodded.

"So why would someone kill Greg now?"

I took a deep breath. I had no idea what anything had to do with anything. John was right. If Greg's murder was payback for Bill Green's, why would whoever killed him wait fifteen years to do it? And why kill Aaron? Greg's and Aaron's deaths were much more likely connected to what they'd been doing recently than what they'd done in 1975. Hard to explain the bodies buried in the same dump, but stranger things had happened. Yet, it was possible that someone who knew the history I'd discovered wanted to open old wounds. I just didn't know why he'd wait until so much time had passed.

I rode the rest of the way deep in thought, but John didn't seem to mind; he drove along, taking in the midday air. I liked that he kept the air conditioning on and the windows open. This was Big John's attitude toward the prescribed way of doing things.

After a long time, I said, "You know, this is weird. And I might be dead wrong. But when I was in the bar yesterday, waiting for you, I saw someone who looked just like that guy Alberto, Ernesto's partner." I told John then about seeing Ernesto and Alberto at Charlie's office.

John turned abruptly. "Whoa. Go over that again."

When I did, John didn't say anything for a couple of miles; then, as we were getting off the Garden State onto the Atlantic City Expressway, he said, "This is a whole new kettle of fish. Why didn't you tell me about those guys before?" The unspoken accusation hung in the air. Had I cost Greg his life, after already getting Ntango shot, by keeping information from John to protect my father's international working-class comrades?

Still, even now, when it came right down to it, I didn't like John suspecting Ernesto and Alberto, despite the fact that I'd brought the subject up. Alberto wasn't the only one with explaining to do, I told John. "What does Charlie being here tell us? And Walter? What does that tell us? Don't we have some questions to ask them, too?"

"Take it easy, bro."

I was still fuming about Charlie and Walter when something else hit me. A connection—far-fetched maybe, but it clanged like a brass bell right at that moment.

"Did Walter know Bill Green or Dave Bradley?"

"What do you mean?"

"Suppose he did. Suppose he and Bill Green were tight. Suppose for years he was trying to find out who killed his friend, but he couldn't be sure because everything had been covered up so well. Suppose he started hanging out with Greg, or even Aaron, trying to find out. And he hooks up with Charlie. Maybe that's the way things point. Then, one night, someone's drunk and talks too much. He finds out Greg killed Green. So he kills Greg."

Something clicked in John. He went on full alert.

"Maybe Aaron was who told Walter that Greg killed Green," I said. "Then Aaron figured out what Walter was up to. He was going to tell Greg, so Walter killed Aaron."

John shook his head. "I don't buy it." He watched the road in front of him and spoke slowly. "Number one, you'd have to believe that Greg killed Green and that Aaron knew. And why wouldn't Greg tell us about Walter after Aaron was killed if that's what happened?"

He was right. Greg even went out to do business with Walter after Aaron was killed. "Maybe he didn't know," I said. "He didn't know Walter killed Aaron."

"Like I said, bro. I don't buy it. Greg didn't kill nobody. But Walter's another story. Walter's someone to think about."

John dropped me at the bus depot. He still had work to do in Atlantic City and I wanted to get home. Before I got out of the car, I noticed him studying me, and his scrutiny made me squirm. "Don't do anything without checking with me first," he said finally. "Too much is going on for you to stick your head up. I don't want anything else to happen, especially to you." His eyes went soft. He put his hand on my shoulder, hauled me in with his arm, and gave me a shake with that big one-armed bear hug of his. "The manager from the Ocean Club called me yesterday. He wanted to fire you for not showing up," he said gruffly as he shoved me toward the passenger door. "I gotta cover for everybody. Someday I'm gonna start hiring reliable help."

I hobbled into the depressing Formica-paneled waiting room and called Linda.

She answered on the first ring, panic in her voice. "The police want to talk to me."

"Don't tell them about the clippings, and call John. He'll know what to do."

"What about you?" she asked in a weak voice.

"I'm going back to New York."

"I'll miss you," said Linda sweetly.

chapter twenty-two

When I got back to the city in the middle of the afternoon, I started to head up to the hospital to see Ntango, but then I got off at 104th Street instead to buy a couple of joints at the dope store on Amsterdam Avenue. I went home, put on the Grateful Dead, and sat down in my blue stuffed chair. After an hour or so, I stopped thinking about Greg and started to feel like myself again. I decided to have dinner before I went to the hospital, so I walked down to the Cathedral Market for a steak and a six-pack of Beck's. On the way back, I ran into Ntango, who was coming out of the Drop Off Your Laundry Laundromat. He had a small bandage on his head, walked slowly, talked more slowly even than he had before. But he assured me he was fine. Dr. Parker had gotten him released from the hospital the night before and had bought him dinner, he told me.

We got another steak and went back to my apartment. After we ate, I told him about Greg's murder. Afterward, we smoked dope, listening to the sound track from *The Harder They Come* over and over again. Sometime after midnight, we decided to go to Oscar's for a drink. Why we thought we needed to go out this late, who we expected to see, why we didn't just pack it in and go to sleep after a pleasant-enough evening—those are the kind of unanswerable questions that have defined my existence. Thinking there must be more to life, then speculating that the extra bit life had to offer would be found at Oscar's in the small hours of the morning is the kind of misguided answer I unfailingly came up with. I'd once worked at Oscar's, after getting fired from the Sheraton the first time and before the union, despite its best efforts to the contrary, got me my job back. So I knew most of the regulars, and the owner, Oscar.

When we came in, Oscar, who suspected Ntango of being a drug dealer—as he suspected most people of the colored persuasion—climbed off his bar stool near the door and went to the far end of the bar, like a fighter going to a neutral corner. Eric the Red, Oscar's cook, who'd already closed up the kitchen, left the end of the bar that Oscar went to and came to sit with us. Carl Van Sagan, my friend the doorman, who'd loaned me the suit for my ill-fated bar manager job at the Ocean Club, came in before we had ordered our first drink. It was a little after 1:00 A.M., gathering hour for the winos.

I was glad to see Carl; I hadn't seen him since I'd returned the suit. He'd been to a couple of other joints before Oscar's and had that pleasant glow and gregariousness that he got after just a few scotches and before he'd had too many. He wore a white shirt and his doorman green pants, and, though he'd been on a diet for a few months, had not lost much of his heft. He'd gotten new glasses, though; these were horn-rimmed and made him look more distinguished than his granny glasses. I also noticed lines in his face, crow's-feet, I guess, around the eyes and mouth, and wisps of gray in his hair. Looking at him this night, for some reason, reminded me of how many years I'd known him—longer than I'd known Big John. Carl's expression was serene; when he looked like this, something in the cast of his eyes reminded me of Snoopy.

The regulars knew Ntango had been shot, but since he was a cabdriver and being shot was part of the territory, they didn't make too big a deal over it. When it came to light that I'd been with Ntango, Carl asked why they hadn't shot me.

"Why should they shoot me?"

He stopped drinking in midsip, raised an eyebrow, and said in his mildest tone, "I didn't mean that they should shoot you."

Carl was nosy enough to want an explanation. But I let him wait for a while. When I did tell him about the whole baffling mess, I did so with a sense of déjà vu. Telling him about Greg reminded me of an awful time a year or so before when a girl we knew was murdered—and I thought Carl had killed her. Eric listened in, and the group pondered the mystery—as likely a brain trust as you'd find on any cluster of bar stools in New York.

"Suspect everyone! Accuse no one!" said Carl after a moment. Having drawn himself up to his full height on the bar stool, he bespoke this wisdom in a strong, shivering baritone. "Sergeant Cuff," he explained.

Eric the Red pondered this before changing the subject. Eric had long black hair to the middle of his back, tied in a ponytail, and a long black beard to the middle of his chest that trails off into ragged threads at the end. He was small, but he looked large because of his hair, his prominent hooked nose, his eyebrows like flourishing shrubs, and because of his hands, which were large and thick workingman's hands. He hailed from Yugoslavia and idolized Tito, who had brought him in from shepherding in the mountains of Serbia and civilized him—or had taken a shot at it at least. "You been working downtown?" he asked. Eric had stalked the streets of New York for six months, an illegal alien, panhandling and living on handouts, looking for work, so he knew what it meant to need a job.

"I was working downtown till all this shit started happening."

"You got fired again?"

"Not exactly. I'm still sort of on the clock," I said, knowing Eric wouldn't understand.

"I don't get it, man."

I nodded.

Carl, on the other hand, got too much. "A PI!" The expression in his small thoughtful eyes was gleeful.

Now I didn't get it.

"A private eye . . . private investigator." When he wasn't writing poetry or reading it, Carl read detective novels in his little doorman's cubicle, often one a night. His favorite was Nero Wolf.

"I'm not a PI; I'm a bartender. Actually, I'm a bar manager; that's how I'm still on the clock. I get a salary. But now that's over. I'm going back behind the stick, where I belong."

"You should get a license and hang up a shingle." Carl said, ordering another round of drinks with a flourish of his hand.

"I don't want a license or a shingle. I don't even want to be a bar manager."

Soon, we were joined by Sam the Hammer and Reuben Foster, both regulars at Oscar's and, interestingly enough, former murderers in their own rights. Reuben was a big barrel-chested guy, who played lineman in the early fifties for his alma mater, Amherst College. A descendant of northwestern Massachusetts free blacks, a writer, and an intellectual, he had squandered his youth in the Village and the Upper West Side with the Beats. He was remarkably well read, could quote Milton from memory—and, in the late 1950s, served a prison term for murdering his first wife.

Sam the Hammer was a neighborhood fixture, one felony short of a habitual criminal sentence, whose name derived from his first felony sentence, manslaughter. Sam wore his hair slicked back, the same way he'd worn it when he began running numbers as a teenager; the hair was gray now, as was his walrus mustache and his thick eyebrows. What I liked about Sam was that he noticed everything and kept his own counsel. Under Carl's tutelage, he'd been preparing for a while now to write a book about characters he'd known.

Oscar, at the far end of the bar, grumbled into the ear of the bartender, John, a tall, thin, soft-spoken lush, who replaced me behind the stick. Given that Oscar hated each and every one of the group gathered around me and since he was now drunk but still lacked the courage to try it himself, he was telling John to throw us all out. John listened attentively to Oscar, then came back to see if we needed another drink.

As the night crawled toward the small hours, with one thing leading to another—mostly the present drink leading to the next one—the case of the murders of Greg Peters and Aaron Adams caught the fancy of the assembled group. A number of suggestions were made, none of them deserving of being taken seriously, yet in the dim alcoholic fog near closing time, Reuben's plan—to find one of the suspects, grab him by the neck, and shake the truth out of him—began to pick up a following. A persistent but resigned and jaded voice deep in my un-conscious whispered that this was a bad idea. But even though I had to squint one eye closed to focus on our merry band gathering in the doorway, I paid no heed.

Ntango hadn't yet gotten his cab back and was in no condition to be driving—with his brain bullet-damaged on the one hand and drink-addled on the other—anyway, so Reuben was dispatched to ex-tricate his ancient Pontiac from the parking garage on 109th Street while the rest of the posse waited in front of Oscar's in the echoing quiet of Broadway at 3:00 A.M. When Rueben pulled up to the curb—over the curb, actually—Ntango and I joined him in the front seat: Sam, Eric, and Carl piled in back. Off we went, gladiators for justice, all of us well beyond the first bloom of youthful fitness, not a push-up among us, except for the occasional barroom dare, in twenty years—fat asses and bulging bellies, sagging into the seats of the old Pontiac, which groaned down on its springs like an old dray horse.

"Go up Amsterdam," Sam said authoritatively.

"No, across One Hundred and tenth," said Carl.

I suggested up Broadway to 125th Street.

"Assholes," said Reuben as he thumped down off of the sidewalk and into Broadway. A screech of brakes, a bleating horn, and a yellow cab fishtailed past us in the outer lane, the only thing visible of the driver his outstretched hand with index finger pointing up.

"Asshole," said Reuben.

"Reuben," said Ntango quietly, "go across Ninety-sixth Street and through the park; it's safer."

"Except for the squirrels," Carl said.

Less than twenty minutes after leaving Oscar's, we turned into East 183rd Street, and I was again squinting out the window, searching the boarded-up and empty-windowed buildings for that faded 92. The street was deserted; the buildings looked abandoned. A pack of dogs, dark and hulking shapes, slunk along the street.

We stopped in front of 92 when I finally spotted it the second time we went past. No light shone from behind the corrugated door this time. I didn't know if it was appropriate for a goon squad to knock, but the point was moot, because while I stood in front of the door pondering this, Alberto pushed his way out through the sheet of metal to loom before us. Reuben and Eric, who had gotten out with me, swayed shoulder-to-shoulder beside me. As Alberto seemed really alarmed by our arrival, my doubts as to the wisdom of this encounter increased rapidly. But before any of us could say anything, smiling and sleepy-eyed Ernesto pushed his way through the doorway.

"Brian," he said. "You're drunk."

I was hard-pressed to deny it.

More of the cadre of revolutionaries emerged from their hovel at this point, all of them angry and serious—at least two of them carrying guns. The older man I'd liked the last time I was there pushed a snub-nosed pistol into my ribs, snarled into my ear, and shoved me toward the tin door. The rest of my elite corps, sullen and scared, were hauled into the building by the scruff of their necks.

I sat at the table while Ernesto argued energetically in Spanish with his comrades for ten minutes. Every now and then, the group would look in my direction, first with anger, then contempt, and finally a bewildered sort of pity. Carl, Sam, and Reuben sagged into an old couch that leaned against a wall, all three of them sinking so far into it and with such misplaced centers of gravity that it would take five minutes of intense struggle for any of them to get out of the couch again if called to battle.

When things calmed sufficiently, the leader, Raol, came and stood over me. "What are you doing here?" he asked. "What do you want?"

Given the superfluousness of preliminaries, I got right to the point. "My friend Greg was murdered," I said in a shaking voice. The adrenaline that had been holding me up deserted me. I felt the room waver. I pointed to Alberto, who was back on duty at the door. "The day Greg was killed, I saw Alberto in Sea Isle City." I fixed my bleary eyes on Raol. He didn't flinch. "I want to know what he was doing there."

"He wasn't there," Raol said quietly.

I don't know what I expected. All along, I'd held onto a faint hope that it hadn't really been Alberto in Sea Isle. But I wasn't reassured. I had no reason to believe Raol. So why ask questions if you aren't going to believe the answer? It wasn't that I expected the truth. Everyone shapes the truth to fit his needs. Still, asking questions sometimes produces something—if not answers, maybe mistakes, contradictions. So I said, "Bay Ridge, Brooklyn. Three nights ago. Dr. Wilson's optometry office. Anyone know anything?" Everyone stared blankly at me. I settled on Ernesto. "How's your eyesight?"

His expression was sad. I checked out Alberto. His dark eyes were as blank as a wall. I tried Raol. His expression was stern. Somewhere a clock ticked. Somewhere the sun shone and children laughed. But not here in Mudville.

"I'm sorry for you, my friend," said Raol. "We did not kill the man. Alberto was not in this seaside city. More than that, no." He squared his shoulders and lifted his chin. "I can see it is hard for you to believe us. But it is as we told you. Ernesto help your friend. No more."

"Who killed Greg?"

"Not us. I'm sorry you don't believe."

Carl cleared his throat a couple of times, so I looked over at him. He wrinkled his brow and narrowed his eyes. "How would this guy you saw in the bar down at the shore have found Greg?"

"He followed me."

Carl tried again. "If he followed you, how could he find Greg before you did?"

The pale light of morning slipped through the gaps in the tin doors and the cracks in the boarded-up windows; a wonderful smell of frying onions, garlic, peppers, and spices drifted out from the kitchen. Raol held up both his hands in a saintlike gesture, as if to bless us all, and insisted we stay for breakfast. I wanted to believe these men. They were my father's comrades, the folks from the Internationale. But a man can't spend most of his life in New York City without cultivating doubts about the motives of his fellowmen. Doubting did not stay me from enthusiastically tearing into my breakfast, but it did keep me from scratching comrade Alberto off my list. He might have tracked Greg down in Sea Isle some other way. I still didn't know why he and Ernesto were at Charlie's office in Brooklyn. And I didn't know if any of the *campañeros* drove a red Jeep Cherokee.

chapter twenty-three

When I woke up in the afternoon with a pounding headache, I called Detective Sergeant Sheehan at the Manhattan Detective Bureau and asked him to meet me at La Rosita, a Cuban-Chinese restaurant in my neighborhood. I read the *Daily News* and drank espresso while I waited.

He arrived discreetly enough but still had a chilling effect on the establishment. For one thing, he was too big and fair-skinned for the place; for another, with that sandy hair and ruddy, weathered face, he looked like a cop. Seats began emptying pretty quickly. Visibly uncomfortable himself for a change, he ordered his espresso to go. We sat on a bench on the island in the middle of Broadway.

"How's your friend?" he asked first.

"He's out of the hospital." I was glad he'd asked. I didn't say so, but he could tell, because he shifted his eyes from mine and moved his body around a great deal without going anywhere, the way big guys do sometimes when they're embarrassed. Neither of us especially wanted this to be a personal relationship. If we'd been stuck somewhere without a problem to solve, I don't know if we would even have been able to carry on a conversation.

"You find out anything about that Cherokee?"

"No." When I looked disappointed, he said, "Remember I'm homicide. I don't get involved until they kill you."

"I'm sure you already know Greg is dead."

Sheehan, reasserting his know-it-all, surprised-by-nothing, superior expression, leaned back expansively on the bench, crossing one leg over the other. "You were quite a hit with the Sea Isle City police."

"Do you guys work together?" I asked. "Do you share information and work on things together? Suppose you thought whoever killed Greg also killed Aaron?"

What I got for an answer was this twinkling of mild amusement in his eyes and a twitching around his mouth that might have passed for a smile in some circles. "My, my! Are you teaming up with the forces of law and order?" When I just looked at him, he said, "Suppose you hold up your end by telling me where that drug-dealing, revolutionary wetback friend of yours is?"

"What? . . . Who's a drug dealer?"

"All your friends . . . Maybe you, too, for all I know." Sheehan's blue eyes reflected a sort of awed perplexity. "Why'd you call me?"

I didn't answer. Maybe I didn't know the answer. Or maybe I didn't want to admit to myself what I'd made up my mind to do. Finally, I said, "I think the two murders are connected and that they might be linked to something that happened years ago in Atlantic City."

"What kinds of things?"

I told him about Bill Green and David Bradley. "Greg may have been killed in revenge for Bill Green being murdered by Greg, and Aaron may have just gotten in the way. There's a guy named Walter Springer. He shared Greg's apartment in Brooklyn, and he's from down at the shore, years ago. Could you find out if he ever knew Bill Green?"

Sheehan stood up. I watched the 104 bus pull away from the curb, waiting until the bellowing of the diesel motor faded. Sheehan seemed to be waiting for something, too. "I'm not looking for things to do, McNulty. You want information, tell me where's that guy Ernesto hiding out?"

I froze. I couldn't do it, so I lied, knowing Sheehan knew I was lying.

Sheehan let his disapproval hang over me like a dark cloud for a few pregnant seconds, then asked, "You got any proof this Greg guy killed this Bill Green?"

"Proof?"

"Proof. In this state, we need proof to convict someone."

"You don't need to convict Greg. He's dead."

"Thanks," Sheehan said sarcastically. "Maybe I can hang a few of my other unsolved murders on him, too, now that he's dead."

"It's okay with me."

Sheehan's expression turned to disgust. I thought he was going to kick my crutch out from under me as he turned to walk away.

"Do you really not believe me?" I asked his retreating back.

"I believe in proof," said Sheehan over his shoulder. "See you around, McNulty."

After striking out with Sheehan, I went in the early evening to Brooklyn to ask Pop what he thought about Sheehan's theory that Ernesto and the comrades were dealing dope. I also hoped to catch up with Dr. Parker while I was in the borough of churches. She must have had her beeper turned off, because I couldn't reach her, so I had to settle for Pop. When he opened the door, he looked at me in this piercing way of his that had seen into my soul since I was a child. I still didn't know what he looked for, but now, just as when I was a kid, I expected he might find something awful. In his own way, he was probably glad to see me, just as, in his own way, he loved me. He couldn't help it that his standards were celestial.

"You look wan and tired. Your skin is a white as a nun's," he said when he finally did speak.

"You look good yourself, Pop."

He didn't miss the sarcasm—I think he invented sarcasm—he ignored it. "I walk an hour a day," he said proudly.

"I walk, too."

"You walk from bar to bar. . . . You should take better care of yourself. I hoped you'd outlive me." He let go of the door, so I followed him in to the dining room with its ancient round mahogany dining room table. As usual, a book, the page carefully marked with a bookmark, lay on the table next to his glasses. Not the least of my childhood transgressions was infuriating my father by laying books facedown on a table, damaging the spines. This time, he was reading Trotsky's *My Life*.

I sat down and Pop went for coffee, fresh this time. When he came back from the kitchen, I picked up the Trotsky book and looked expectantly at him. But no explanation was forthcoming. Since Pop eschewed small talk, I didn't beat around the bush with him, either. I told him Greg had been killed, about Sandra, although not about sleeping with her, about seeing Alberto and Ernesto at Dr. Wilson's office and maybe seeing Alberto in Sea Isle and maybe not. I told him Sheehan said Ernesto was a drug dealer and about meeting with the *compañeros* in the South Bronx the night before, editing out the burlesque.

"I'm trying to convince myself the Chileans didn't have anything to do with the murders," I said.

"Good for you. Then perhaps you can get their country back for them."

"I wish I believed they could."

Pop heard the despair behind my cynicism but was having none of it. Communists are optimists, my father no exception. "Fortunately, unlike you, your Chilean comrades believe man can determine his fate." He sat back in his chair like a stern judge. "You're sure you saw this man both times?"

"I'm sure I saw him at Charlie's office. I'm not sure it was Alberto in Sea Isle City."

"Could the Chileans have a different reason for doing business with this Charlie?"

"Maybe they went to get their eyes checked."

Pop didn't lose his concentration. "There are reasons why progressives from Latin America might do business with gangsters in America. Two that come to mind are guns and papers."

I loved the orderliness of my father's thinking. My own thinking wasn't like his. Despite being his son, I was inherently chaotic. Those genes came from my mother, the Irish romantic from County Cavan. Pop went for facts. I used leaps of imagination to bridge the gaps between the facts. But this time he leaped further than I could. "What do you do with papers and guns? I don't see the connection."

"That's because your brain is addled from too many nights in barrooms." He took a deep breath. "Guns, for obvious reasons, to send back to those doing the fighting. Papers—passports, green cards, driver's licenses—identification for those on the run to get work. Political refugees who need to lose their identities—Palestinians, Irish, Guatemalans—and Chileans, too, I would bet."

"Maybe. Do you suppose they'd be riding around in a red Cherokee, taking potshots at me?"

Pop looked me over like he suspected I was coming down with something. "I beg your pardon. You don't know who shot at you—and what in God's name is a Cherokee?"

"It's sort of like a van or a jeep, kind of boxy. . . ." I felt my voice dropping off. Already, he had that uncomprehending cast to his eyes. "It's like a station wagon. It's got big wheels. . . . Well, not big exactly, I guess, just high off the ground. . . . It was red. . . . It had Cherokee written on it."

Pop picked up his book, deciding, it seemed, I had all the advice I needed. "If you keep at it long enough, life will probably drop something into place."

"And if life doesn't drop something into place?"

"If it doesn't, there won't be an answer. That happens, too." He took his glasses off again, but impatience showed in the gesture. He knew I was stalling, and he wanted to get back to his reading. "Let me know what I can do." He put the glasses back on.

After I left Pop's apartment, I debated with myself over a couple of beers at Farrell's bar in Windsor Terrace—an undocumented historical landmark, where, back in the 1920s, elevator operators and window washers met to amalgamate their unions. Why didn't I just let someone else handle this? That was the question I began the debate with. People get murdered all the time. In New York, during the busy season, two or three unfortunate souls a day—not counting mass murders or vengeful arson. Curiosity wasn't a reason to risk life and limb in pursuit of whatever truth I might come up with in the end. Yet, sipping my draft beer in the musty late-afternoon sunlight that filtered into the venerable dark mahogany, brass, and mirrored bar, I realized I would follow this out with the same certainty with which I followed my nose—and for the same reasons. Why I would follow this senseless trail to the end had nothing to do with what I thought now, everything to do with what life had already made me into. So I surrendered the debate and thought about Charlie. He had his imprint on every shady deal I'd come across. Here, he was tied up in some nasty business with Greg and Walter. Over there, he had business with Ernesto and Alberto. I'd have bet he was the older man at the Ocean Club the night Aaron was murdered. He was in Sea Isle the night Greg was murdered. I first met the Cherokee folks in his office. On the plus side, he was John's father and had tightened me up with a set of cheaters. And maybe I liked him, and maybe he liked me. I knew I might have some bad moments. But that wasn't going to keep me from sending him over if he shot Miles. I mean, stabbed Greg.

At this moment, with the white remains of the beer head drying against the side of the pilsner glass, I felt a sense of déjà vu. In a bar like this, not long before, I'd sat like this, not knowing what to do. That night, I went to pee, found the gin mill's back door open, walked out into the alley below Greg's apartment, thought of a plan, climbed a tree—and the rest was history. Once more, I had to pee. And, even though this joint didn't have a back door and no one lived upstairs, the plan was already hatched before I pulled down my zipper.

Fate dictated no one would answer the door at Charlie's office. Fate determined I would notice a side window off Charlie's porch was open a half inch on the bottom. Fate, not thought, led me into the forsythia bush alongside the porch. Fate, again, as I gave a shove and the window went up.

Crouched in the bushes—my eyes flashing, I'm sure, with the cunning of the fox outside the open chicken coop—I saw trees, empty porches, blank walls, and not a living soul. Using my one crutch as a pole, I vaulted for the open window and made it about halfway through before losing momentum and beaching myself on the windowsill. Half in and half out, I wiggled and squirmed, kicked and grunted, grasped and pulled, until I hoisted myself through and poured myself onto the floor. A bit more experienced at this sort of thing now, I looked out the window carefully to make sure no one had seen my entrance. Satisfied no one had seen because the window faced the blank wall of the house next to it and the bushes blocked it from the street, I pulled down the shades and turned on the light. Quickly, I went about my work, searching through Charlie's desks, cabinets, and files. I didn't know what I was looking for, but I was sure I'd know it when I found it.

What I did find, after shuffling through papers, insurance forms, charts, and photocopied articles, was a metal box, not unlike a safe-deposit box, on a shelf in a metal cabinet. I figured it might contain eyeglass lenses or frames, or it might contain sophisticated laser machine parts. Then again, it might contain whatever it was I was searching for. The only way to know was to break it open—but if I did, Charlie would know someone had broken in. I could take the box with me, but he'd still know, and on top of that, I'd have to carry the goddamn box with me. With my luck, there'd be twenty pounds of uncut cocaine in the box. Then someone would kill me for sure. So I grabbed a screwdriver-type instrument from another cabinet and pried the box open.

It was filled with small booklets with dark blue heavy-stock covers. When I opened one, I discovered it was a passport. In small boxes underneath the passports were blanks for driver's licenses from California, New York, Florida and packets of Social Security cards. This was enough for me. I was a nervous wreck anyway in the deathly quiet, antiseptic room. The shadow of the examining chair, with all its arms and levers, started my imagination working, so I expected it might start up and come after me any minute, grabbing me with its levers and strapping me into the chair, holding me there until sourpuss the receptionist showed up in the morning to turn me over to the cops.

I went back out the window, leaving it open wider than I'd found it, hoping Charlie might figure some neighborhood kids had broken in. I took a car-service cab back to Pop's apartment in Flatbush, where I recounted my adventures.

"I admire your flair for the dramatic," Pop said when I told him what had happened.

Flair maybe. But for once I was glad to have worked without an audience. With a burglary charge already hanging over my head, another arrest would send me up the river. Even though I knew I'd acted with the best of intentions—and that I wasn't a second-story man in the real sense of the word—any judge I tried to explain this to would have as much compassion as one of Kafka's judges.

"The passports mean you were right about Ernesto having a different reason for hooking up with Charlie," I told him.

Pop nodded. "So whom do you point the finger at now?"

"Walter," I said without hesitation.

Before leaving, I called Sheehan to see if he might have had a change of heart and gotten the information I'd asked him for.

"I'll tell you what I know when you tell me how you knew where Greg Peters's body was buried," Sheehan said by way of hello. "Who tipped you off?"

"A reporter I know down there. They listen to the police scanner."

"Bullshit," said Sheehan. "How'd you know it would be Peters?" When I didn't answer, Sheehan said, "Sorry I can't help you. Police information is confidential."

"Wait." I thought this over quickly. I needed to trade, and since I'd already let most of the cats out of the bag anyway, I told him about the newspaper articles.

What I got for my trouble was a long silence.

"C'mon," I said. "Fair's fair. What's good for the goose is good for the gander." This last was an oft-used phrase of my mother's, one that never in my wildest dreams did I expect I would use myself.

"What they told me," Sheehan said, the flatness of his tone worthy of a twenty-year veteran of New York's finest, "was that they made no connection between this case and the earlier case or between the two earlier cases. In one of the earlier cases, the cause of death was a drug overdose. The other is an open murder case."

"They don't think it's strange that all the bodies were buried in the same garbage dump?"

"You see a connection, McNulty. No one else does. Two guys were stabbed to death fifteen years apart. They're buried in the same place. Could it have been the same murderer? Yes. Could it have been a different murderer? Yes. Then you have an overdose. You're telling me that was a murder also. All I want to know, McNulty, is how do you know? What's the motive? Who's the perpetrator?"

"Why do I gotta do all the work? You guys are the ones on the clock. What cop did you talk to down there? That guy Carney seems like he should know better."

"I didn't talk to him. I spoke to the chief."

"Doesn't it sound like bullshit to you no matter who you talked to? The bodies in the same place? The guys knowing one another? There's no connection?" I said this a little louder than was probably appropriate.

Sheehan's voice rose to fill the telephone receiver. "If you know how these deaths are linked, why were you sending me to find out about it from the Sea Isle cops? Don't talk to me about goosing no fucking gander!" He sputtered for a few seconds but then quieted. "I'm not a fucking messenger."

"If Greg killed Bill Green, then it's possible he was killed in revenge."

"By who?"

"I don't know. That's why I asked you to find out about that guy Walter."

Sheehan didn't say anything, but I sensed something might be coming, so I kept quiet. "This Walter Springer . . ." he said.

"Yeah?" My heart stopped.

"I couldn't find anything on him."

"What?"

"There wasn't anything there." Sheehan sounded uncomfortable. He was a guy used to saying things directly, not good at pussyfooting around.

I didn't believe him, but I knew better than to argue. It was one of those times when the unsaid says a whole lot more than the said.

Pop watched me hang up the phone. "You're not planning on a diplomatic career, I hope."

I ignored him and called Sue Gleason. Although she'd already come up with more than her share of startling information, this time she might as well have whacked me between the eyes with a two-by-four. I mumbled something, hung up, and stood in front of the phone, staring into the space behind it.

Pop didn't interrupt my trance. Some time later, I found myself sitting across from him at the dining room table. "John's father, Charlie, went to prison for murdering someone in the 1950s," I told him. "Sue Gleason has the lurid and graphic newspaper story on the murder. But the intriguing thing is how: The guy who was killed was stabbed once, up under the ribs and into the heart, just like Aaron was killed, like Greg was killed, and the way, many years ago, Bill Green was killed."

We sat in silence, which was interrupted only by the creaking of the old wooden dining room chairs. The dark wood of the sideboard behind me, the glass-fronted china cabinet across the room, the ancient round table itself—these and everything else in the room shone with a dull light, like a sanctuary. I began to remember things we'd talked about sitting around this table. Once, when I was seventeen, shortly after my mother died, my father and I talked for hours, and I decided I would go to Columbia University. That night, I was prouder of myself, and more determined to make my father proud of me, than I'd ever been before or would ever be again. The son of a blacklisted outcast had been accepted at one of the country's most exalted seats of learning. Even though Pop required a blood oath that I wouldn't forsake the working class when I entered college, I knew it was a moment of great pride for him, this man who had spent a lifetime in quixotic battles without ever giving up his belief that mankind might one day end its inhumanity to man. It was at this same table three years later that I told him I was dropping out of Columbia because I was failing and just couldn't do it anymore. The room and the table were filled with the memories of my life and my father. My eyes filled with tears. I thought of John and his father and wondered what in the world I would tell John now that I knew.

"It's got to be Walter," I said.

Pop heard the desperation in my voice, so his own voice was kind, reminding me of how he'd sounded the night my mother died and we sat at this table long, long into the night. Back then, the gentleness didn't help. I was lost and alone and bitter in a way I thought I'd never recover from. Perhaps I never had. But when I looked back over the years, the gentleness of that talk with my father was one of the beautiful things I remembered in my life. Now, the gentleness came again, because he knew I grieved for John. But Pop's gentleness didn't allow for ignoring the truth. His tone was gentle, but the expression in his eyes was unwavering. "You can despise this Walter person, but nothing that you know makes him a killer."

"Well, if Charlie did it, Walter was with him. He was with him every single time." My voice cracked, the tears welling up behind my eyes.

I stormed out of my father's house, as I'd done so many times in my life, leaving Pop sad and brooding, behind me. I headed straight down Flatbush, through neighborhoods that would normally scare me to death. This night, with my gimpy gait, one crutch, and unseeing eyes, I must truly have looked like the one carrying the ax. I slowed down as the pain in my leg caught up with me, and the late-summer night and the gentle evening calmed me a bit. A stickball game between the parked cars, down one of the side streets, brought back my childhood with a pang of nostalgia. As a kid, I was warned not to talk to strangers. There were gangs and junkies, but I wasn't afraid all the time. My head full of summer evenings, stickball games, love affairs on stoops, and the safety of childhood, I was at Grand Army Plaza before I realized where I'd gotten to. I turned at Seventh Avenue and backtracked toward Walter's apartment. Heedless and incautious, I should have considered that Walter might have a gun. I should have at least noticed that there was a red Cherokee parked half a block from Walter's apartment.

chapter twenty-four

My hand was poised in front of Walter's bell when for no reason other than instinct I looked back over my shoulder for a second. Out of the corner of my eye, I caught a glimpse of a gleaming dark blue Cadillac Eldorado parked at the curb on the far side of the street, and my hand froze. I turned and began to casually haul myself across the street—and almost got creamed by a *Daily News* truck thundering down Seventh Avenue with the early edition.

I didn't really think it was John's car. But I needed to make sure. Since I had no idea what John's license plate number was, I didn't know what looking at the car would prove. As it turned out, I didn't have to know the number. The plates read BIGJON. John was not someone to slink around under the cover of darkness.

It was while contemplating this turn of events that I caught sight of the red Cherokee I'd walked past back on the other side of the street. It was parked a few doors down from Walter's apartment. There are many red Cherokees, as there are many blue Eldorados, and no reason to assume this was the one that had been stalking me. But, using my imagination, I came up with a couple of possibilities. One, John had been captured by Walter and the goons. Two, John, Walter, and the goons in the red Cherokee were in cahoots.

The situation called for action. I pictured myself scaling the side of the building across the street from Walter's apartment, swinging across Seventh Avenue on a rope, swooping through the front window of the apartment, rescuing John—or capturing him, depending on the circumstances—catching the bad guys dead to rights, rounding them up, and turning the whole passel of thieves over to the coppers. I think I had myself mixed up with Zorro. When, in my mind's eye, I replaced the lithe figure of Zorro with that of an aging and sagging bartender, the doorbell seemed more practical. But I hesitated doing this, too, because if either of my theories was right, I'd be in more trouble than I could handle.

Under the circumstances, I decided to have a drink before taking any action. Given my druthers, I'd have gone into the Hourglass and sipped manhattans with the old ladies, but I wanted to keep an eye on both the Cherokee and John's car, so I went into Dominick's Den to drink with the hairy chests and inhale the cologne. Sipping a beer, I leaned my body and my one crutch on the dry bar next to the picture window, where I could watch the street. When I went back for my second beer, I noticed two swarthy guys among the many swarthy guys. These two were bent over the bar together in quiet and intent conversation, indifferent to the activity around them. Every other guy floated through the bar, patting a pal on the shoulder, muscling up to one of the girls in tight white jeans. These two guys talked. And the smaller one, dark-haired, hard-eyed, square-jawed, I'd seen before: in Bay Ridge one sunny morning, holding a gun in his hand.

It is the experience of experiences, let me tell you, to find yourself a few bar stools away from a man who has shot you. I froze to the spot just as I had when I saw that *Daily News* truck bearing down on me. One more step and wham! Stepping back from the wham this time, too, I set my beer glass down, and, grabbing my crutch, I limped as quickly as I could out of the bar, not looking back, but cringing nonetheless, waiting for a bullet in the back.

As luck would have it, at the same moment I walked out of the bar, Big John came charging out of Walter's building. I hesitated a quick second, then called him. He turned sharply, his eyes bright and alert. John moved through his life like a fox in the field, enjoying it to the fullest but constantly on guard.

"Yo, bro!" he hollered cheerfully when he saw it was me. "What's going on?"

"C'mere," I said in a low voice, trying to hush him, as if the goons in the bar could hear. I pushed him into the Hourglass and, before we had ordered a drink, told him about the guys in the next bar. John took off his glasses and went stone-faced.

"Two double shots of tequila," he said when the bartender showed up.

As we sucked them down, I kept watch out the window.

"Let's go," John said, throwing down the last of his tequila.

I did the same and followed him toward the door. "Where we going?"

"To snatch those goons."

"Oh?" I hesitated. "Are you sure that's a good idea?" What I meant was, "Please, Mr. Custer, I don't want to go." But I stiffened my back and gritted my teeth.

Reaching into a locked box under the seat of the Eldorado, John took out two little snubbed-nose guns. He stuck one of them into his belt and handed the other one to me.

"Are you really going to shoot someone with that?"

John rolled his eyes. "Just scare them. You don't have to shoot them."

"What if they don't scare?"

John shook his head. "You shoot them in the leg. You don't have to kill anybody."

"I don't want it," I said, backing away from him.

John looked like he wanted to throttle me.

"I wouldn't use it."

He rolled his eyes, then stared at me for a few seconds; finally, his face took on that wistful, perplexed expression he often got when I tried to explain why I didn't want to be a boss or why I thought it was terrible for people to be rich. I liked the expression, because it seemed to have in it some weird form of admiration mixed with the incredulity.

"Suit yourself," he said. "I'll whack both of them if I have to."

We sat in John's car and waited. I thought about telling him then what I'd learned about Charlie's past, but it didn't seem like the right time. Instead, I pestered him with questions, asking him when he thought the goons would come out, and if he thought they'd see us when they did. When I asked him if he thought they had guns, he gave me a scornful glance, so I shut up. John seemed to take our stake-out in stride, like a veteran soldier going into battle. It didn't make any difference how far up the corporate ladder he'd climbed. You could take the kid away from the mean streets, but you couldn't take the streets out of the kid. Big John settled his own scores.

It dawned on me that once more, after all these years, I was follow-ing him. Even though this was my battle, he'd taken over and now led the charge. I didn't like what we were doing; I wouldn't have chosen this way. But I was drawn to this as if John were leading me around by a chain. I didn't have to remind myself that the two guys we were af-ter made their living killing people. They weren't normal in any sense I understood. Calling them down wasn't going to be a grade-school fight. Even Sam and Reuben, the only murderers I knew on a first-name basis, when they killed people, had done it almost by accident—in fear or rage. The guys we were after were execution-style killers. When you read about them in the paper, you understand that a cold, calculated, immeasurably cruel act of premeditated, conscienceless killing has taken place. They were like those governors who so cold-bloodedly order the executioner to throw the switch.

Sitting in the car waiting was gloomy and nerve-racking. Each time the door of Dominic's Den opened, my heart stopped beating. Each time it turned out not to be them, I felt a surge of relief and a strange sense of disappointment. I don't know why I doubted the inevitable. Was I thinking they'd never come out? That maybe a higher power would turn them into bar stools?

Despite my anxiety, I noticed that Seventh Avenue was pleasant as the evening progressed. The streetlights shone dully on the flat brown-faced four- and five-story buildings. Cars passed by in each direction; the street was crowded, jostling, but no traffic jam, no blaring horns. Some cars were double-parked in front of the fruit stand a couple of doors from us, or in front of a Korean grocery store on the far corner. Well-dressed, nicely groomed young men and women, forced across the river by high rents in Manhattan, sauntered toward the Japanese restaurant on one corner or the Mexican restaurant across from it. In the second-floor storefront directly opposite us, I saw a sign that read FORTUNE-TELLER AND ADVISER. Looking through the plate-glass window, I watched a large woman in a flowing red-and-green-flowered gown and black shawls, wearing dangling chains and bracelets, walk in and out from behind a curtain made of shiny beads. I thought I might run in and get a quick glimpse of the future. "You're not a happy man," she would say. "But don't worry about it. Your lifeline stops about thirty seconds after you walk out my door."

At one point, a Camaro double-parked in front of Dominic's, blocking in the Cherokee. I thought this might complicate things. But the night wore on; the Camaro moved, but still no sign. The guys we waited for were in for the long haul.

Then, the inevitable. The smaller guy came through the door first. I recognized him before I saw his face. His gestures were animated but unsteady. The other guy bumped into the first guy and then bounced off the door; they talked to each other in louder voices than they needed to. When they bumped into each other, they giggled. Two contract murderers giggling like schoolgirls.

John was out of the car and crossing the street before I'd hoisted myself out of the car and up on my crutch. Because they were drunk, they missed what they should have seen coming. John stuck his gun into the back of the bigger one as the guy stood next to the Cherokee, shuffling through his pockets for his keys. I came up behind the smaller guy on the curb side, dropped my crutch into the gutter, grabbed his arm, and twisted it up behind his back—a hold I'd learned the hard way from a cop. By bending and pushing up my arm behind me, the cop had first bent me over and then lifted me by the force of excruciating pain onto my tiptoes, where I wriggled like Eliot's bug. This approach worked on the goon, too; he danced on his toes like a ballerina. John let the little guy see the gun, found the bigger guy's keys for him, opened the door, and we all climbed into the

Cherokee—the bad guys in front, the good guys in the backseat.

"Drive," John said.

The driver sat stiffly.

"Drive this fucking car," John said menacingly, sticking the gun into the driver's neck. The driver stiffened some more but didn't move to start the car. I thought, Man, this is it, murder on Seventh Avenue. John didn't want to shoot the guy, but what do you do when you've got the gun and the other guy balks? Fortunately, my faithful reading of the *New York Daily News* over more than a quarter of a century came to my rescue: Hit men were often imported from Latin American countries to do a particular job.

I leaned through the gap between the two front seats, turned the ignition, and started the car. "*¡Andele! ¡Andele!*" I said, waving my hand toward the windshield. The driver dropped the car in gear and off we went. "I don't think they speak English very well," I told John.

For a moment, he looked as if he might explode, but quickly that sheepish, boyish look he got when the absurdity of life caught up with him took over. We'd also, I realized, forgotten to frisk them. When I told this to John, he rolled his eyes and nodded. "Tell them to drive out to Rockaway," he said.

"I don't speak enough Spanish."

"Try," John insisted.

"*¡Andele!* To Rockaway," I commanded. The driver sank down into his seat. His partner stared sullenly out through the windshield. We were headed out Seventh Avenue, which was more or less the right direction, so I let it go for the moment.

"Why do we want to go to Rockaway?" I asked.

John rubbed his chin. "I don't know. I want to ask them some questions." After a few more moments, he began to eye the front seat suspiciously; his face took on that wrinkled look of someone who smells a rat. "Maybe these guys are lying."

I wasn't impressed. "Maybe they are. What are we going to do, torture them?"

John winked at me, gesturing with his gun. I didn't know what the hell he was doing. "Here," he said in a whisper, but loudly enough to be easily overheard from the front seat. "Take this other gun, wrap it in this jacket, and put a hole right behind that little fucker's ear." His voice sounded so cruel, I believed he wanted me to do it. But he winked again, so I caught on.

Neither of the guys in front flinched, so John sat back against the seat. But he didn't relax his gun hand. "This is ridiculous," he said.

"Why don't we drive them out to Charlie's office? Somebody might do some explaining." I sounded like George Raft.

John took off his glasses, cocking his head in my direction, like a dog not able to identify the sound he's hearing. "What would who explain?" He sounded so uncertain that my theory began to leak.

"About these guys?" I tried to sound like it hadn't really been my idea after all.

"What about these guys?"

"I don't know. That's why we'd ask them. So they'd tell us."

John's eyes opened wider. He put his glasses back on. "You think these guys work for Charlie?"

I lost my nerve and hesitated, trying to regain some standing in the conversation. For one thing, I wasn't ready to accuse Charlie yet. For another, it was John's fault we were in this car with these gunmen who didn't speak English. Why shouldn't he be embarrassed? "They might know something. . . ." I tried to add a hint of truculence to my tone, but it came out closer to a whine.

"You think my father sicced these jerks on you?" John's gaze was hard enough for me to avert my eyes. He was also not paying attention to the guys in the front seat.

I pointed at them. "Those guys may still have guns."

Now he panicked. He waved the gun at the front seat, and I thought he was going to pull the trigger.

"I don't know," I shouted. "If I'm wrong, I'm wrong. You tell me who they're working for."

By a visible act of will, John regained his old form, pulling himself up straight, narrowing his eyes with concentration. Each movement and gesture suggested authority. "Tell him to turn around," John ordered. "We'll find out who they're working for."

I looked at him blankly while I tried to think of how you might say turn around. I'd already used up the store of Spanish I'd learned watching Speedy Gonzales cartoons.

By grunting, shouting, pointing, and thumping the driver on the shoulder, I got him to alter direction. We went back down dark, quiet Sixth Avenue and turned left onto Union Street, following it across the Gowanus Canal from Park Slope into Carroll Gardens—Red Hook—and the Amalgamated Industrial workers union hall.

I don't know how John knew someone would be there. But sure enough, a light was on. When I pushed the bell, a bulky, broad-shouldered young man, resembling a junkyard dog in demeanor and attitude, came to the door. He received John's message wordlessly, walked away, then came back a few minutes later and opened the door. John walked our pals in. The junkyard dog frisked them, removing a good-size handgun from the smaller guy and a small gun like John's from the bigger guy, then watched over them while John spoke on the phone for a few minutes. After the phone call, John and I sat in straight-backed chairs in the shape-up room, waiting out the night.

Just after dawn, Frank Carlucci and his entourage—two assistants the size of defensive tackles and a small dour-looking man in rumpled clothes walking unhappily between them—burst through the door. Dressed impeccably in a gray Italian-cut suit and a blue shirt with a pastel pink silk tie and matching handkerchief, Carlucci was brisk and businesslike, not to say angry. It was 5:30 A.M.

"These guys belong to you, Peter?" Carlucci asked the rumpled man as soon as they entered the room. The light of recognition had gone on in the eyes of both the characters he was talking about when Peter came through the door, so the question wasn't misplaced.

Peter looked sick. He fawned after Carlucci, ignoring the rest of us, including the thugs on either side of him. "Frankie," he said in a cajoling voice. "I told them to lay off." He gestured toward the two hit men, who by this time of the morning, their drunks wearing off, their lives on the line, looked ready to raise the white flag. "I sent them the fucking message: 'Don't hurt him.' Maybe they didn't understand the language." The sincerity in his tone, the sadness in his eyes, it was pure obsequiousness. But Frank ate it up. Then Peter looked at me. Red-faced, his eyes bulging and misty with tears of frustration and anger, he looked like he'd finally found the one to blame for everything. "You tell this fucking guy, too," he cried out. "Tell him to cut the shit. You want him to be running the fucking union?"

By this time, I'd recognized him. Here was Peter Kelly, president of Local 1101 of the United Bartenders of America: my first line of defense against exploitation and abuse by the bosses. Poor Pop would break down in tears.

"Don't worry about him. Worry about you. We had an agreement. You fuck up again," Frank said, "I'll whack you and them."

"It was a mistake, Frankie," Peter said, holding up his hands once more to placate his pal. "I never cross anyone, Frankie. You know that." He gestured toward his hired hands. "They fuck up again, I'll whack them myself."

Frankie dismissed the whole group with a wave of his hand. The goons followed Peter out the door like truants following dad out of the principal's office. When they left, Carlucci looked at John, and for a split second, I caught a whiff of something like friendship. "It happens that way sometimes," he said to John.

That was the apology. For me, the marked man, nothing. I was still trying to digest the idea that my own union had been trying to kill me. If not for John, they might have, and in spite of John's efforts, they'd almost killed Ntango.

One of Carlucci's henchmen drove us back to John's car, and John drove me back to the Upper West Side in the early light before the morning traffic. The trip was quick: Flatbush Avenue to the Brooklyn Bridge, then up the remnants of the West Side Highway. Going along the river, past the abandoned slips down near the Village, where gay lovers strolled on the wooden piers in the pale morning light, up through the Thirties and Forties, where hookers in tight, garishly colored shorts and white boots waited for the truck drivers, and finally, bouncing over potholes that would put a tank-testing ground to shame, climbed onto what was left of the elevated part of the old highway at 57th Street.

All the way uptown, I looked out the open window and listened to WQXR on John's car radio, inhaling the rush of wind, which smelled faintly of salt and the sea, laying my head back against the seat and feeling the rush of air against my hair. Before dropping me off, John broke into my dream, telling me I had to get back to work; he couldn't keep me on salary anymore. He started to tell me to leave the union alone, then thought better of it and changed direction in midsentence. "—so if you want to beat these guys, it's got to be everybody. One guy is too easy to get rid of."

I nodded. It was the same advice Pop had given me.

John sighed. "What a fucking day! Maybe things can get back to normal now."

"Maybe not," I said. "What about Greg? Who killed Greg? Those guys?" I asked him.

John shook his head.

When we pulled up across the street from my building, he shoved the shifting lever into park and leaned against the door. He took off his glasses and rubbed his eyes; then he closed his eyes and just sat there.

"Why were you at Walter's?" I asked. John's eyes sprang open. Once again, I'd asked for more information than he was willing to give me. For years, I'd never asked anything more than he was willing to tell me. Despite his grand public manner, John was a private man; he kept his own counsel, made his own way. We were as good friends as we were because I'd respected that. When I covered for him at the Dockside years before, I never asked where he'd been or what he'd been doing. I had my own secrets. I respected his. He understood this, so we became friends. Even more than this, John ran every show he was in. You accepted him as boss, or you found your own show. Now, in ways that Greg never had been able to, I'd found my own show. This was treacherous territory. So I tread carefully, speaking softly, talking with my eyes, backing away from what John might feel was a challenge. "We still don't know what happened with Greg and Aaron."

"We may never find out, bro," he said softly.

"Walter and Charlie were at the Ocean Club the night Aaron was killed. They were in Sea Isle when Greg got killed." I hesitated because I didn't want to tell John I knew about Charlie's murder conviction. But he'd have to have pretty bad eyesight not to see the handwriting on the wall. I tried to stick to Walter, but we both knew I was talking about Charlie, too.

"Walter just shows up one day," I went on. "He says he's from down the shore. But no one remembers him." I caught John's eye. "Why did Greg and your old man hook up with him?"

"I do wonder about him," John said. "Something's not right about Walter." He gripped the steering wheel. "That's why I went to see him tonight."

John looked worn-out, circles under his eyes, gently nodding back and forth like he was rocking himself to sleep while he looked at me for a long time. His expression was hard to describe—like a father might look at his son, a tender look, but not soft, one that makes you feel cared for and protected from things you don't even know about. John smiled slightly. "Maybe you've done enough for a while. Is that what you were doing, checking up on Walter?"

I nodded sheepishly. "Yeah, but then I got a little confused when I saw you were there, so I went for a beer to think things over; then I saw those guys. . . ." I stopped because John looked confused.

"How did you know I was there?"

"Your car. Those license plates."

John winced and held up his hands in exasperation. "Of course, the goddamn car." He nodded a few more times. "The goddamn license plates. I shoulda known."

"John," I said, still working up my courage. "Why did your father go see Greg on the day he was killed?"

John's response was softer than I expected. "You tell me," he said sadly.

I thought maybe I would. "They were working together. Something went wrong years ago, so a guy got killed. Maybe something went wrong this time, too." I locked eyes with John and made the leap. "I gotta tell you this, John. You know goddamn well there's a good chance Charlie or Walter or both of them together killed Aaron and Greg."

John stared out the window in front of him and spoke softly. "I don't know that, bro. And neither do you." He sounded even wearier. "Do me a favor. Just let me get my old man out of here. You can do anything you want after that. I don't care anymore."

When I got inside my apartment, instead of going to bed, I paced around, nosing into the refrigerator and the kitchen cabinets, looking for something to eat. Too tense to sleep, I found a joint and was about to light it, then decided not to. I was too confused and tense—and afraid, I figured out finally—to smoke a joint. Instead, I picked up William Butler Yeats's *Collected Poems* and sat down with it in my overstuffed chair. There was solace from the poets after all.

chapter twenty-five

I woke up in the early afternoon, feeling depressed. It was a hot, muggy, gray smog sort of day, and Broadway stank of garbage. I walked to an Arab lunch counter for shish kebab and hummus, drank two beers at the West End, went back home, and called Kevin. I wanted to tell him Big John and I had found the guys who'd shot me and Ntango.

He perked up much more dramatically than he usually did during my calls. "What'd you do to them?"

"Nothing really."

"What's gonna happen to them?"

I told him they'd probably get fired and maybe deported.

"That's all?" said Kevin. "If they did that to me, I'd kill them both. You guys are really lame."

Pretty lame indeed. Another lesson in life for Kevin, another disappointment. His father would not wreak vengeance; the wrongdoers would not be brought to justice. Once more, the phony grown-ups, his father included, had come up short. I knew the myth Kevin adhered to; it was as old as the ages: Be a man. Settle your scores. Part of me yearned to subscribe to it, too. So why didn't I go kill them both? There was an answer, not something I could explain to Kevin, maybe not even to myself. But I knew I was right, and part of my job as his dad was to try to tell him that when the cards were laid out on the table, what he'd see is that Rambo is wrong. Too many kids his age died facedown in the gutter after dissing or being dissed and seeking revenge.

"This is why, Kevin," I said, with little hope he'd believe me. "Because if you killed them, then you'd be like them."

"That's bullshit, Dad. . . . That's just being weak."

"I love you, buddy," I said then. "Good-bye."

The conversation with my son helped neither my mood nor my view of what the world had to offer, although when I talked with him, no matter how combative or sullen his mood, it helped me get my bearings. I remembered I had a purpose in life, that there was reason to battle the chaos and the meaninglessness, and that despite the emptiness of the uncaring universe, I knew, like the guy in the rowboat in the middle of the ocean, I wanted to embrace life. But not at the moment. I shut off my phone and read until I fell asleep.

When I woke up next time, it actually was morning, and I didn't know what day it was. Realizing that with all that was going on I should probably be paying more attention to the world around me, I called for messages. There were three calls from Sandra, beginning early that morning.

"I was really worried. I thought something happened to you," she said when I called her back. She sounded breathless and unsettled.

"Why did you think that? Is something wrong there?"

She hesitated. "No . . ." But it was the kind of no that took a long time to say and ended up meaning yes.

"What happened?"

"Someone broke into my house." She paused. Her breathing sounded like gasping. Finally, she screeched, "Brian, I'm terrified. Please come here. Please . . . please come here."

Shit, I said to myself. I'd been planning to give Dr. Parker a call to see if we could have an early dinner before I went to work. And I sure as hell didn't want to trek all the way back to the Jersey shore. "I gotta work tonight," I said weakly. "Maybe you could come up here?"

Sandra began weeping quietly. "I know it's not right to ask you. I only asked because I was really afraid. . . . Don't worry. I'll be okay."

"If you're afraid, go somewhere. Did you call the police?"

"I didn't call the police, because nothing was missing. Someone was just here. I have this terrible premonition that someone sat here all night waiting for me to come home. I can't explain it."

"Why weren't you home?"

"I was in the hospital to have my catheter changed. They didn't like some of the tests, so they kept me over. I have a feeling that if I'd been home last night, whoever killed Greg would have killed me."

"Stay right there. I'll call you back." I hung up and called Charlie's office. When Sourpuss answered, I altered my voice to sound like one of the pious Brooklyn Irish Catholics I'd known as a kid. "Father Mc-Nulty here," I said. "Dr. Wilson, please."

"He's not here, Father," she answered very politely, as I knew she would because I remembered the pictures of people with halos I'd seen on her desk. "Are you sure it's this Dr. Wilson you're looking for?"

"Yes, yes, I need to speak to him on a pressing business matter," I said in the lilting tones of a New Testament shepherd. "Do you know where I might reach him?"

She stuttered a bit. "I'm sorry, Father. He's out of town."

"Oh, praise the Lord. Is he still in Atlantic City?"

"Why yes, father."

"Then he must have remembered. God bless you," I said. I hung up and called Sandra back. "I'll be there this afternoon. Call the police and keep your eyes open."

When I left my apartment, morning was in full swing. Pretty young Upper West Side women in their business suits, wearing Nikes and carrying attaché cases, ran neck and neck and elbow-to-elbow with worsted-suited and silk-tied Upper West Side men, all heading for the subway with grit and determination. The neighborhood was an awful lot more respectable than when I first moved there in the 1970s. These days, on a New York City morning, no one sauntered, no one stood aside to let another pass. Those already too late to take the subway leaned out into Broadway, bodies braced, arms jabbing at the air, flagging down a cab.

I couldn't handle either the subway or the four or five Yuppies already leaning into Broadway from my corner, so I walked downtown a few blocks on the off chance I might find an empty space on one of the blocks, and on the even more remote chance I might find a cabdriver having coffee in La Rosita.

As luck would have it, Ntango was having coffee at La Rosita— with Dr. Parker. They sat together at a small table, engrossed in each other, and then shame-faced when they saw me. Until I saw their embarrassment, I thought they'd just run into each other. With my usual aplomb in delicate situations, I stared at them. They stared at me. Finally, Dr. Parker stood. She said she had to leave and asked me to walk her to her car. On the way, she told me she'd gone to see Ntango, as I had asked her to. She got him released from the hospital; they had dinner together that evening, then again last night, and one thing led to another. She looked at me with those beautiful eyes and smiled that secret smile, too happy to be ashamed.

Since, during one of the times she and Ntango were having dinner, I was in the sack with Sandra, I couldn't conjure up much moral outrage. Ntango really was a wonderful man in all respects—in all respects I knew about anyway—and Dr. Parker's blushing suggested she was quite pleased with any additional respects she'd discovered.

I asked her if Ntango had his cab back yet. She said no. Feeling some dowry might be in order, I asked if I could borrow Ntango and her car to go to the Jersey Shore. I didn't know if the Hippocratic oath extended to loaning your car, but it was a matter of life and death. Despite her profession, Dr. Parker had those salt-of-the-earth instincts. She went back in to La Rosita, talked to Ntango, and gave him the keys. In her self-possessed way, she came back, hugged me, then actually sauntered over to the curb. An uptown cab did a quick U-turn around the center island and picked her up as soon as she raised her hand.

Ntango was eating eggs and reading the *News* when I came back in and ordered my own *huevos rancheros*. He was polite and embarrassed but, like Dr. Parker, unapologetic. I didn't talk about her. There wasn't anything to say. I liked her. At moments, I'd dreamed we'd spend our lives together. But once more, I'd bet on the wrong horse.

I told Ntango who the guys were who'd shot him and said that they
were really after me. There was nothing personal, just a couple of guys
trying to make a buck. They wouldn't shoot him again, nor would they
shoot me, presumably, for the foreseeable future. Ntango showed no
particular anger that the villains wouldn't be brought to justice. Like
most of us, he'd come to accept daily injustice. I brooded about it,
though. Most corruption, I could take. But the older I got, unconsciously and absolutely involuntarily, the more I began to pick up Pop's
traits. Reverence for the union was one of them. They could step on
Superman's cape, spit in the wind, pull the mask off the old Lone
Ranger, but this desecration of the last best hope of the working people, this would be avenged someday.

Ntango looked at me in that sympathetic, bored way of his as I told
him this. After all, someone had stolen his country and murdered his
father; what was a corrupt union or two to him? But he did care that
Sandra might be in danger. Murderers sometimes travel in packs, he
said, so he'd drive me back to the shore.

By the time we reached south Jersey and the ocean breezes, the afternoon was sunny and clear. The parkway ran straight through a field
of marsh grass that looked and felt like a prairie—everything low to
the ground, nothing protruding, the marsh grass shifting in the breeze
like Nebraska wheat, flowing toward the horizon, where the sea and
the sky came together. The air was warm, but the breeze was strong
off the ocean. I liked the coastal wetlands flashing by the car window.
I liked the emptiness and peacefulness, and that the wetlands belonged to no one. I didn't get scared until we turned off the parkway
and headed east through the marsh grass to the bridge that led into
Sea Isle City. By the time we'd crossed into town, slowed in front of
the police station, and turned right to head out on Central Avenue toward Sandra's house, a sickening fear came over me, like the night
John and I started out in search of Greg.

Sandra's street was quiet, the air dead. Her house was dark, as dark
as it could be in the sparkling sunlight. The outside was bright enough,
but nothing came from the inside; the house was lifeless. I had the eerie
feeling you get sometimes that no one is home, even before you can

reasonably know this to be true. I went up the walk and then up the ramp to the porch. I knocked and waited and then knocked again. No answer. I hollered to Ntango that I was going to wait, so he could go get lunch or coffee if he wanted, but he joined me on the porch instead. We sat on ancient dark green Adirondack chairs that were much more comfortable than they looked, with their hard wooden angles and straight backs. Sitting on the porch might have been quite pleasant, even in the heat, if I hadn't secretly dreaded that Sandra might be dead in her darkened house. "If I had any balls, I'd go look," I told Ntango.

He agreed.

But before I could take action—if, in fact, I was going to take any action—Sandra called me from a grove of bayberry a little way up the street. I sprang out of the Adirondack chair—no mean feat, given the shape of the chair and the shape of me—and half-ran, half-vaulted myself to her. She held my head in an armlock while I hugged her as best I could with the edge of the wheelchair arm sticking in my ribs. She clutched at me, as if what she was describing were happening that minute. Someone had been in the house, she'd swear to it, but she didn't see anyone or any signs that someone had been there. The police didn't believe her. They'd asked her questions about Greg and drugs, as if whatever had happened, if indeed something had, was because of drugs.

"As if that made it okay to break into someone's house—because someone else was involved in drugs," she said through her tears.

On the way down to the shore, I'd figured out what was nagging at me about Sandra's house being broken into. Aaron's apartment had been broken into, too, right after he was murdered. On top of this, the cops had accused me of jimmying open the window to Greg's apartment. Since I hadn't, it was likely someone had broken in before I got there.

"Is anything missing?"

She shook her head. "Not that I could tell. But I think things were moved around. It feels like something's been disturbed, though I can't say what's been moved."

Sandra and I took a quick look through the house while Ntango went around the side and back of the house to check the doors and windows. I was particularly interested in Greg's things, which, true to form, were stacked or placed or arranged in perfect symmetry: his records, his tapes, his paperback works of Shakespeare and a few other books on a bookshelf. Also, on one of the shelves was a row of videotapes—a Shakespeare collection, as I might have guessed. Laurence Olivier as Hamlet, James Earl Jones as Othello. What caught my eye was that the row of tapes was askew, the plays out of order, some leaning on others, disorder very unlike Greg.

"Could something have been hidden behind the tapes?" I asked Sandra.

"Like what?"

"I don't know like what," I said irritably. "Did you ever look behind there?"

My tone had gotten her dander up, so she was a bit testy herself. "I think I would have seen something if it was there. But the tapes are messed up. They shouldn't be jumbled up like that."

"Are any of them missing?"

Sandra threw up her hands. "I don't know. I don't remember all of them. Why would someone want one of Greg's tapes?"

I threw up my own hands, too. "I have no idea."

Ntango came back to report no signs of a break-in. But this turned out not to make any difference, because Sandra remembered she hadn't locked her doors. My trained eye was unable to find any evidence of anything, except the evidence that Sandra was about to become hysterical and shouldn't be trusted alone. I told her she needed to stay with her family or a friend. She insisted there was no one she could stay with.

"You can't stay here. You can go stay with someone, or you can ride around with Ntango and me while I check on some things. But you'll have to wait in the car."

She decided to come along.

Ntango drove us back to Atlantic City and the Claridge. In the doldrums of midafternoon, it wasn't hard to find Charlie at a craps table. He wasn't holding the dice, and he wasn't sweating. There was a pretty good stack of chips in front of him. As unobtrusively as possible, given that I was the only one in the place with a crutch, I slid in beside him, nudging him so as not to disturb the half a dozen others concentrating on the dice.

"If you're not on a roll at the moment, I'd like to talk to you," I said.

Charlie's brown eyes usually had this warm and friendly expression about them—disarming, you might say. Now was no exception. He picked up his chips, put his arm around my shoulder, and led me away from the table to a small bar off the mezzanine above the lobby: half a dozen bar stools, three or four tables against the wall. Even at its busiest, one bartender and a waitress could handle it. Charlie ordered a couple of Beck's from a bartender who called him Charlie, and we sat down. There was no one else at the bar.

"This bar used to be a lot bigger," I told Charlie.

Charlie waved his arm in the direction of the rest of the hotel. "They want all the space they can get for gambling. They'll put the bar in a broom closet next."

When Charlie paid for the drinks, he handed the bartender a ten. "Swing it," Charlie said, winking at the barman.

The guy instinctively looked up, so I noticed a video camera in the ceiling, trained on the cash register, and another over the doorway covering the service bar. He rolled his eyes and went to the register.

"What can I do for you?" Charlie asked me after taking a satisfying sip of his beer.

"You could stop killing my friends."

He took another generous swallow of his beer. His expression didn't change—the warmth was still there in his eyes—and he didn't take his eyes from mine until he had put together what he wanted to say. "I don't know why I have to be the guy to straighten you out. You know John all these years, and still you don't know anything." Sitting back in the plush bar stool, he gave every appearance that this was one of the more pleasant afternoons he'd spent in a while.

"I'm going to name four people," I said. "All of them had some connection to you. You tell me why and how they died. David Bradley, Bill Green, Aaron Adams, and Greg."

Charlie looked at his beer glass for quite a while. I didn't know if he'd say anything at all. I couldn't think of any reason he should, but he must have thought of one. "Put it this way. A guy doesn't get whacked for no reason. You know what I mean?"

I didn't, but he didn't really care.

"You know the rules. You follow the rules. You do okay. You don't wanna follow the rules? Maybe that's okay, too. But you better be damn good. Because you know what happens if you aren't good enough."

Charlie ordered two more beers, not saying anything while we waited for them.

"Put it this way," he said after he poured some of his new beer into a clean glass, which he'd asked for. "My son, John . . . He's smarter and tougher than all of them. He does what he wants. Everybody respects him. Me? I was pretty good in my time, too. I took my chances and came out on my feet." He knocked on the dark wooden surface of the bar with his knuckles. "Those other guys, even Greg, who I knew since he was a kid, they weren't smart. They thought they could do like John or like me. They thought they could get away not following the rules." Charlie's eyes narrowed and bored into mine. "They knew goddamn well what happens if you fuck up."

Perspiration beaded on Charlie's forehead. He didn't look nervous or angry so much as intent, breathing hard through his nostrils. "In this game, if you go off on your own and you win, you make a bundle. You know what I mean? But if you're not tough enough to win, you get whacked. That's all there is to it. You don't wanna take a chance on getting whacked, then do what you're fucking told." Charlie's intensity was amazing. He explained this way of life to me as if his depended on it. "Let me tell you. None of them guys had to get killed. Like in the Old West when you give the guy a chance to go for his gun, it's a fair fight. Any one of them could have just done what he was told. But each guy took his chances. If they'd won, maybe someone else would be dead. Maybe I whacked them. Maybe someone else did. It's none of your fucking business. You're a lunch-box guy. No one's going to whack you. You got me? Forget about it." Charlie turned back to his beer and sat hunched over the bar, looking into his glass.

"That's it, then? You're telling me that's what happened?" I leaned toward Charlie, trying to make him look at me.

When my eyes finally caught up with his, he said. "I'm not tellin' you nothin', except I'll tell you one more time: Forget about this. I'm gonna forget about it, too. John's shipping me back to Arizona." Charlie leaned forward a little unsteadily to clap me on the shoulder, willing to let bygones be bygones.

"Why should I believe you're telling the truth?"

"Son, no one ever tells you the truth about everything. Your father should have taught you that when you were a boy."

I bristled. "My father taught me a lot."

Charlie laughed comfortably again, nodding his head with approval. "That's right, stick up for your old man; even an old outlaw like me got a son to stick up for him." Charlie switched to scotch. I stayed with beer.

While he sipped his scotch, I thought about how easily he sucked me in with his charm, just like his son did. I really wanted him to tell me about life. I wanted to know what made fathers proud of their sons. But there were other things I needed to find out first. I wasn't exactly plying Charlie with liquor to get him to open up. But since he was doing a pretty good job on his own, it didn't take long for him to begin babbling about how unjust the world was to a gangster trying to make a buck, and how hard it was to hold on to your son's respect when everyone was down on you. "I never pushed John to do anything. But he wasn't ashamed of me, even though they tried to get him to be." Charlie developed this sappy smile as he ordered another scotch.

John and I had been down this road back in the old days. We'd passed a lot of nights talking about our reprobate dads. As a kid, I reluctantly stood by my father—just as John had stood by his—even when I suspected he really might be a traitor. I worried about him; that's why I did it. He was my dad, and when I was eight or nine years old, I thought it was my job to watch out for him.

"Most people wouldn't understand," Charlie said. "My son won awards. He was elected things and appointed to places. He made a speech when he graduated from high school. I got proclamations from the mayor from him doing things to help old people. They could say what they wanted about his father being a jailbird, but John was up there with the doctors' kids and the bankers' kids. And he stuck up for his old man. When he was getting one of those awards or whatever, he'd always want me to come with him. In that speech when he graduated, he said his dad had taught him what he knew."

"So you taught him how to become an outlaw?"

"Hey," Charlie said, sitting up and pointing his finger in my face. "He never looked down on how I made a living. When he got out of high school, he worked with me. That's how he got started. I taught him a lot."

"Did you teach him to use a knife?"

Charlie looked stunned. I'd gotten him right up under the ribs, and he was reeling. For a long time, he didn't say anything. Then he spoke in a whisper that resembled a growl. "I did my time. You may be too fucking smart for your own good. People kill for money everywhere; they always have. Grow up." Charlie glowered at his rocks glass, brooding, knowing he'd let his guard down, that he must be slipping—knowing, too, that in his line of work if you start slipping, you're done for.

"I got one more problem, Charlie, and then I'll leave you alone. What was someone looking for in Sandra's house?"

"What?" Charlie shook his head to clear it. "Whose house?"

"Sandra. The woman Greg was living with."

Charlie's face gave too much away after the scotch; he showed too much interest.

"What was someone looking for in Sandra's house?" I asked again.

Charlie shook his head. "I don't know what you're talking about."

"And Aaron's apartment. Who broke in after Aaron was killed. You? Walter?"

"What are you talking about?"

"Was it Walter? What was he looking for?"

"Ask Walter."

"Why Sandra's house?"

Charlie stared at me with a drunk's stupid expression. He waved his hand in my direction. "You're nuts. No one's breakin' into places." He sat up straight on his bar stool, trying to regain the stature he dimly realized was gone for good. But it didn't work, so I left Charlie with his scotch and found Ntango and Sandra in the car on the street.

"I got one more stop. And I'll be awhile." I said, then gave Ntango directions to Linda's house.

Sandra questioned me with her eyes but didn't ask me anything. Neither did Ntango. I wouldn't have known what to tell them anyway.

"Tell me again what you saw the night Greg disappeared," I asked Sandra. My voice sounded harsh and demanding.

I startled her, so she stammered. "I saw a car going up the street. I heard something. Then I heard the car. Maybe I didn't see a car. I don't remember. Maybe I just heard it."

"You told me and John you saw it."

"Maybe I did." Her eyes were pleading. I could see Ntango's shoulders tensing. I didn't like the sound of my voice, either. I didn't like what I was doing. But I didn't stop.

"Maybe you don't want to remember. You don't want to think about it. You want someone else to do all the work."

Sandra turned on me. There were tears in her eyes. "Why are you doing this to me? Why are you talking like this?"

I didn't know. I didn't know where the rage was coming from. "You gotta get out of here," I said. There was no caring in my tone at all, as if it were her fault she had to get out of there, that she'd caused all the trouble. In a strange way, I realized, this was true. Like Charlie'd said. Just as it had been Greg's fault and Aaron's, and before them Bill Green's and David Bradley's, that they got themselves killed. They made their choices, took their chances.

"Why should I?" Sandra asked petulantly.

"If you stay here, you might get murdered."

She looked stricken.

"Come with us back to New York. If I'm wrong, you'll spend a couple of days in the city. That's not so bad."

She chewed on her lower lip. "Why should I believe you?"

For the next few seconds, we shot pain and anger back and forth at each other. Finally, something happened: The anger cooled, replaced by an unspoken sympathy for each other that words couldn't pull off right then. "Okay," she said.

Ntango dropped me off at Linda's and headed back to Sandra's so she could pack. Linda called to me from the backyard when I rang the bell. When I caught up with her, she was sitting in what was left of the sun, holding the baby, smiling at me, then nudging the baby with her nose, bopping the kid's forehead with her own, poking her gently in her little dimples to make her smile. "Look who's here, Jenny. It's Brian. Say hi to Brian." I waved to the kid, who looked at me suspiciously.

The baby's skin was darker than Linda's. Her eyes were dark, too. But they shone and sparkled like Linda's when she smiled. Linda wore a brightly flowered two-piece bathing suit and was as unconsciously lovely as she always was. I didn't know how she wouldn't notice my eyes devouring her or feel the wanton lasciviousness in my heart. But she was as cheerfully glad to see me as ever, hugging me, her flesh, hot from the sun, burning in my hands as I held her against me after she'd placed the baby gently in the wading pool.

"You feel wonderful," I said.

"You look awful." She leaned back to take a better look.

Leaving me to watch the baby, she went inside to get me a beer. As soon as she left, I got scared the tyke would drown, so I hovered over the pool and kept my eyes glued on the child, who slapped at the water, making big splashes, giggling and screeching. She was adorable, with her sparkling eyes, her two tiny white teeth, and her dimples.

Linda handed me the beer, then sat down in her sling-back beach chair. She watched the baby and made cooing sounds in tune with her daughter's sounds as she splashed about. Linda looked content, sitting in the yard of her own house in the sun, watching her baby, waiting for her husband to come home, waiting to go to work herself. It was a reasonable-enough life. I didn't know what the hell I was doing in the middle of it. She seemed as if she traveled in the right orbit, like a star. I'd rejected a similar life myself many years before when I first had my own child, because I thought then that life owed me better. By the time I realized life didn't owe me anything and had probably already given me more than I deserved, I was already pretty far down that lost highway.

The wonder and innocence in Linda's eyes matched that of her little girl's. She was either totally guileless or the world's best liar. And she certainly wasn't in any hurry to find out what I wanted.

"I hate to bring this up again," I said.

Those beautiful eyes searched mine. "I knew you would. I knew it wouldn't be over."

"How did you know all that?"

"I just knew," Linda said quietly.

I wasn't finding Linda as cute as I usually did. I was tired of her playing coy. "Sometimes you know too much," I said. "Sometimes you know things you wish you didn't know. How are things working out with Ralph?"

"Better" was all she said; then her face took on this expression Kevin used to get when he was small and I'd wrongfully accused him of something. Not accustomed to unfairness, he was more than hurt by the accusation; such injustice was something he, until that moment, had thought was impossible. Linda looked like that. But since she was over thirty, I figured she should know better—and expect less from her friends, particularly me, than she seemed to. But I still felt like a rat.

I'd come there to check up on Charlie. Instead, I asked her about something else that had nothing to do with Charlie and was probably none of my business. "A few years ago, Greg was arrested for punching Ralph. Why?"

The expression on her face was so incredulous and so damning that I felt like I'd finally done the thing for which there was no forgiveness. "You come so close," she said, "and then you always do something to screw it up." She glared at me for a second and then closed her eyes. When she opened them, they reddened, as if she would cry. "I'm going to tell you," she said. She reached behind her for a white beach robe that had been draped over the back of the chair and put it on. That beach robe was a barrier. Like Eve putting on clothes when the sense of shame was born. Evil had entered the garden; innocence was lost. "I'm going to tell you," she said again. "Maybe I was wrong and should have told you before. But even if I am wrong, so are you, because you should never have had to test me. I loved you and was your friend. That was as important as anything in the world to me. Like my baby." Her eyes pinned me against the sky.

"You don't understand—"

"Yes I do. You're going to think I'm terrible. But so do I, so it doesn't make any difference anymore. . . . All those years ago, John and I were lovers. You never knew that. I don't know why he didn't tell you. I didn't because I was ashamed."

Sitting down awkwardly in the grass in my stiff and heavy dungarees, the sun beating down, I listened like the child I all along had thought Linda was.

"Since the time I was seventeen, John summoned me whenever he wanted me."

We stared at each other over this piece of information for a long time.

"Ralph knew about you and John? Is that what the fight was about?"

"Not exactly. Ralph never liked John. Maybe he knew about John and me, or maybe he suspected something, but we never talked about it. That night, we were at some party in a bar. Ralph was drinking. He doesn't ever drink, so he's a real asshole when he does. John was toying with him for a while, sort of helping him to become more and more of an asshole and making fun of him. I got John to stop. But Ralph kept it up. John wasn't even paying attention to him by then. He was talking to someone else. Ralph went after him, so Greg dragged Ralph outside just to get him out of trouble. I guess he pissed Greg off, too. Greg punched him. A cop happened to be passing by and arrested Greg. That's the story. Something stupid. Something embarrassing. Something private and none of your business."

I felt a place inside me start to crumble, another section of my self-respect probably. I was embarrassed for Linda, and even more for myself, because I began to understand something. "You were seeing John even then?"

Linda's eyes went wild, her look mocking and angry, filled with triumph and despair. "John and I were together before I met you, when you and I were together, and after you left."

"When did you stop seeing him?" I asked, despite the cold, sick feeling in my chest.

She didn't answer. The look in her eyes, so angry and triumphant, began to weaken, until she looked down and wouldn't look up again. And then I knew the answer. I remembered what I'd always known about John. He made every man who knew him jealous because we all knew he could take any woman he wanted anytime. John—ever noble and chivalrous—would never tell. So I remembered now asking him where he was the night Aaron was killed. I remembered the song I'd kidded him about. The missing line: ". . . I was locked in the arms of my best friend's wife." I knew the last time Linda had been with John.

She was crying now, pulling her robe around her, crying and watching the baby. "You found out what you had to find out," she said between sobs. "I was with John in the Sheraton in New York the night Aaron was killed. He said he'd never tell. But once the murder happened, I knew it would come up. Someone would ask where John was that night. I would have to tell them, and it would ruin my life. And it had to be you. Are you satisfied?"

The baby must have gotten cold by then. Or maybe she just caught her mother's terrible unhappiness. Whatever the reason, she let out a series of bloodcurdling blats that shredded what was left of my nerves. "She needs a nap," Linda said, cuddling her daughter as she walked away from me. I watched her walk to the kitchen, her blond hair, whitened by the summer sun, against the white robe, the white robe against the backs of her tanned legs. She walked erectly and proudly.

Linda hadn't told me to stay or go, so I stayed. I'd come there to find out about Charlie and the alibi they'd made for the night Bill Green was killed. Instead, I found out this innocent love I'd remembered all my life had been sordid and corrupt. I stretched out on the lawn and stared at the sky. I felt like I hadn't lain on my back and looked at the sky like that since I was a kid. Fascinated, I watched the deep blue, the wisps of clouds, a bird scooting once in a while from one end of my vision to the other. For the rest of the time, Linda was gone, which may have been a few minutes or may have been many. I didn't think about anything except the sky.

When she came back, she'd pulled herself together. Even the color in her face had improved. It had been drawn and pale when she was so angry and scared; now that she'd gotten control again, her complexion was as pink and healthy as her baby's. She handed me a beer and sat down on the grass beside me. I watched the robe slide away from her pretty legs.

"I'm not sure why I married Ralph. Maybe I shouldn't have. Maybe it will just make terrible unhappiness for both of us forever. I didn't love him. But look what love had done to me. There was John, who treated me like a princess with caviar and champagne in luxury hotel suites one day and was gone then for the next six months, leaving me a couple of hundred bucks on the bureau, so I knew I was a whore and not a princess after all. Then there was you. You with your 'Love is all you need.' Did you really believe that, Brian? Or was I the only one dumb enough to believe it? . . . I'm such an idiot. I just loved and loved." Her expression was pained and cold and she was so alone behind it. "Well, love wasn't enough, was it, Brian?"

I didn't want to be with her now. I didn't want her looking at me anymore.

"I told you I made a mess of everything. But lots of times I've thought of you, and thought that you would have been enough for me. I really did love you. And I would have been enough for you, too. You were just too dumb to know it. Now, I see John sometimes—once or twice a year, sometimes not for a couple of years. I spend the night in a luxury suite, drinking hundred-dollar bottles of champagne." She turned on me. Her eyes drilled into mine. "You know about that kind of stuff, too. You're corrupt in your own way. Just like John. Just like me." She waited for this to sink in. "Now I wish I'd never known anything about either you or John." She began crying. "I just want my baby and my life and Ralph."

"What do you want Ralph for?" I asked. I said it without thinking. It wasn't what I meant. Really, what I meant was that I wished life had been different; that's all. I wished life had turned out happily for everyone.

But Linda didn't understand, of course. She turned to ice in front of me, then said, "Please leave."

I said, "Linda, I didn't—"

She said, "Please get out of my house."

I wasn't actually in her house. But I didn't see how pointing this out would help anything. So I trudged away.

chapter twenty-six

When I left Linda's, Ntango and Sandra were waiting
for me in the car at the corner. I told them I was staying
on in Atlantic City for a while longer and sent them back to New York.
At first, I thought Sandra should stay at my apartment for a few days.
But I realized my apartment wasn't any safer than her house. My
friend Carl had a spare bedroom in his rent-controlled apartment,
where I, along with everyone else we knew on the Upper West Side,
had crashed during one crisis or another in our lives. So I told Ntango
to take her there, and said I'd call Carl to tell him Sandra was coming.

When they left, I limped along Atlantic Avenue, back toward the
casinos. Not only were things going badly in the present; I'd now also
managed to screw up the past. After a couple of blocks, I stopped at a
sidewalk pay phone and called Sue Gleason, asking her if she might be
able to find any additional information on the deaths of David
Bradley and Bill Green and anything at all on Walter and Charlie. She
said she'd meet me at the Atlantic City police station in an hour.

I ate a red snapper dinner at Dock's Oyster House on Atlantic Avenue and then called a cab to take me to the police station. As drawn
and tired and tense as I was, despite the meal, I'm sure the cabdriver
thought I was going there to turn myself in for murdering my wife.

Sue was sitting on the steps of the police station, reading a book,
when I got out of the cab. "You have your father's instincts for investigative reporting," she said.

I sat down beside her.

"The connections are astounding." She rattled some papers in a manila folder. "One of the better ones is that Walter Springer was a patrolman on the Atlantic City police force from 1971 until 1975."

"A cop? Walter?"

"That's not all. After 1975, he disappeared. There's no record of him ever again."

"Why would that happen?"

"Two possibilities I can think of," said Sue. "One, he went into a witness protection program of some sort. Or he went undercover for some organization—CIA, FBI, some other police department—so they pulled his file to protect his cover."

She handed me the papers, some of which were handwritten police reports and were virtually impossible to read. "There are a few things not in the file—off-the-record things I can tell you but that we don't have in writing." She told me Greg and John had been questioned about both David Bradley's death and Bill Green's. But the police didn't seem to have any evidence against them, and both had strong alibis: proof they'd been at work. The police hadn't questioned Charlie about either death. Another interesting piece of news was that David Bradley had been arrested a couple of weeks before he died in a car carrying four hundred pounds of marijuana. Because of the arrest, he was cooperating with police at the time of his death.

"A snitch?"

Sue nodded. "Does this help?"

"I don't know. It's more things to try to fit together. Reminds me of when I used to try to fix my bike when I was a kid. I'd have it all fixed and put back together; then I'd notice a part on the ground that I'd forgotten to put back in." I stared at the photocopied reports Sue had hustled out of the police station. After a long time of my looking at it, a name at the bottom started to come up off the page at me.

"What's that name?" I asked Sue.

"Sam Roberts. He used to be a narcotics detective here in Atlantic City. Even though the bodies were found in Sea Isle, the Atlantic City police had an interest because David Bradley was their informer.

Roberts moved over to Sea Isle in the late 1970s, and a couple of years ago, he became chief. Does that tell you anything?"

"Yeah. Now I've got two parts lying on the ground."

Once more, I rode the New Jersey Transit bus from Atlantic City to New York City, sleeping fitfully and having dreams that frightened me and that I forgot as soon as I woke up. Greg was in one dream. We were all back at the Dockside and Walter and I were the bartenders. I kept telling Walter I needed to find Greg. When I woke up, I remembered the last conversation I'd had with John, sitting in the car in front of my building. He said that something was wrong about Walter. I should have thought about that more, but it slipped by me.

When I got home near 11:00 P.M., I called John's home number. He answered on the first ring. "Jesus, bro," he said in his most mournful voice. "I told you to go to work tonight."

I was contrite. "Sorry, John." I wanted to remind him that he'd gotten me into this mess in the first place, but I decided to wait and let him talk himself into straightening things out, like he usually did.

"It's okay," John said. "You're on the clock. But you'd better get over there. I can't keep saving your ass forever."

"I went to Atlantic City and I forgot."

"What were you doing down there?"

"It's a long story," I said. "Sandra called me. She was scared."

"Scared? What was she scared of?"

I told him what had happened with Sandra, and that I'd talked to Charlie.

"Why Charlie? What are you trying to do, Brain? And where's Sandra now?"

"It's a long story. Come over to the Sheraton and have a drink. I'll tell you about it."

"I'm working on a problem," John said. "I don't think I'll get there tonight."

"Walter?"

"My problem, bro. Go to work. Call me later."

I put in the last three hours of my shift and gave all of the tips I

picked up to the bar back who'd covered for me. It felt great to be behind the stick again, even if I was a bit gimpy. Around 1:00 A.M.,
there was a bit of rush, so I got the rhythm back, soda bottle in one
hand, liquor bottle in the other, shaking the whiskey sour behind my
ear, pouring in front of a woman in an evening dress, her breasts
pushing over the top of her gown, pouring the drink, with a half inch
of froth, perfectly filling the glass, not a drop to spare, her eyes rising
from the glass to meet mine, my eyes rising from the glass and then
passing over her breasts to meet hers. It was fun, and, for the first time
in weeks, I was in control of something.

John never came in, and when I called, his machine was on. I went
home around three and slept like the dead. In the morning, I called
Carl's house. He hadn't gone to bed yet, so he was pleasant enough.
Sandra was gleeful; Carl was taking her out for a job interview. "New
York is wonderful," she said.

"Fun City," I told her. "Keep your head up and don't talk to
strangers."

Somewhere between waking and finishing breakfast, the jam broke;
the pieces tumbled into place. Someone once told me that everyone
can be bought. This theory didn't speak very highly of humankind,
but it did help the picture emerge. Half a dozen pieces of information
that until that moment had made no sense at all now fit so snugly, I
couldn't pry them loose.

I called Sue Gleason and asked her to find the security director
from the old Dockside and ask him a couple of questions for me. I
started to call Sandra to ask her the one question I had for her, but I
hung up on the first ring. I wanted to check on a couple of other
things first. I wanted to check on them because I hoped I was wrong.
I did my laundry in the machines in the basement of my building,
washed some food-encrusted dishes in my sink, and took a shower. I
kept remembering my life in Atlantic City, trying to recapture something from that time. The longer I thought about it and the more I remembered, the further away it slipped, until it seemed like I didn't
really know anyone who'd been there—not even myself.

Late in the afternoon, I called John again.

"Let's have dinner," he said.

"Where?"

"You could come up here." There was a little hesitation, almost shyness, in the invitation.

"Sure. You want me to bring anything?"

"Bring something Polish."

I took a cab down to First Avenue near Ninth Street and picked up a couple of kielbasa dinners and some pierogi from a Polish lunchcounter restaurant. John's apartment was smaller than his office, as he'd said, a one-bedroom walk-up on the second floor of a nondescript town house on Eleventh Street in the West Village.

John had St. Pauli Girls in his refrigerator, so we drank beer and ate kielbasa and pierogi at his table.

"Tell me about your trip to the shore," he said.

"Linda said you were lovers."

John looked embarrassed. He stared at his plate and chewed distastefully. "That was a long time ago, bro." He looked at me sheepishly.

"That's not what she said."

John nodded as he chewed. "Linda's okay," he said noncombatively. "She just don't know to shut up." He ate for a few minutes, then asked without looking up, "What about Sandra?"

I told him about the break-in at Sandra's. He ate his dinner impassively.

"Where is she now?"

Right at that moment, I got this horrible flashback to Greg's body half-buried in the soft spongy dirt of the garbage dump. When I came to my senses, John was watching me carefully. I froze. I couldn't bring myself to talk. He asked if I was sick. Then he said, "Where'd you say Sandra was now?"

I didn't tell him. He waited, then smiled a kind of rueful smile, like the joke was on him, and asked about work.

"It was great. I can't wait to go back."

"Tonight?"

"Yeah. You wanna come by?"

"Maybe." But I still got that problem to deal with."

"What's that?"

Usually, I wouldn't ask a question like that, and if I did, it would have no effect on John, but this time he told me. "You're right about Walter," he said.

When I left John's apartment, I walked around the Village, examining my theory, which wouldn't go away. I walked down Christopher Street, crossed Sixth Avenue, and walked across Eighth Street to Mac-Dougal. I'd been coming to the Village since I was twelve, looking for excitement. MacDougal intersected with Bleecker, and at that corner were Le Figaro and the Crossroads, and along Bleecker were the cafés where I had first heard Joan Baez, Bob Dylan, and the whole generation of 1960s folksingers. The streets had changed and not changed, maybe the way I had changed and not changed; some part of us both defined forever in those early days. I stopped into Kenny's Castaways well before the music began. I drank two beers and realized I wasn't going to work that night, nor would I call John to cover for me.

I made a stop at a Crazy Eddie's on Sixth Avenue to have them demonstrate a telephone answering machine for me. Then I called Carl. Because he was a union delegate, he knew just about every doorman in New York. I asked if he could make some arrangements for me and he said he would. An hour later, I was riding the freight elevator to the forty-first floor of the Omnibus Building. The United Maintenance Workers business agent for midtown was at the controls. Short and dumpy and smoking a cigar, he looked like he'd been raised in a kennel and brought out into the world to be a steward in a building-maintenance workers' union. It turned out he'd graduated from the Cornell School of Industrial and Labor Relations and spoke like an English professor.

"If for some reason you're found in here, it would not be good form to mention how you got in," he said without removing the cigar.

"I won't," I said solemnly.

"I know Carl well." He gave this statement added significance by glaring at me.

"So do I." I glared myself.

He stopped the elevator and shook my hand before he opened the door. "Come down in the main elevator. There's a button alongside the door to call it."

I crossed the darkened anteroom and tried the door to John's office, which was open. I fumbled with the desk drawer in the dim light from the large windows, but in the dark, I couldn't make sense of the answering machine, so I turned on the desk light and put on my new specs. I could find the play button, but I couldn't figure out how to get the machine to reverse, and I was afraid I was going to erase whatever was on it. My nerves were rattling and I wanted to get out of there. I would have taken the machine and screwed, but I'd promised the union guy I wouldn't take anything from the office. After going to the reception area every time I heard a creak or a groan, I realized that even if I heard a noise and it turned out to be something, I wouldn't know what to do. Hide behind the couch? Jump out the forty-first-floor window? So I said, Fuck it, and concentrated on fiddling with the machine. Finally, I got it to work. I rewound it to the beginning and let it play.

The sound from the anteroom when it came was not a creak or a groan anyway. It was more like a bam and a swish. By the time I looked up, Big John was halfway across the room. His expression was more disappointed than angry. He certainly didn't look surprised. I would just as soon have melted into a puddle on the thick pile rug. The first thing I thought was that he would fire me because I wasn't at work.

I stood and walked to the visitor side of the desk; he walked right past me and sat behind it. We both listened to the tape recorder playing Greg's message from my answering service, telling me to come to the shore but not to tell anyone. After we listened, John sat back in his chair, looking like a boxer taking a flurry of punches, waiting for his shot.

"Just out of curiosity," I asked, "do you have the videotape in that drawer?"

He opened the bottom drawer and held up a black videotape case.

John hadn't been at work on June 17, 1975, just like I hadn't been on time for work at the Sheraton last night, but we both had been on the clock all the same. The problem for John was that the security tape for that June night, which he now held in his hand and which Aaron had held on to all those years, showed he wasn't there.

"I should have left you out of it, bro. I didn't think it would come down this way." John tried for that reassuring expression I'd seen so often, when to look at him was to believe firmly that he'd find a way out of whatever jam we were in. Not this time. John couldn't come up with the expression. And I couldn't come up with the belief. He sagged in his chair like an old man. "You make a mistake and you spend your whole life covering it up. For what? For this?" He gestured theatrically about him. "I told you it was lonely at the top. All alone with your bodies."

"David," I said.

"David was wired. The stupid bastard got caught and they turned him. He was going to give me up to save his ass."

"That guy who's the chief of police now told you about David."

"That's right. The AC cops had David. But I had Sam Roberts—a narcotics cop on the take."

"So you killed David. Then you killed Bill Green."

"I had to get somethin' from Green to give David the hot shot, so Green knew I killed David. He thought David had a lot of money, so he tried to shake me down."

"Aaron fixed your time card the night you killed David and then came back years later with the security tape to get paid off. Why did Aaron wait all this time?"

John shrugged his shoulders. "Maybe he didn't want to do it—or have nerve enough—until he was desperate. Maybe he waited until I was in a position where I could really do something for him. He wanted to manage a hotel. He thought I could get it for him."

"But why Greg? Why would you kill Greg?" It took a few seconds for me to catch the import of what I'd said.

John's expression was pained, his eyes misty. "For all those years, Greg thought Bill Green killed David. Then dumb fucking Aaron—when he was trying to shake me down, thought he'd get to me through Greg, so he told Greg I'd killed David. He didn't know Greg loved David like a brother. Greg would've killed Green if I hadn't, and he might've killed me then, if he'd known the truth.

"I didn't know Aaron had told Greg, so I left Aaron for Greg to dump later, after the bar closed. He acted like nothin' had happened and took care of the body. But he also must have clipped the tape from Aaron, because I'd told Aaron to bring it that night, but then I couldn't find it. When Greg took off and I didn't find the tape at Aaron's apartment, I began to suspect somethin'. When we found Greg that night at the shore, I pretty much knew. I thought I could straighten him out. But when he left that message for you, I knew he'd tell you about the tape and me killing David." All of John's arrogance was gone when he leaned across the desk; he pleaded with me. "I didn't know what Greg would do next. I couldn't trust him."

With this, John pushed back his sumptuous leather chair, resting both his arms on the arms of the chair, and I realized he had a gun in his lap. He brushed back his hair with his hands and took off his glasses. "Jesus, bro, can you believe someone ends up like this? I never wanted to hurt anyone in my life."

Something frightful was happening to him, like Dorian Gray's face in the portrait. His whole expression seemed to disintegrate, as if he'd had a stroke. I felt sorry for him. Once more, I was edging toward Big John's side. Just like the old days, I found myself thinking if Big John did it, it must be all right; I must have missed something. Even if there were bodies strewn all over the waterways, it wasn't what it looked like. But this time, the doubt overwhelmed the belief. Faith can't be explained when you have it, nor can its lack be explained when you've lost it. Brian, the Wayward Disciple. I'd lost my faith.

"And Sandra?"

John put the gun on the desk. He looked up and spoke apologetically. "She saw my car driving away with Greg. I knew she recognized my car the day of the funeral. It just didn't register. But you know my goddamn license plate; she'd remember soon enough."

"And Linda?"

"Linda knew all along how this added up. We grew up together. She'd cover for me. She always has." He held up his hands.

"And me?"

"Now you know." John's expression had regained its wisdom, and his movements their decisiveness. My chest froze and my breath stopped.

There were noises in the hall. John picked up the gun and stood up. The door swung open. It was Walter, leading a phalanx of police wearing bulletproof vests.

"Hold it. Police," Walter said.

John just stood there. Walter fired.

I didn't go to Big John's funeral. I don't know if anyone did. I guess Charlie went. Maybe Linda. I called her that night to tell her John was dead.

"Why did you have to hunt him down?" she screamed, and then she cried.

I knew part of what Linda had told me about her and John wasn't true. She hadn't been in New York with John at the Sheraton the night Aaron was killed. I wanted to ask about the rest—if she really had been seeing him while we were together. I tried. But her grief seemed more important than my memories, so I just said I was sorry and hung up. I told Sheehan that sleezeball Walter shot John in cold blood. Sheehan told me I was nuts to file a charge, because no one would ever find Walter guilty if John had a gun in his hand.

I'd had a hard time telling Kevin right after it happened. He didn't get sad so much as really angry at me. The day of the funeral, I'd called him again. I thought he, my dad, and I might go to the funeral together. But my ex-wife didn't want him to go. She said he was still sad and angry and suffering, so I should leave him alone. We argued for a few minutes. But I lost heart pretty quickly and gave up. I didn't even call Pop.

The night of John's funeral I went to Oscar's. I sat at the bar reading the *Daily News* with my new specs on, waiting for someone to make a remark. As the night moved toward morning, the usual crowd drifted in. I was a little put out when Ntango came in with Dr. Parker. Even though I didn't have much to say and was just as glad they sat at a table, I bought them a drink and let bygones be bygones.

Then Carl came in pushing Sandra's wheelchair. As soon as they stopped giggling with each other and looked at me with those guilty and embarrassed expressions, I caught the drift of that one, too. They said hello and slunk off to a table, which was fine with me. They could buy their own fucking drinks.

It was one of those nights when drinking didn't do anything but make me feel worse. So I had one last beer around two A.M. and left. It had been raining most of the night and really picked up before I'd gone a block. I didn't much care about that, either—just walked along getting soaked—until when I was crossing 110th Street, a red Jeep Cherokee came down Broadway. No one shot at me this time. It just splashed through the glistening intersection, spraying muddy water. I stood on the corner, watching it speed down rain-slicked Broadway, watching the windshield wiper slapping back and forth, clearing the back window.